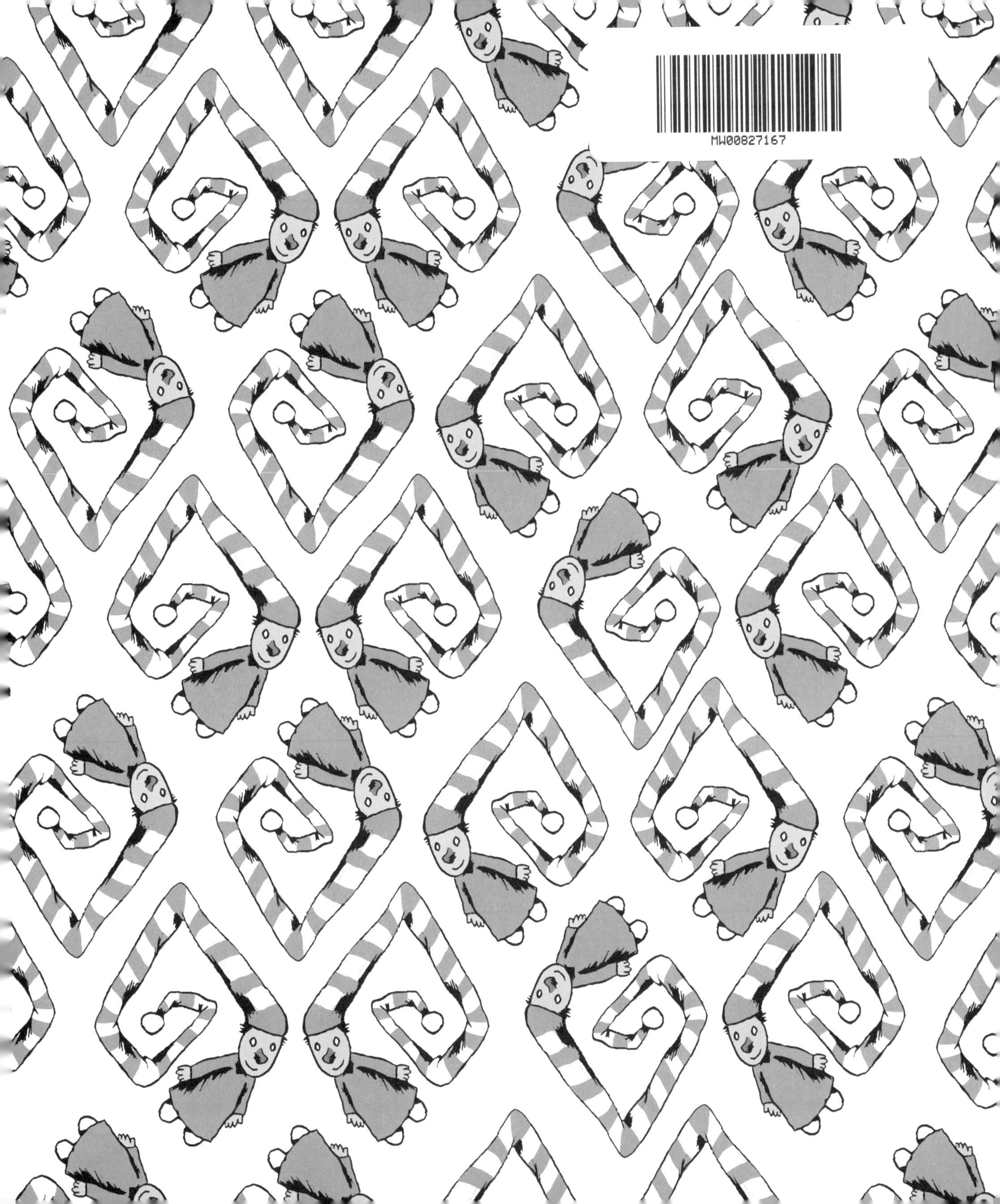

To my parents, for understanding
that the jokes were a serious thing.

First American edition published in 2014 by Enchanted Lion Books
351 Van Brunt Street, Brooklyn, NY 11231
English-language translation Copyright © 2014 by Mara Faye Lethem
English-language edition Copyright © 2014 by Enchanted Lion Books
Layout and design for the English-language edition by Sarah Klinger

Originally published in Spanish as *Macanudo #2* by Ediciones de la Flor S.R.L.
Copyright © 2004 by Ediciones de la Flor S.R.L, Buenos Aires, Argentina
All rights reserved under International and Pan-American Copyright Conventions
A CIP record is on file with the Library of Congress

Printed in China in August 2014 by the South China Printing Co.

MACANUDO #2

BY LINIERS

TRANSLATED FROM THE SPANISH BY MARA FAYE LETHEM

ENCHANTED LION BOOKS

NEW YORK

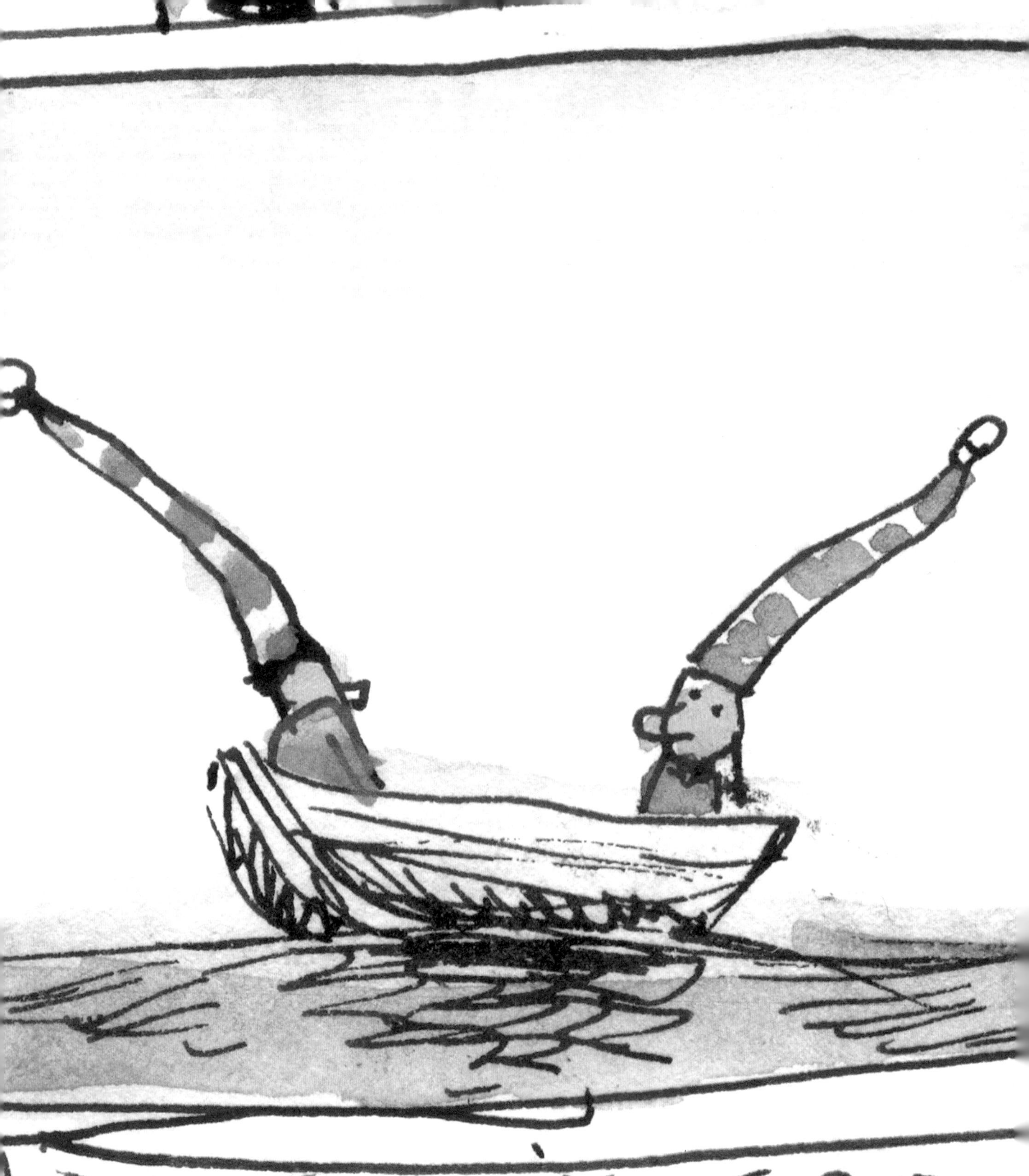
PERO SE
¡SABE QUE

PROLOGUE

I consider reading Liniers to be a "demanding pleasure," though not necessarily in that order.

Honestly, the "demanding" part of reading his jokes (Liniers likes the term) comes later, because if he catches you off guard, you've probably missed the joke already! On one hand, the twists in his jokes are immediate, but they also leave a kind of aftertaste that you only really catch later. I think this might be what gives them their durability, unlike so many comic strips, which are ephemeral.

Still, his strips don't presume to be profound or anything like that, because Liniers is always showing his deeply superficial side, like the true fan of surrealism that he is.

Perhaps what I like best about *Macanudo* is that it doesn't have regularly recurring characters. I'm sure Liniers does this on purpose, just to torture us, because I for one am always hoping for a strip with "People About Town" or "Oliverio the Olive." Or at least for Henrietta to show up in a hurry!

Mark Twain said, "The problem with humor is that no one takes it seriously." But the thing about *Macanudo* is that we know it's serious. And that's the trick to it and that's where the pure pleasure—with no demands—comes in.

I'm sure, tomorrow, Liniers will be walking down the street and some fan will shout, "I love the Bovine Movie Buff!" And we'll all know what he's talking about.

—Kevin Johansen

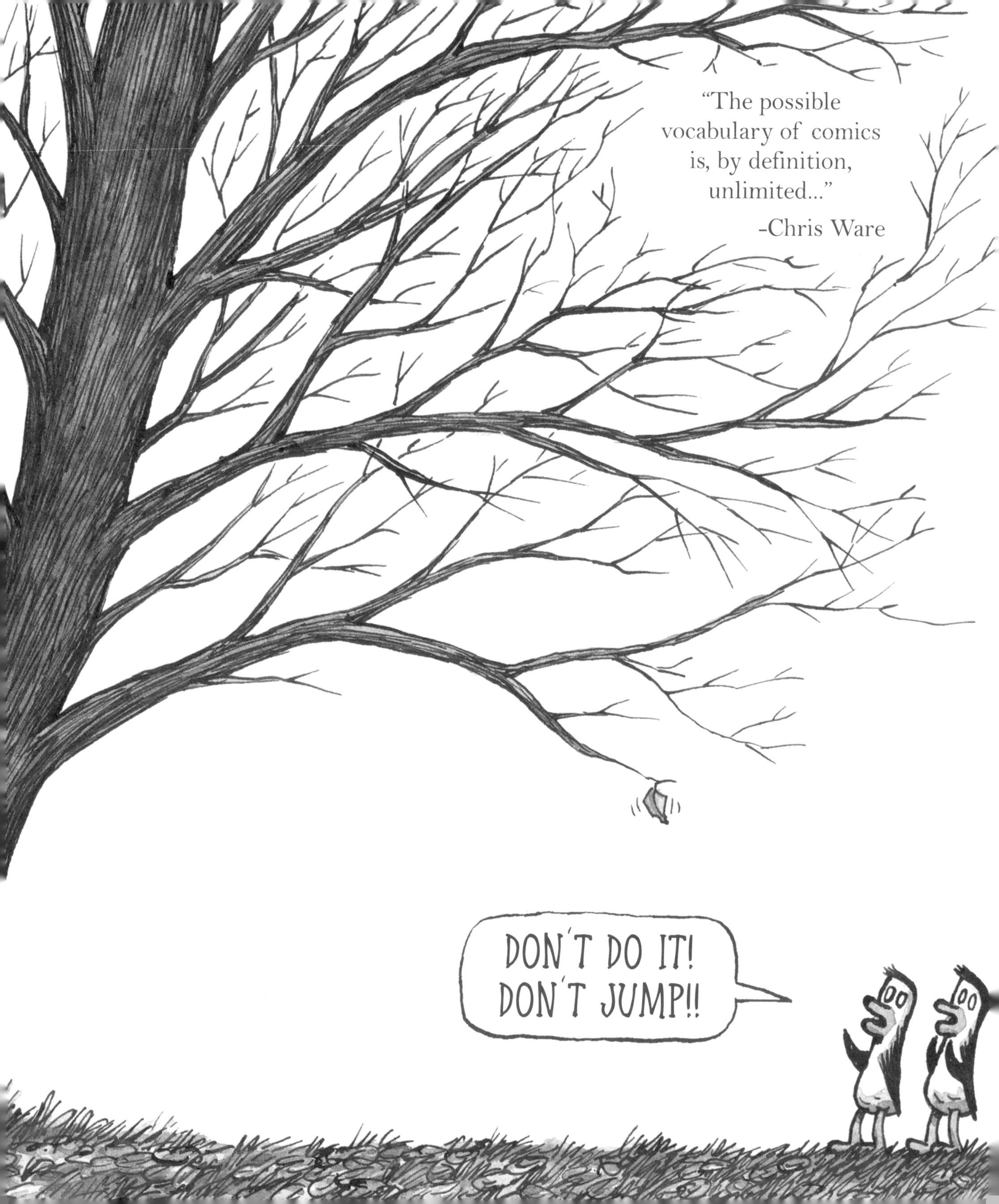
"The possible vocabulary of comics is, by definition, unlimited..."
-Chris Ware
DON'T DO IT! DON'T JUMP!!

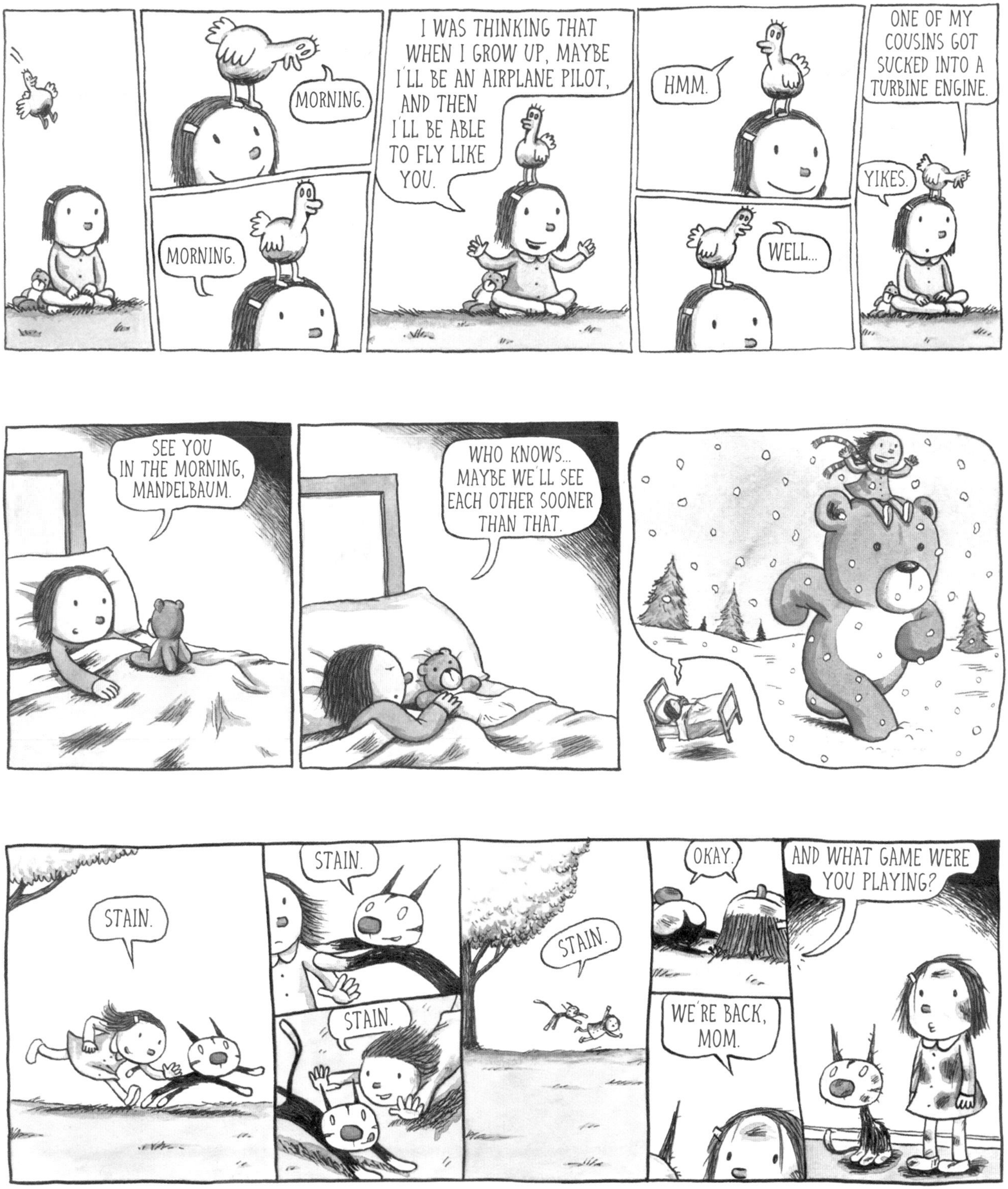
MORNING.
MORNING.
I WAS THINKING THAT WHEN I GROW UP, MAYBE I'LL BE AN AIRPLANE PILOT, AND THEN I'LL BE ABLE TO FLY LIKE YOU.
HMM.
WELL...
ONE OF MY COUSINS GOT SUCKED INTO A TURBINE ENGINE.
YIKES.
SEE YOU IN THE MORNING, MANDELBAUM.
WHO KNOWS... MAYBE WE'LL SEE EACH OTHER SOONER THAN THAT.
STAIN.
STAIN.
STAIN.
STAIN.
OKAY.
WE'RE BACK, MOM.
AND WHAT GAME WERE YOU PLAYING?

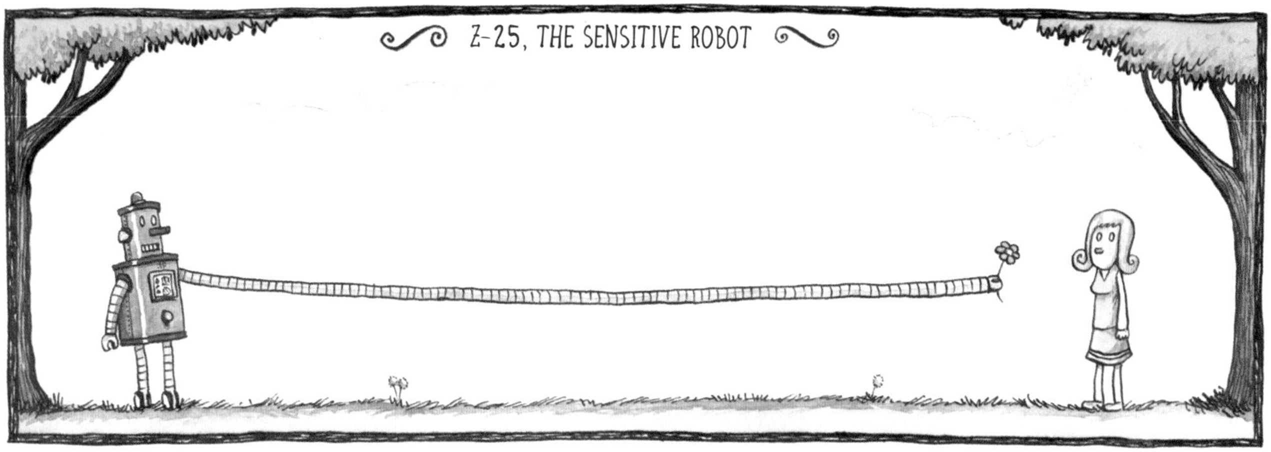
Z-25, THE SENSITIVE ROBOT

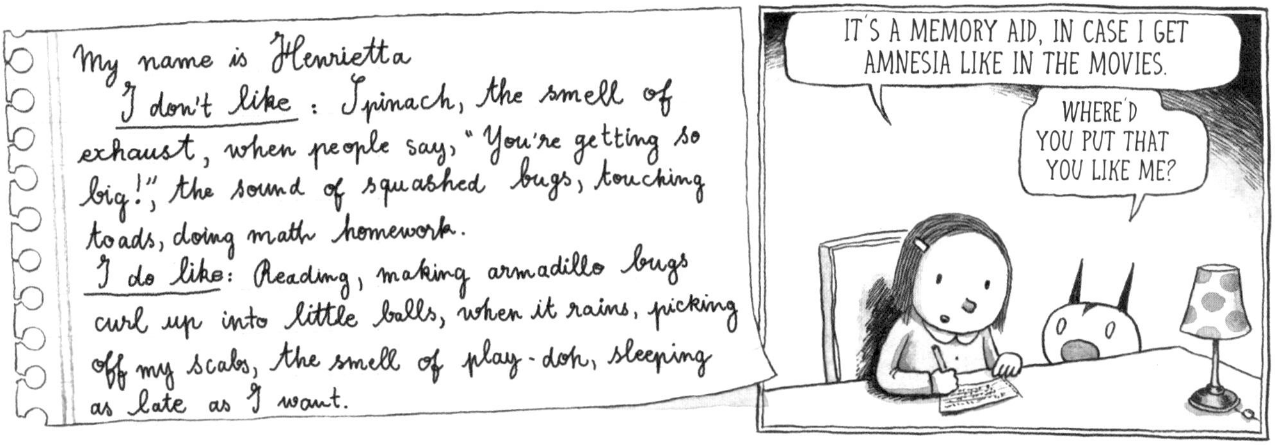
My name is Henrietta
I don't like: Spinach, the smell of exhaust, when people say, "You're getting so big!", the sound of squashed bugs, touching toads, doing math homework.
I do like: Reading, making armadillo bugs curl up into little balls, when it rains, picking off my scabs, the smell of play-doh, sleeping as late as I want.
IT'S A MEMORY AID, IN CASE I GET AMNESIA LIKE IN THE MOVIES.
WHERE'D YOU PUT THAT YOU LIKE ME?

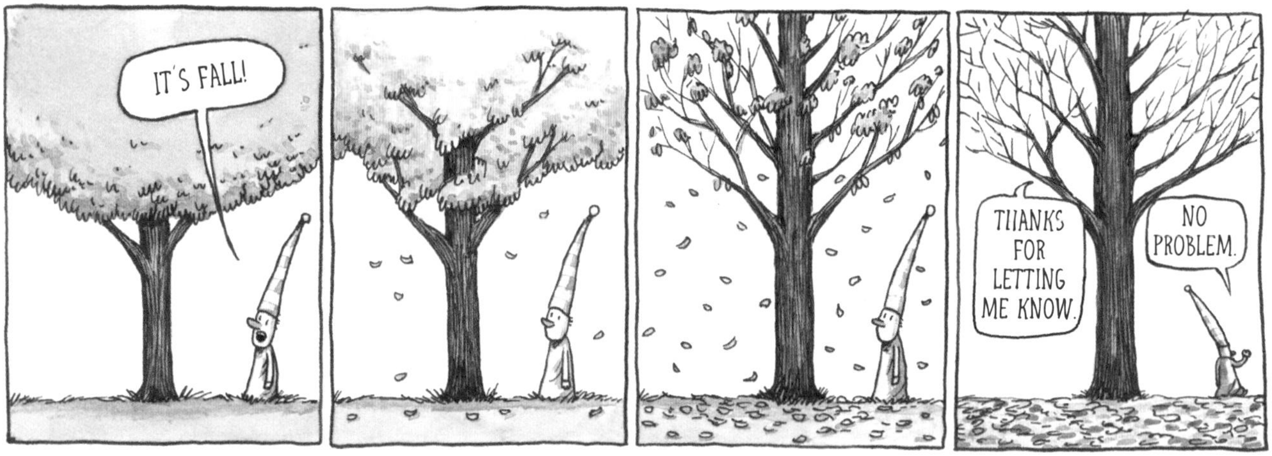
IT'S FALL!
THANKS FOR LETTING ME KNOW.
NO PROBLEM.

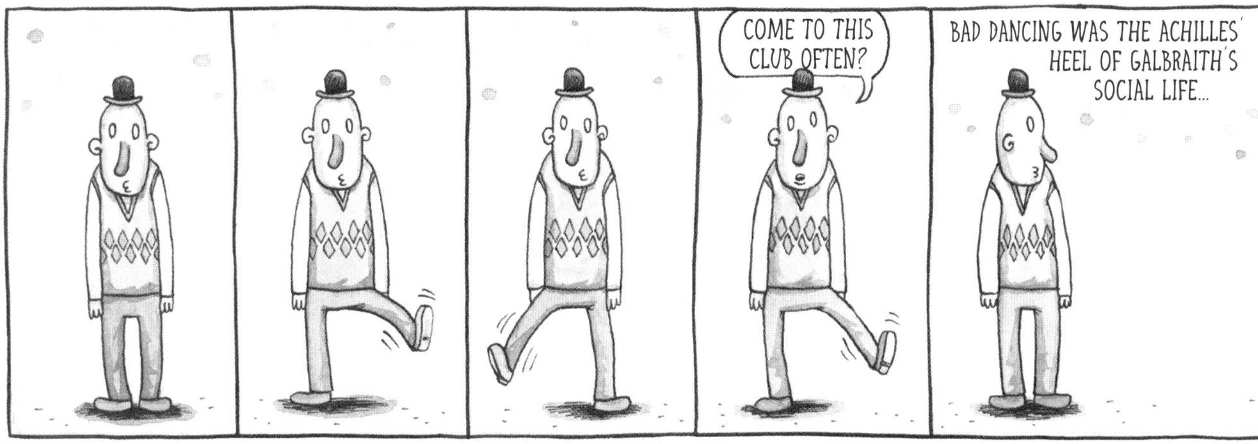
COME TO THIS CLUB OFTEN?
BAD DANCING WAS THE ACHILLES' HEEL OF GALBRAITH'S SOCIAL LIFE...

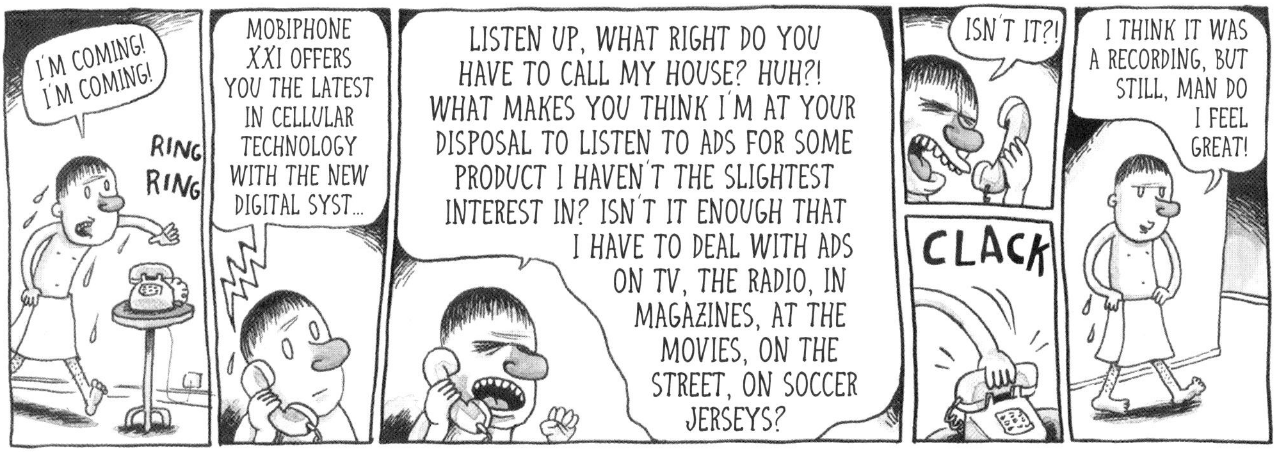
I'M COMING! I'M COMING!
RING RING
MOBIPHONE XXI OFFERS YOU THE LATEST IN CELLULAR TECHNOLOGY WITH THE NEW DIGITAL SYST...
LISTEN UP, WHAT RIGHT DO YOU HAVE TO CALL MY HOUSE? HUH?! WHAT MAKES YOU THINK I'M AT YOUR DISPOSAL TO LISTEN TO ADS FOR SOME PRODUCT I HAVEN'T THE SLIGHTEST INTEREST IN? ISN'T IT ENOUGH THAT I HAVE TO DEAL WITH ADS ON TV, THE RADIO, IN MAGAZINES, AT THE MOVIES, ON THE STREET, ON SOCCER JERSEYS?
ISN'T IT?!
CLACK
I THINK IT WAS A RECORDING, BUT STILL, MAN DO I FEEL GREAT!

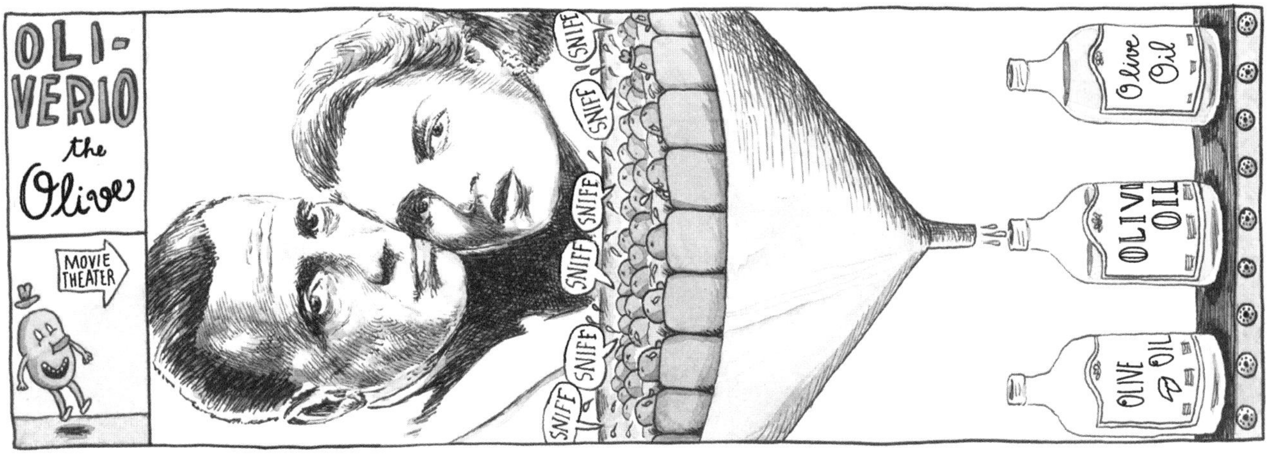
OLI-VERIO the Olive
MOVIE THEATER
SNIFF
SNIFF
SNIFF
SNIFF
SNIFF
SNIFF
SNIFF
SNIFF
SNIFF
Olive Oil
OLIVE OIL
OLIVE OIL

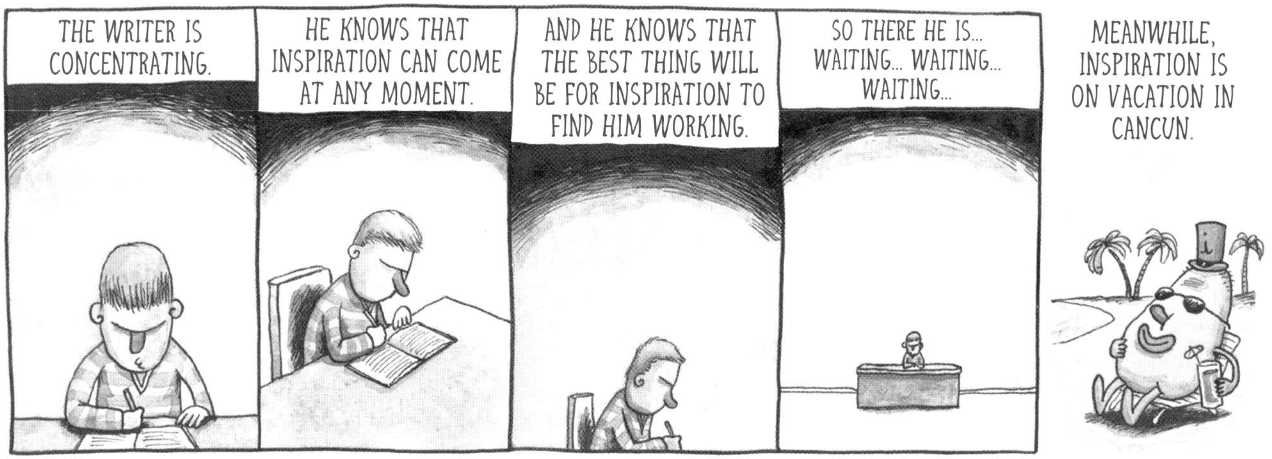
THE WRITER IS CONCENTRATING.
HE KNOWS THAT INSPIRATION CAN COME AT ANY MOMENT.
AND HE KNOWS THAT THE BEST THING WILL BE FOR INSPIRATION TO FIND HIM WORKING.
SO THERE HE IS... WAITING... WAITING... WAITING...
MEANWHILE, INSPIRATION IS ON VACATION IN CANCUN.

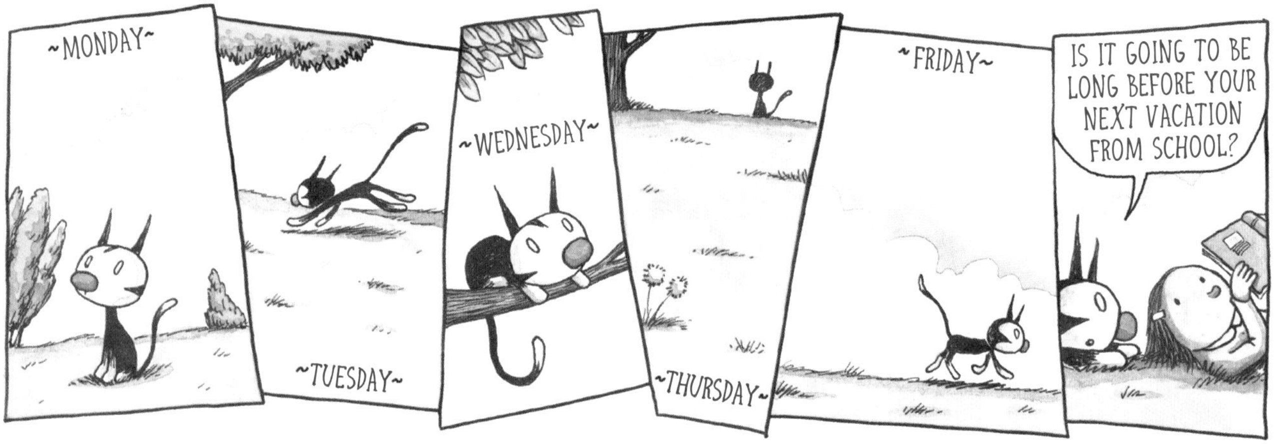
~MONDAY~
~TUESDAY~
~WEDNESDAY~
~THURSDAY~
~FRIDAY~
IS IT GOING TO BE LONG BEFORE YOUR NEXT VACATION FROM SCHOOL?

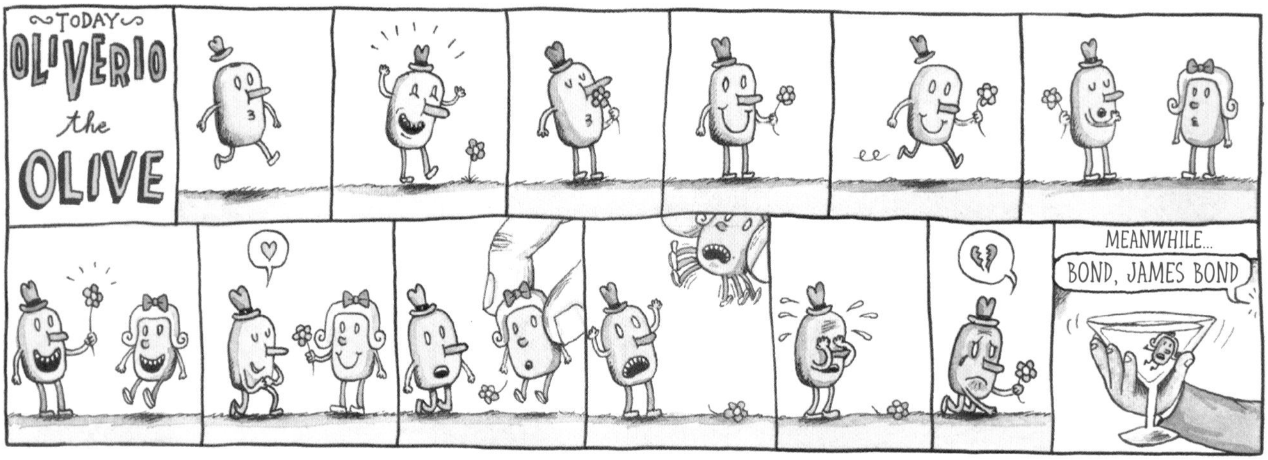
TODAY
OLIVERIO the OLIVE
MEANWHILE...
BOND, JAMES BOND

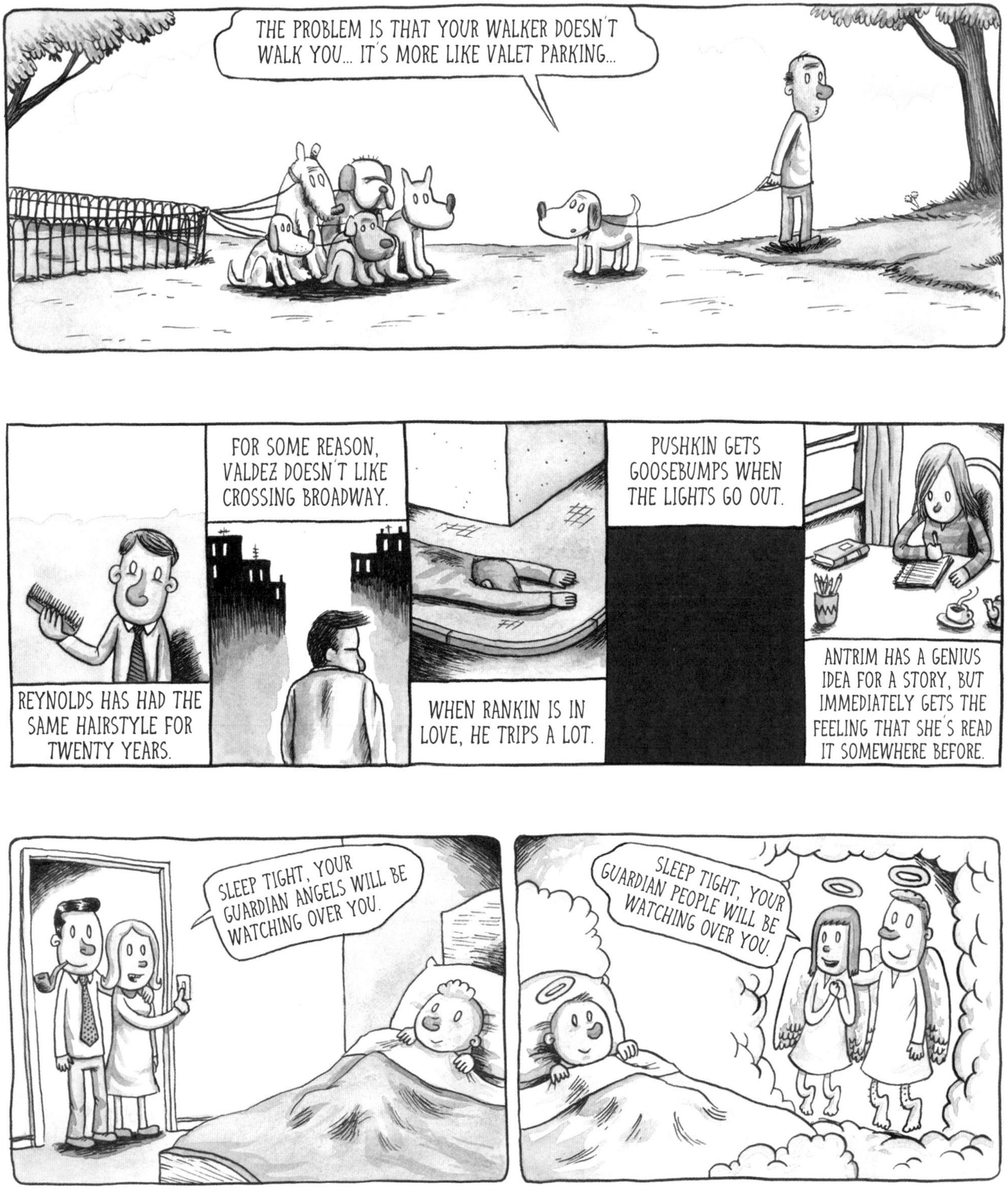
THE PROBLEM IS THAT YOUR WALKER DOESN'T WALK YOU... IT'S MORE LIKE VALET PARKING...
REYNOLDS HAS HAD THE SAME HAIRSTYLE FOR TWENTY YEARS.
FOR SOME REASON, VALDEZ DOESN'T LIKE CROSSING BROADWAY.
WHEN RANKIN IS IN LOVE, HE TRIPS A LOT.
PUSHKIN GETS GOOSEBUMPS WHEN THE LIGHTS GO OUT.
ANTRIM HAS A GENIUS IDEA FOR A STORY, BUT IMMEDIATELY GETS THE FEELING THAT SHE'S READ IT SOMEWHERE BEFORE.
SLEEP TIGHT, YOUR GUARDIAN ANGELS WILL BE WATCHING OVER YOU.
SLEEP TIGHT, YOUR GUARDIAN PEOPLE WILL BE WATCHING OVER YOU.

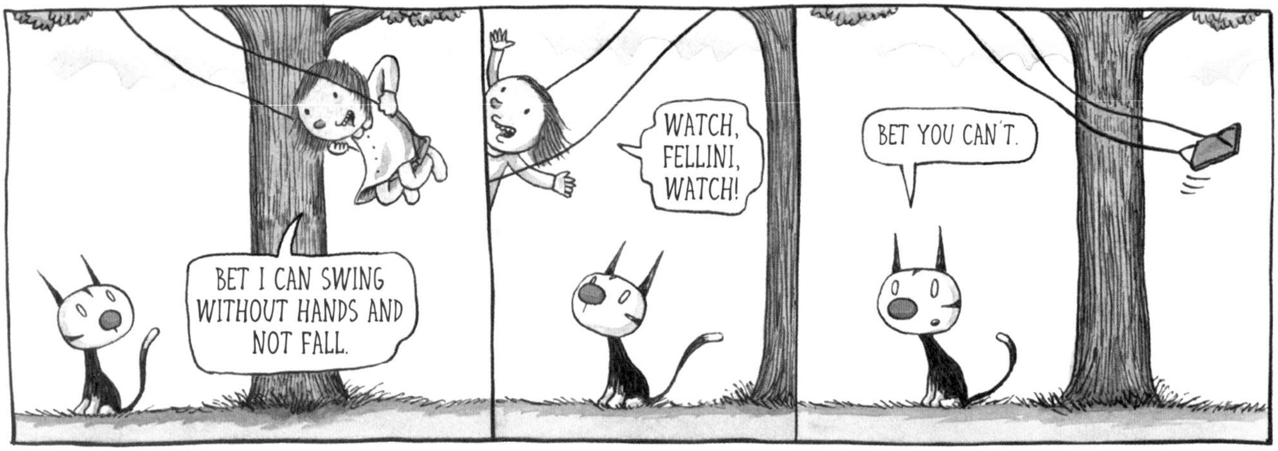
BET I CAN SWING WITHOUT HANDS AND NOT FALL.
WATCH, FELLINI, WATCH!
BET YOU CAN'T.

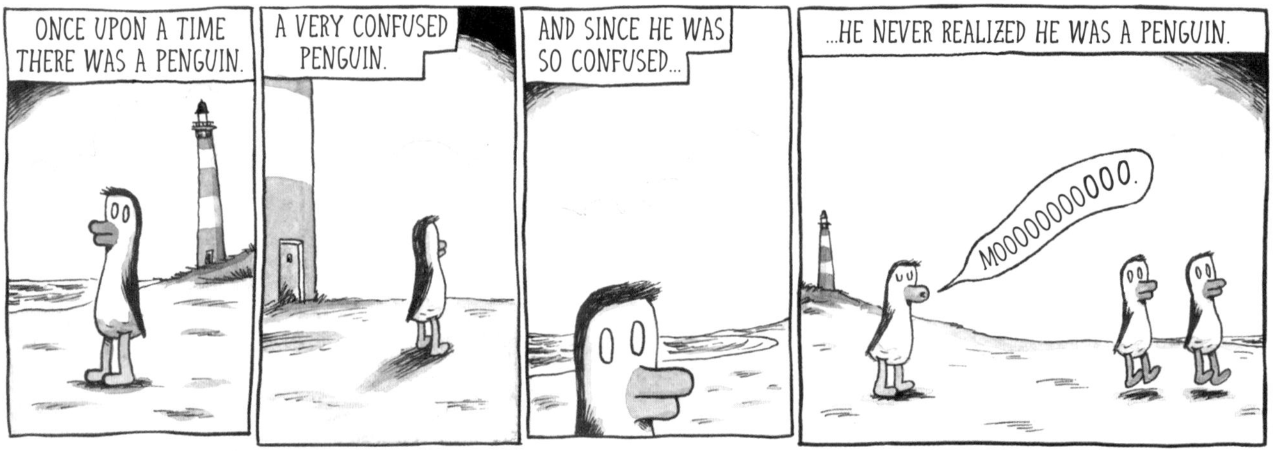
ONCE UPON A TIME THERE WAS A PENGUIN.
A VERY CONFUSED PENGUIN.
AND SINCE HE WAS SO CONFUSED...
...HE NEVER REALIZED HE WAS A PENGUIN.
MOOOOOOOOOOOO.

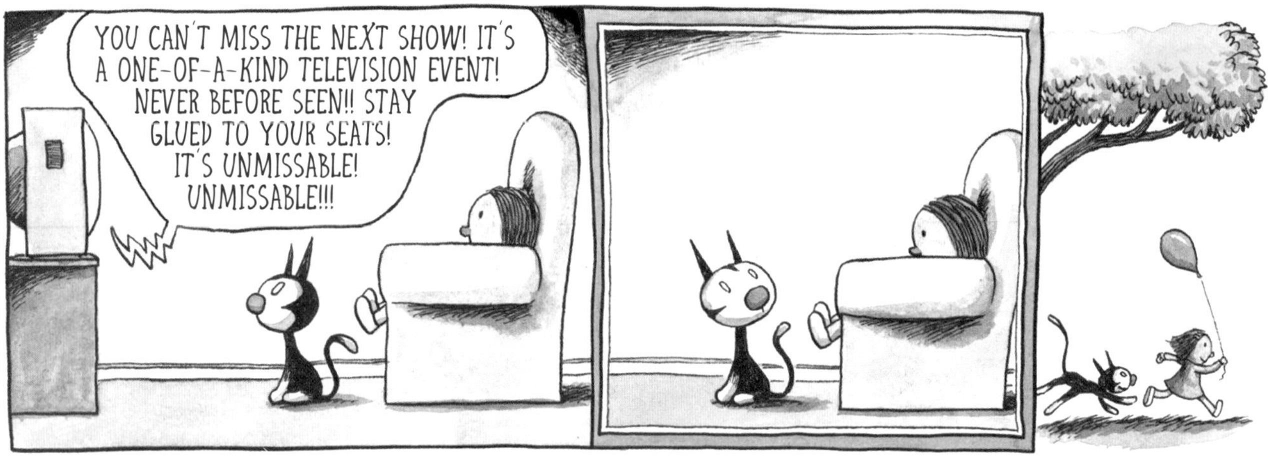
YOU CAN'T MISS THE NEXT SHOW! IT'S A ONE-OF-A-KIND TELEVISION EVENT! NEVER BEFORE SEEN!! STAY GLUED TO YOUR SEATS! IT'S UNMISSABLE! UNMISSABLE!!!

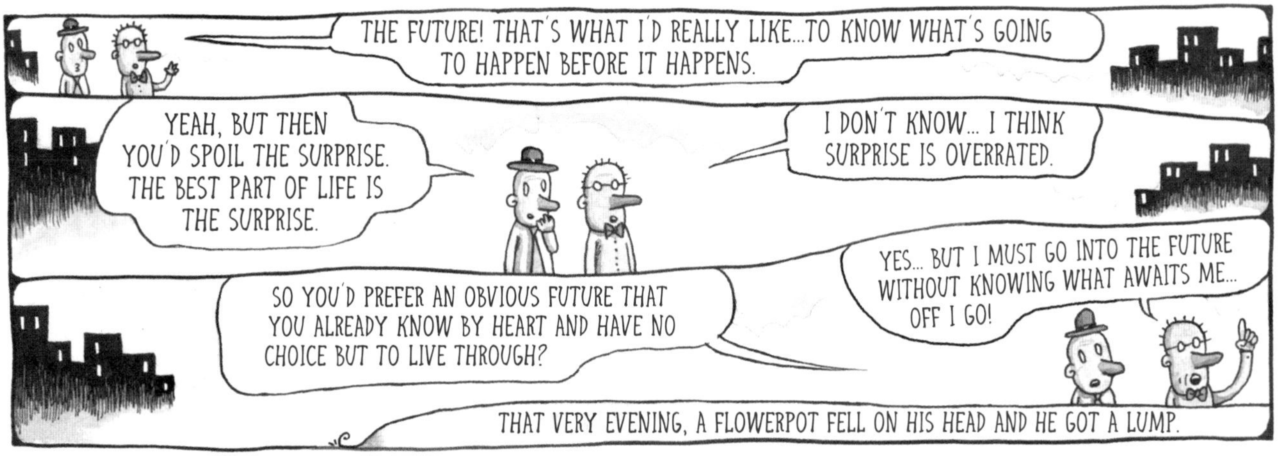
THE FUTURE! THAT'S WHAT I'D REALLY LIKE...TO KNOW WHAT'S GOING TO HAPPEN BEFORE IT HAPPENS.
YEAH, BUT THEN YOU'D SPOIL THE SURPRISE. THE BEST PART OF LIFE IS THE SURPRISE.
I DON'T KNOW... I THINK SURPRISE IS OVERRATED.
SO YOU'D PREFER AN OBVIOUS FUTURE THAT YOU ALREADY KNOW BY HEART AND HAVE NO CHOICE BUT TO LIVE THROUGH?
YES... BUT I MUST GO INTO THE FUTURE WITHOUT KNOWING WHAT AWAITS ME... OFF I GO!
THAT VERY EVENING, A FLOWERPOT FELL ON HIS HEAD AND HE GOT A LUMP.

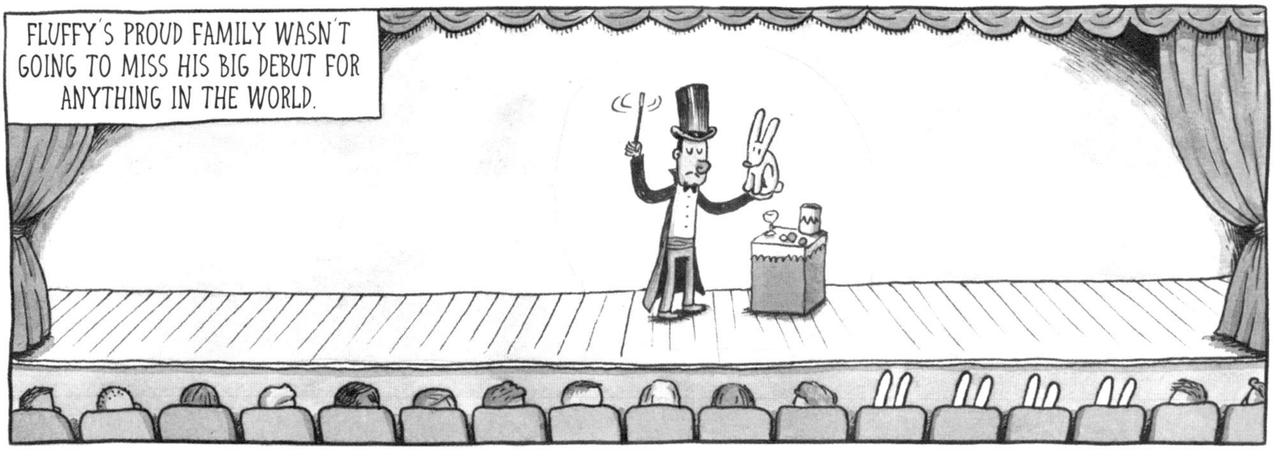
FLUFFY'S PROUD FAMILY WASN'T GOING TO MISS HIS BIG DEBUT FOR ANYTHING IN THE WORLD.

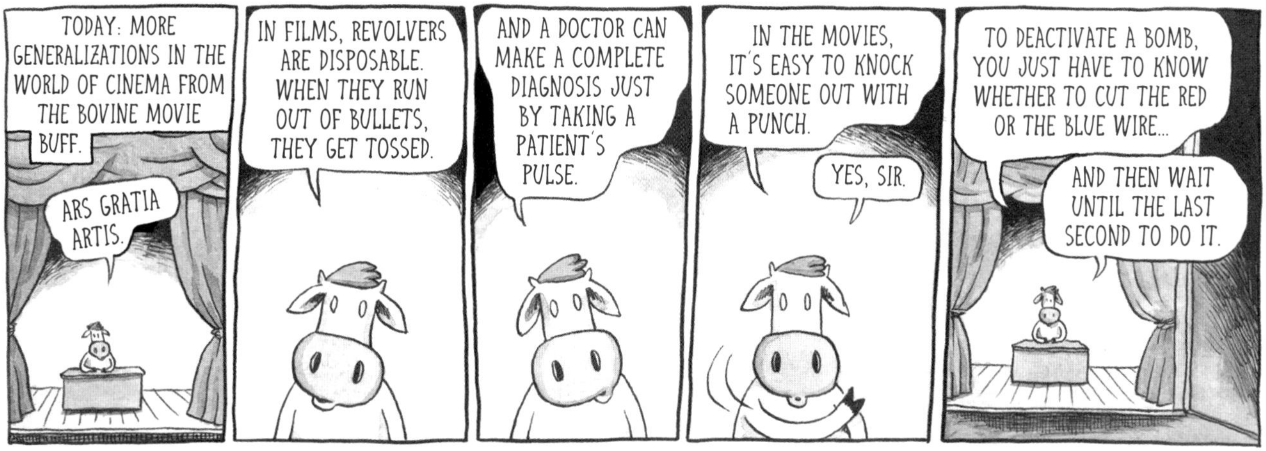
TODAY: MORE GENERALIZATIONS IN THE WORLD OF CINEMA FROM THE BOVINE MOVIE BUFF.
ARS GRATIA ARTIS.
IN FILMS, REVOLVERS ARE DISPOSABLE. WHEN THEY RUN OUT OF BULLETS, THEY GET TOSSED.
AND A DOCTOR CAN MAKE A COMPLETE DIAGNOSIS JUST BY TAKING A PATIENT'S PULSE.
IN THE MOVIES, IT'S EASY TO KNOCK SOMEONE OUT WITH A PUNCH.
YES, SIR.
TO DEACTIVATE A BOMB, YOU JUST HAVE TO KNOW WHETHER TO CUT THE RED OR THE BLUE WIRE...
AND THEN WAIT UNTIL THE LAST SECOND TO DO IT.

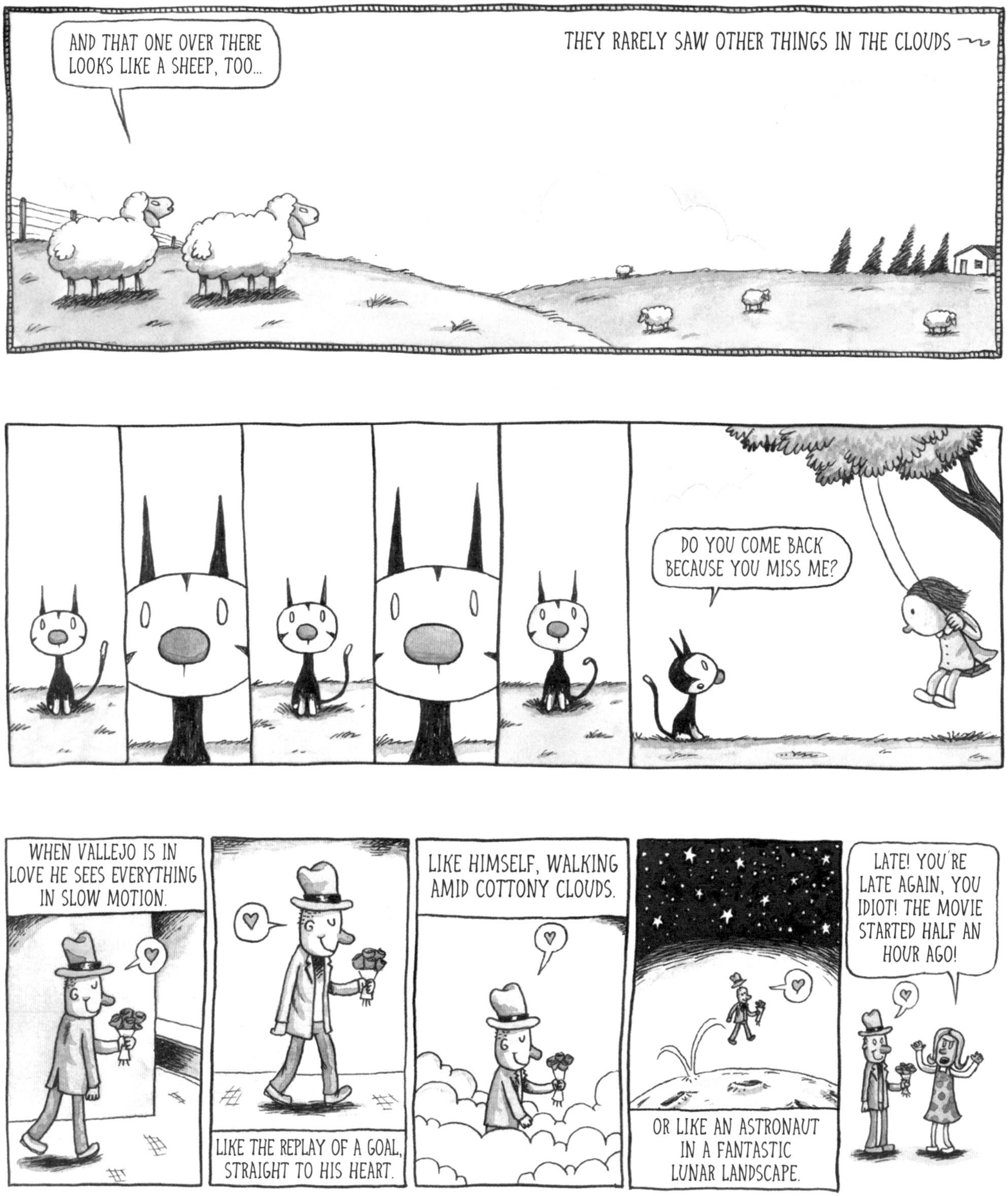
AND THAT ONE OVER THERE LOOKS LIKE A SHEEP, TOO...
THEY RARELY SAW OTHER THINGS IN THE CLOUDS
DO YOU COME BACK BECAUSE YOU MISS ME?
WHEN VALLEJO IS IN LOVE HE SEES EVERYTHING IN SLOW MOTION.
LIKE THE REPLAY OF A GOAL, STRAIGHT TO HIS HEART.
LIKE HIMSELF, WALKING AMID COTTONY CLOUDS.
OR LIKE AN ASTRONAUT IN A FANTASTIC LUNAR LANDSCAPE.
LATE! YOU'RE LATE AGAIN, YOU IDIOT! THE MOVIE STARTED HALF AN HOUR AGO!

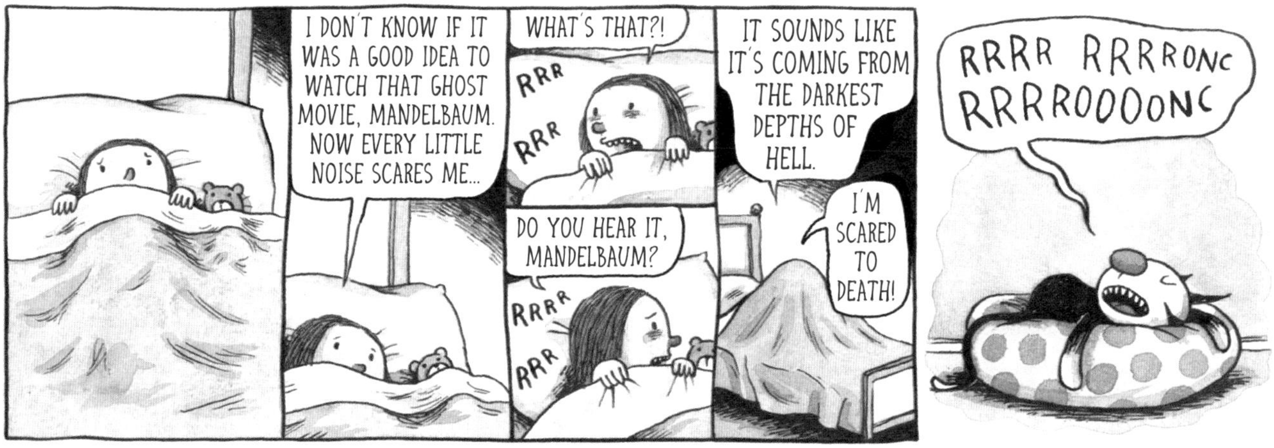
I DON'T KNOW IF IT WAS A GOOD IDEA TO WATCH THAT GHOST MOVIE, MANDELBAUM. NOW EVERY LITTLE NOISE SCARES ME...
WHAT'S THAT?!
RRR
RRR
DO YOU HEAR IT, MANDELBAUM?
RRRR
RRR
IT SOUNDS LIKE IT'S COMING FROM THE DARKEST DEPTHS OF HELL.
I'M SCARED TO DEATH!
RRRR RRRRONC RRRROOOONC

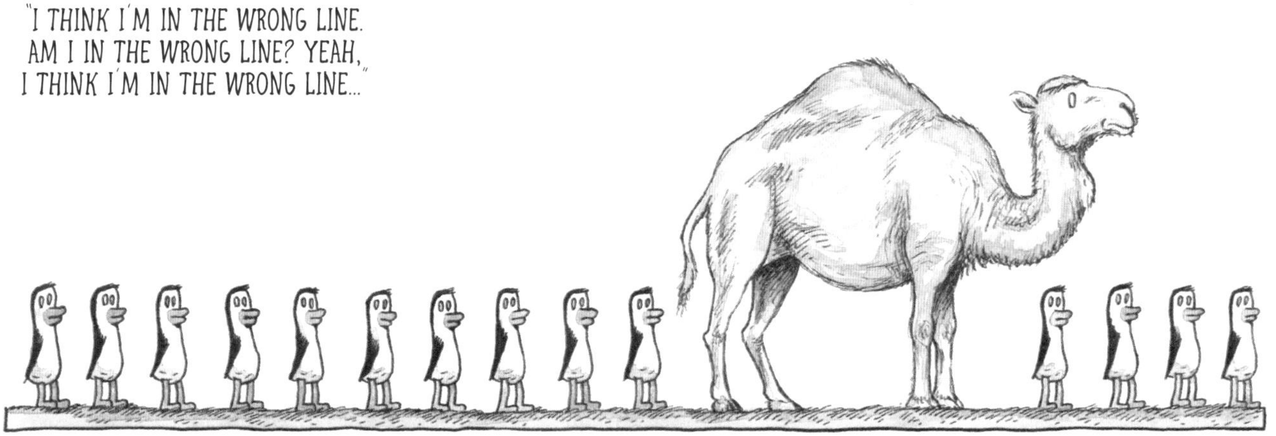
"I THINK I'M IN THE WRONG LINE. AM I IN THE WRONG LINE? YEAH, I THINK I'M IN THE WRONG LINE..."

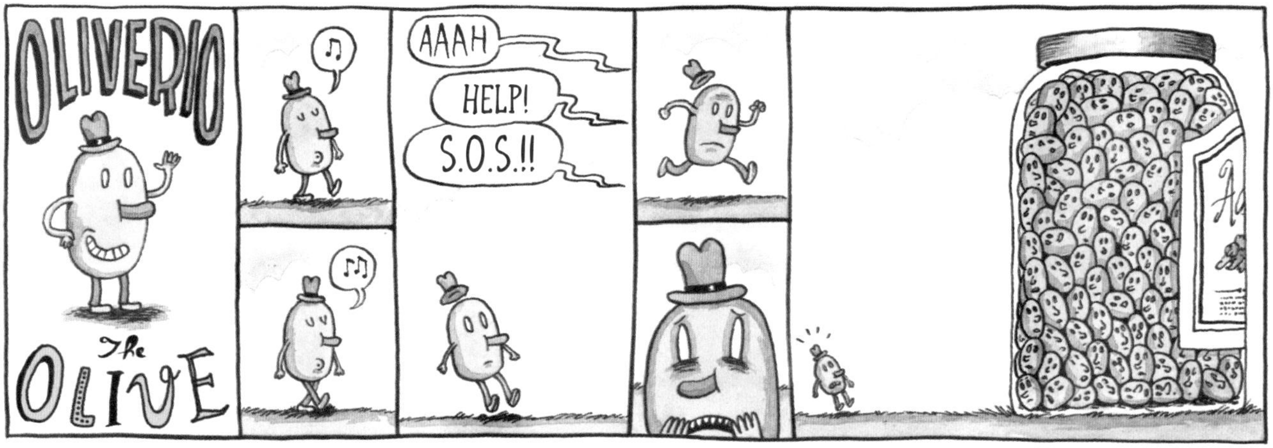
OLIVERIO
The
OLIVE
AAAH
HELP!
S.O.S.!!

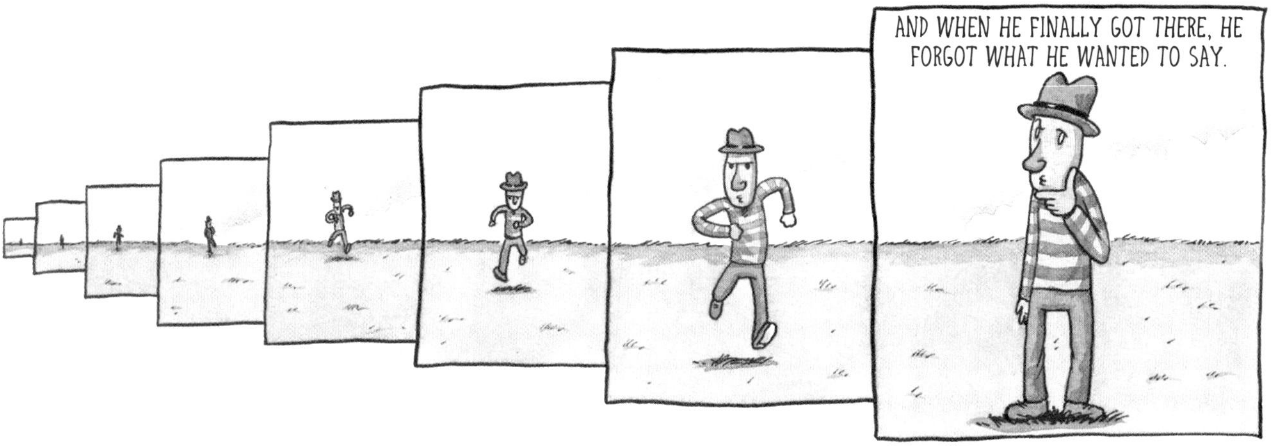
AND WHEN HE FINALLY GOT THERE, HE FORGOT WHAT HE WANTED TO SAY.

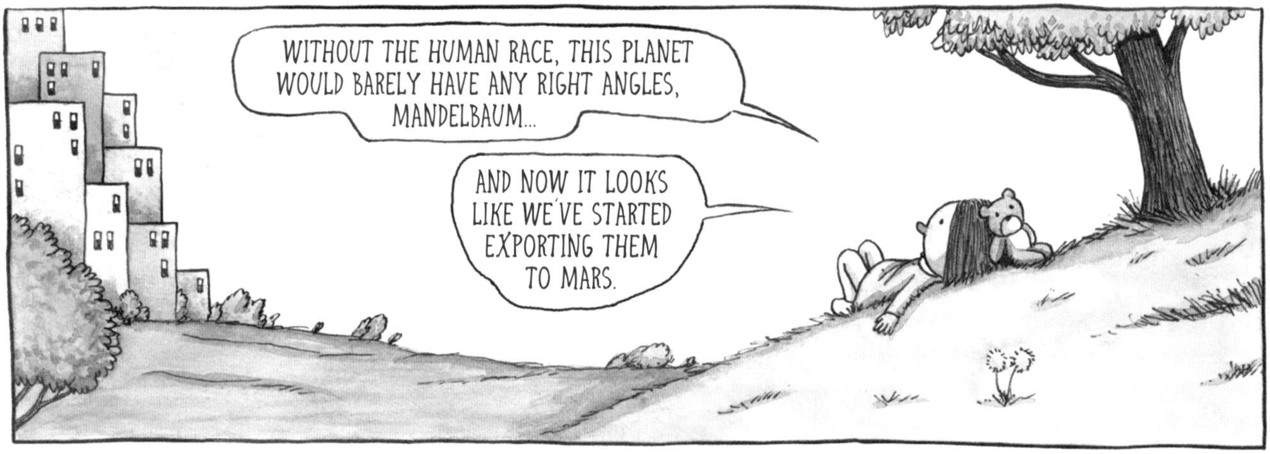
WITHOUT THE HUMAN RACE, THIS PLANET WOULD BARELY HAVE ANY RIGHT ANGLES, MANDELBAUM...
AND NOW IT LOOKS LIKE WE'VE STARTED EXPORTING THEM TO MARS.

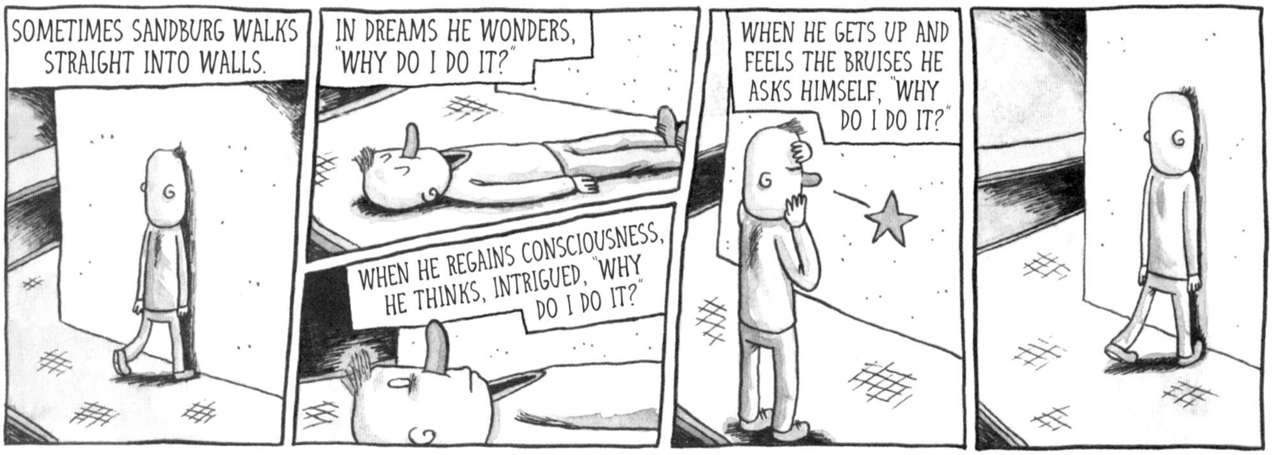
SOMETIMES SANDBURG WALKS STRAIGHT INTO WALLS.
IN DREAMS HE WONDERS, "WHY DO I DO IT?"
WHEN HE REGAINS CONSCIOUSNESS, HE THINKS, INTRIGUED, "WHY DO I DO IT?"
WHEN HE GETS UP AND FEELS THE BRUISES HE ASKS HIMSELF, "WHY DO I DO IT?"

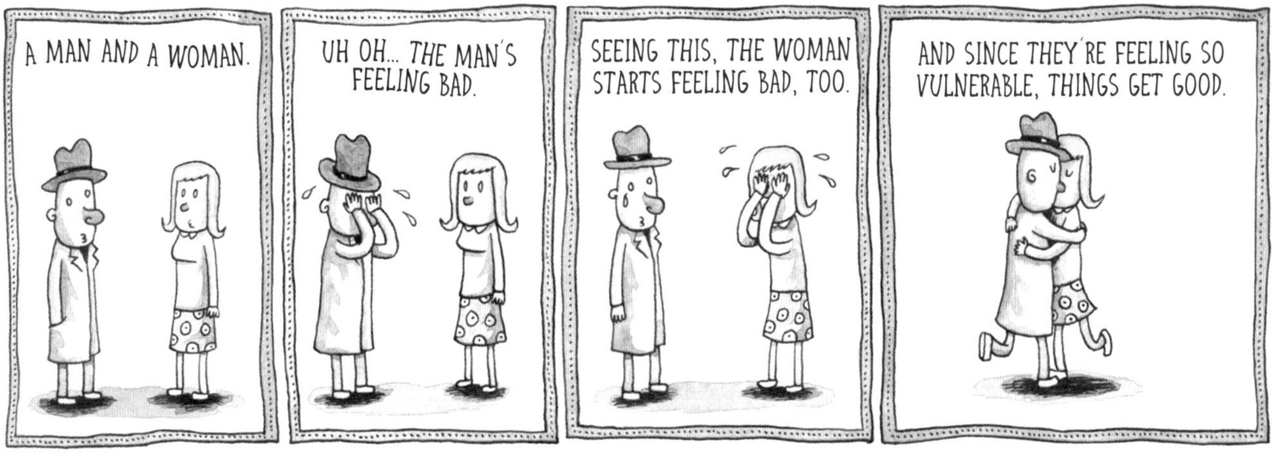
A MAN AND A WOMAN.
UH OH... THE MAN'S FEELING BAD.
SEEING THIS, THE WOMAN STARTS FEELING BAD, TOO.
AND SINCE THEY'RE FEELING SO VULNERABLE, THINGS GET GOOD.

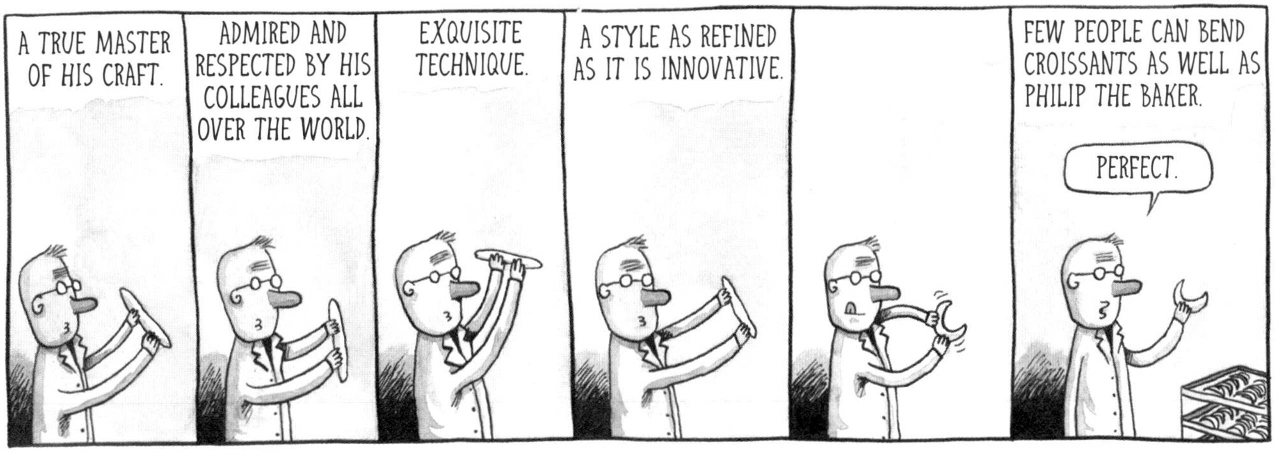
A TRUE MASTER OF HIS CRAFT.
ADMIRED AND RESPECTED BY HIS COLLEAGUES ALL OVER THE WORLD.
EXQUISITE TECHNIQUE.
A STYLE AS REFINED AS IT IS INNOVATIVE.
FEW PEOPLE CAN BEND CROISSANTS AS WELL AS PHILIP THE BAKER.
PERFECT.

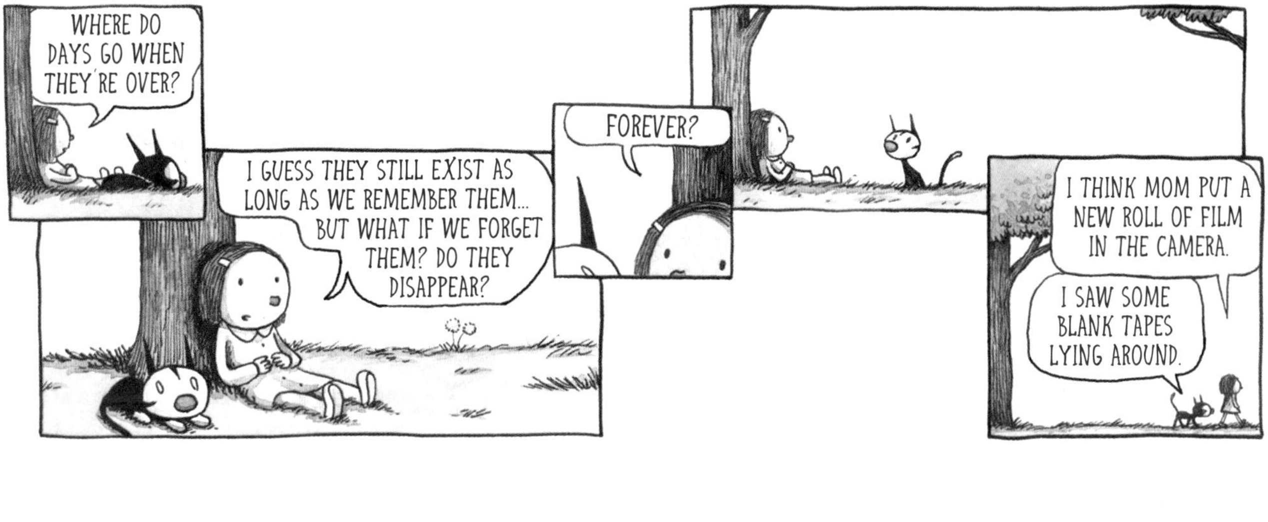
WHERE DO DAYS GO WHEN THEY'RE OVER?
I GUESS THEY STILL EXIST AS LONG AS WE REMEMBER THEM... BUT WHAT IF WE FORGET THEM? DO THEY DISAPPEAR?
FOREVER?
I THINK MOM PUT A NEW ROLL OF FILM IN THE CAMERA.
I SAW SOME BLANK TAPES LYING AROUND.

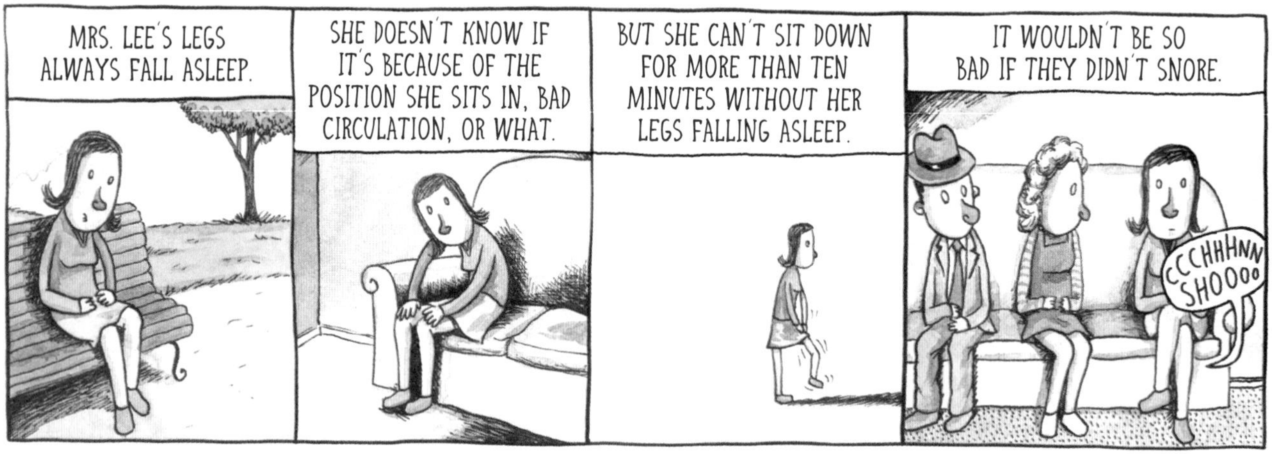
MRS. LEE'S LEGS ALWAYS FALL ASLEEP.
SHE DOESN'T KNOW IF IT'S BECAUSE OF THE POSITION SHE SITS IN, BAD CIRCULATION, OR WHAT.
BUT SHE CAN'T SIT DOWN FOR MORE THAN TEN MINUTES WITHOUT HER LEGS FALLING ASLEEP.
IT WOULDN'T BE SO BAD IF THEY DIDN'T SNORE.
CCCHHHNN SHOOOo

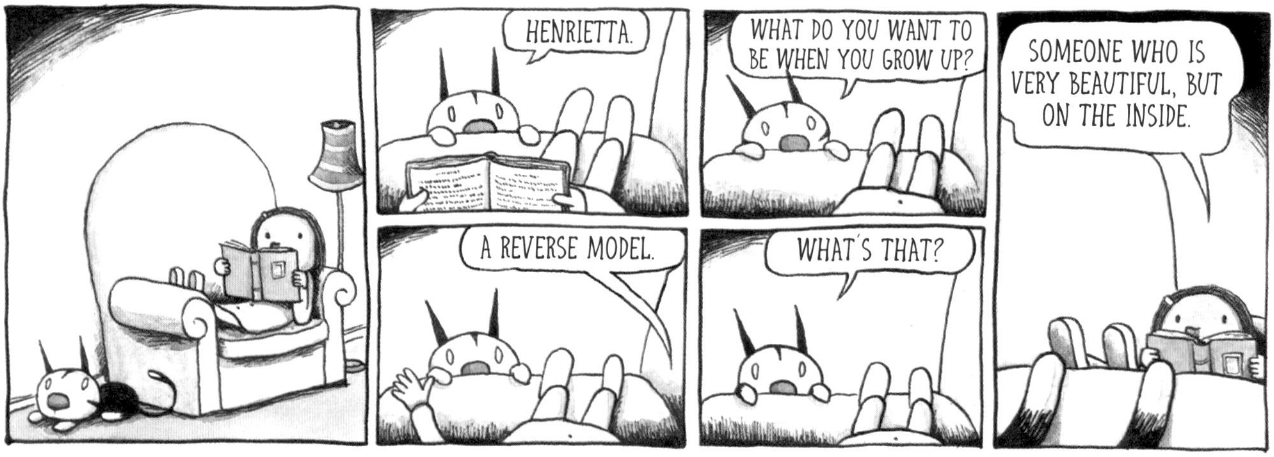
HENRIETTA.
WHAT DO YOU WANT TO BE WHEN YOU GROW UP?
A REVERSE MODEL.
WHAT'S THAT?
SOMEONE WHO IS VERY BEAUTIFUL, BUT ON THE INSIDE.

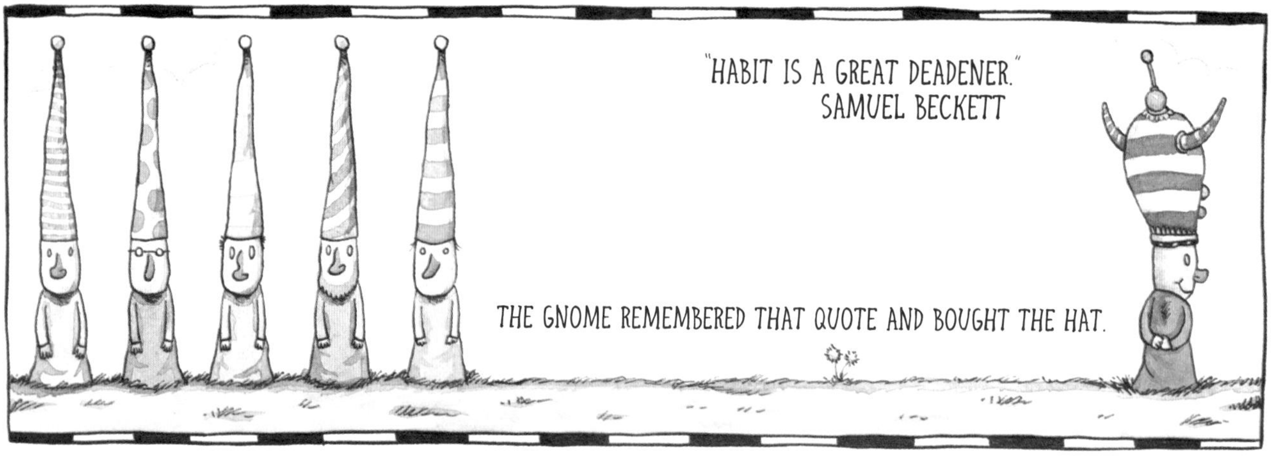
"HABIT IS A GREAT DEADENER."
SAMUEL BECKETT
THE GNOME REMEMBERED THAT QUOTE AND BOUGHT THE HAT.

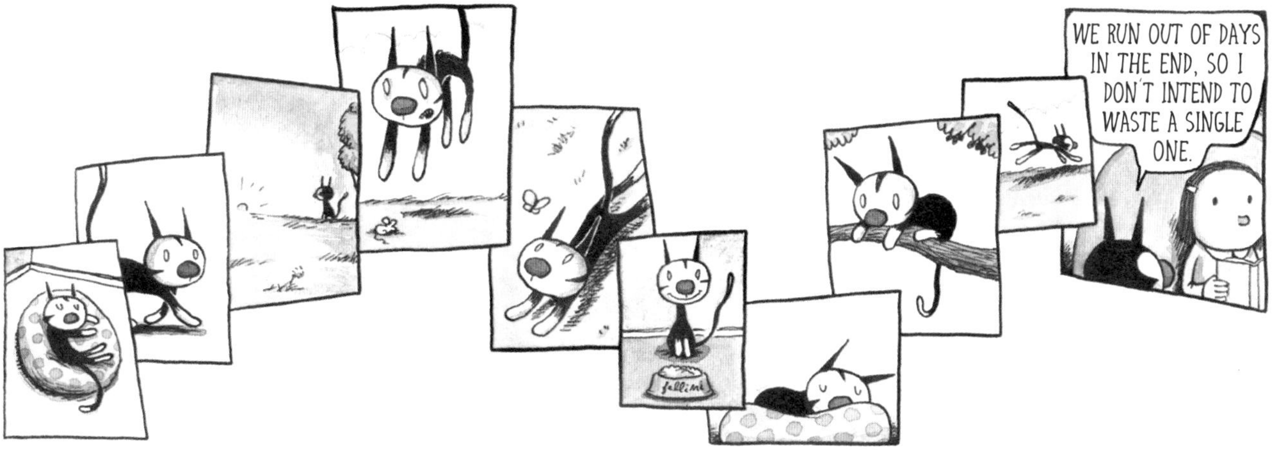
WE RUN OUT OF DAYS IN THE END, SO I DON'T INTEND TO WASTE A SINGLE ONE.

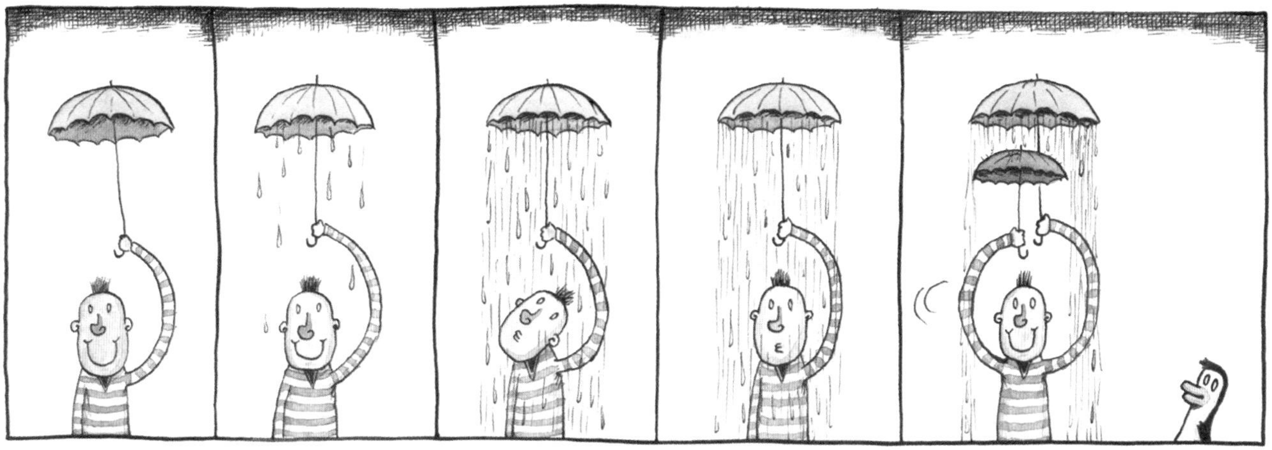

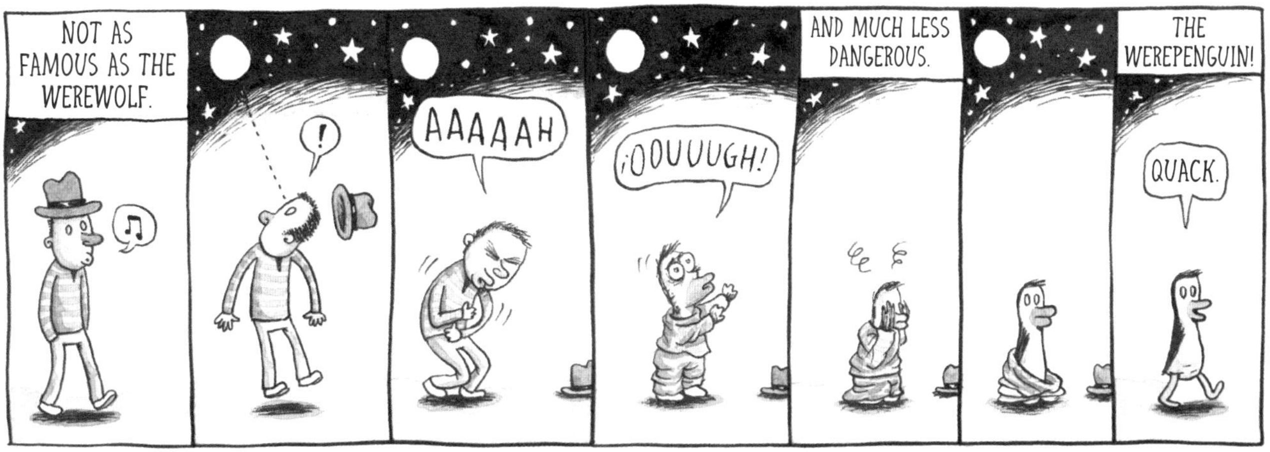
NOT AS FAMOUS AS THE WEREWOLF.
!
AAAAAH
¡OOUUUGH!
AND MUCH LESS DANGEROUS.
THE WEREPENGUIN!
QUACK.

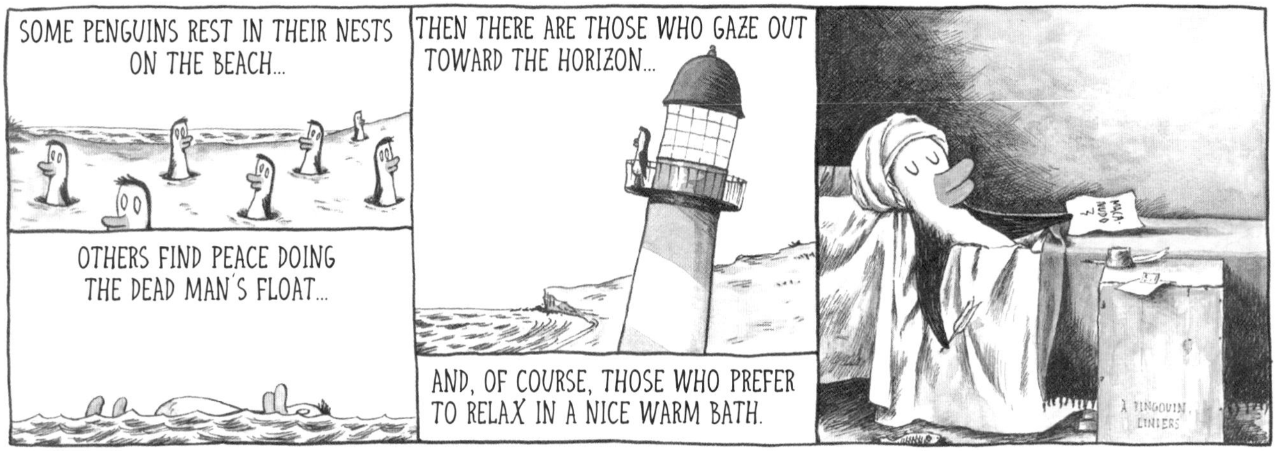
SOME PENGUINS REST IN THEIR NESTS ON THE BEACH...
OTHERS FIND PEACE DOING THE DEAD MAN'S FLOAT...
THEN THERE ARE THOSE WHO GAZE OUT TOWARD THE HORIZON...
AND, OF COURSE, THOSE WHO PREFER TO RELAX IN A NICE WARM BATH.

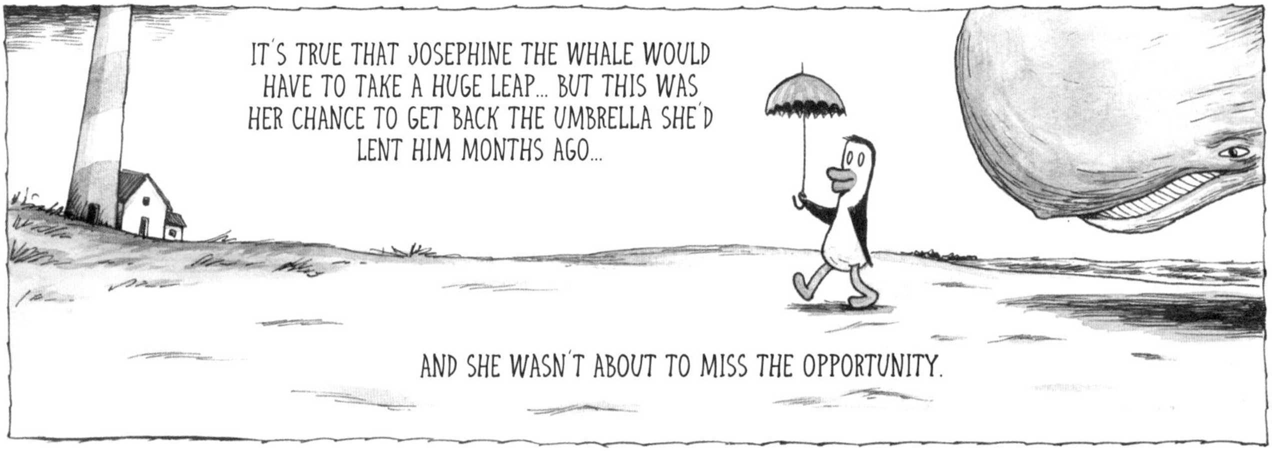
IT'S TRUE THAT JOSEPHINE THE WHALE WOULD HAVE TO TAKE A HUGE LEAP... BUT THIS WAS HER CHANCE TO GET BACK THE UMBRELLA SHE'D LENT HIM MONTHS AGO...
AND SHE WASN'T ABOUT TO MISS THE OPPORTUNITY.

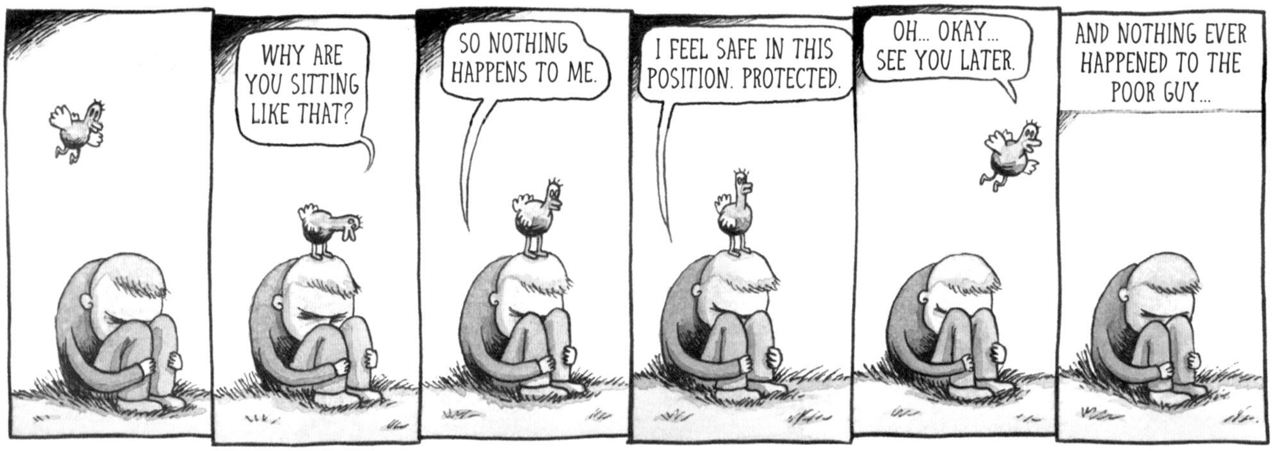
WHY ARE YOU SITTING LIKE THAT?
SO NOTHING HAPPENS TO ME.
I FEEL SAFE IN THIS POSITION. PROTECTED.
OH... OKAY... SEE YOU LATER.
AND NOTHING EVER HAPPENED TO THE POOR GUY...

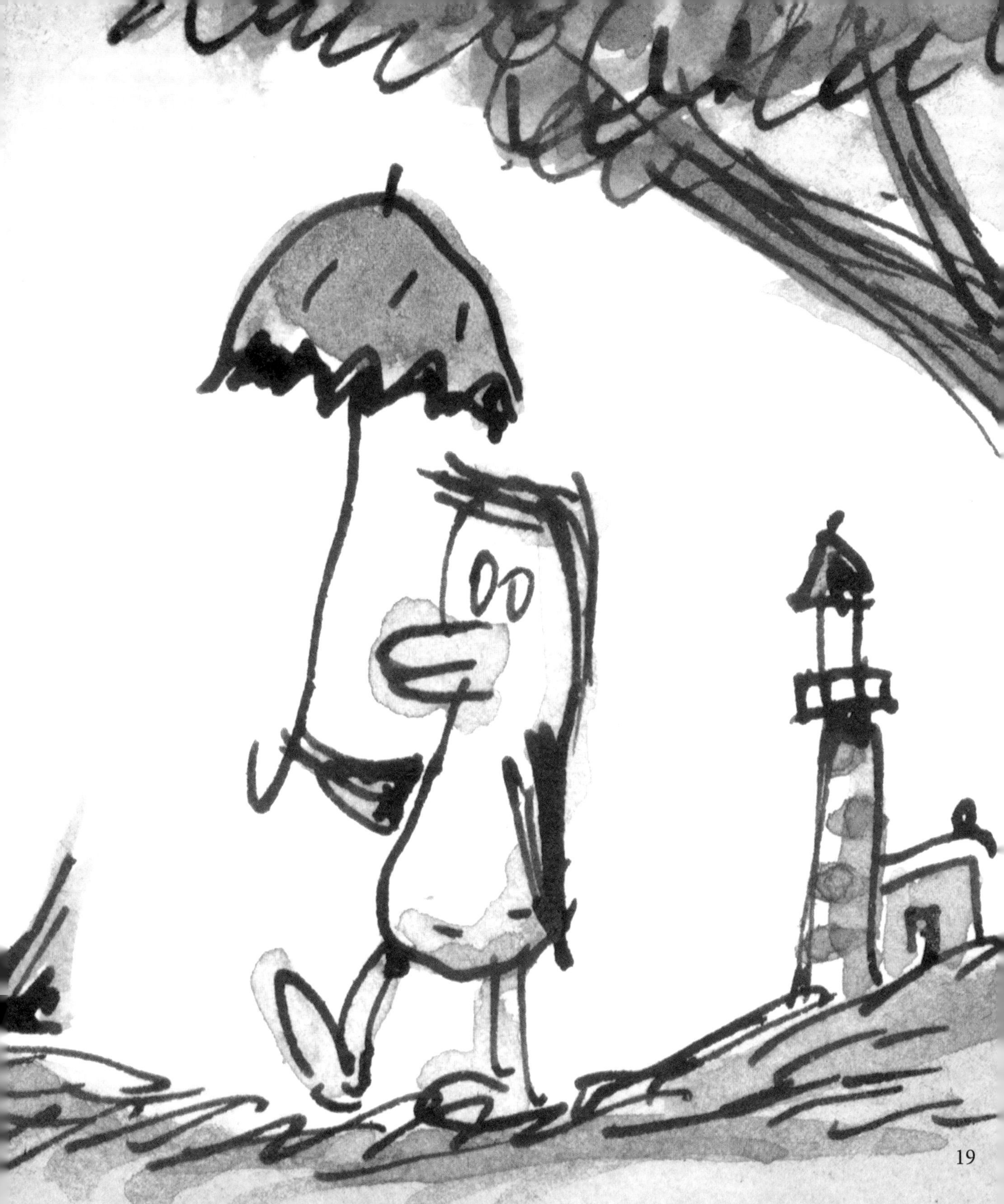

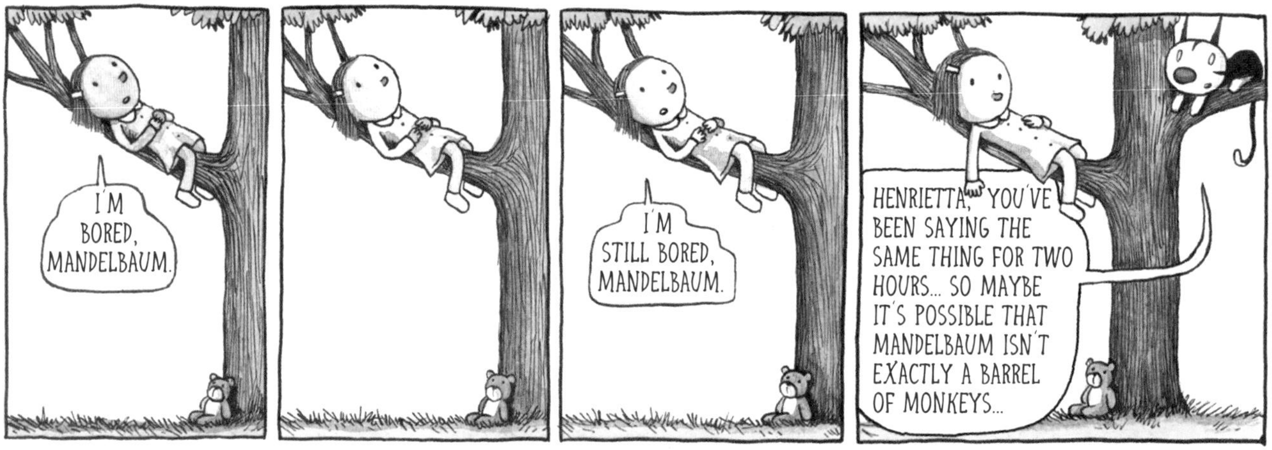
I'M BORED, MANDELBAUM.
I'M STILL BORED, MANDELBAUM.
HENRIETTA, YOU'VE BEEN SAYING THE SAME THING FOR TWO HOURS... SO MAYBE IT'S POSSIBLE THAT MANDELBAUM ISN'T EXACTLY A BARREL OF MONKEYS...

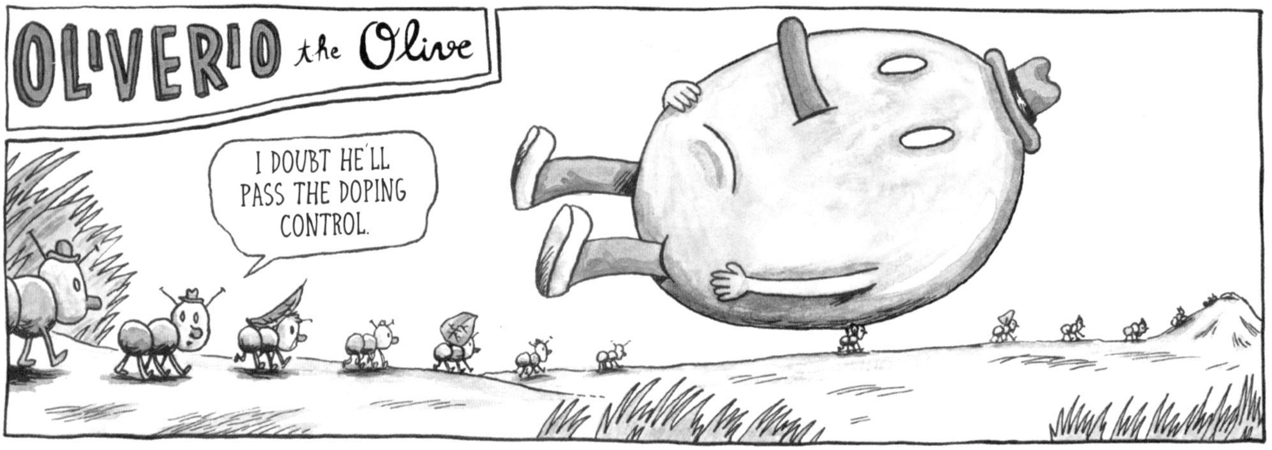
OLIVERIO the Olive
I DOUBT HE'LL PASS THE DOPING CONTROL.

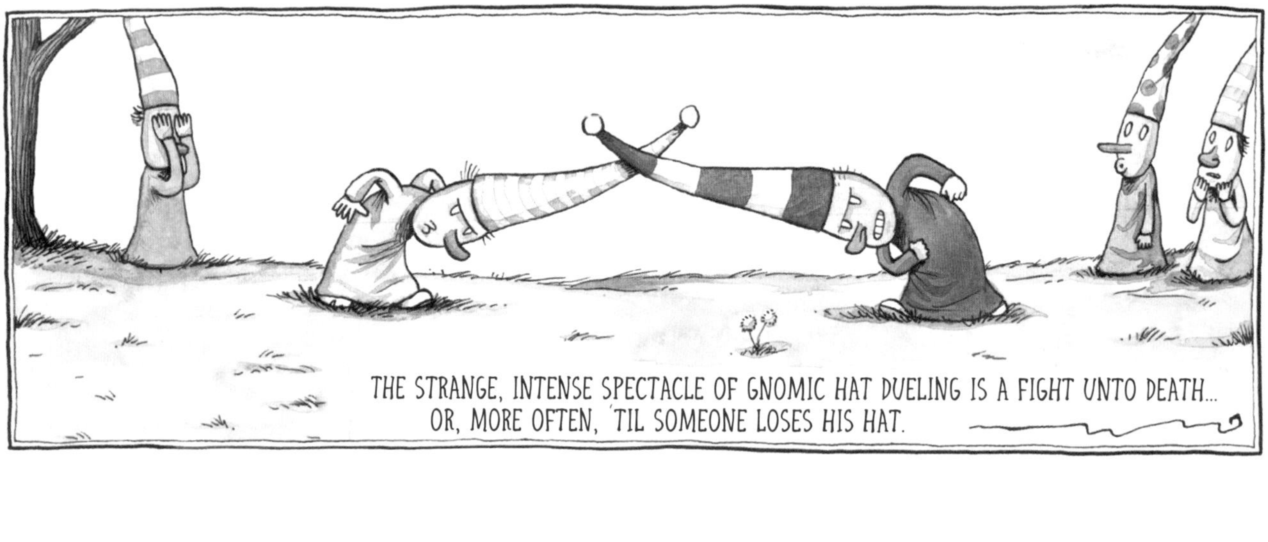
THE STRANGE, INTENSE SPECTACLE OF GNOMIC HAT DUELING IS A FIGHT UNTO DEATH...
OR, MORE OFTEN, 'TIL SOMEONE LOSES HIS HAT.

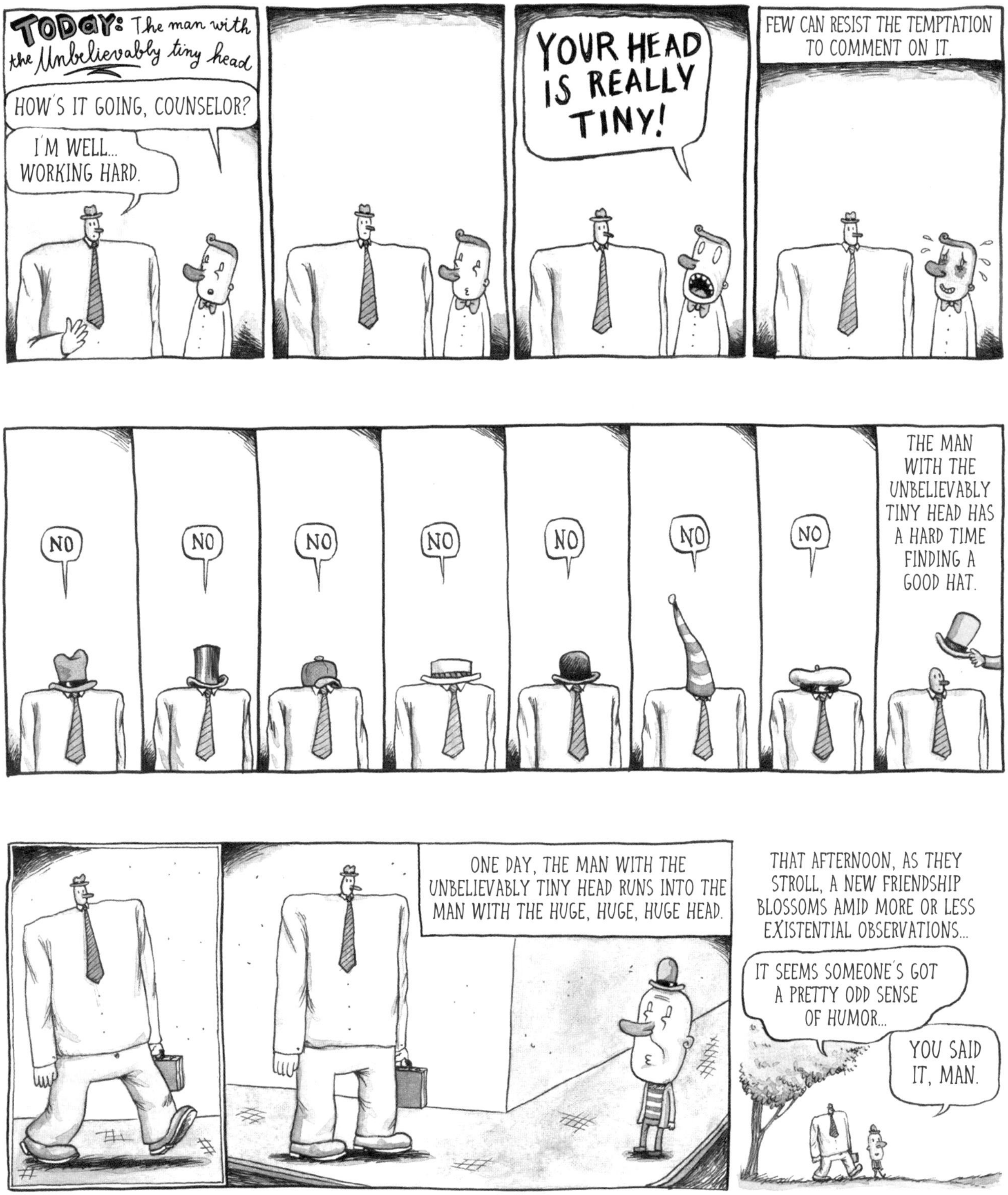
TODAY: The man with the Unbelievably tiny head
HOW'S IT GOING, COUNSELOR?
I'M WELL... WORKING HARD.
YOUR HEAD IS REALLY TINY!
FEW CAN RESIST THE TEMPTATION TO COMMENT ON IT.
NO
NO
NO
NO
NO
NO
NO
THE MAN WITH THE UNBELIEVABLY TINY HEAD HAS A HARD TIME FINDING A GOOD HAT.
ONE DAY, THE MAN WITH THE UNBELIEVABLY TINY HEAD RUNS INTO THE MAN WITH THE HUGE, HUGE, HUGE HEAD.
THAT AFTERNOON, AS THEY STROLL, A NEW FRIENDSHIP BLOSSOMS AMID MORE OR LESS EXISTENTIAL OBSERVATIONS...
IT SEEMS SOMEONE'S GOT A PRETTY ODD SENSE OF HUMOR...
YOU SAID IT, MAN.

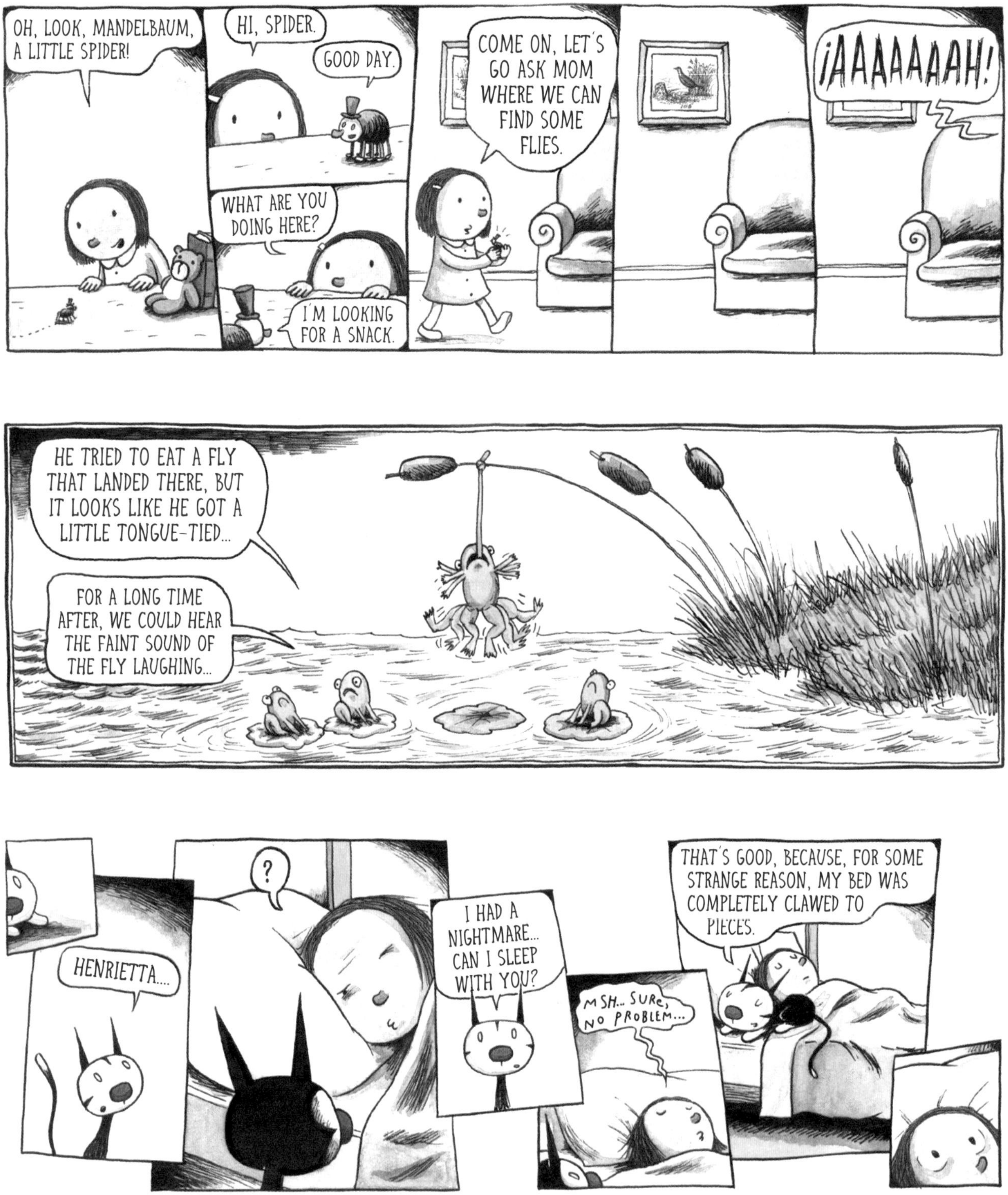
OH, LOOK, MANDELBAUM, A LITTLE SPIDER!
HI, SPIDER.
GOOD DAY.
WHAT ARE YOU DOING HERE?
I'M LOOKING FOR A SNACK.
COME ON, LET'S GO ASK MOM WHERE WE CAN FIND SOME FLIES.
¡AAAAAAAH!
HE TRIED TO EAT A FLY THAT LANDED THERE, BUT IT LOOKS LIKE HE GOT A LITTLE TONGUE-TIED...
FOR A LONG TIME AFTER, WE COULD HEAR THE FAINT SOUND OF THE FLY LAUGHING...
HENRIETTA....
?
I HAD A NIGHTMARE... CAN I SLEEP WITH YOU?
MSH... SURE, NO PROBLEM...
THAT'S GOOD, BECAUSE, FOR SOME STRANGE REASON, MY BED WAS COMPLETELY CLAWED TO PIECES.

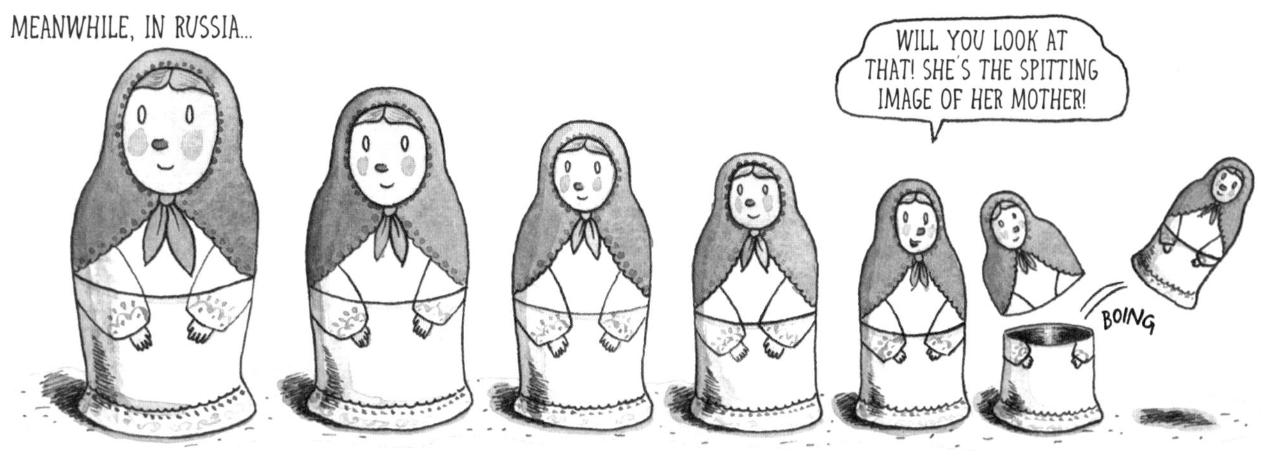
MEANWHILE, IN RUSSIA...
WILL YOU LOOK AT THAT! SHE'S THE SPITTING IMAGE OF HER MOTHER!
BOING

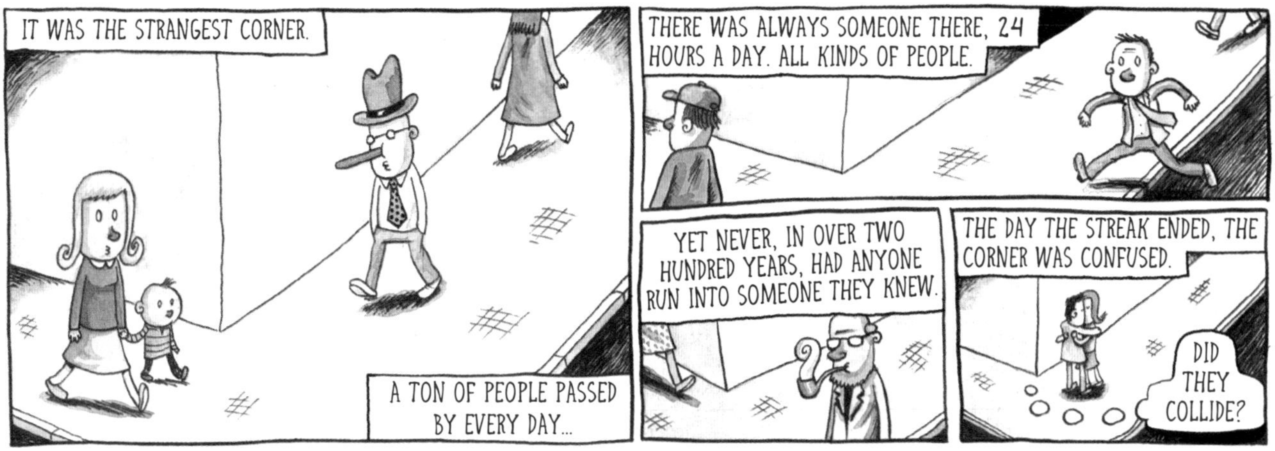
IT WAS THE STRANGEST CORNER.
A TON OF PEOPLE PASSED BY EVERY DAY...
THERE WAS ALWAYS SOMEONE THERE, 24 HOURS A DAY. ALL KINDS OF PEOPLE.
YET NEVER, IN OVER TWO HUNDRED YEARS, HAD ANYONE RUN INTO SOMEONE THEY KNEW.
THE DAY THE STREAK ENDED, THE CORNER WAS CONFUSED.
DID THEY COLLIDE?

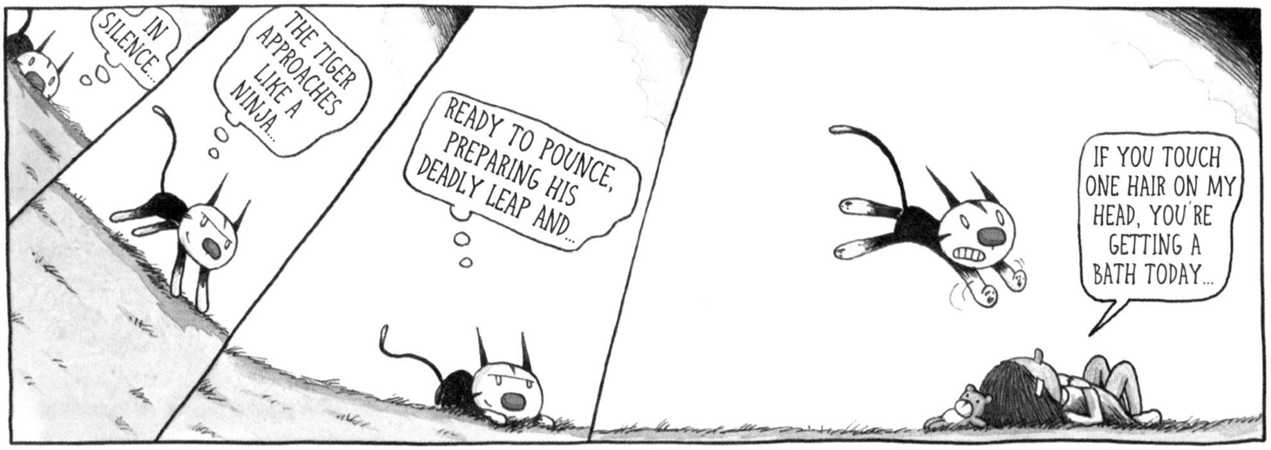
IN SILENCE...
THE TIGER APPROACHES LIKE A NINJA...
READY TO POUNCE, PREPARING HIS DEADLY LEAP AND...
IF YOU TOUCH ONE HAIR ON MY HEAD, YOU'RE GETTING A BATH TODAY...

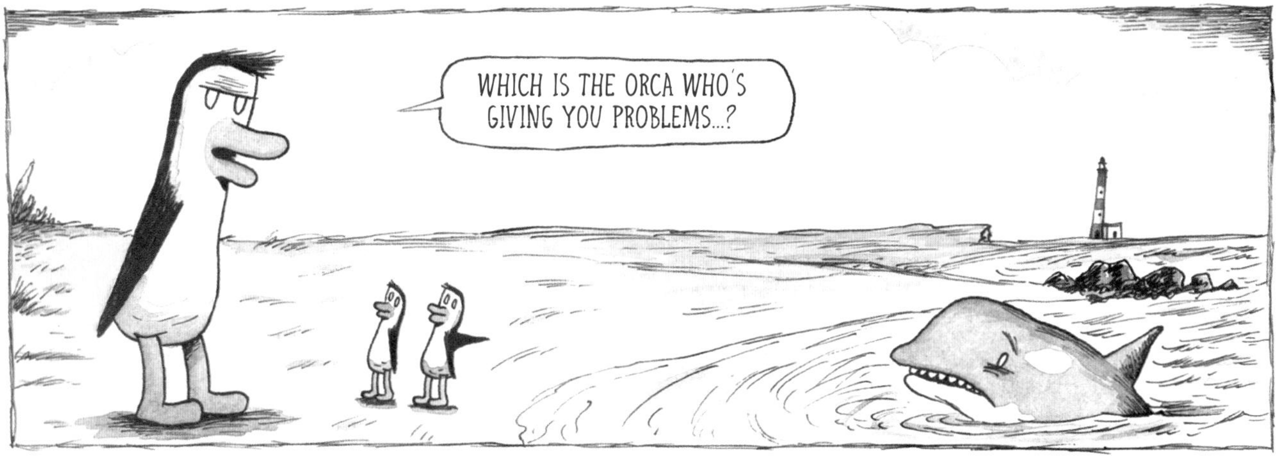
WHICH IS THE ORCA WHO'S GIVING YOU PROBLEMS...?

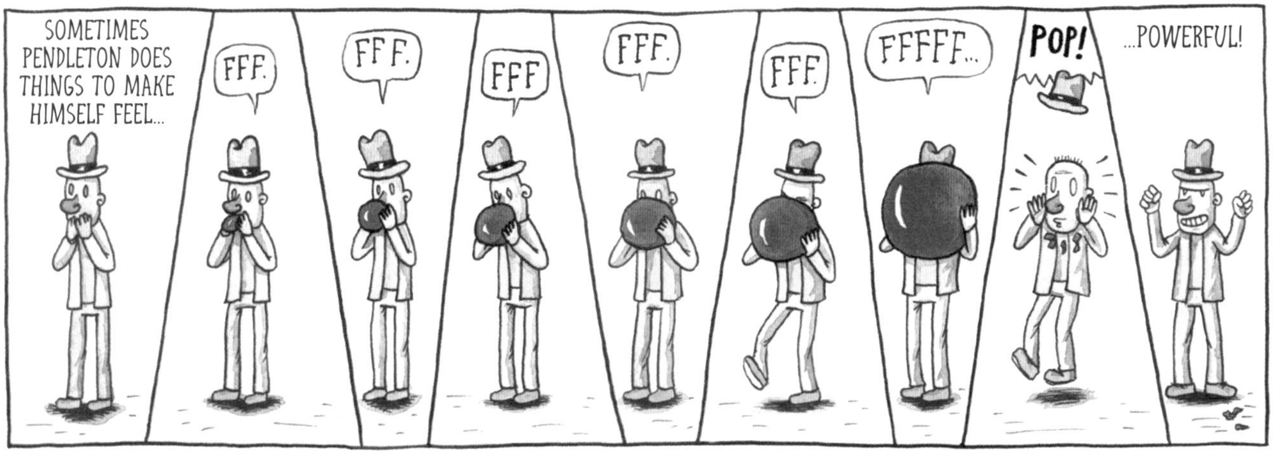
SOMETIMES PENDLETON DOES THINGS TO MAKE HIMSELF FEEL...
FFF.
FFF.
FFF
FFF.
FFF.
FFFFF...
POP!
...POWERFUL!

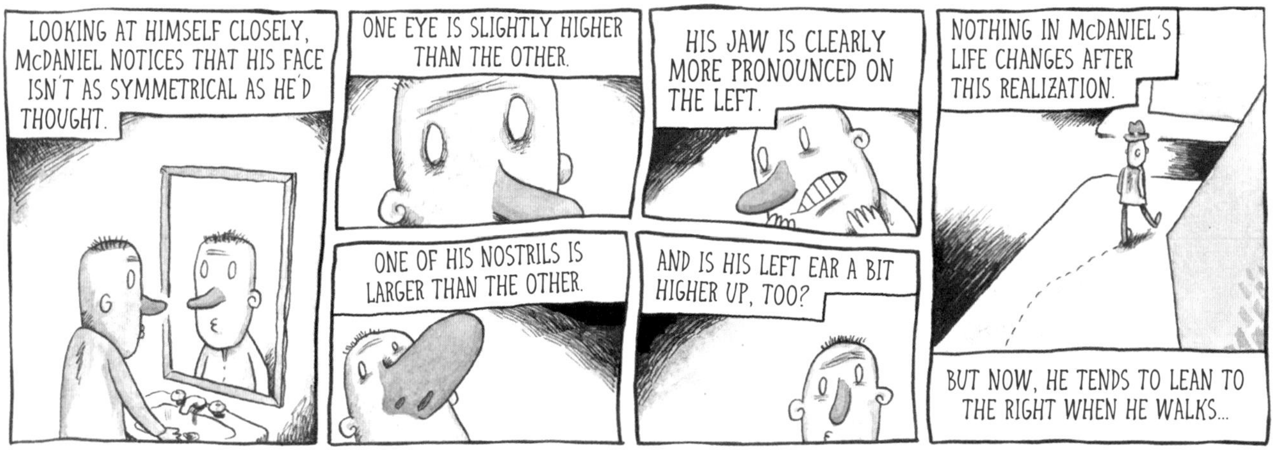
LOOKING AT HIMSELF CLOSELY, McDANIEL NOTICES THAT HIS FACE ISN'T AS SYMMETRICAL AS HE'D THOUGHT.
ONE EYE IS SLIGHTLY HIGHER THAN THE OTHER.
ONE OF HIS NOSTRILS IS LARGER THAN THE OTHER.
HIS JAW IS CLEARLY MORE PRONOUNCED ON THE LEFT.
AND IS HIS LEFT EAR A BIT HIGHER UP, TOO?
NOTHING IN McDANIEL'S LIFE CHANGES AFTER THIS REALIZATION.
BUT NOW, HE TENDS TO LEAN TO THE RIGHT WHEN HE WALKS...

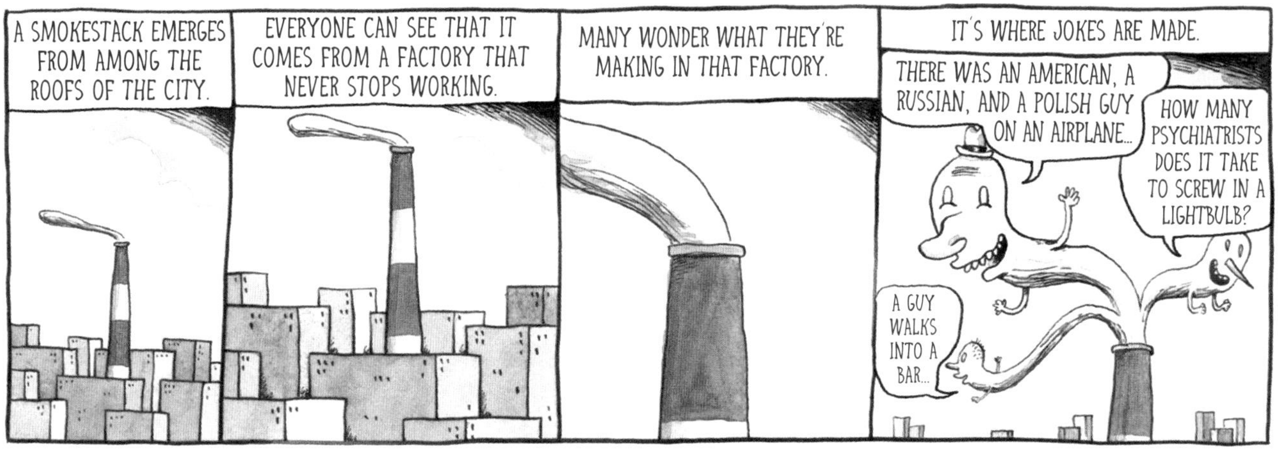
A SMOKESTACK EMERGES FROM AMONG THE ROOFS OF THE CITY.
EVERYONE CAN SEE THAT IT COMES FROM A FACTORY THAT NEVER STOPS WORKING.
MANY WONDER WHAT THEY'RE MAKING IN THAT FACTORY.
IT'S WHERE JOKES ARE MADE.
THERE WAS AN AMERICAN, A RUSSIAN, AND A POLISH GUY ON AN AIRPLANE...
HOW MANY PSYCHIATRISTS DOES IT TAKE TO SCREW IN A LIGHTBULB?
A GUY WALKS INTO A BAR...

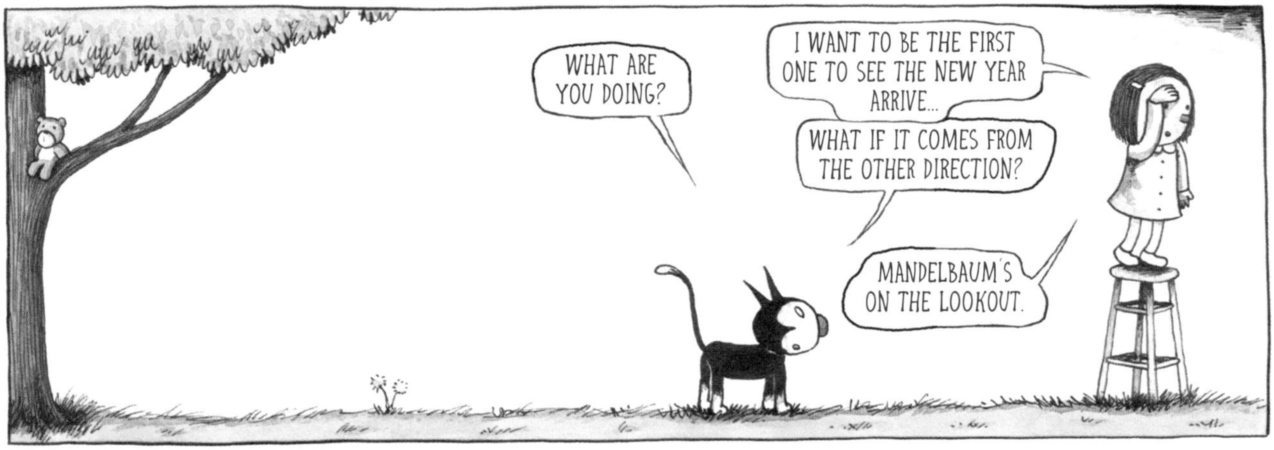
WHAT ARE YOU DOING?
I WANT TO BE THE FIRST ONE TO SEE THE NEW YEAR ARRIVE...
WHAT IF IT COMES FROM THE OTHER DIRECTION?
MANDELBAUM'S ON THE LOOKOUT.

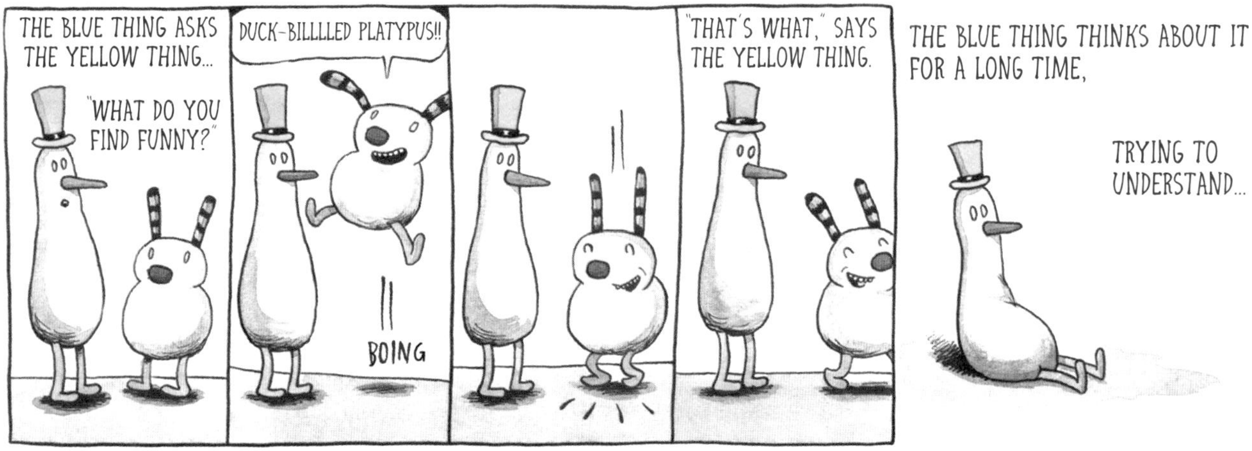
THE BLUE THING ASKS THE YELLOW THING...
"WHAT DO YOU FIND FUNNY?"
DUCK-BILLLLED PLATYPUS!!
BOING
"THAT'S WHAT," SAYS THE YELLOW THING.
THE BLUE THING THINKS ABOUT IT FOR A LONG TIME,
TRYING TO UNDERSTAND...

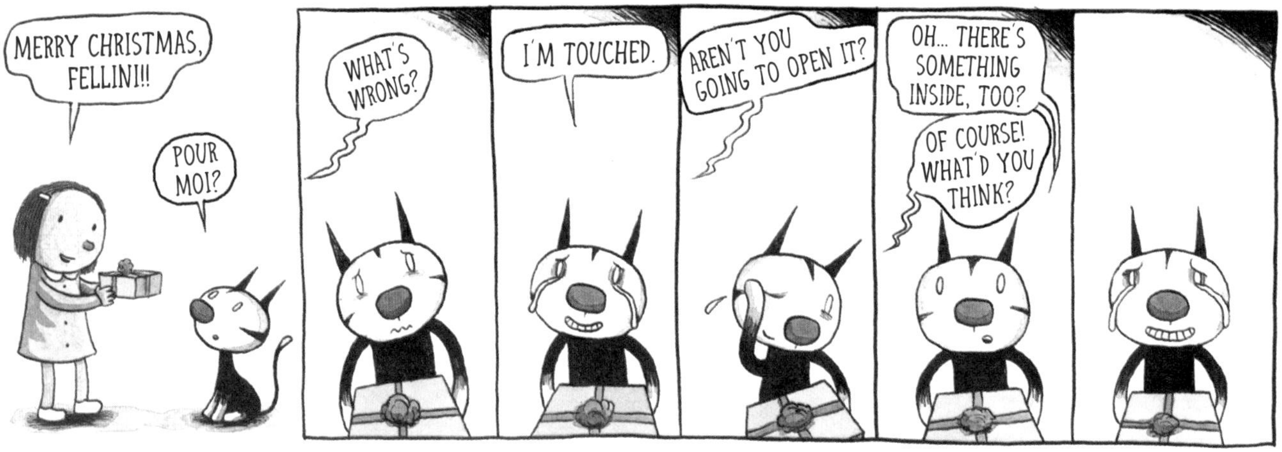
MERRY CHRISTMAS, FELLINI!!
POUR MOI?
WHAT'S WRONG?
I'M TOUCHED.
AREN'T YOU GOING TO OPEN IT?
OH... THERE'S SOMETHING INSIDE, TOO?
OF COURSE! WHAT'D YOU THINK?

IN ADDITION TO DEVOTING THEIR LIVES TO THE STUDY OF FISH, ICHTHYOLOGISTS ARE PRETTY TEMPERMENTAL FOLK.

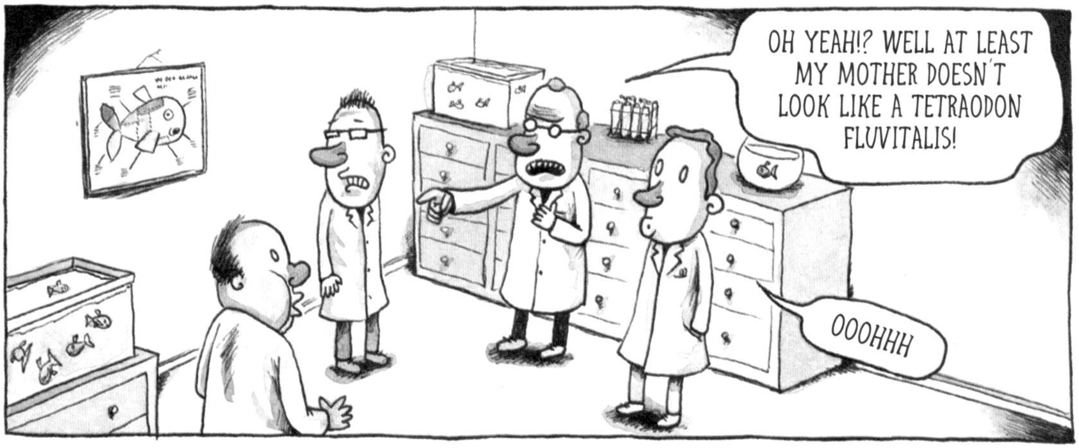
OH YEAH!? WELL AT LEAST MY MOTHER DOESN'T LOOK LIKE A TETRAODON FLUVITALIS!
OOOHHH

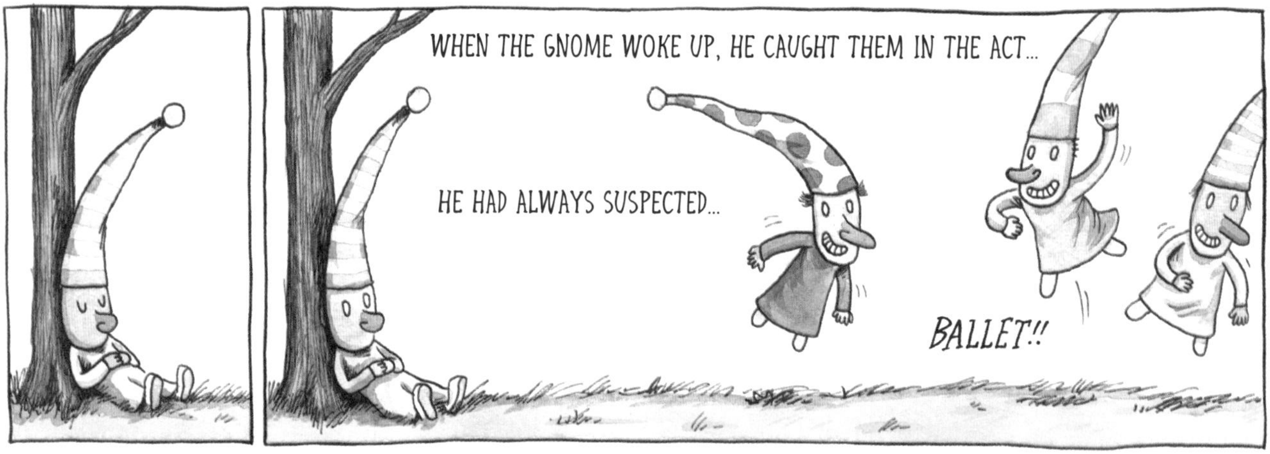
WHEN THE GNOME WOKE UP, HE CAUGHT THEM IN THE ACT...
HE HAD ALWAYS SUSPECTED...
BALLET!!

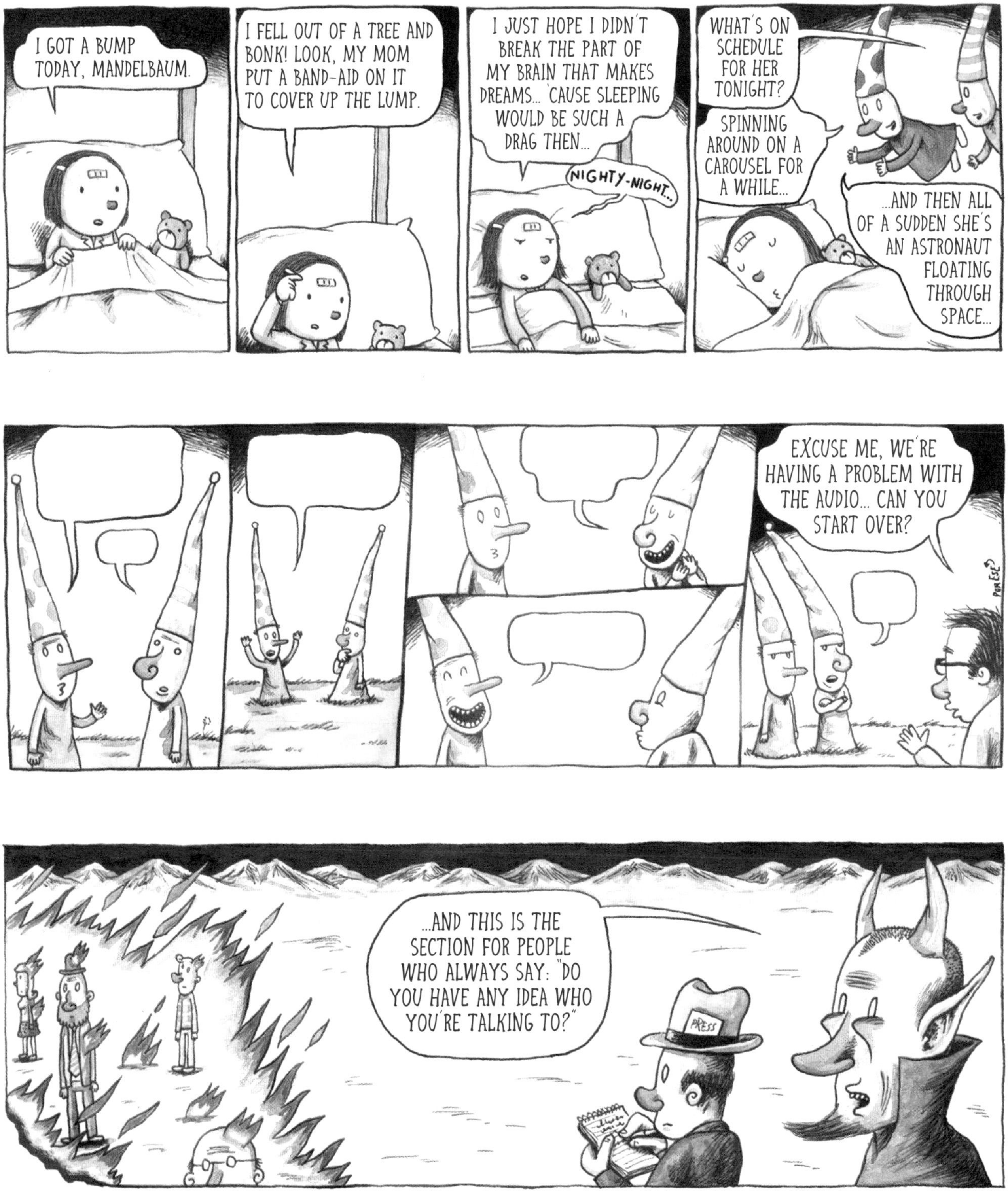

I GOT A BUMP TODAY, MANDELBAUM.
I FELL OUT OF A TREE AND BONK! LOOK, MY MOM PUT A BAND-AID ON IT TO COVER UP THE LUMP.
I JUST HOPE I DIDN'T BREAK THE PART OF MY BRAIN THAT MAKES DREAMS... 'CAUSE SLEEPING WOULD BE SUCH A DRAG THEN...
NIGHTY-NIGHT...
WHAT'S ON SCHEDULE FOR HER TONIGHT?
SPINNING AROUND ON A CAROUSEL FOR A WHILE...
...AND THEN ALL OF A SUDDEN SHE'S AN ASTRONAUT FLOATING THROUGH SPACE...
EXCUSE ME, WE'RE HAVING A PROBLEM WITH THE AUDIO... CAN YOU START OVER?
...AND THIS IS THE SECTION FOR PEOPLE WHO ALWAYS SAY: "DO YOU HAVE ANY IDEA WHO YOU'RE TALKING TO?"
PRESS

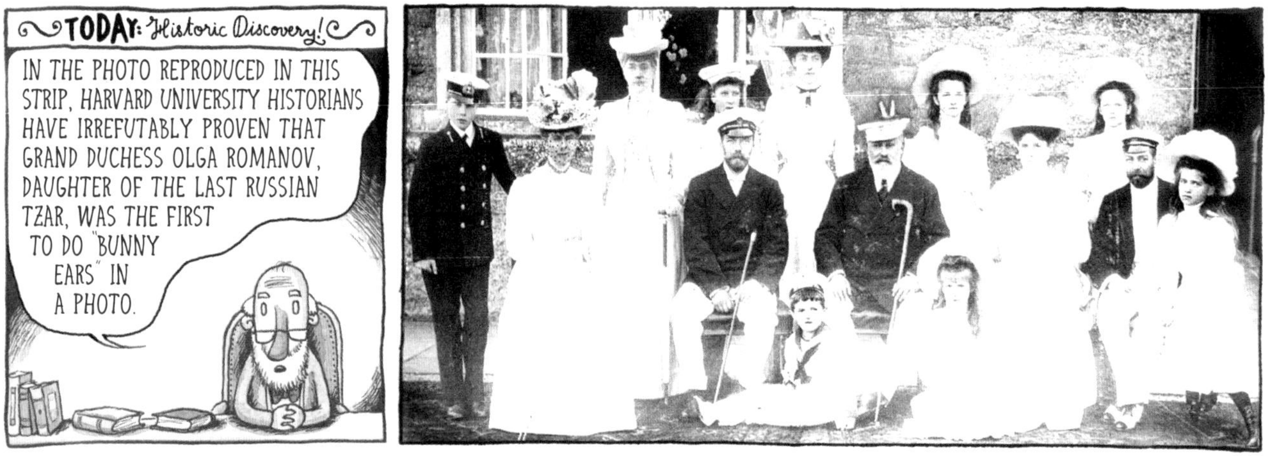
TODAY: Historic Discovery!
IN THE PHOTO REPRODUCED IN THIS STRIP, HARVARD UNIVERSITY HISTORIANS HAVE IRREFUTABLY PROVEN THAT GRAND DUCHESS OLGA ROMANOV, DAUGHTER OF THE LAST RUSSIAN TZAR, WAS THE FIRST TO DO "BUNNY EARS" IN A PHOTO.

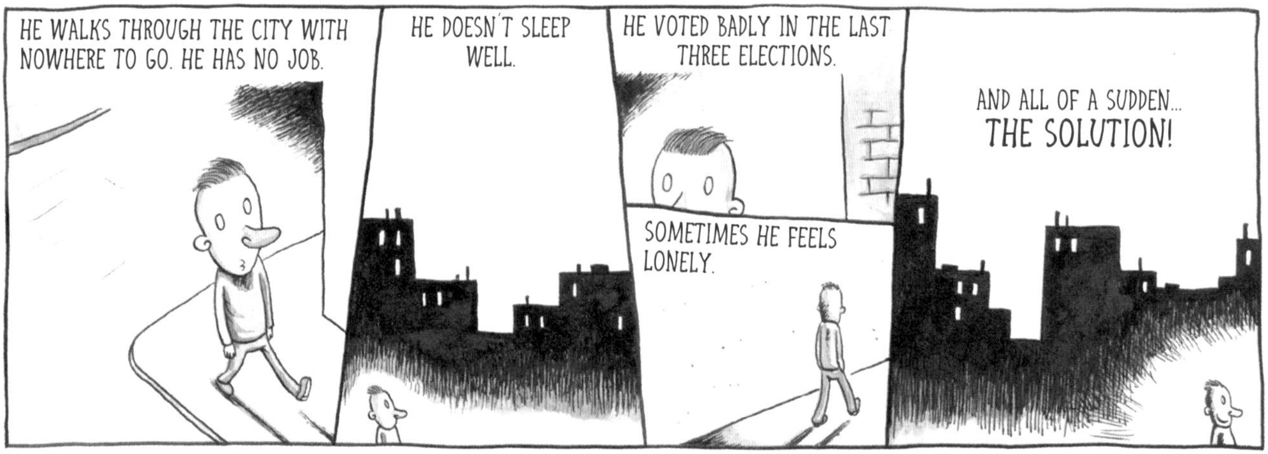
HE WALKS THROUGH THE CITY WITH NOWHERE TO GO. HE HAS NO JOB.
HE DOESN'T SLEEP WELL.
HE VOTED BADLY IN THE LAST THREE ELECTIONS.
SOMETIMES HE FEELS LONELY.
AND ALL OF A SUDDEN... THE SOLUTION!

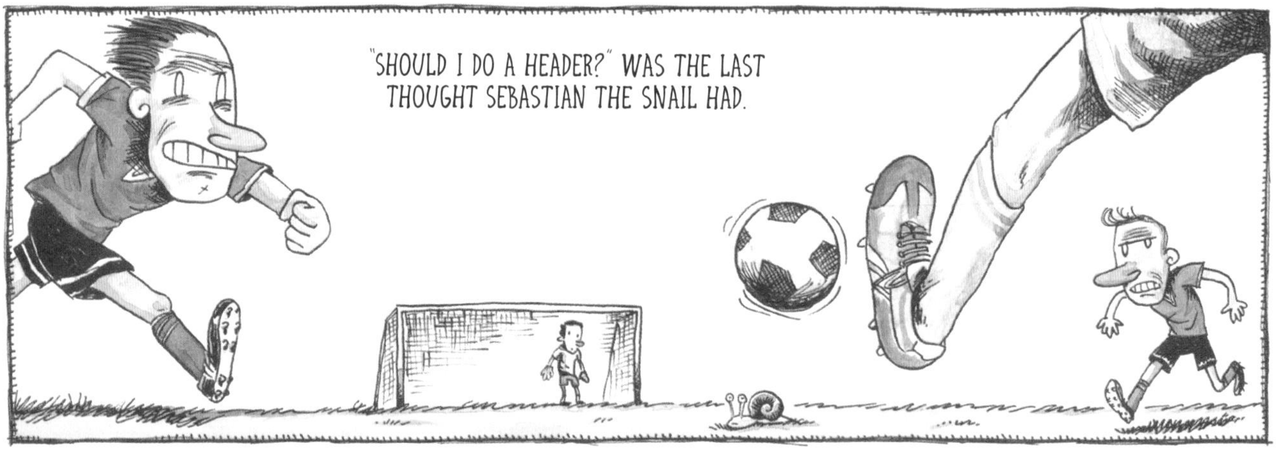
"SHOULD I DO A HEADER?" WAS THE LAST THOUGHT SEBASTIAN THE SNAIL HAD.

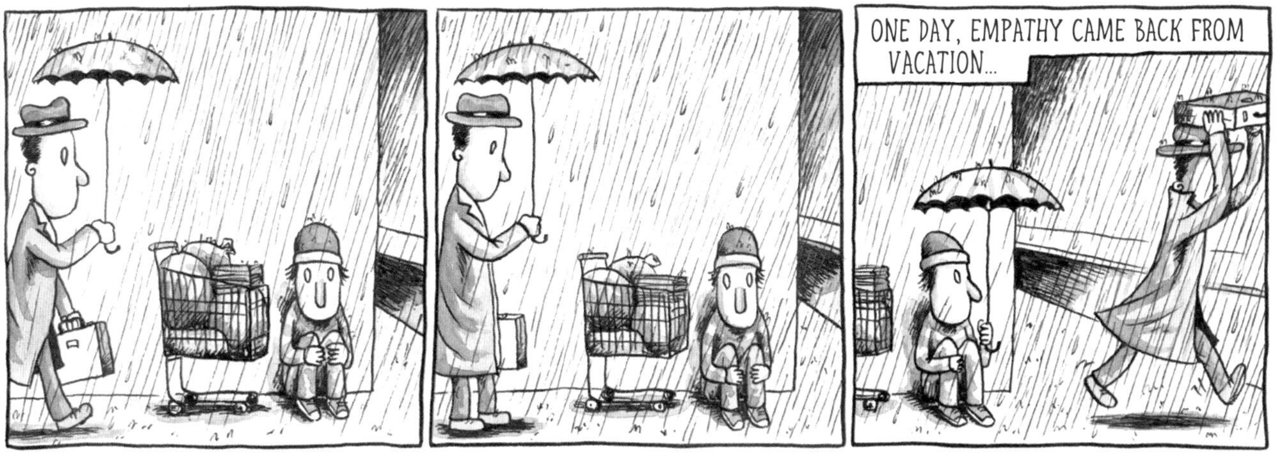
ONE DAY, EMPATHY CAME BACK FROM VACATION...

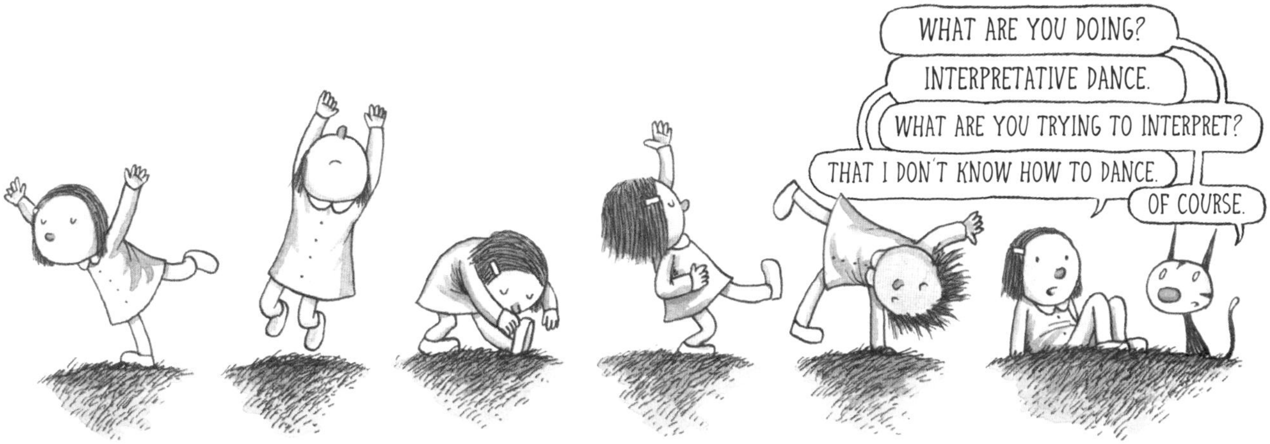
WHAT ARE YOU DOING?
INTERPRETATIVE DANCE.
WHAT ARE YOU TRYING TO INTERPRET?
THAT I DON'T KNOW HOW TO DANCE.
OF COURSE.

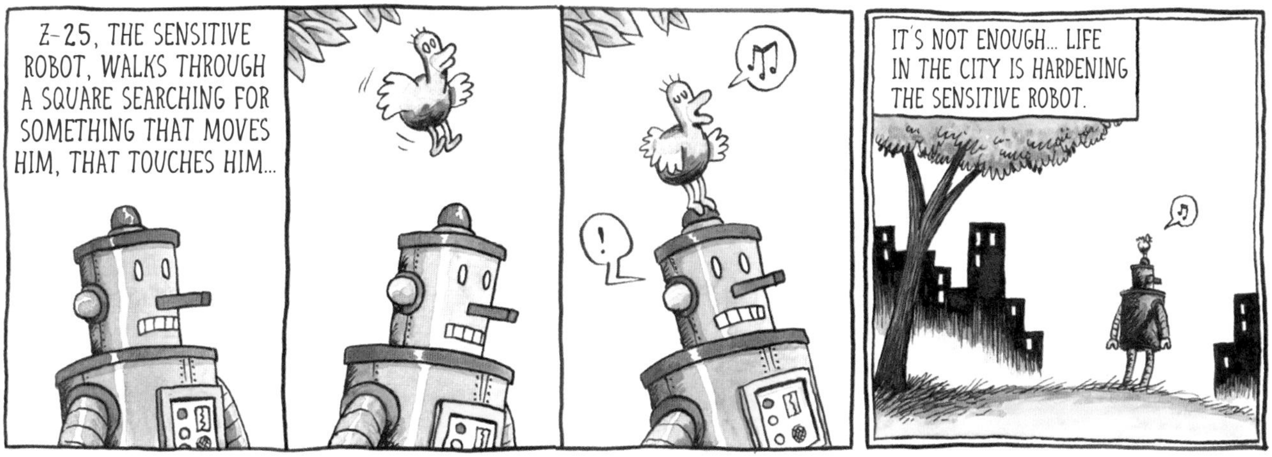
Z-25, THE SENSITIVE ROBOT, WALKS THROUGH A SQUARE SEARCHING FOR SOMETHING THAT MOVES HIM, THAT TOUCHES HIM...
!
IT'S NOT ENOUGH... LIFE IN THE CITY IS HARDENING THE SENSITIVE ROBOT.

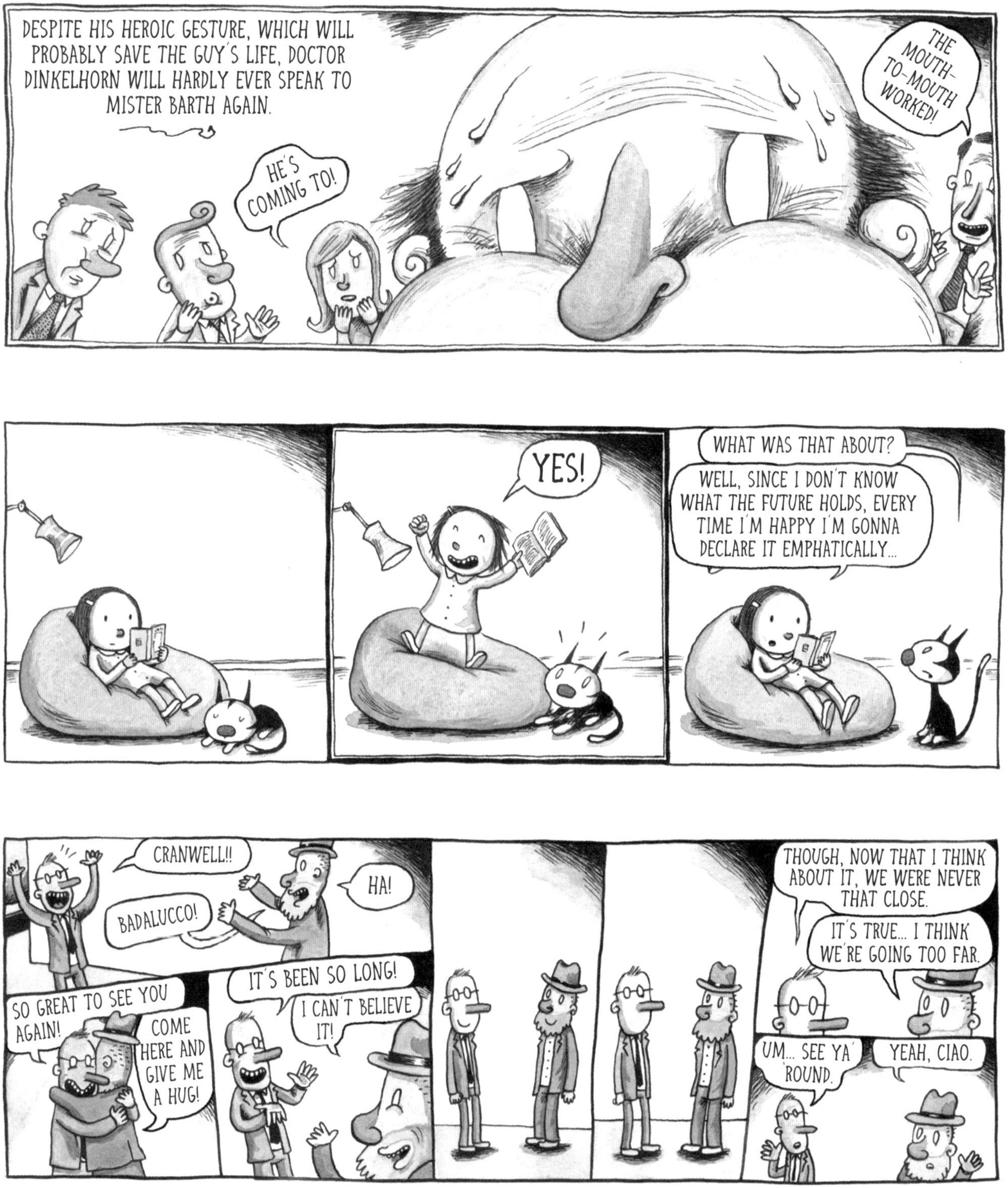
DESPITE HIS HEROIC GESTURE, WHICH WILL PROBABLY SAVE THE GUY'S LIFE, DOCTOR DINKELHORN WILL HARDLY EVER SPEAK TO MISTER BARTH AGAIN.
HE'S COMING TO!
THE MOUTH-TO-MOUTH WORKED!
YES!
WHAT WAS THAT ABOUT?
WELL, SINCE I DON'T KNOW WHAT THE FUTURE HOLDS, EVERY TIME I'M HAPPY I'M GONNA DECLARE IT EMPHATICALLY...
CRANWELL!!
HA!
BADALUCCO!
SO GREAT TO SEE YOU AGAIN!
COME HERE AND GIVE ME A HUG!
IT'S BEEN SO LONG!
I CAN'T BELIEVE IT!
THOUGH, NOW THAT I THINK ABOUT IT, WE WERE NEVER THAT CLOSE.
IT'S TRUE... I THINK WE'RE GOING TOO FAR.
UM... SEE YA' 'ROUND.
YEAH, CIAO.

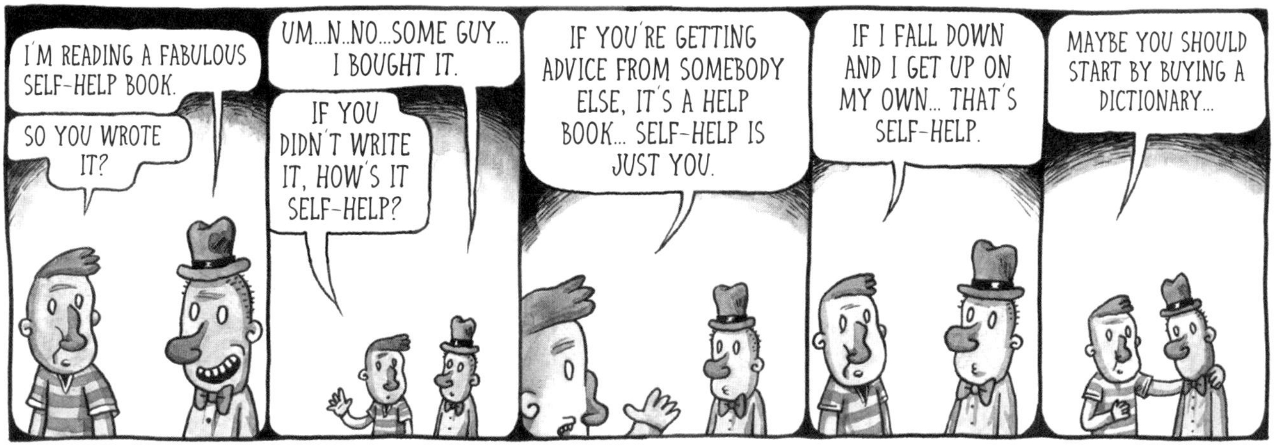
I'M READING A FABULOUS SELF-HELP BOOK.
SO YOU WROTE IT?
UM...N..NO...SOME GUY... I BOUGHT IT.
IF YOU DIDN'T WRITE IT, HOW'S IT SELF-HELP?
IF YOU'RE GETTING ADVICE FROM SOMEBODY ELSE, IT'S A HELP BOOK... SELF-HELP IS JUST YOU.
IF I FALL DOWN AND I GET UP ON MY OWN... THAT'S SELF-HELP.
MAYBE YOU SHOULD START BY BUYING A DICTIONARY...

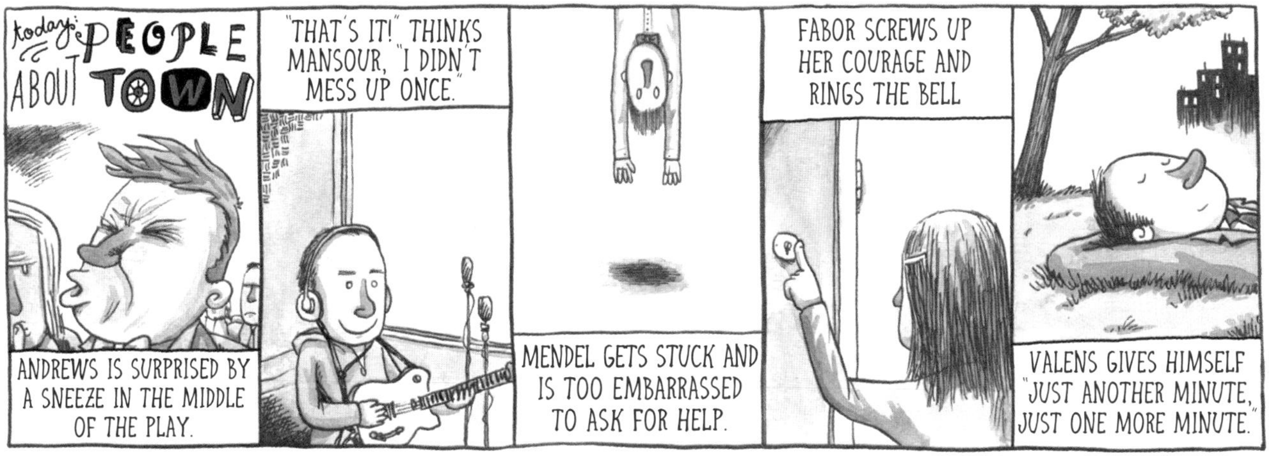
today: PEOPLE ABOUT TOWN
ANDREWS IS SURPRISED BY A SNEEZE IN THE MIDDLE OF THE PLAY.
"THAT'S IT!" THINKS MANSOUR, "I DIDN'T MESS UP ONCE."
MENDEL GETS STUCK AND IS TOO EMBARRASSED TO ASK FOR HELP.
FABOR SCREWS UP HER COURAGE AND RINGS THE BELL
VALENS GIVES HIMSELF "JUST ANOTHER MINUTE, JUST ONE MORE MINUTE."

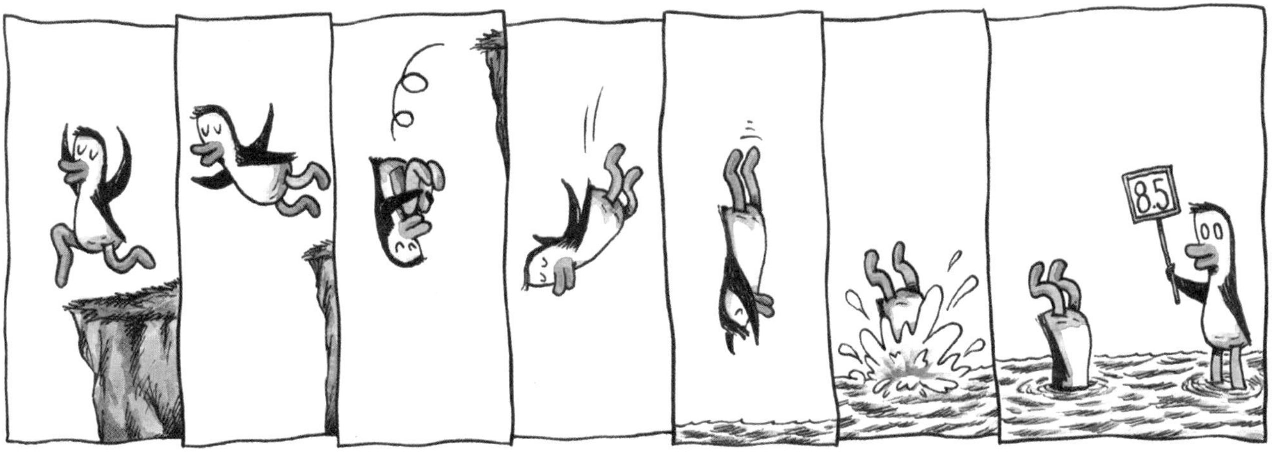
8.5

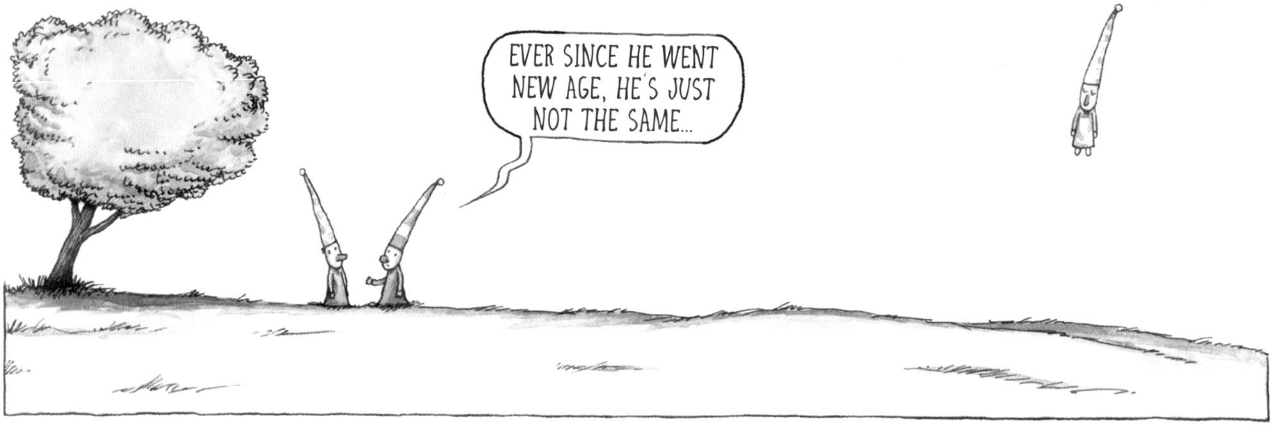
EVER SINCE HE WENT NEW AGE, HE'S JUST NOT THE SAME...

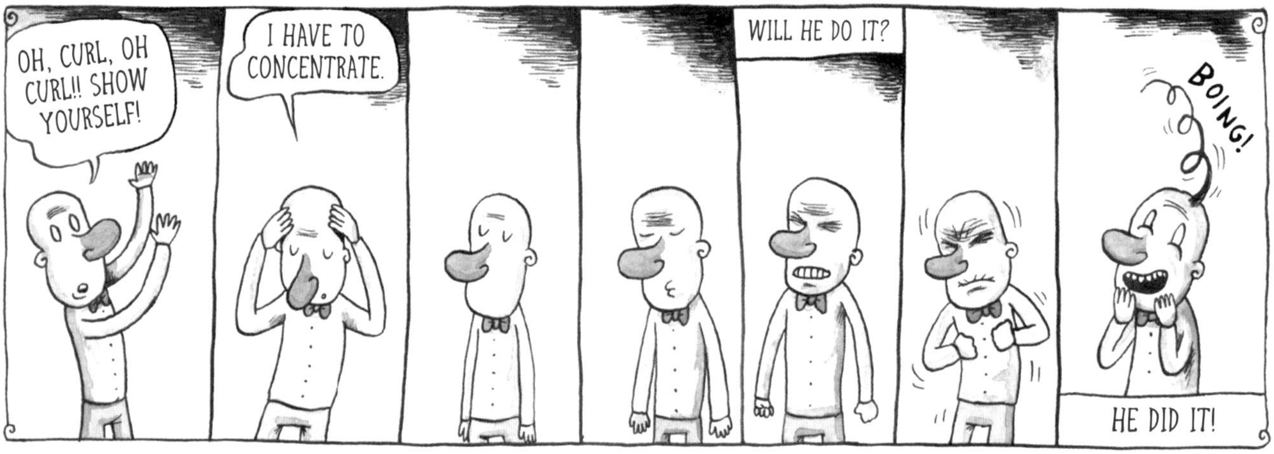
OH, CURL, OH CURL!! SHOW YOURSELF!
I HAVE TO CONCENTRATE.
WILL HE DO IT?
BOING!
HE DID IT!

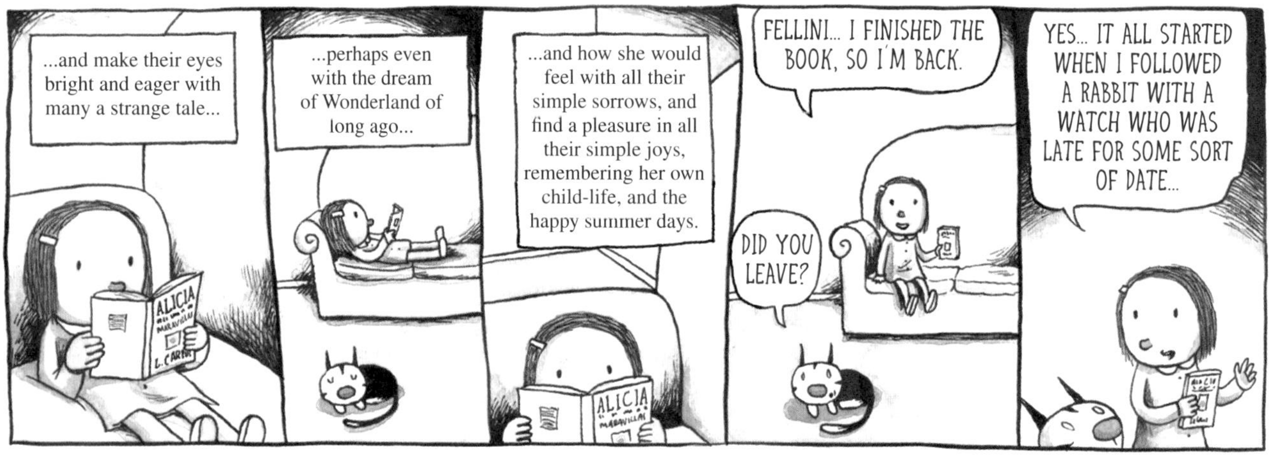
...and make their eyes bright and eager with many a strange tale...
ALICIA
L. CARR
...perhaps even with the dream of Wonderland of long ago...
...and how she would feel with all their simple sorrows, and find a pleasure in all their simple joys, remembering her own child-life, and the happy summer days.
ALICIA
FELLINI... I FINISHED THE BOOK, SO I'M BACK.
DID YOU LEAVE?
YES... IT ALL STARTED WHEN I FOLLOWED A RABBIT WITH A WATCH WHO WAS LATE FOR SOME SORT OF DATE...

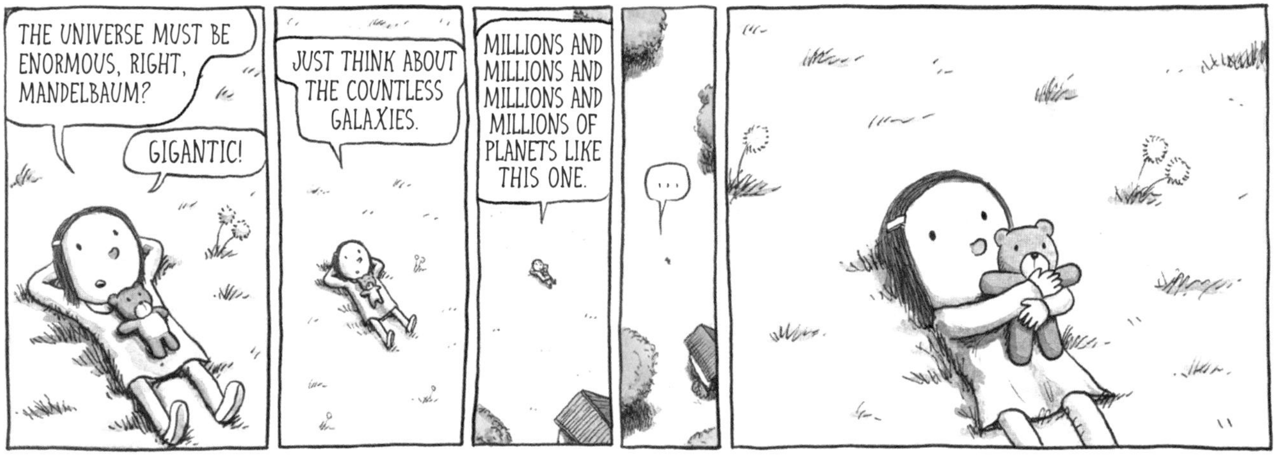
THE UNIVERSE MUST BE ENORMOUS, RIGHT, MANDELBAUM?
GIGANTIC!
JUST THINK ABOUT THE COUNTLESS GALAXIES.
MILLIONS AND MILLIONS AND MILLIONS AND MILLIONS OF PLANETS LIKE THIS ONE.
...

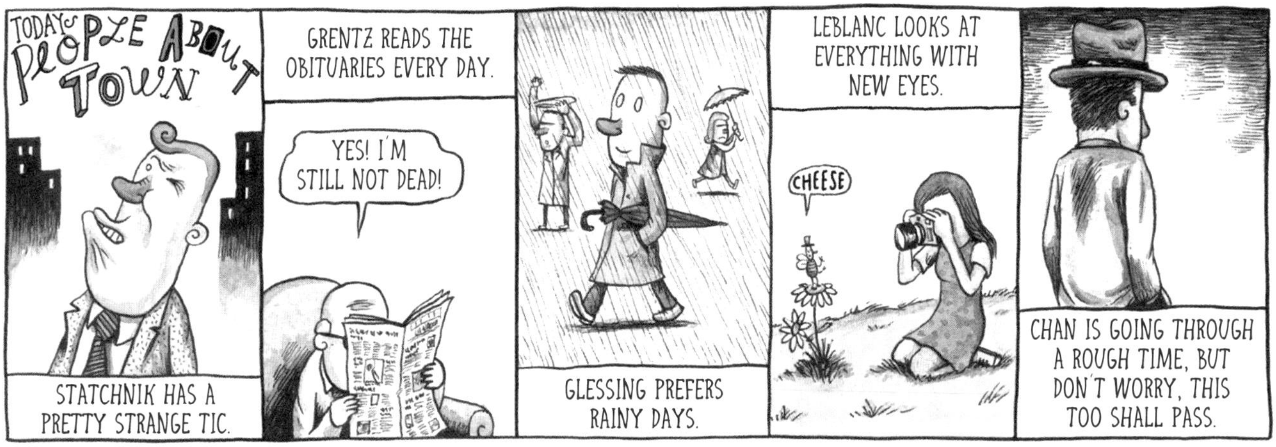
TODAY'S PEOPLE ABOUT TOWN
STATCHNIK HAS A PRETTY STRANGE TIC.
GRENTZ READS THE OBITUARIES EVERY DAY.
YES! I'M STILL NOT DEAD!
GLESSING PREFERS RAINY DAYS.
LEBLANC LOOKS AT EVERYTHING WITH NEW EYES.
CHEESE
CHAN IS GOING THROUGH A ROUGH TIME, BUT DON'T WORRY, THIS TOO SHALL PASS.

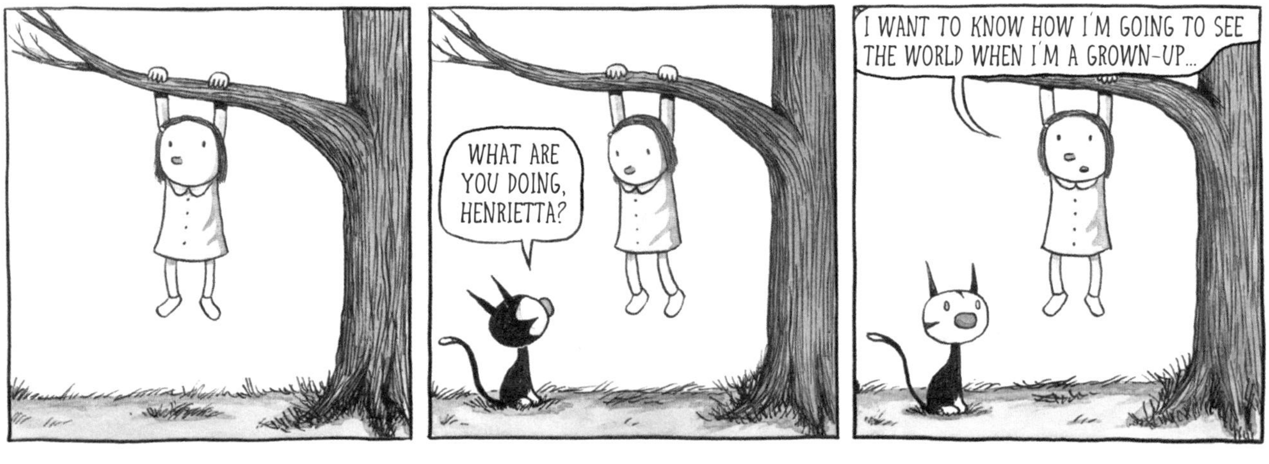
WHAT ARE YOU DOING, HENRIETTA?
I WANT TO KNOW HOW I'M GOING TO SEE THE WORLD WHEN I'M A GROWN-UP...

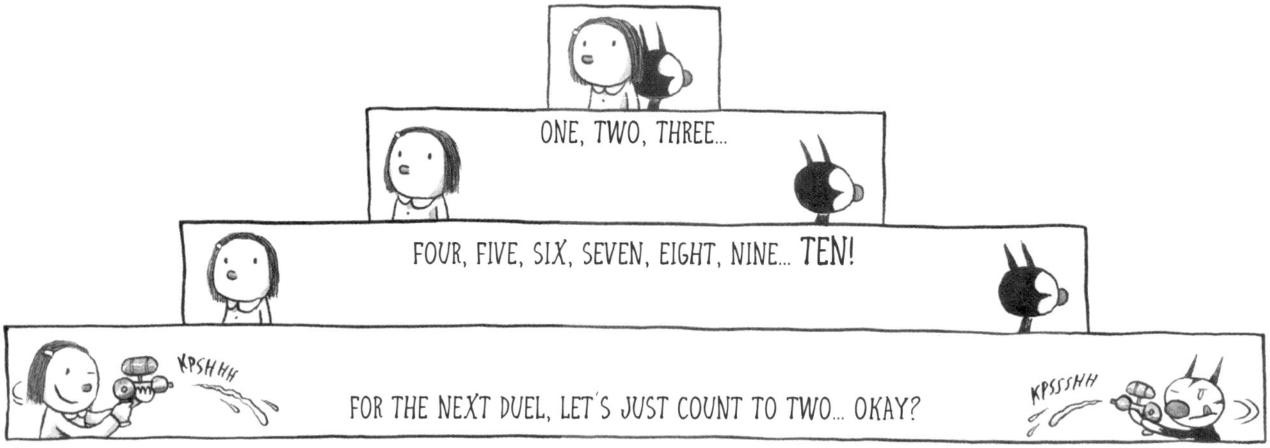
ONE, TWO, THREE...
FOUR, FIVE, SIX, SEVEN, EIGHT, NINE... TEN!
KPSHHH
FOR THE NEXT DUEL, LET'S JUST COUNT TO TWO... OKAY?
KPSSSHH

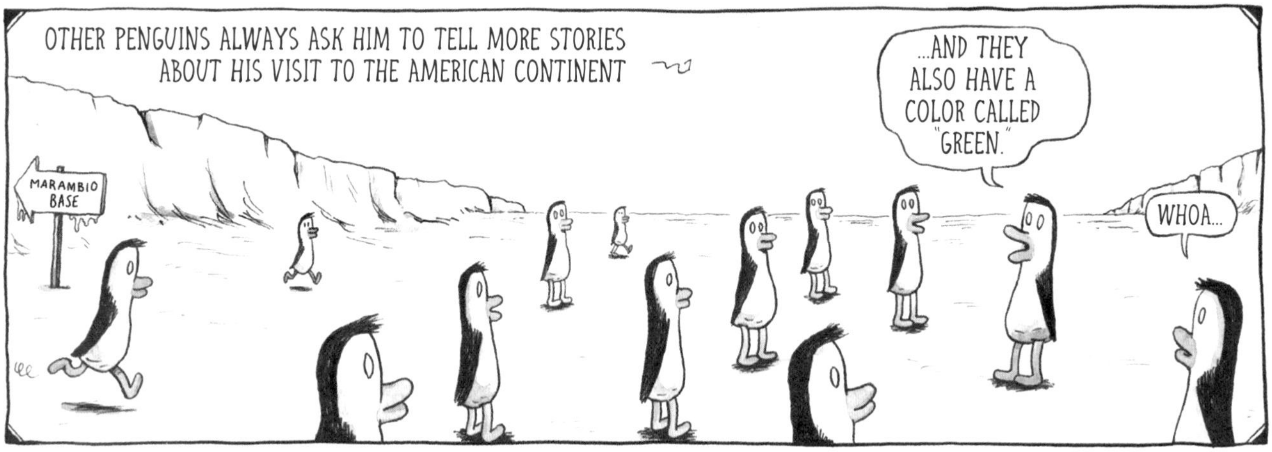
OTHER PENGUINS ALWAYS ASK HIM TO TELL MORE STORIES ABOUT HIS VISIT TO THE AMERICAN CONTINENT
MARAMBIO BASE
...AND THEY ALSO HAVE A COLOR CALLED "GREEN."
WHOA...

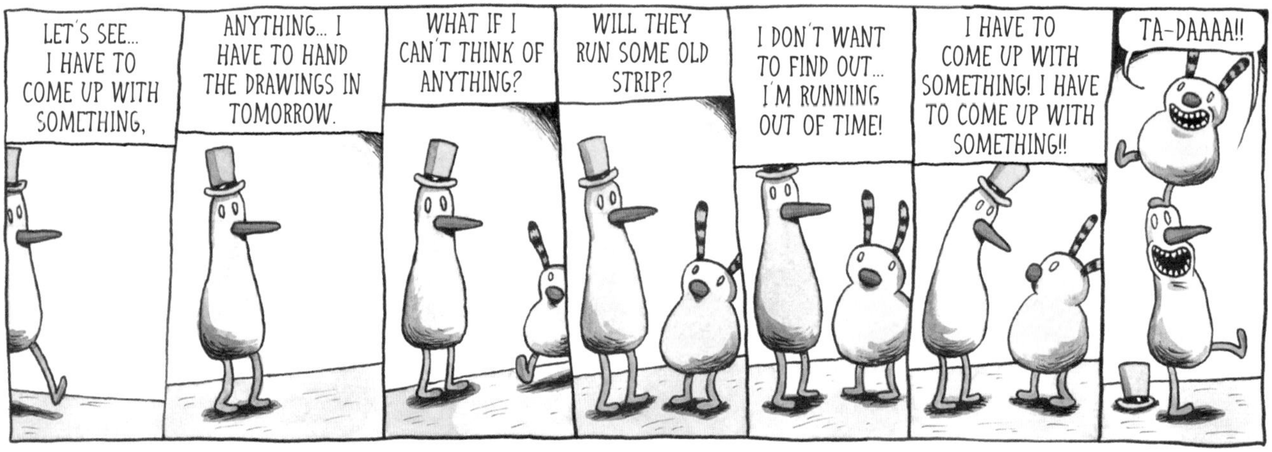
LET'S SEE... I HAVE TO COME UP WITH SOMETHING,
ANYTHING... I HAVE TO HAND THE DRAWINGS IN TOMORROW.
WHAT IF I CAN'T THINK OF ANYTHING?
WILL THEY RUN SOME OLD STRIP?
I DON'T WANT TO FIND OUT... I'M RUNNING OUT OF TIME!
I HAVE TO COME UP WITH SOMETHING! I HAVE TO COME UP WITH SOMETHING!!
TA-DAAAA!!

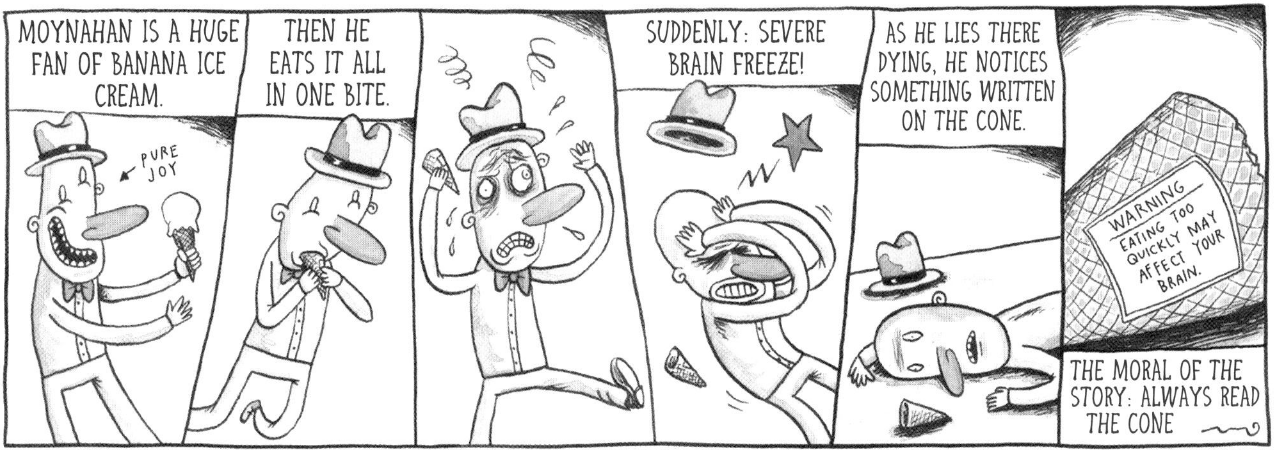
MOYNAHAN IS A HUGE FAN OF BANANA ICE CREAM.
PURE JOY
THEN HE EATS IT ALL IN ONE BITE.
SUDDENLY: SEVERE BRAIN FREEZE!
AS HE LIES THERE DYING, HE NOTICES SOMETHING WRITTEN ON THE CONE.
WARNING
EATING TOO QUICKLY MAY AFFECT YOUR BRAIN.
THE MORAL OF THE STORY: ALWAYS READ THE CONE

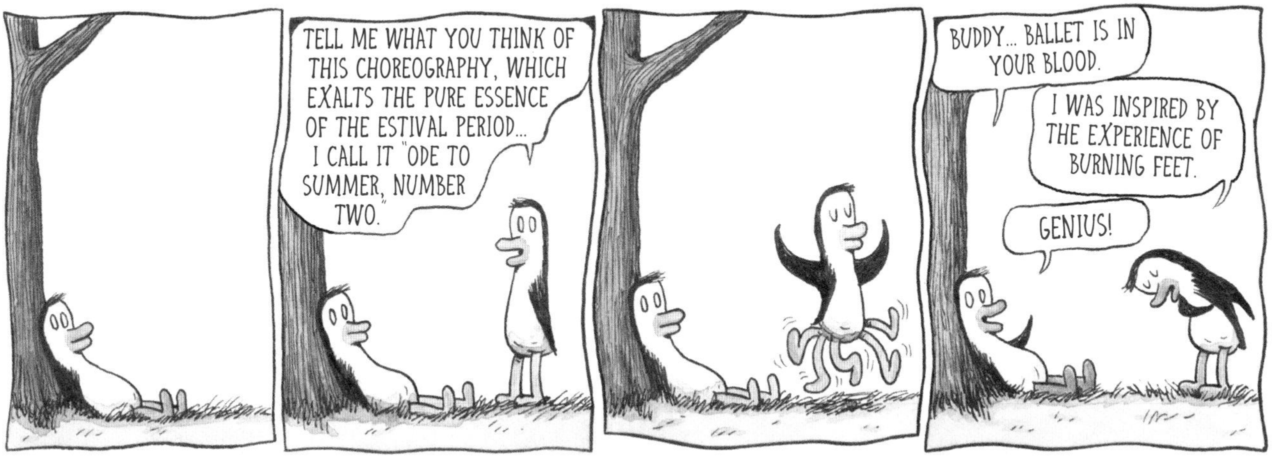
TELL ME WHAT YOU THINK OF THIS CHOREOGRAPHY, WHICH EXALTS THE PURE ESSENCE OF THE ESTIVAL PERIOD... I CALL IT "ODE TO SUMMER, NUMBER TWO."
BUDDY... BALLET IS IN YOUR BLOOD.
I WAS INSPIRED BY THE EXPERIENCE OF BURNING FEET.
GENIUS!

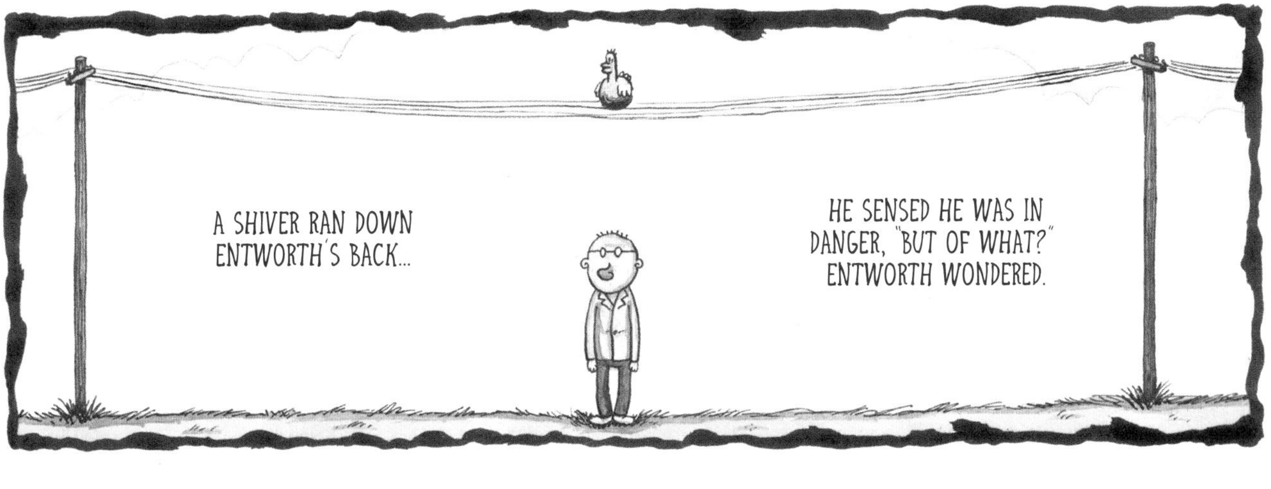
A SHIVER RAN DOWN ENTWORTH'S BACK...
HE SENSED HE WAS IN DANGER, "BUT OF WHAT?" ENTWORTH WONDERED.

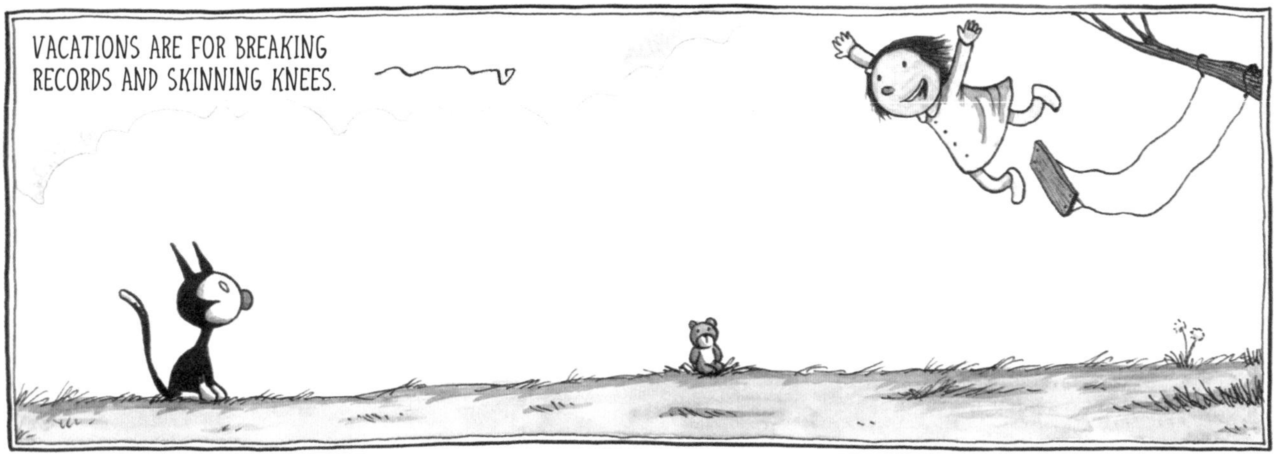
VACATIONS ARE FOR BREAKING RECORDS AND SKINNING KNEES.

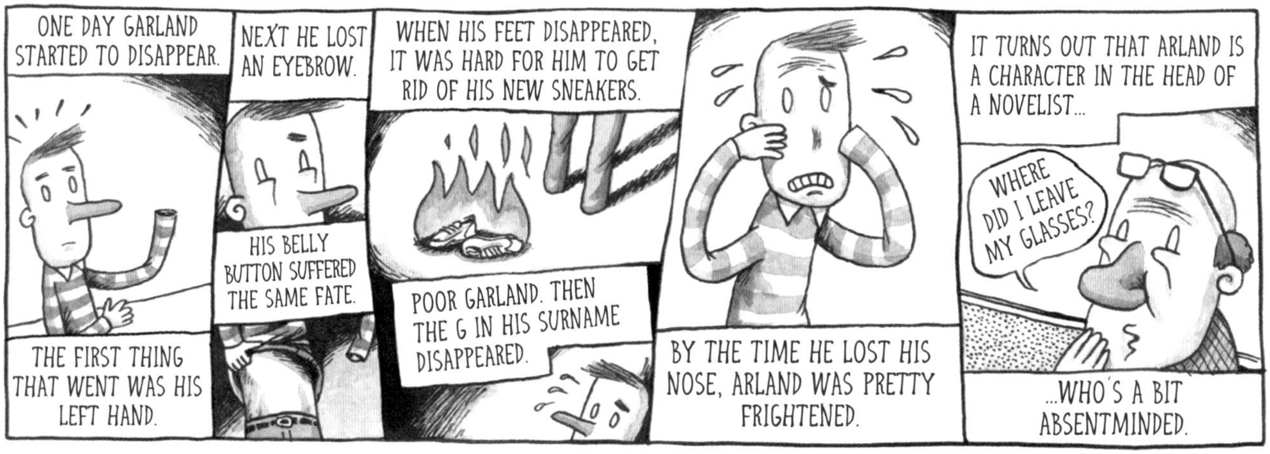
ONE DAY GARLAND STARTED TO DISAPPEAR.
THE FIRST THING THAT WENT WAS HIS LEFT HAND.
NEXT HE LOST AN EYEBROW.
HIS BELLY BUTTON SUFFERED THE SAME FATE.
WHEN HIS FEET DISAPPEARED, IT WAS HARD FOR HIM TO GET RID OF HIS NEW SNEAKERS.
POOR GARLAND. THEN THE G IN HIS SURNAME DISAPPEARED.
BY THE TIME HE LOST HIS NOSE, ARLAND WAS PRETTY FRIGHTENED.
IT TURNS OUT THAT ARLAND IS A CHARACTER IN THE HEAD OF A NOVELIST...
WHERE DID I LEAVE MY GLASSES?
...WHO'S A BIT ABSENTMINDED.

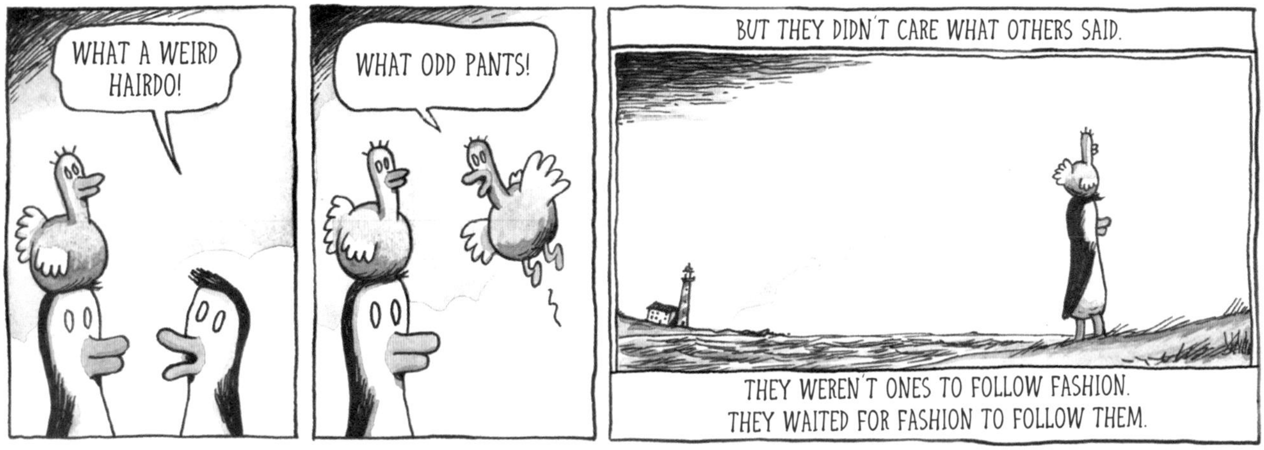
WHAT A WEIRD HAIRDO!
WHAT ODD PANTS!
BUT THEY DIDN'T CARE WHAT OTHERS SAID.
THEY WEREN'T ONES TO FOLLOW FASHION.
THEY WAITED FOR FASHION TO FOLLOW THEM.

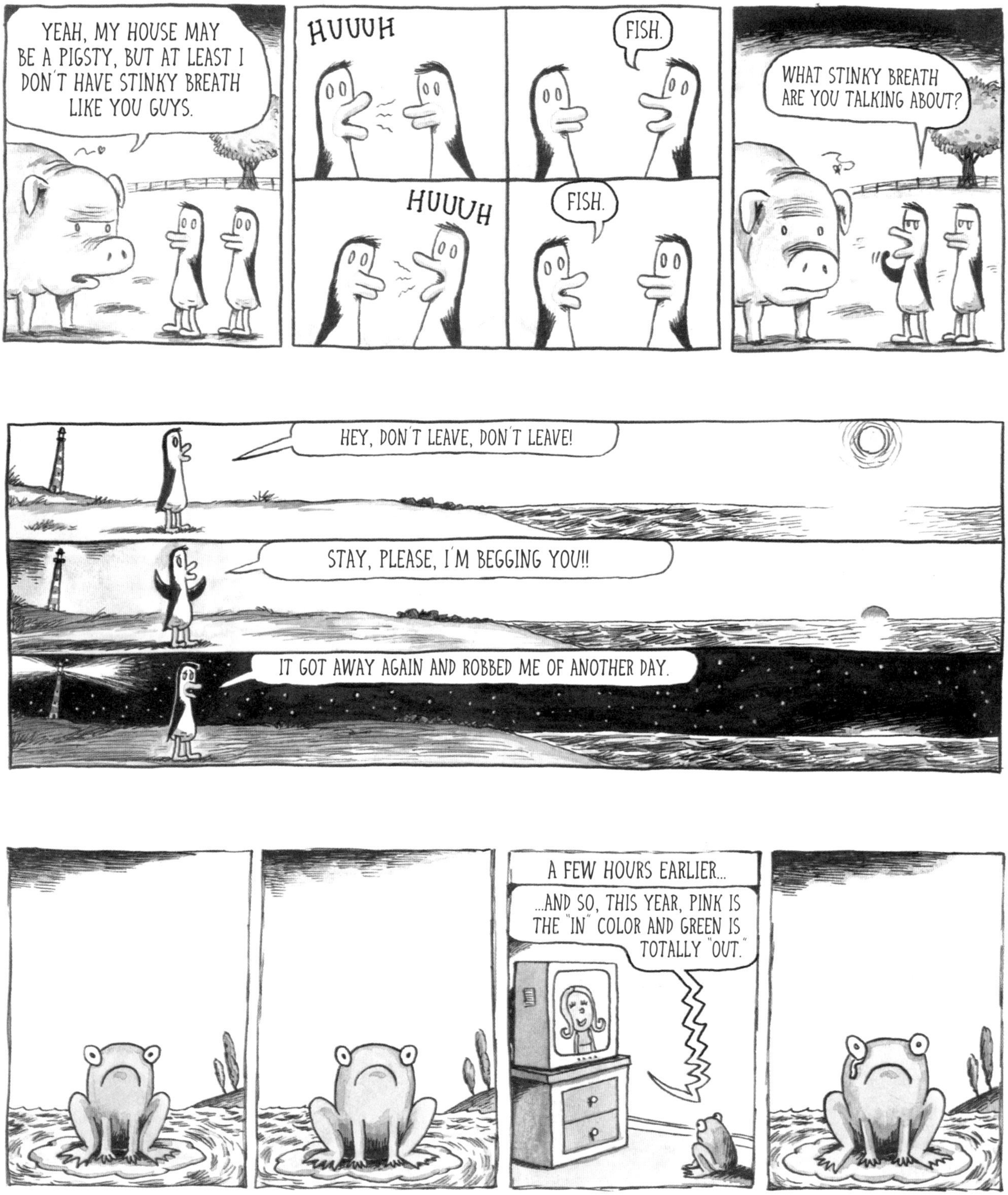
YEAH, MY HOUSE MAY BE A PIGSTY, BUT AT LEAST I DON'T HAVE STINKY BREATH LIKE YOU GUYS.
HUUUH
FISH.
HUUUH
FISH.
WHAT STINKY BREATH ARE YOU TALKING ABOUT?
HEY, DON'T LEAVE, DON'T LEAVE!
STAY, PLEASE, I'M BEGGING YOU!!
IT GOT AWAY AGAIN AND ROBBED ME OF ANOTHER DAY.
A FEW HOURS EARLIER...
...AND SO, THIS YEAR, PINK IS THE "IN" COLOR AND GREEN IS TOTALLY "OUT."

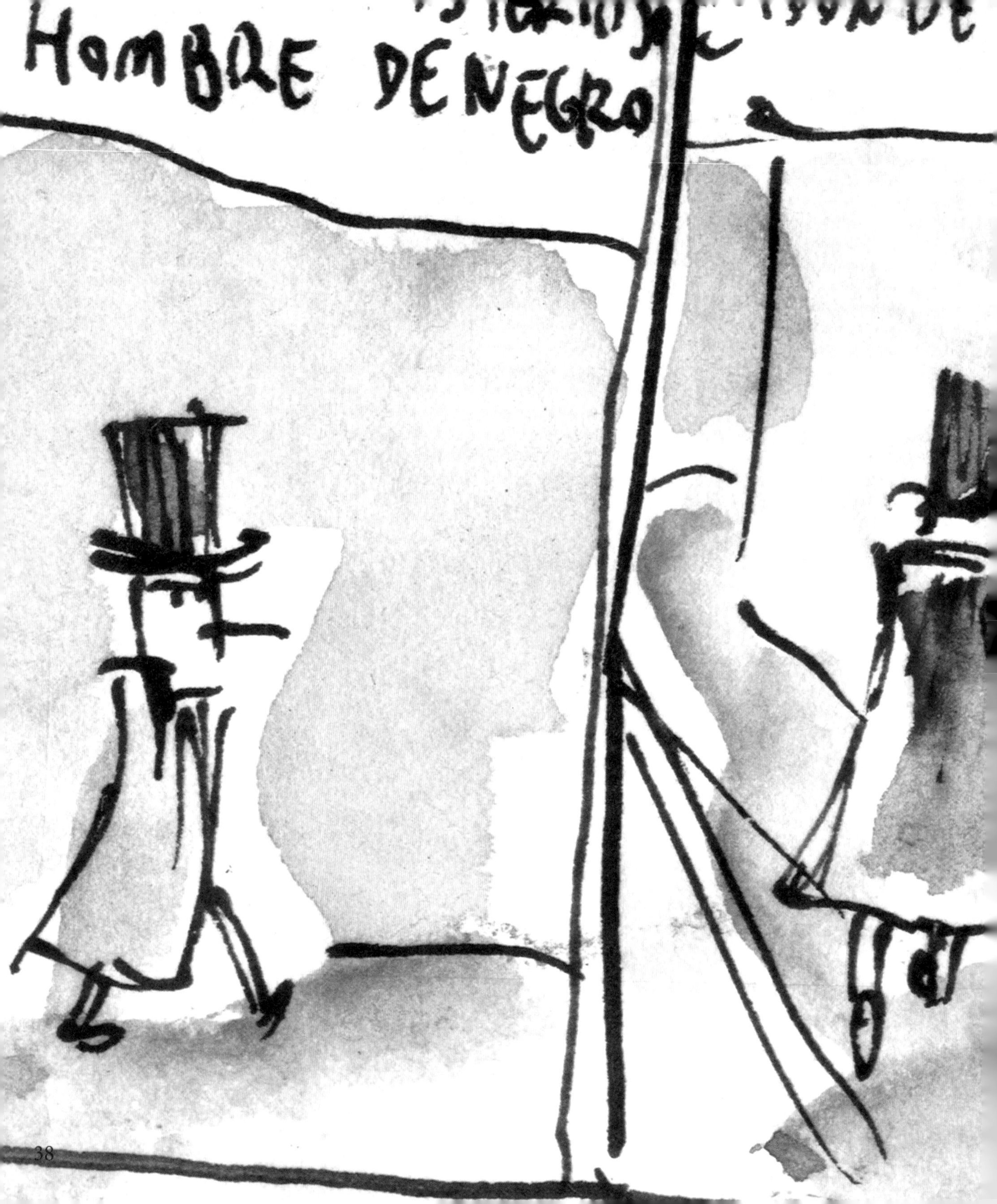
HOMBRE DE NEGRO

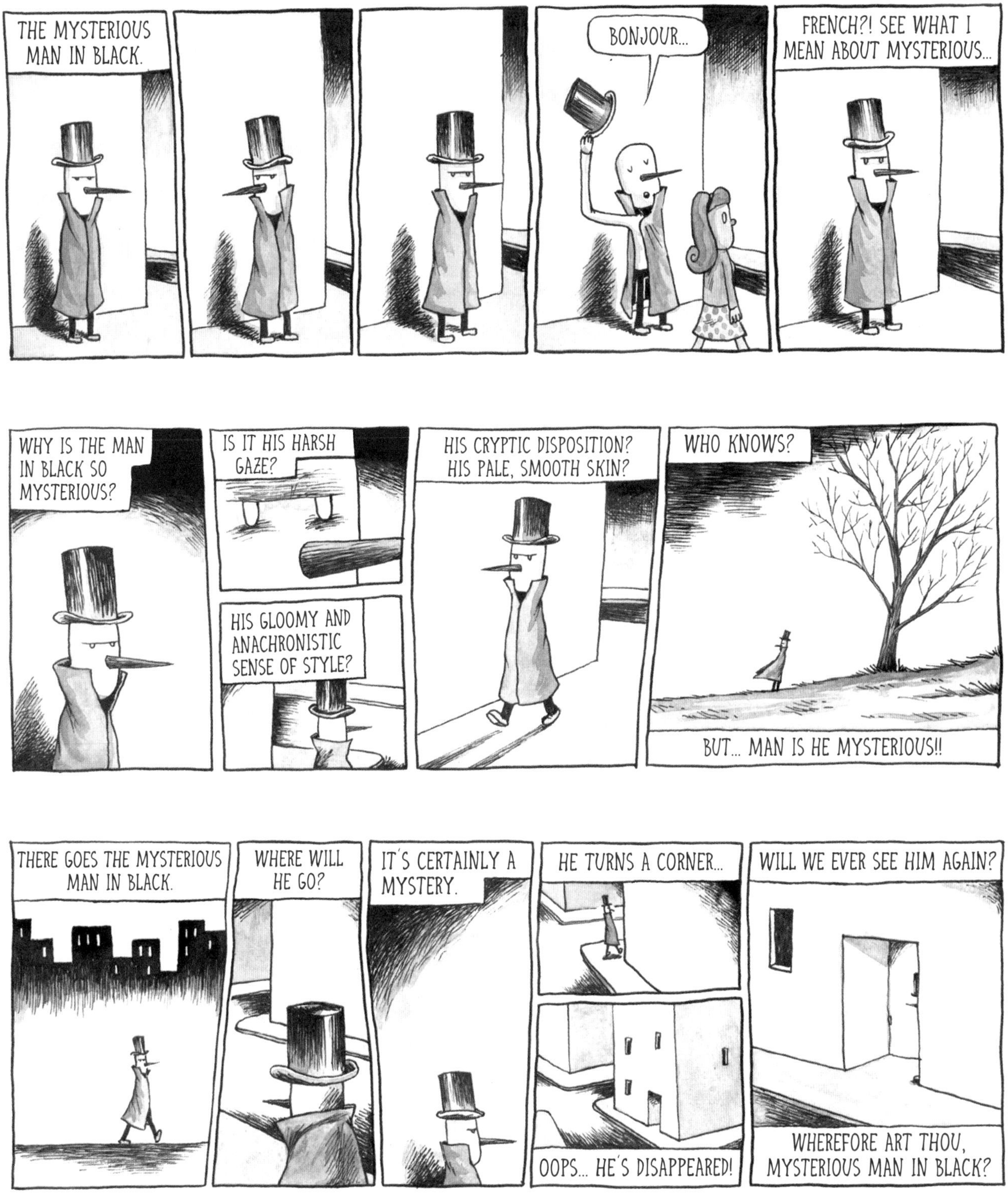
THE MYSTERIOUS MAN IN BLACK.
BONJOUR...
FRENCH?! SEE WHAT I MEAN ABOUT MYSTERIOUS...
WHY IS THE MAN IN BLACK SO MYSTERIOUS?
IS IT HIS HARSH GAZE?
HIS GLOOMY AND ANACHRONISTIC SENSE OF STYLE?
HIS CRYPTIC DISPOSITION? HIS PALE, SMOOTH SKIN?
WHO KNOWS?
BUT... MAN IS HE MYSTERIOUS!!
THERE GOES THE MYSTERIOUS MAN IN BLACK.
WHERE WILL HE GO?
IT'S CERTAINLY A MYSTERY.
HE TURNS A CORNER...
OOPS... HE'S DISAPPEARED!
WILL WE EVER SEE HIM AGAIN?
WHEREFORE ART THOU, MYSTERIOUS MAN IN BLACK?

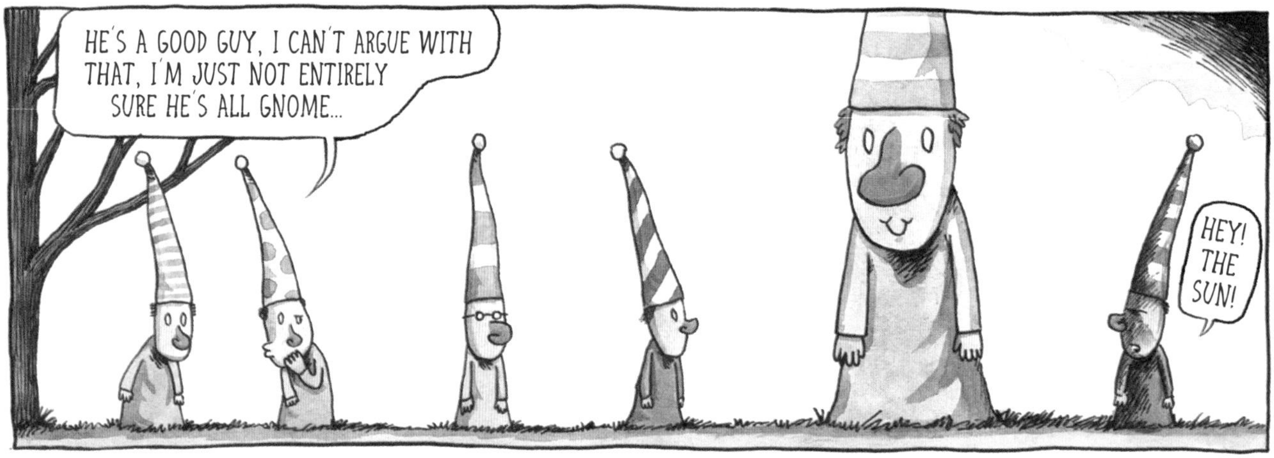
HE'S A GOOD GUY, I CAN'T ARGUE WITH THAT, I'M JUST NOT ENTIRELY SURE HE'S ALL GNOME...
HEY! THE SUN!

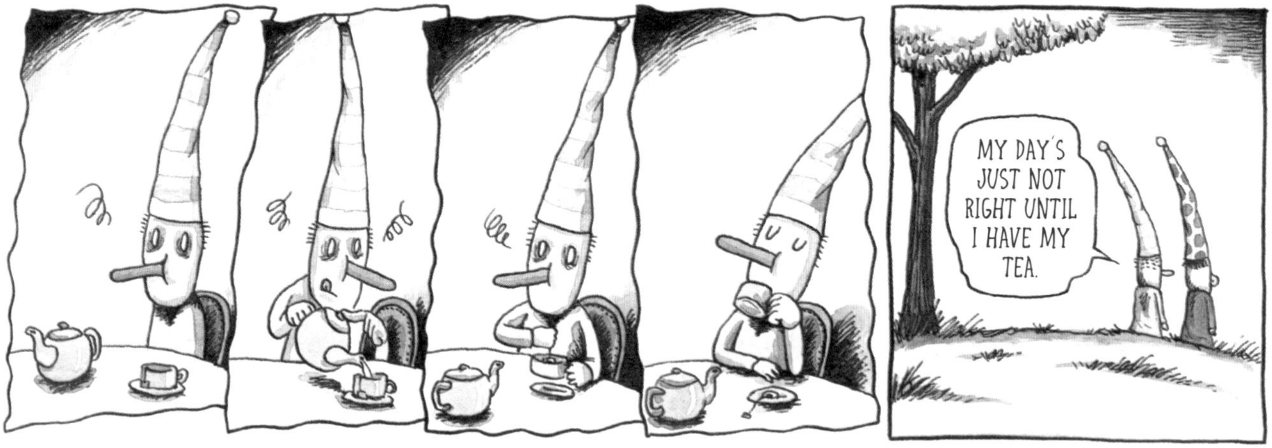
MY DAY'S JUST NOT RIGHT UNTIL I HAVE MY TEA.

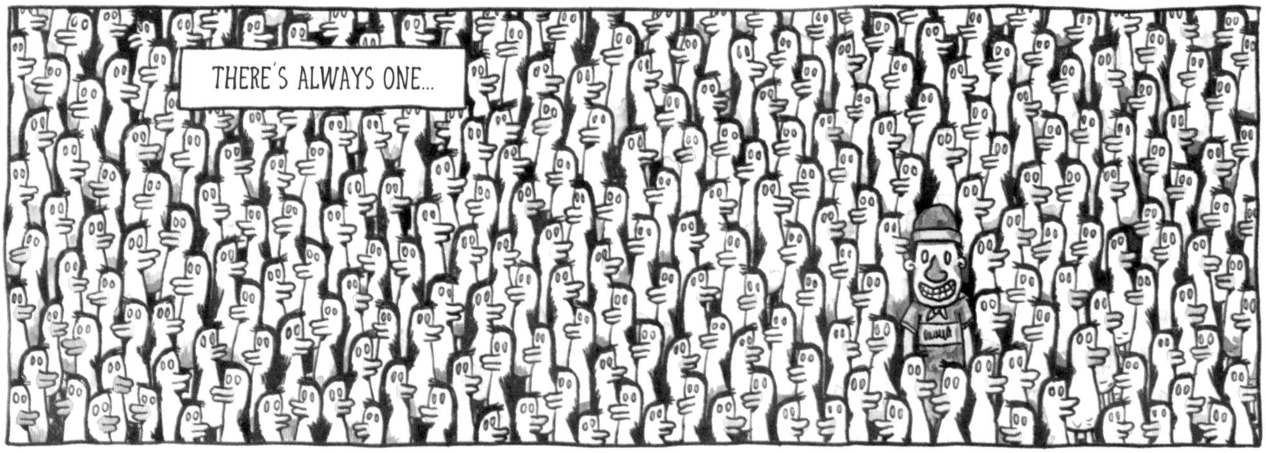
THERE'S ALWAYS ONE...

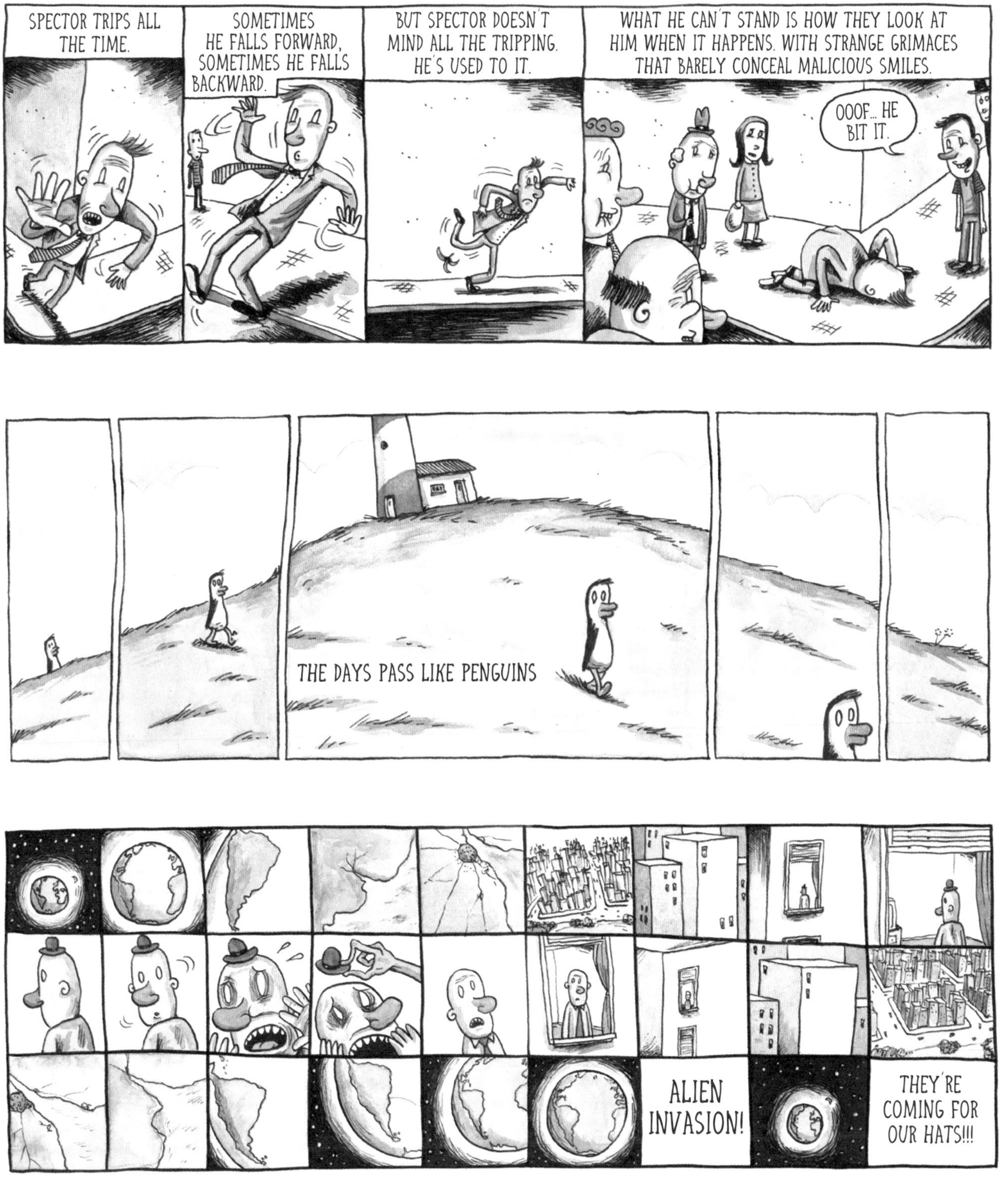
SPECTOR TRIPS ALL THE TIME.
SOMETIMES HE FALLS FORWARD, SOMETIMES HE FALLS BACKWARD.
BUT SPECTOR DOESN'T MIND ALL THE TRIPPING. HE'S USED TO IT.
WHAT HE CAN'T STAND IS HOW THEY LOOK AT HIM WHEN IT HAPPENS. WITH STRANGE GRIMACES THAT BARELY CONCEAL MALICIOUS SMILES.
OOOF... HE BIT IT.
THE DAYS PASS LIKE PENGUINS
ALIEN INVASION!
THEY'RE COMING FOR OUR HATS!!!

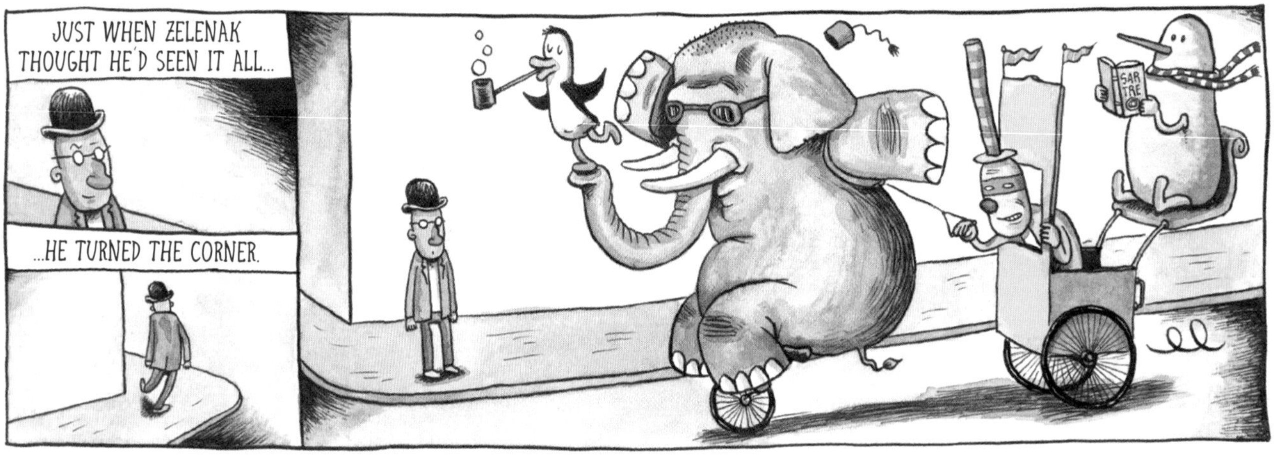
JUST WHEN ZELENAK THOUGHT HE'D SEEN IT ALL...
...HE TURNED THE CORNER.
SAR TRE

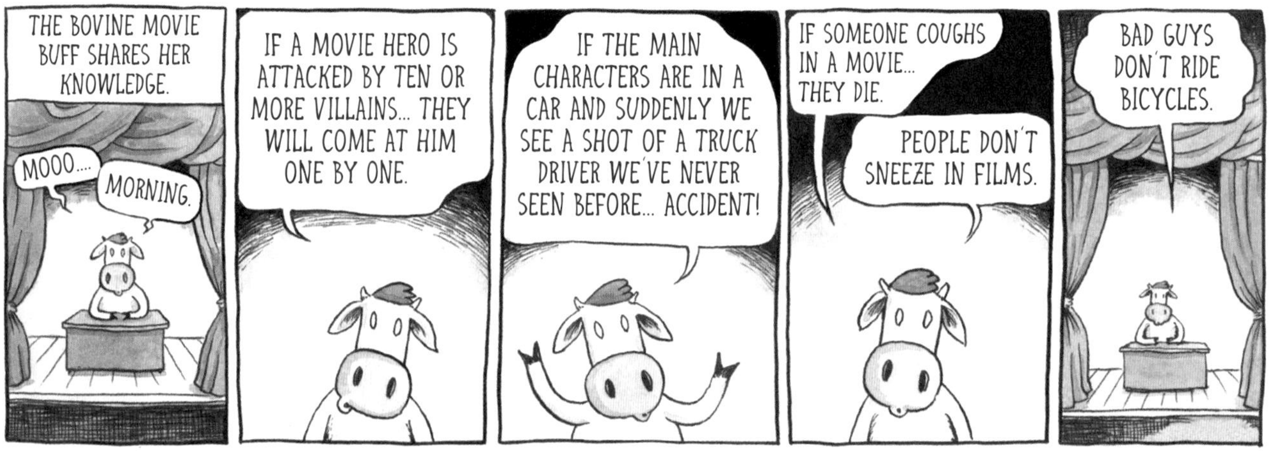
THE BOVINE MOVIE BUFF SHARES HER KNOWLEDGE.
MOOO....
MORNING.
IF A MOVIE HERO IS ATTACKED BY TEN OR MORE VILLAINS... THEY WILL COME AT HIM ONE BY ONE.
IF THE MAIN CHARACTERS ARE IN A CAR AND SUDDENLY WE SEE A SHOT OF A TRUCK DRIVER WE'VE NEVER SEEN BEFORE... ACCIDENT!
IF SOMEONE COUGHS IN A MOVIE... THEY DIE.
PEOPLE DON'T SNEEZE IN FILMS.
BAD GUYS DON'T RIDE BICYCLES.

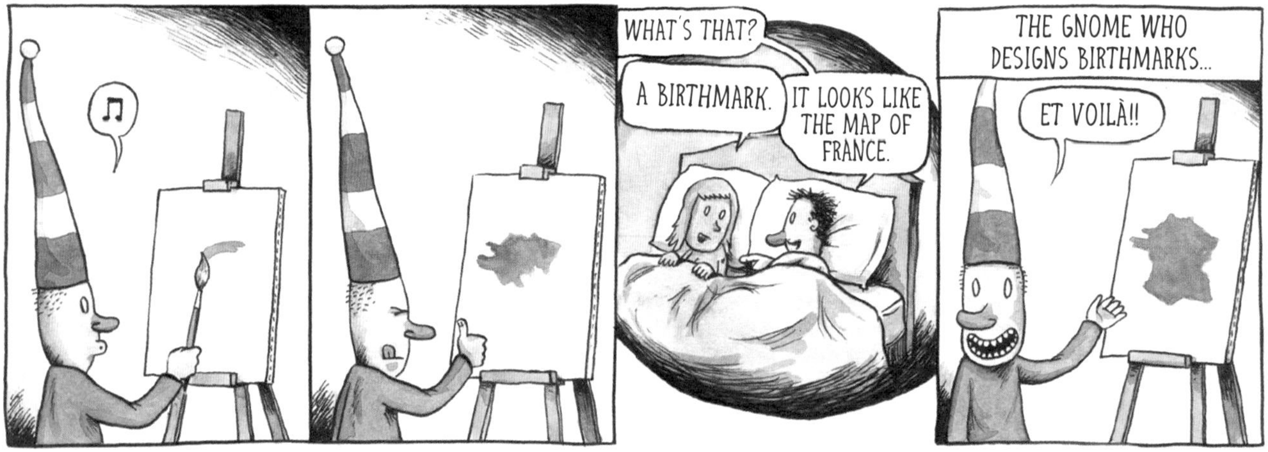
♫
WHAT'S THAT?
A BIRTHMARK.
IT LOOKS LIKE THE MAP OF FRANCE.
THE GNOME WHO DESIGNS BIRTHMARKS...
ET VOILÀ!!

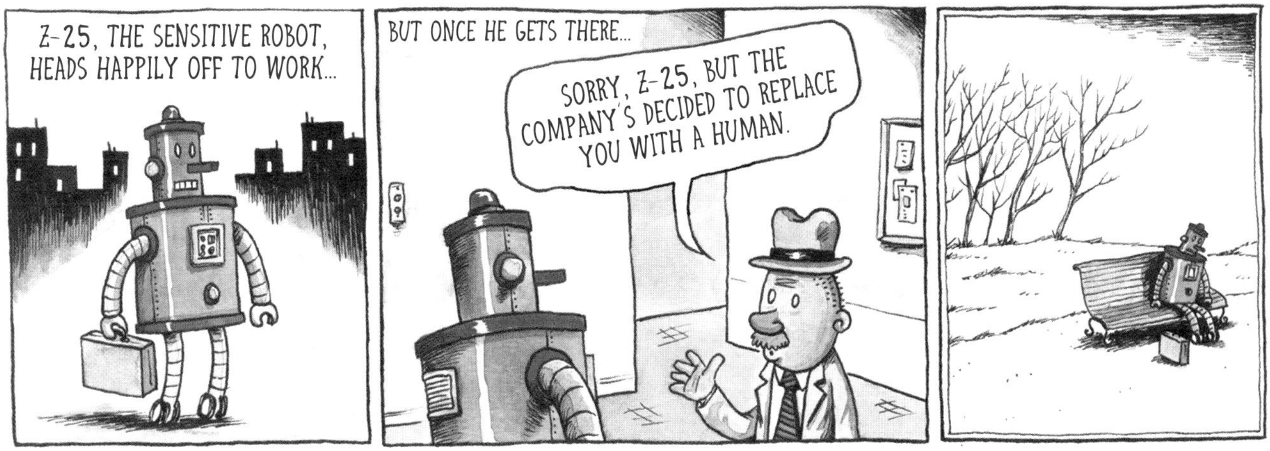
Z-25, THE SENSITIVE ROBOT, HEADS HAPPILY OFF TO WORK...
BUT ONCE HE GETS THERE...
SORRY, Z-25, BUT THE COMPANY'S DECIDED TO REPLACE YOU WITH A HUMAN.

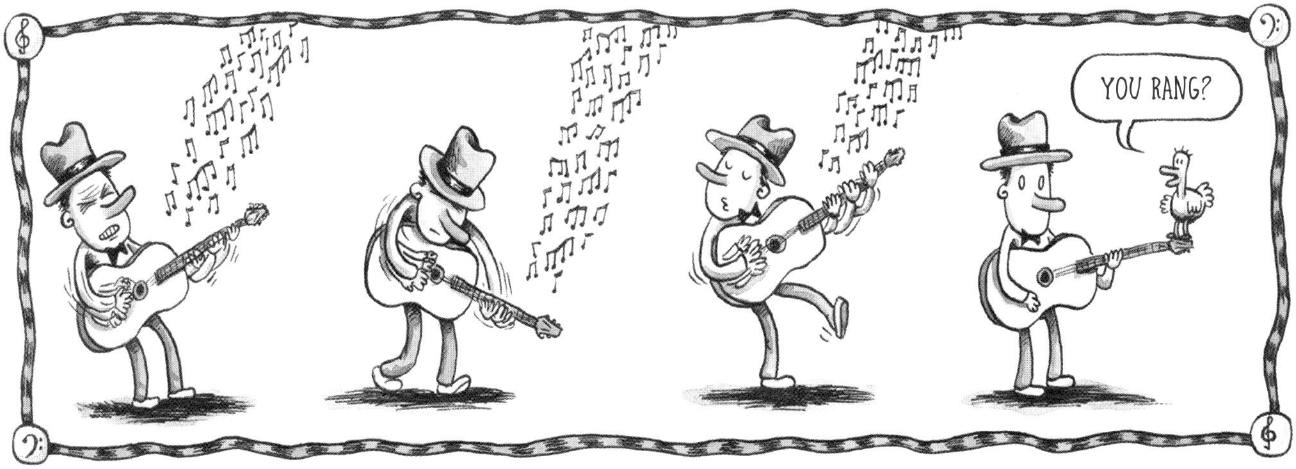
YOU RANG?

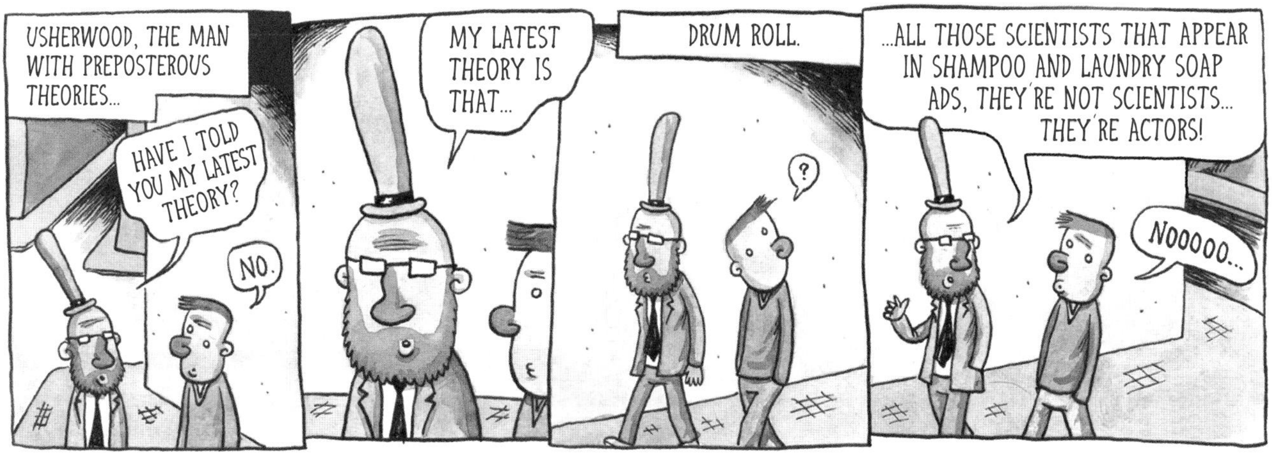
USHERWOOD, THE MAN WITH PREPOSTEROUS THEORIES...
HAVE I TOLD YOU MY LATEST THEORY?
NO.
MY LATEST THEORY IS THAT...
DRUM ROLL.
?
...ALL THOSE SCIENTISTS THAT APPEAR IN SHAMPOO AND LAUNDRY SOAP ADS, THEY'RE NOT SCIENTISTS... THEY'RE ACTORS!
NOOOOO...

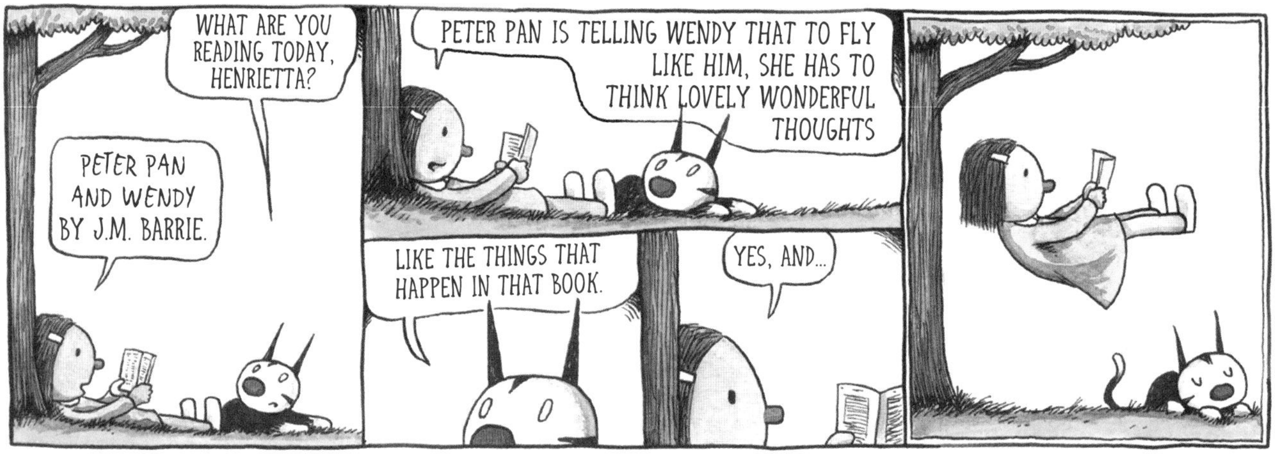
WHAT ARE YOU READING TODAY, HENRIETTA?
PETER PAN AND WENDY BY J.M. BARRIE.
PETER PAN IS TELLING WENDY THAT TO FLY LIKE HIM, SHE HAS TO THINK LOVELY WONDERFUL THOUGHTS
LIKE THE THINGS THAT HAPPEN IN THAT BOOK.
YES, AND...

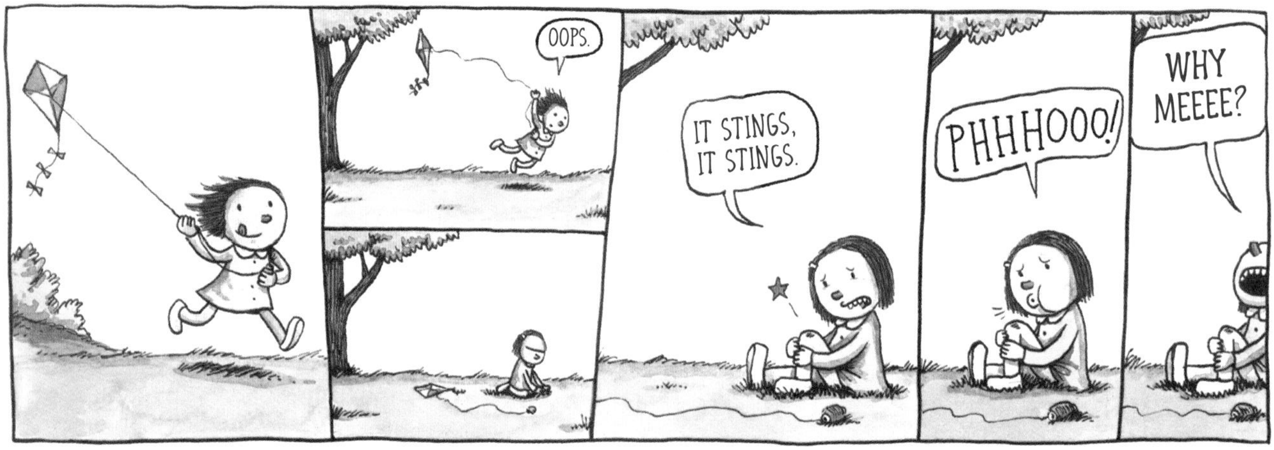
OOPS.
IT STINGS, IT STINGS.
PHHHOOO!
WHY MEEEE?

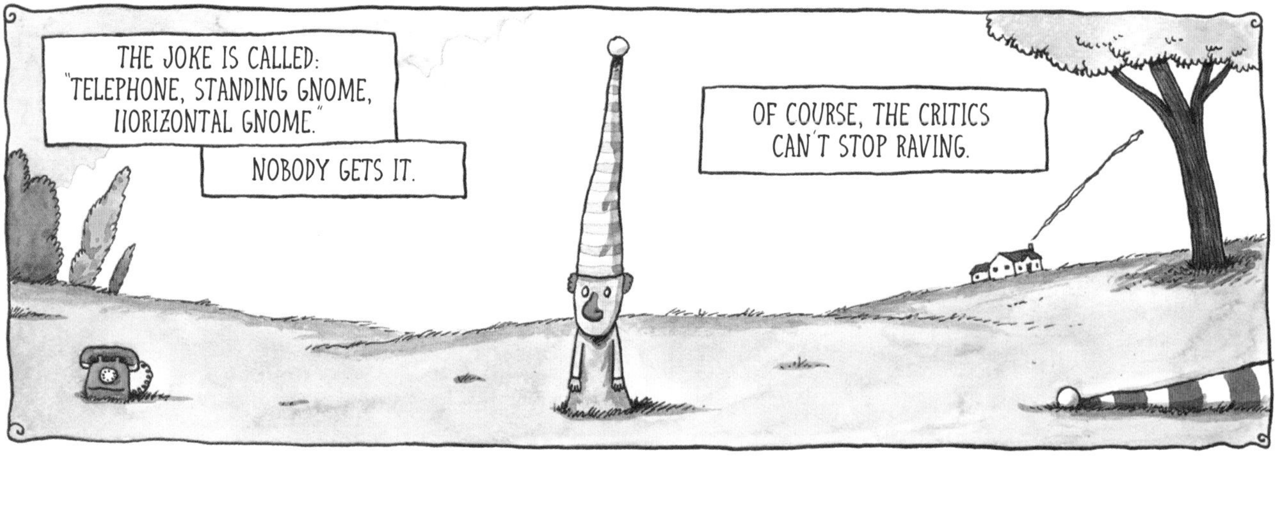
THE JOKE IS CALLED: "TELEPHONE, STANDING GNOME, HORIZONTAL GNOME."
NOBODY GETS IT.
OF COURSE, THE CRITICS CAN'T STOP RAVING.

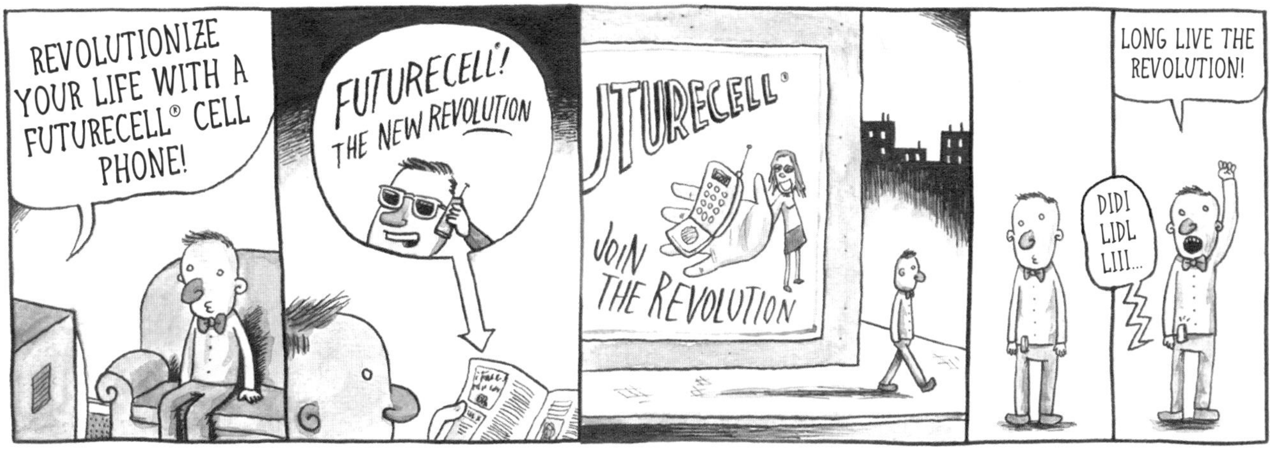
REVOLUTIONIZE YOUR LIFE WITH A FUTURECELL® CELL PHONE!
FUTURECELL®! THE NEW REVOLUTION
UTURECELL®
JOIN THE REVOLUTION
DIDI LIDL LIII...
LONG LIVE THE REVOLUTION!

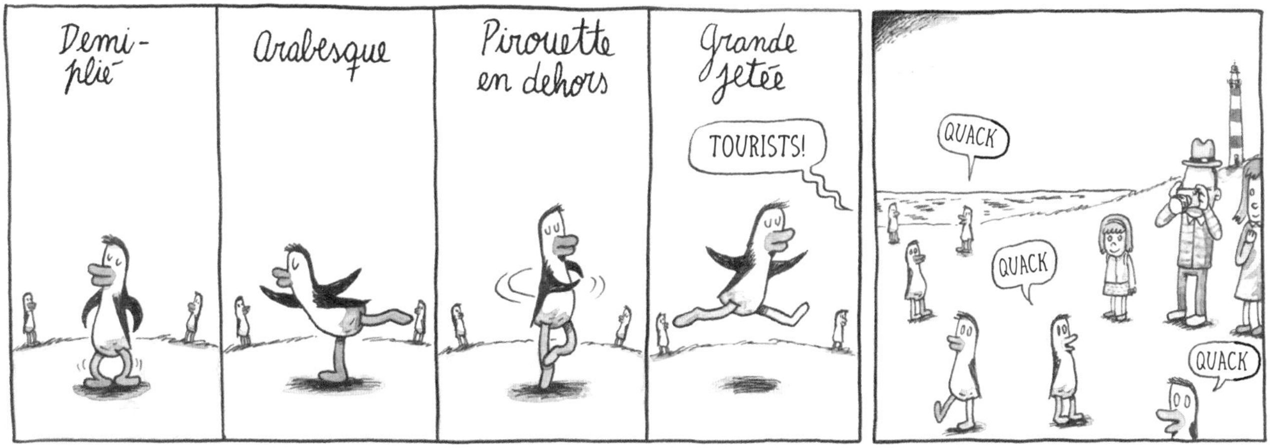
Demi-plié
Arabesque
Pirouette en dehors
Grande jetée
TOURISTS!
QUACK
QUACK
QUACK

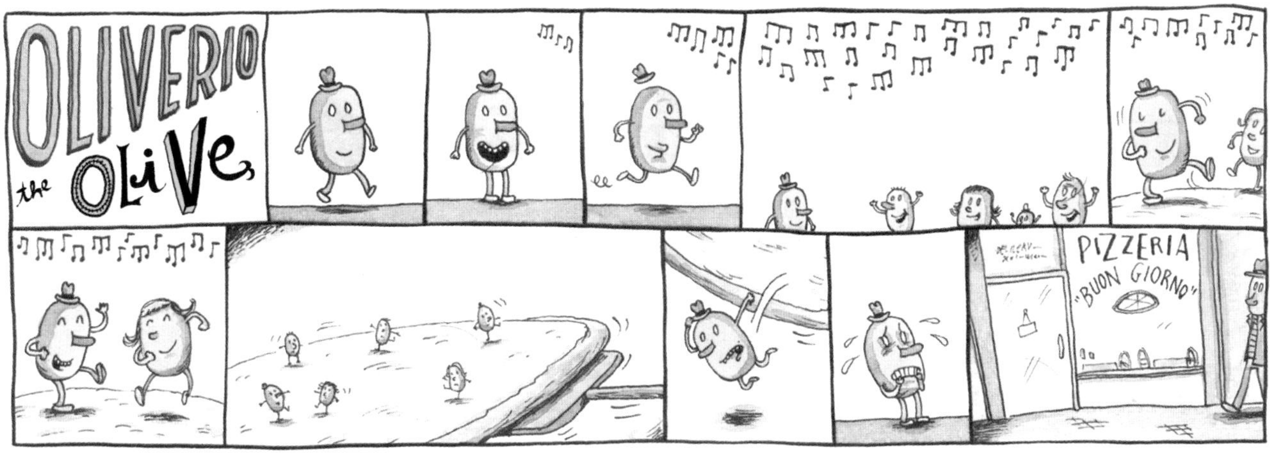
OLIVERIO the OLIVE
PIZZERIA
"BUON GIORNO"

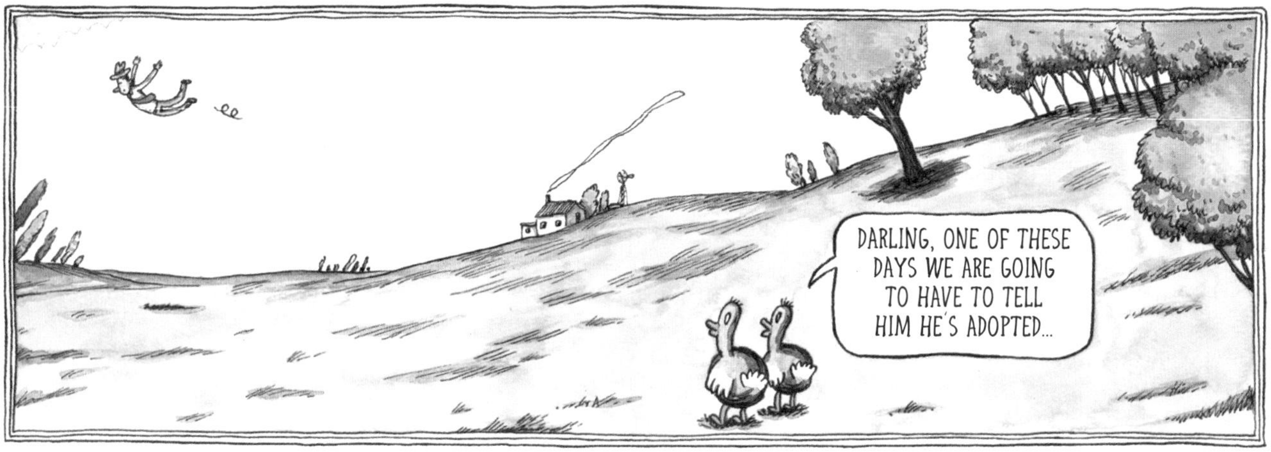
DARLING, ONE OF THESE DAYS WE ARE GOING TO HAVE TO TELL HIM HE'S ADOPTED...

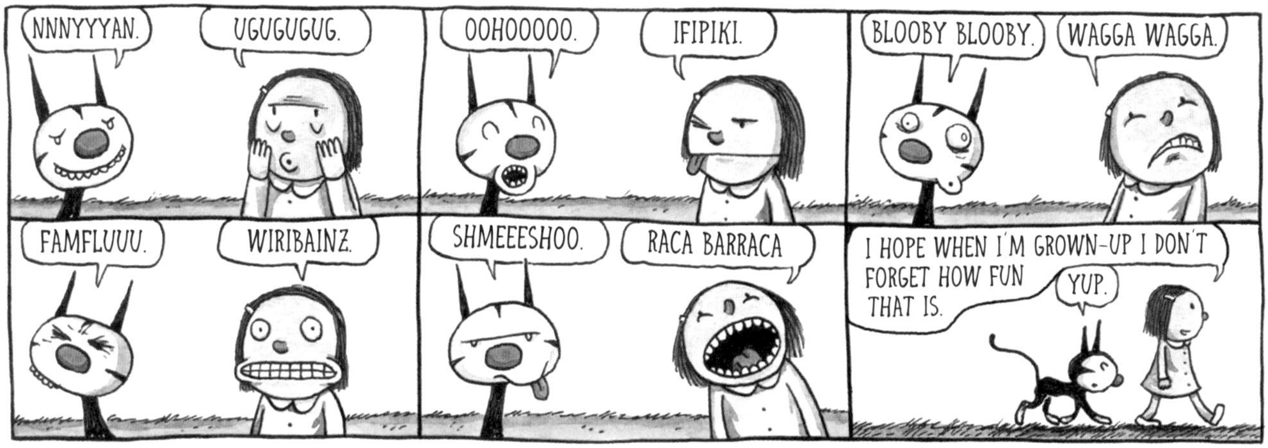
NNNYYYAN.
UGUGUGUG.
OOHOOOOO.
IFIPIKI.
BLOOBY BLOOBY.
WAGGA WAGGA.
FAMFLUUU.
WIRIBAINZ.
SHMEEESHOO.
RACA BARRACA
I HOPE WHEN I'M GROWN-UP I DON'T FORGET HOW FUN THAT IS.
YUP.

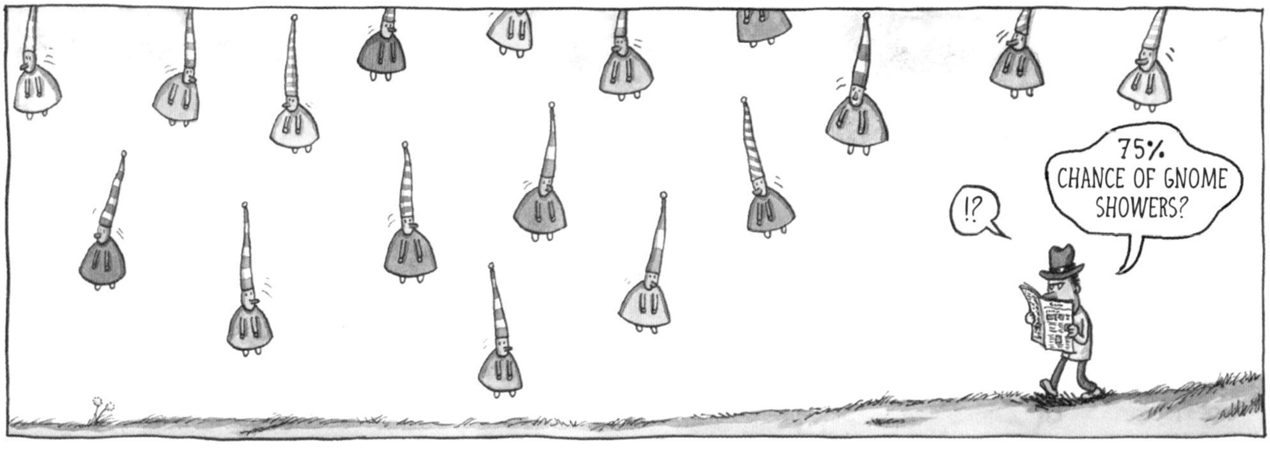
!?
75% CHANCE OF GNOME SHOWERS?

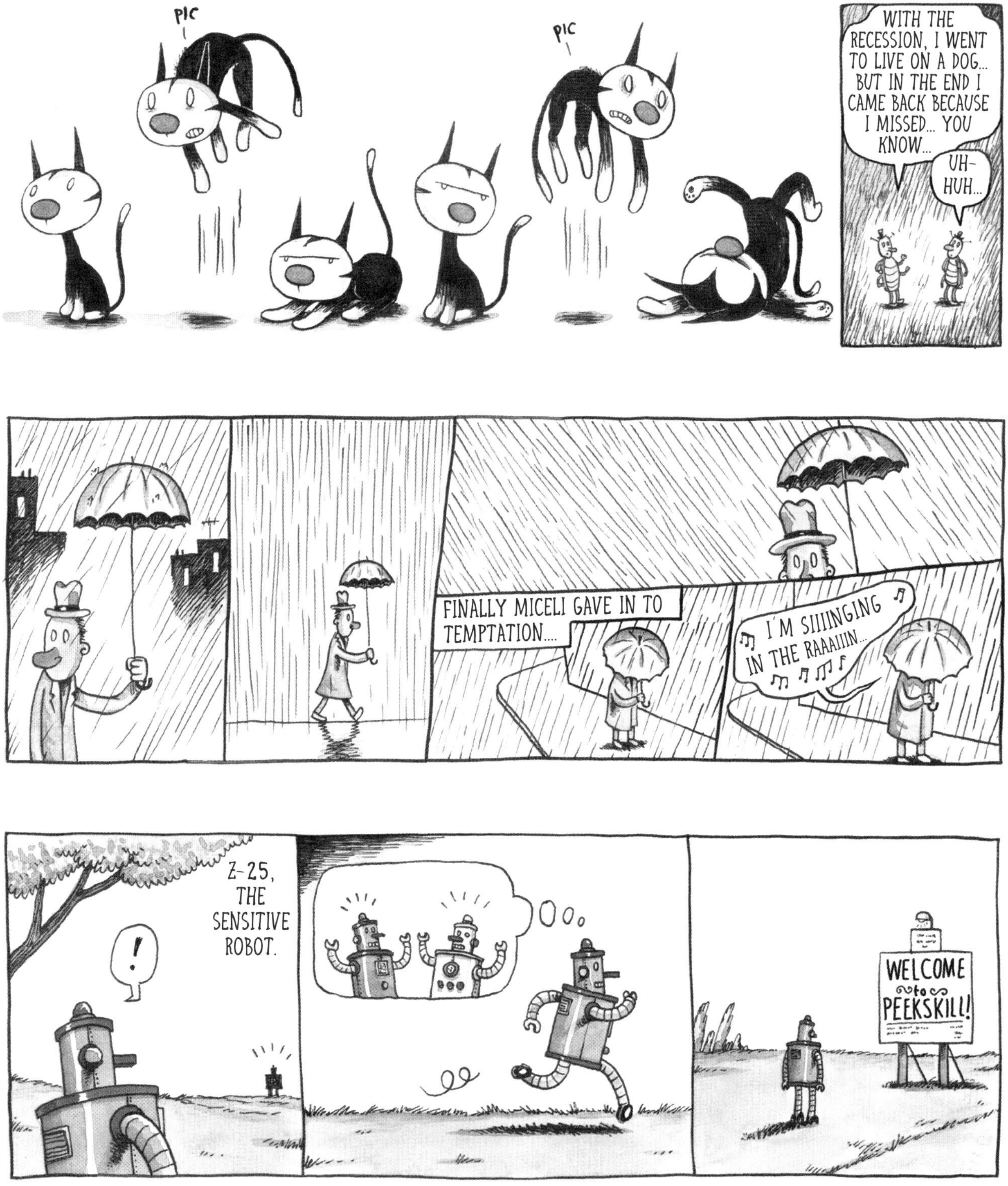
PIC
PIC
WITH THE RECESSION, I WENT TO LIVE ON A DOG... BUT IN THE END I CAME BACK BECAUSE I MISSED... YOU KNOW...
UH-HUH...
FINALLY MICELI GAVE IN TO TEMPTATION....
I'M SIIIINGING IN THE RAAAIIIN...
Z-25, THE SENSITIVE ROBOT.
!
WELCOME to PEEKSKILL!

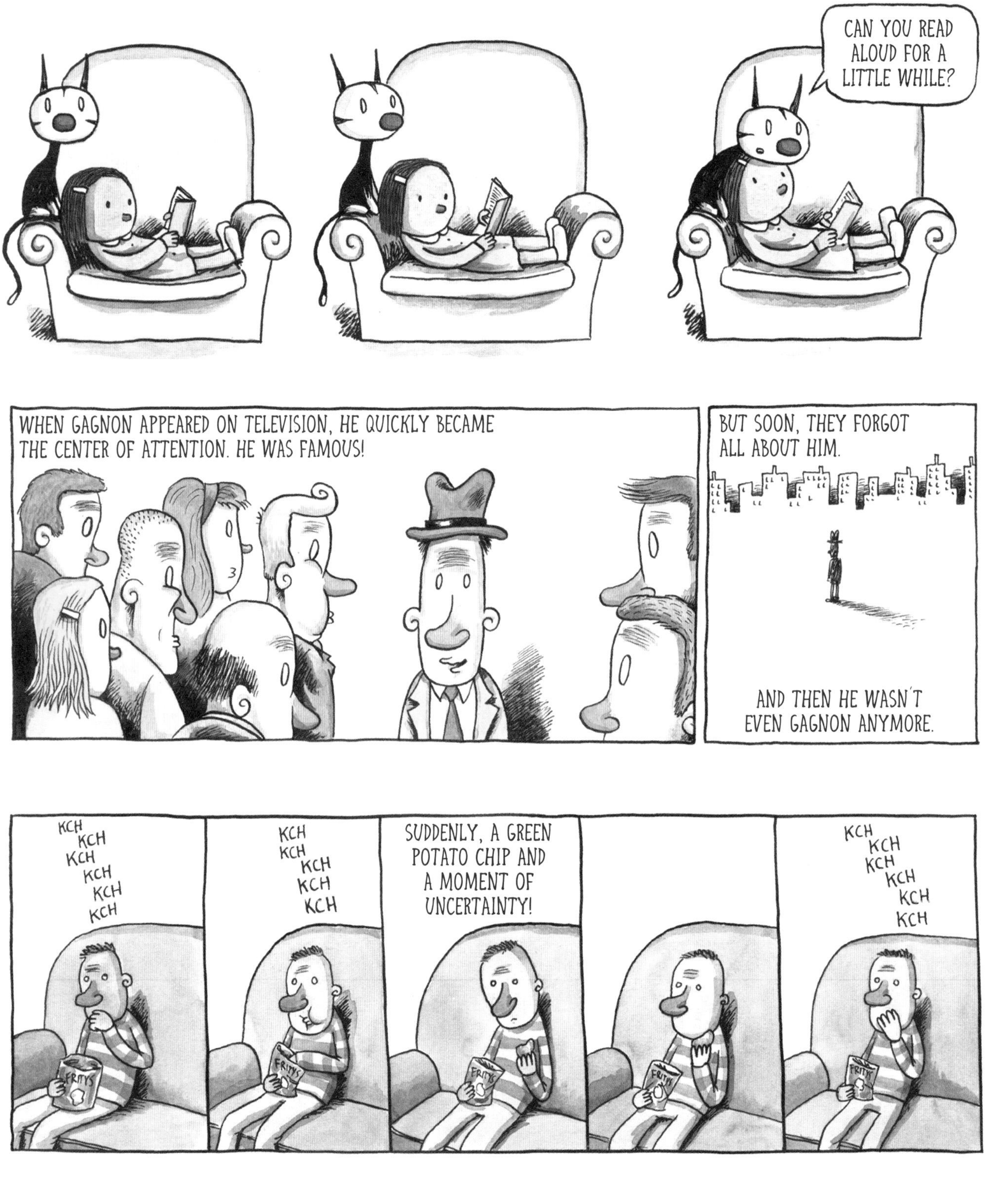
CAN YOU READ ALOUD FOR A LITTLE WHILE?
WHEN GAGNON APPEARED ON TELEVISION, HE QUICKLY BECAME THE CENTER OF ATTENTION. HE WAS FAMOUS!
BUT SOON, THEY FORGOT ALL ABOUT HIM.
AND THEN HE WASN'T EVEN GAGNON ANYMORE.
KCH KCH KCH KCH KCH KCH
FRITYS
KCH KCH KCH KCH KCH
FRITYS
SUDDENLY, A GREEN POTATO CHIP AND A MOMENT OF UNCERTAINTY!
FRITYS
FRITYS
KCH KCH KCH KCH KCH KCH
FRITYS

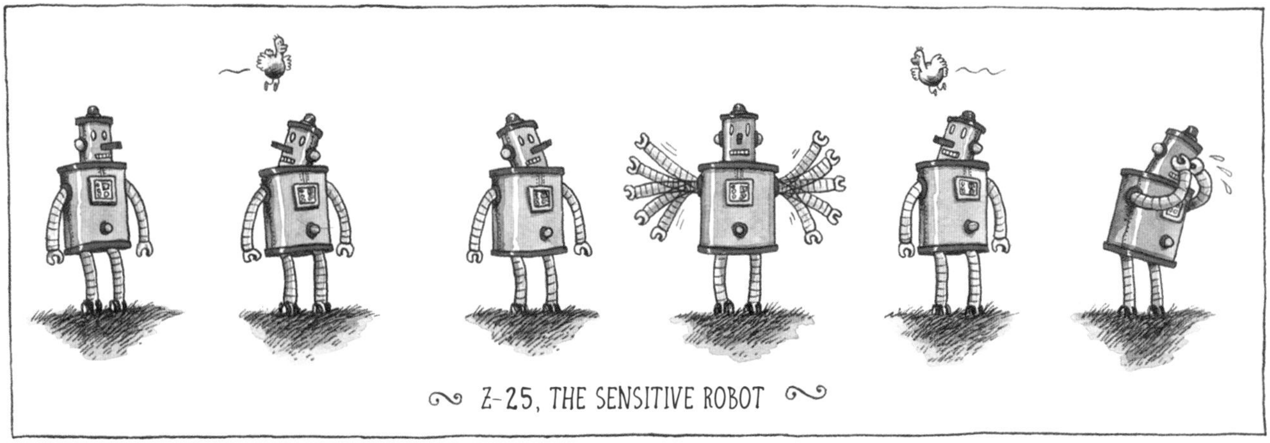
Z-25, THE SENSITIVE ROBOT

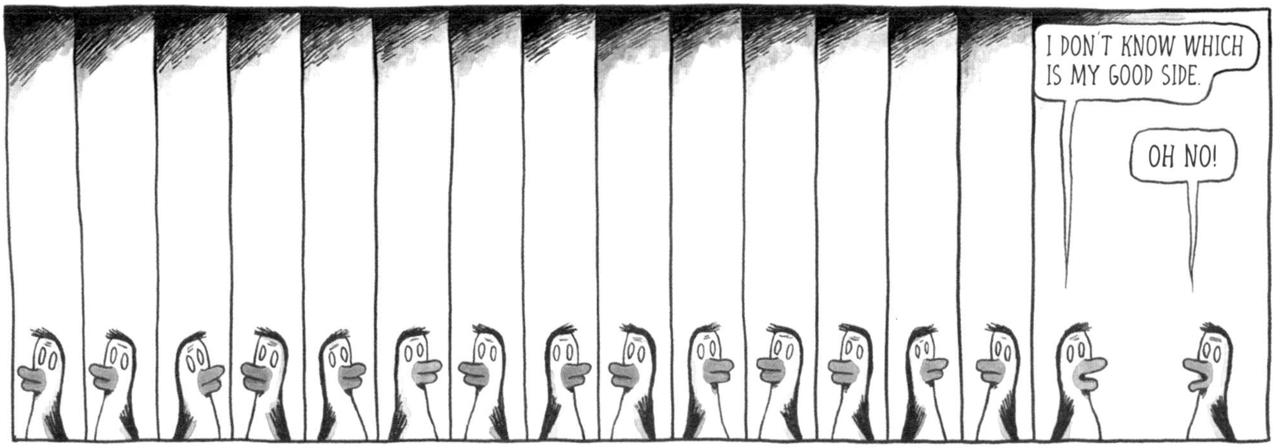
I DON'T KNOW WHICH IS MY GOOD SIDE.
OH NO!

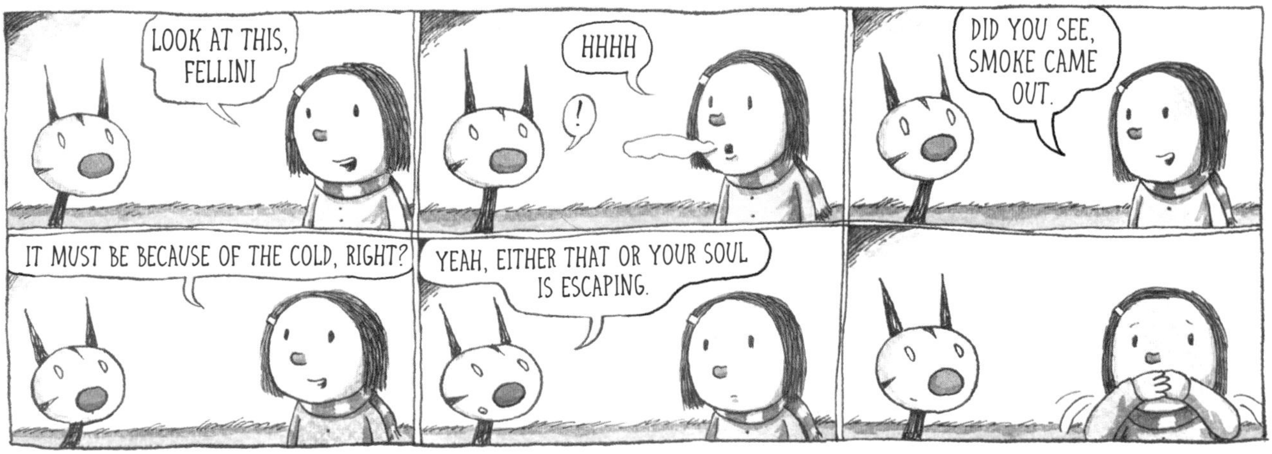
LOOK AT THIS, FELLINI
HHHH
!
DID YOU SEE, SMOKE CAME OUT.
IT MUST BE BECAUSE OF THE COLD, RIGHT?
YEAH, EITHER THAT OR YOUR SOUL IS ESCAPING.

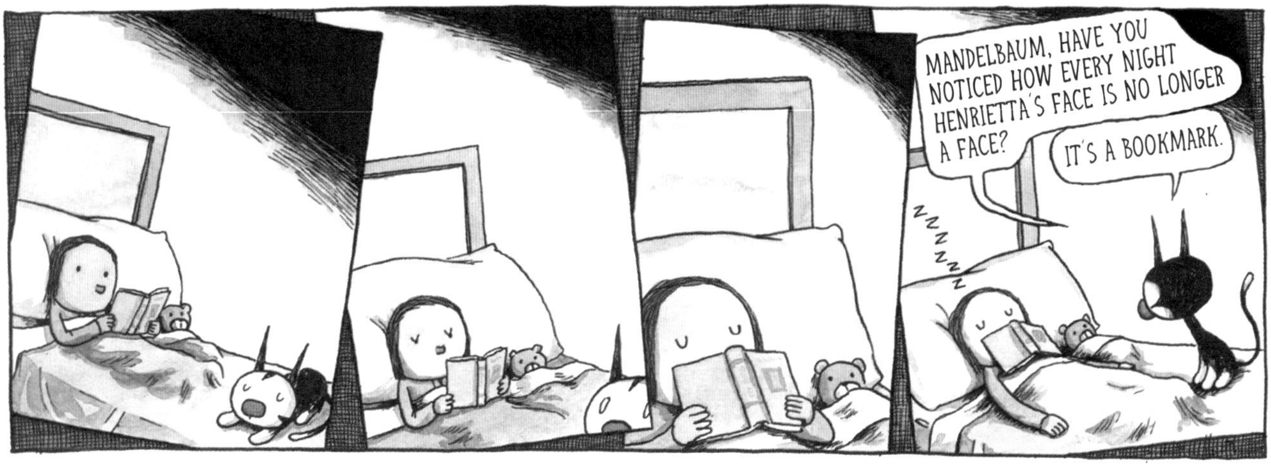
ZZZZZ
MANDELBAUM, HAVE YOU NOTICED HOW EVERY NIGHT HENRIETTA'S FACE IS NO LONGER A FACE?
IT'S A BOOKMARK.

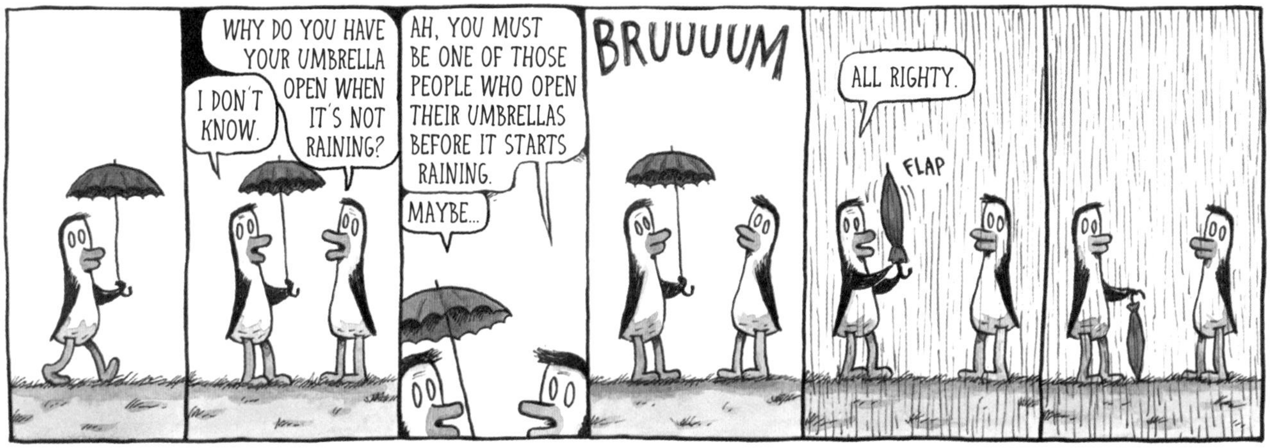
WHY DO YOU HAVE YOUR UMBRELLA OPEN WHEN IT'S NOT RAINING?
I DON'T KNOW.
AH, YOU MUST BE ONE OF THOSE PEOPLE WHO OPEN THEIR UMBRELLAS BEFORE IT STARTS RAINING.
MAYBE...
BRUUUUM
ALL RIGHTY.
FLAP

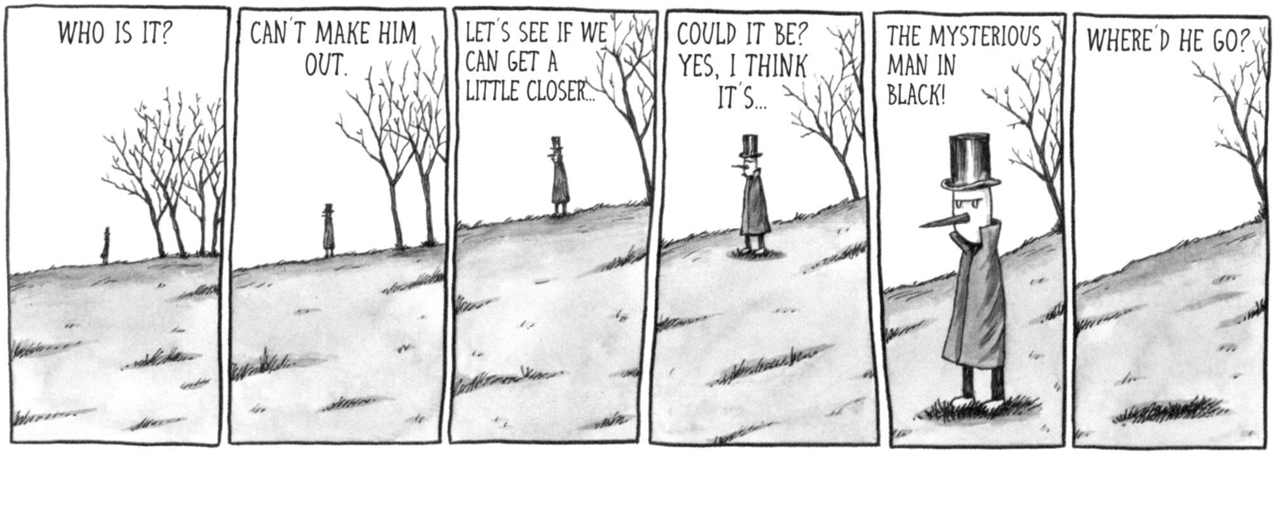
WHO IS IT?
CAN'T MAKE HIM OUT.
LET'S SEE IF WE CAN GET A LITTLE CLOSER...
COULD IT BE? YES, I THINK IT'S...
THE MYSTERIOUS MAN IN BLACK!
WHERE'D HE GO?

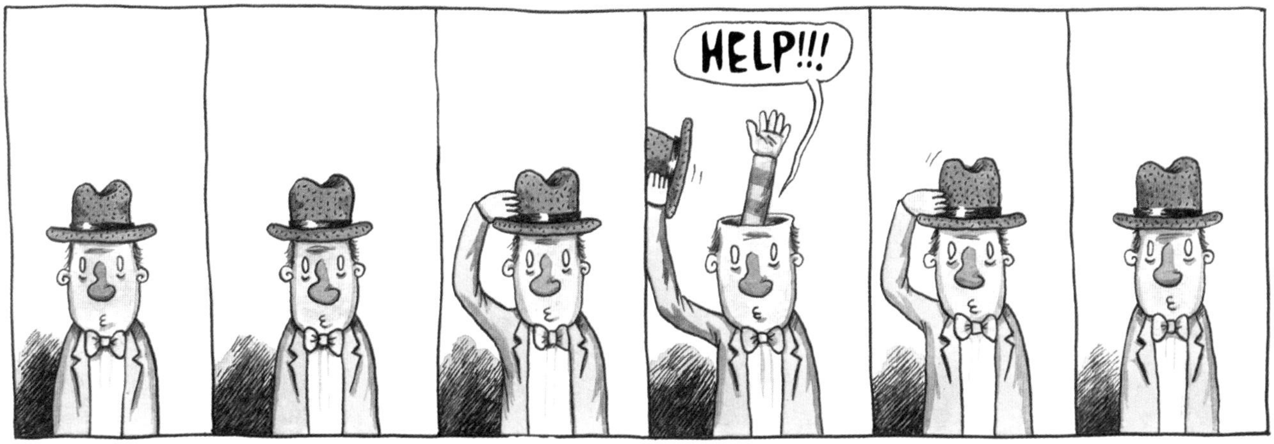
HELP!!!

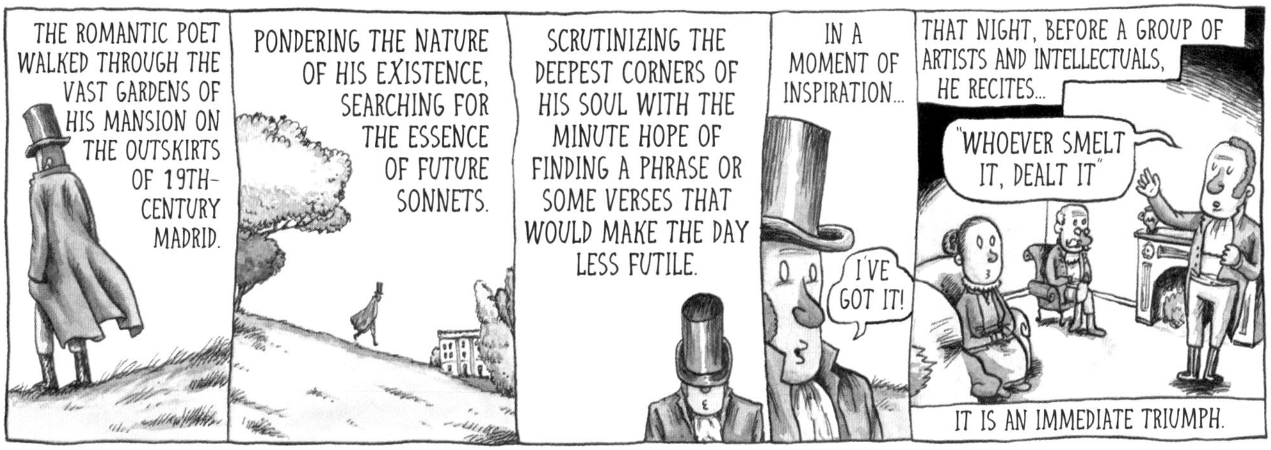
THE ROMANTIC POET WALKED THROUGH THE VAST GARDENS OF HIS MANSION ON THE OUTSKIRTS OF 19TH-CENTURY MADRID.
PONDERING THE NATURE OF HIS EXISTENCE, SEARCHING FOR THE ESSENCE OF FUTURE SONNETS.
SCRUTINIZING THE DEEPEST CORNERS OF HIS SOUL WITH THE MINUTE HOPE OF FINDING A PHRASE OR SOME VERSES THAT WOULD MAKE THE DAY LESS FUTILE.
IN A MOMENT OF INSPIRATION...
I'VE GOT IT!
THAT NIGHT, BEFORE A GROUP OF ARTISTS AND INTELLECTUALS, HE RECITES...
"WHOEVER SMELT IT, DEALT IT"
IT IS AN IMMEDIATE TRIUMPH.

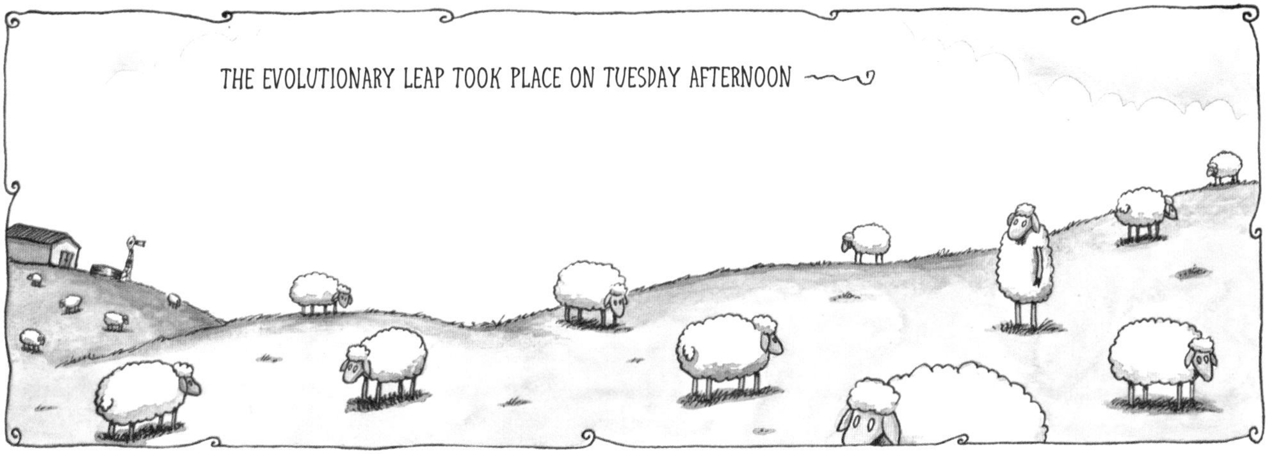
THE EVOLUTIONARY LEAP TOOK PLACE ON TUESDAY AFTERNOON

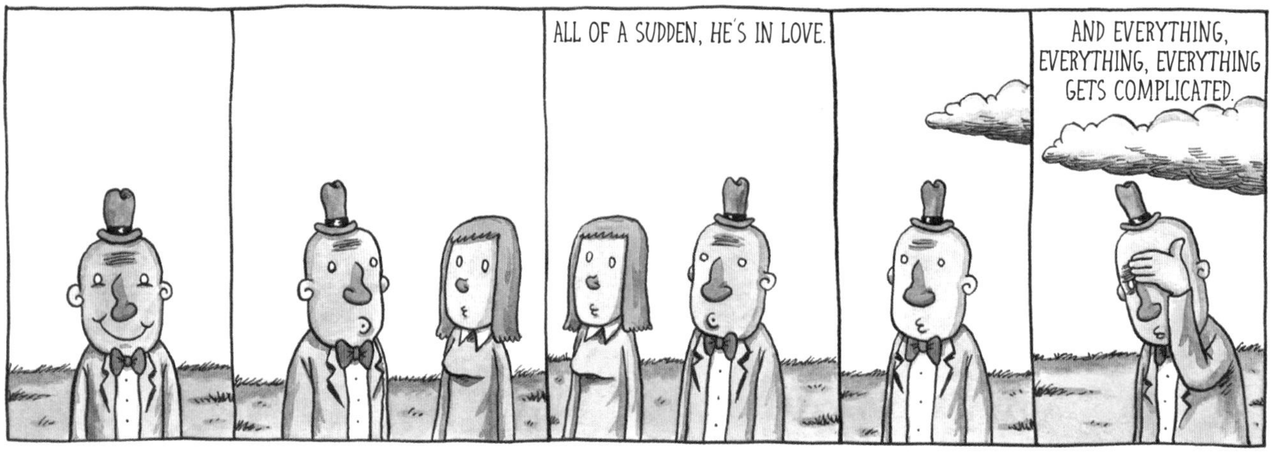
ALL OF A SUDDEN, HE'S IN LOVE.
AND EVERYTHING, EVERYTHING, EVERYTHING GETS COMPLICATED.

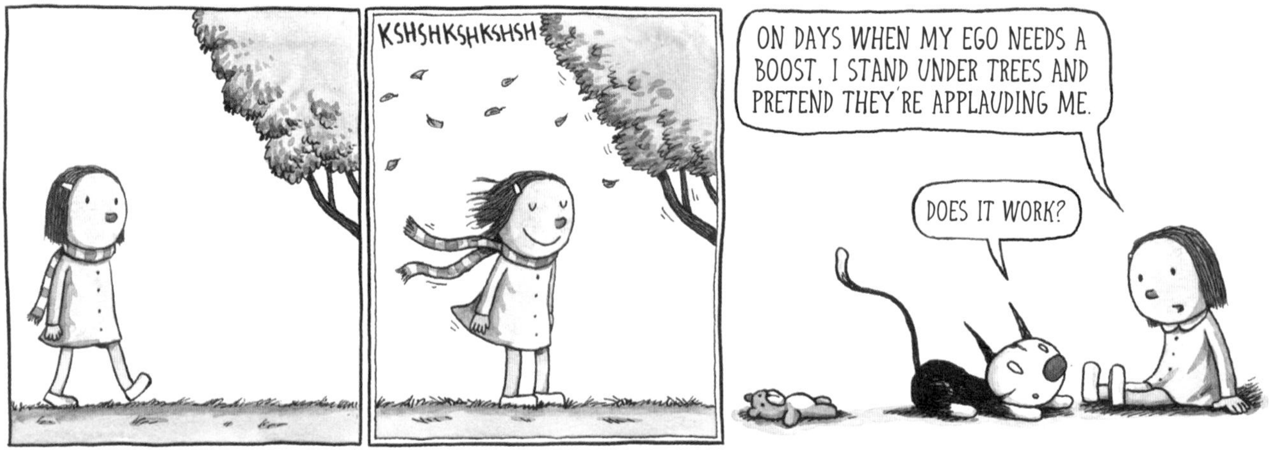
KSHSHKSHKSHSH
ON DAYS WHEN MY EGO NEEDS A BOOST, I STAND UNDER TREES AND PRETEND THEY'RE APPLAUDING ME.
DOES IT WORK?

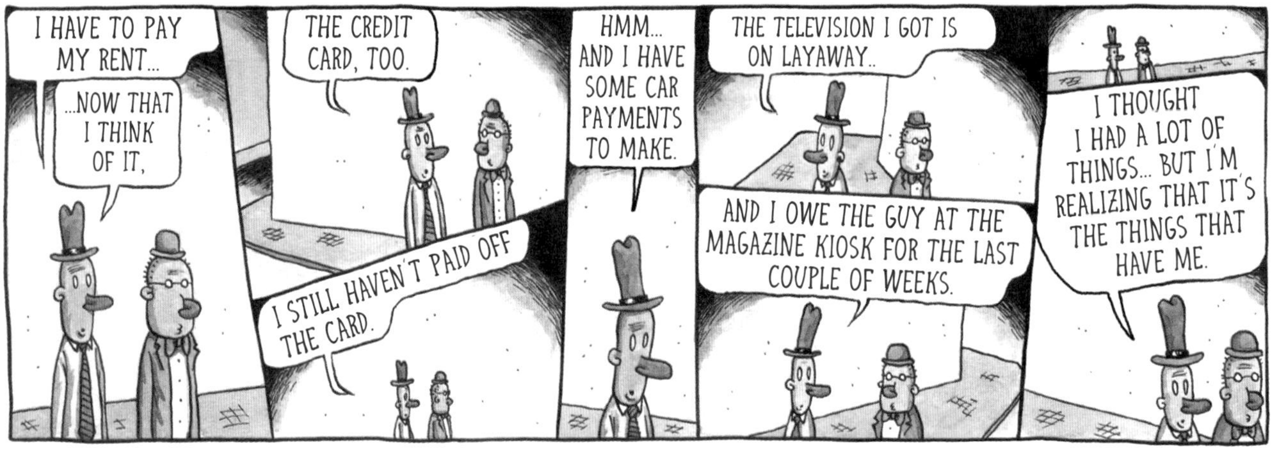
I HAVE TO PAY MY RENT...
...NOW THAT I THINK OF IT,
THE CREDIT CARD, TOO.
I STILL HAVEN'T PAID OFF THE CARD.
HMM... AND I HAVE SOME CAR PAYMENTS TO MAKE.
THE TELEVISION I GOT IS ON LAYAWAY..
AND I OWE THE GUY AT THE MAGAZINE KIOSK FOR THE LAST COUPLE OF WEEKS.
I THOUGHT I HAD A LOT OF THINGS... BUT I'M REALIZING THAT IT'S THE THINGS THAT HAVE ME.

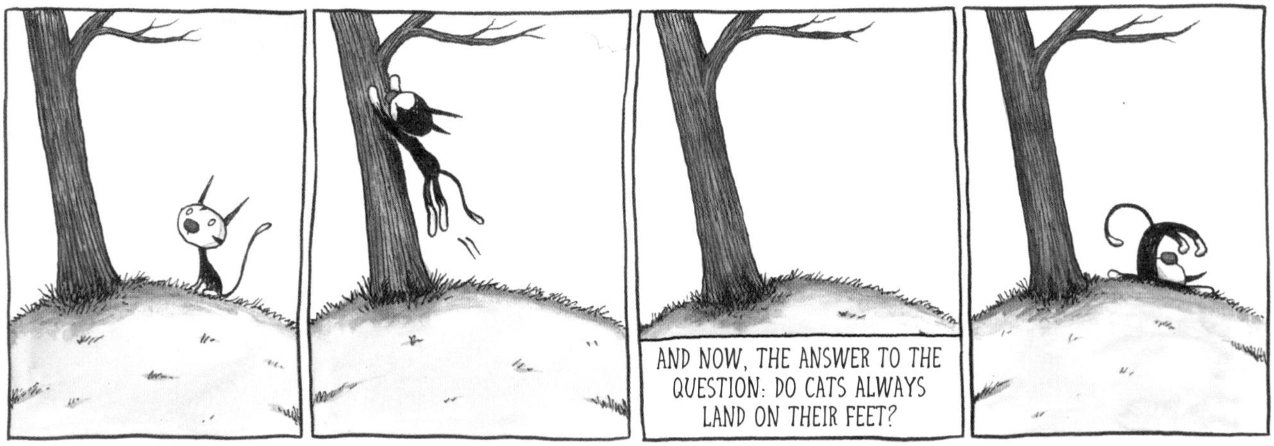
AND NOW, THE ANSWER TO THE QUESTION: DO CATS ALWAYS LAND ON THEIR FEET?

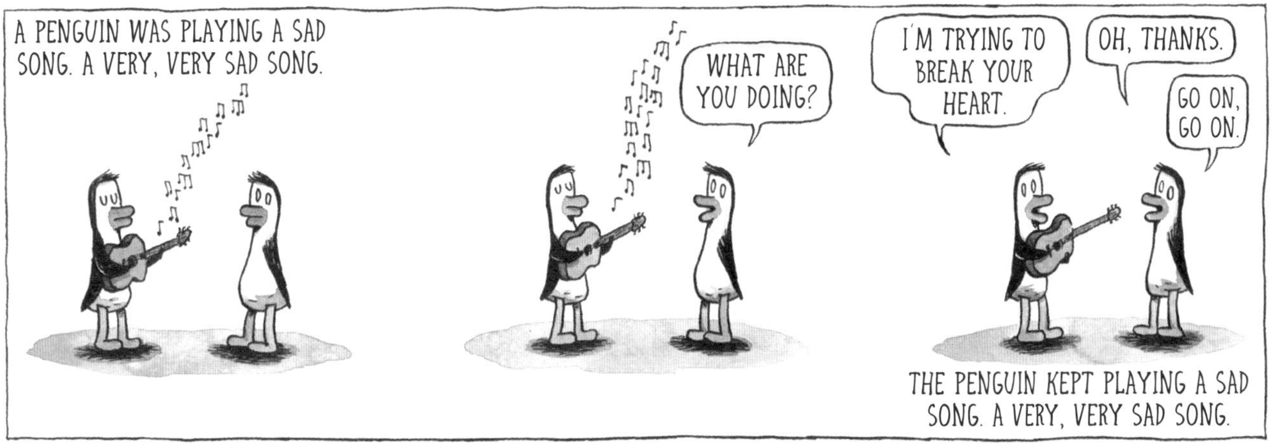
A PENGUIN WAS PLAYING A SAD SONG. A VERY, VERY SAD SONG.
WHAT ARE YOU DOING?
I'M TRYING TO BREAK YOUR HEART.
OH, THANKS.
GO ON, GO ON.
THE PENGUIN KEPT PLAYING A SAD SONG. A VERY, VERY SAD SONG.

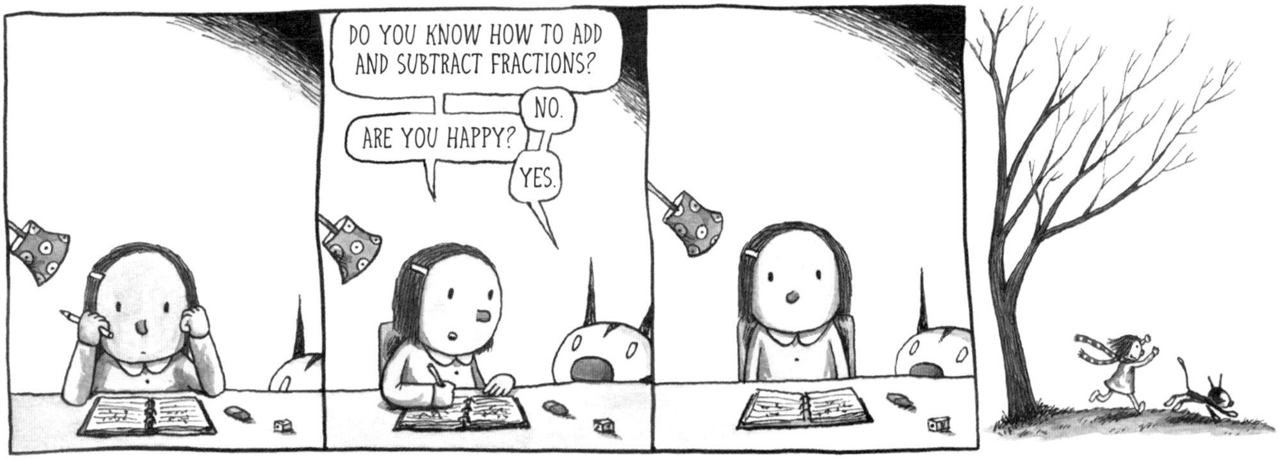
DO YOU KNOW HOW TO ADD AND SUBTRACT FRACTIONS?
NO.
ARE YOU HAPPY?
YES.

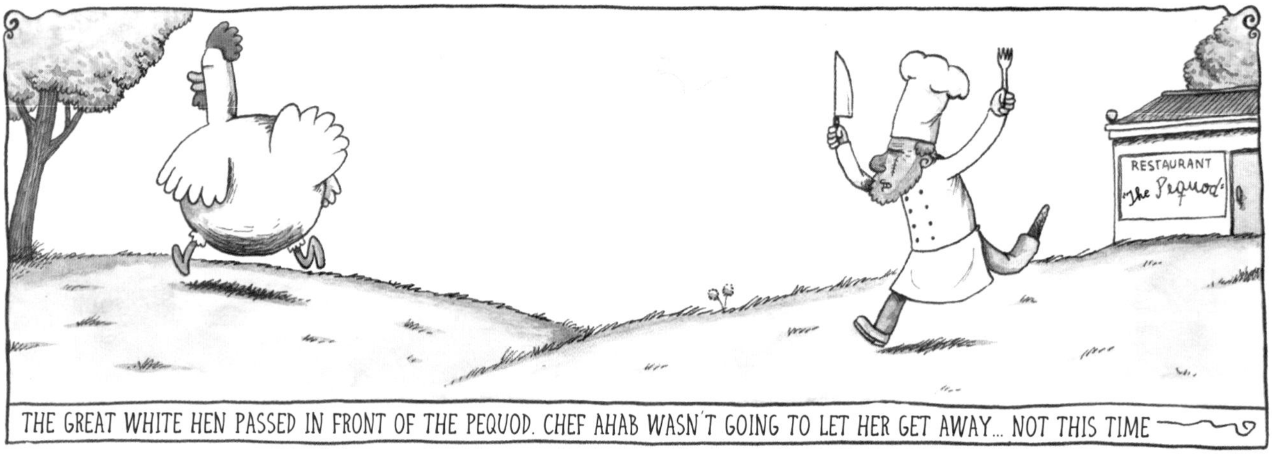
RESTAURANT
The Pequod
THE GREAT WHITE HEN PASSED IN FRONT OF THE PEQUOD. CHEF AHAB WASN'T GOING TO LET HER GET AWAY... NOT THIS TIME

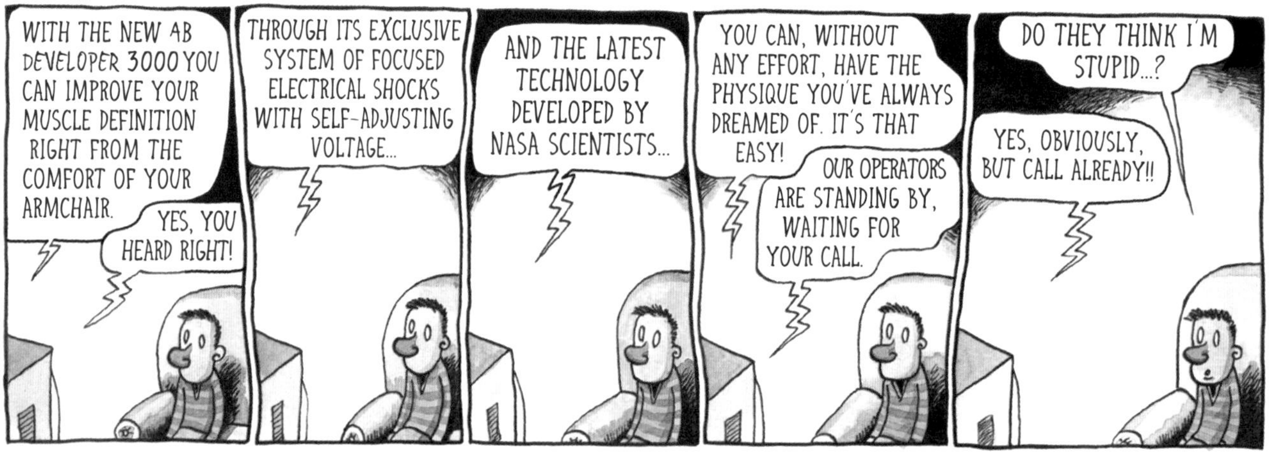
WITH THE NEW AB DEVELOPER 3000 YOU CAN IMPROVE YOUR MUSCLE DEFINITION RIGHT FROM THE COMFORT OF YOUR ARMCHAIR.
YES, YOU HEARD RIGHT!
THROUGH ITS EXCLUSIVE SYSTEM OF FOCUSED ELECTRICAL SHOCKS WITH SELF-ADJUSTING VOLTAGE...
AND THE LATEST TECHNOLOGY DEVELOPED BY NASA SCIENTISTS...
YOU CAN, WITHOUT ANY EFFORT, HAVE THE PHYSIQUE YOU'VE ALWAYS DREAMED OF. IT'S THAT EASY!
OUR OPERATORS ARE STANDING BY, WAITING FOR YOUR CALL.
DO THEY THINK I'M STUPID...?
YES, OBVIOUSLY, BUT CALL ALREADY!!

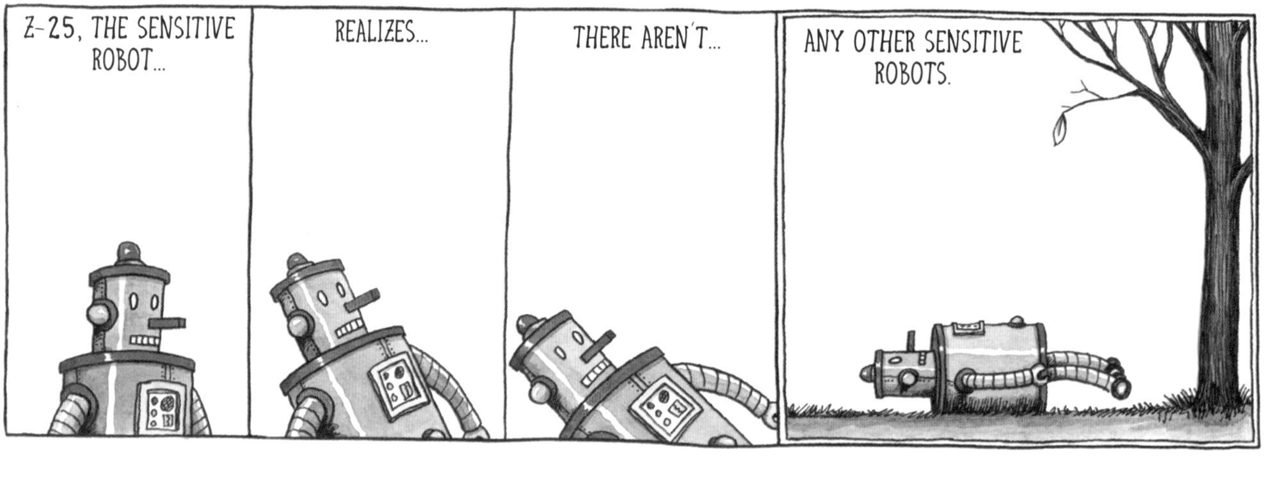
Z-25, THE SENSITIVE ROBOT...
REALIZES...
THERE AREN'T...
ANY OTHER SENSITIVE ROBOTS.

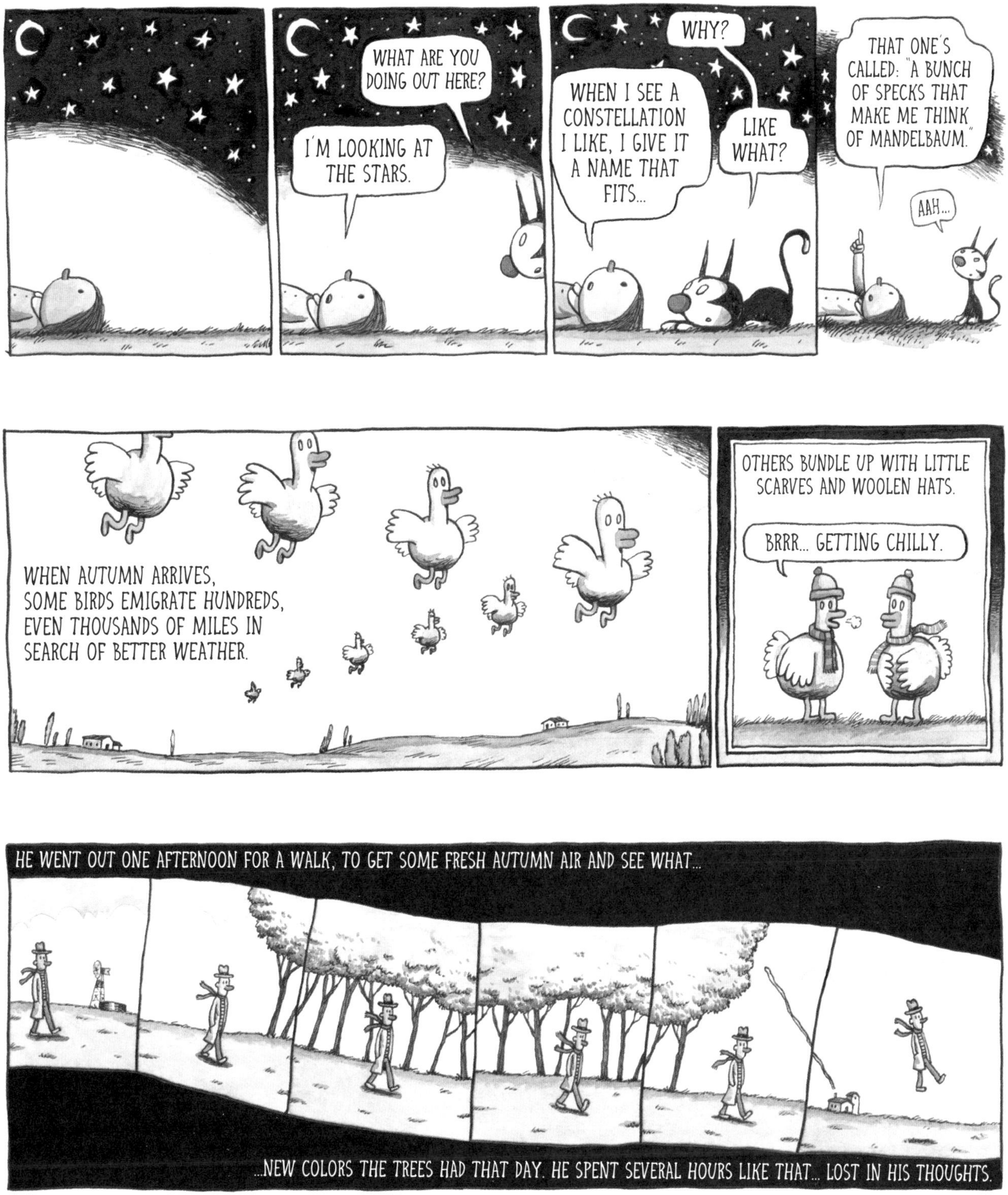

WHAT ARE YOU DOING OUT HERE?
I'M LOOKING AT THE STARS.
WHEN I SEE A CONSTELLATION I LIKE, I GIVE IT A NAME THAT FITS...
WHY?
LIKE WHAT?
THAT ONE'S CALLED: "A BUNCH OF SPECKS THAT MAKE ME THINK OF MANDELBAUM."
AAH...
WHEN AUTUMN ARRIVES, SOME BIRDS EMIGRATE HUNDREDS, EVEN THOUSANDS OF MILES IN SEARCH OF BETTER WEATHER.
OTHERS BUNDLE UP WITH LITTLE SCARVES AND WOOLEN HATS.
BRRR... GETTING CHILLY.
HE WENT OUT ONE AFTERNOON FOR A WALK, TO GET SOME FRESH AUTUMN AIR AND SEE WHAT...
...NEW COLORS THE TREES HAD THAT DAY. HE SPENT SEVERAL HOURS LIKE THAT... LOST IN HIS THOUGHTS.

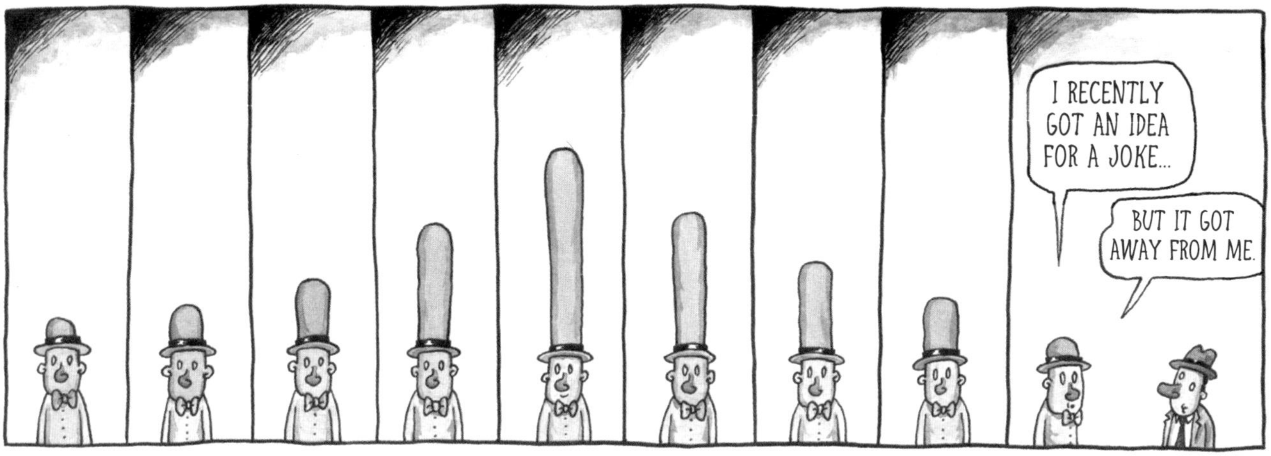
I RECENTLY GOT AN IDEA FOR A JOKE...
BUT IT GOT AWAY FROM ME.

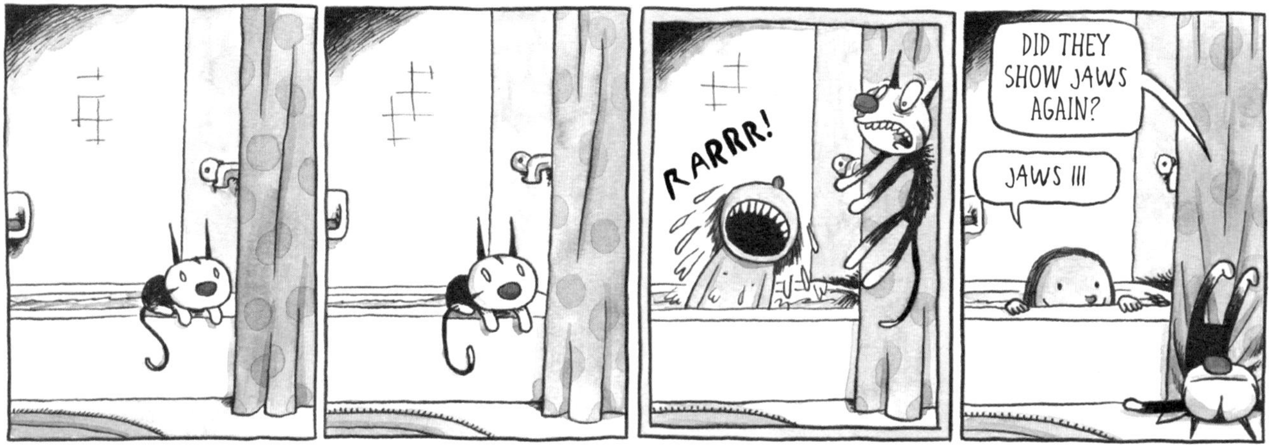
RARRR!
DID THEY SHOW JAWS AGAIN?
JAWS III

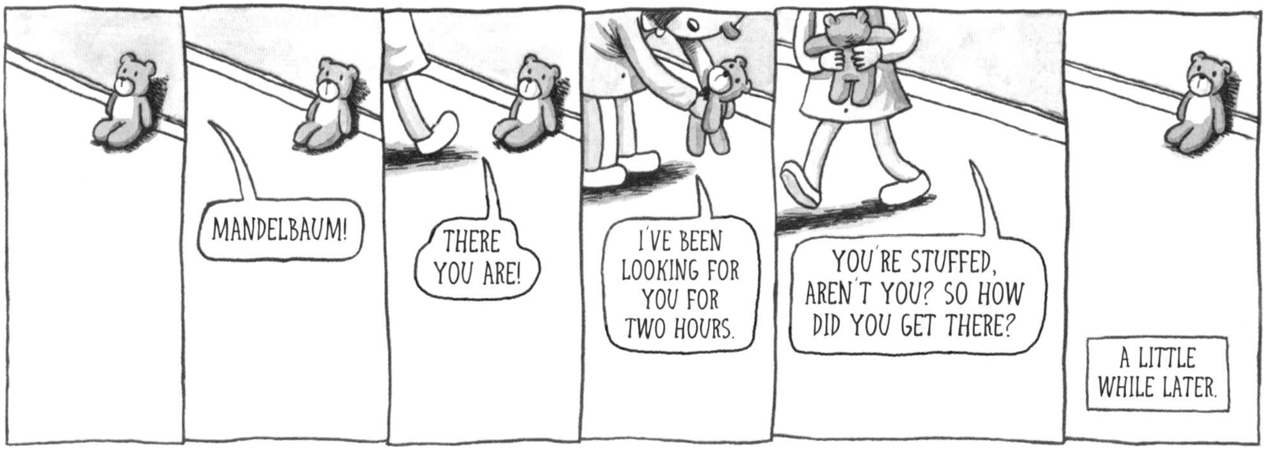
MANDELBAUM!
THERE YOU ARE!
I'VE BEEN LOOKING FOR YOU FOR TWO HOURS.
YOU'RE STUFFED, AREN'T YOU? SO HOW DID YOU GET THERE?
A LITTLE WHILE LATER.

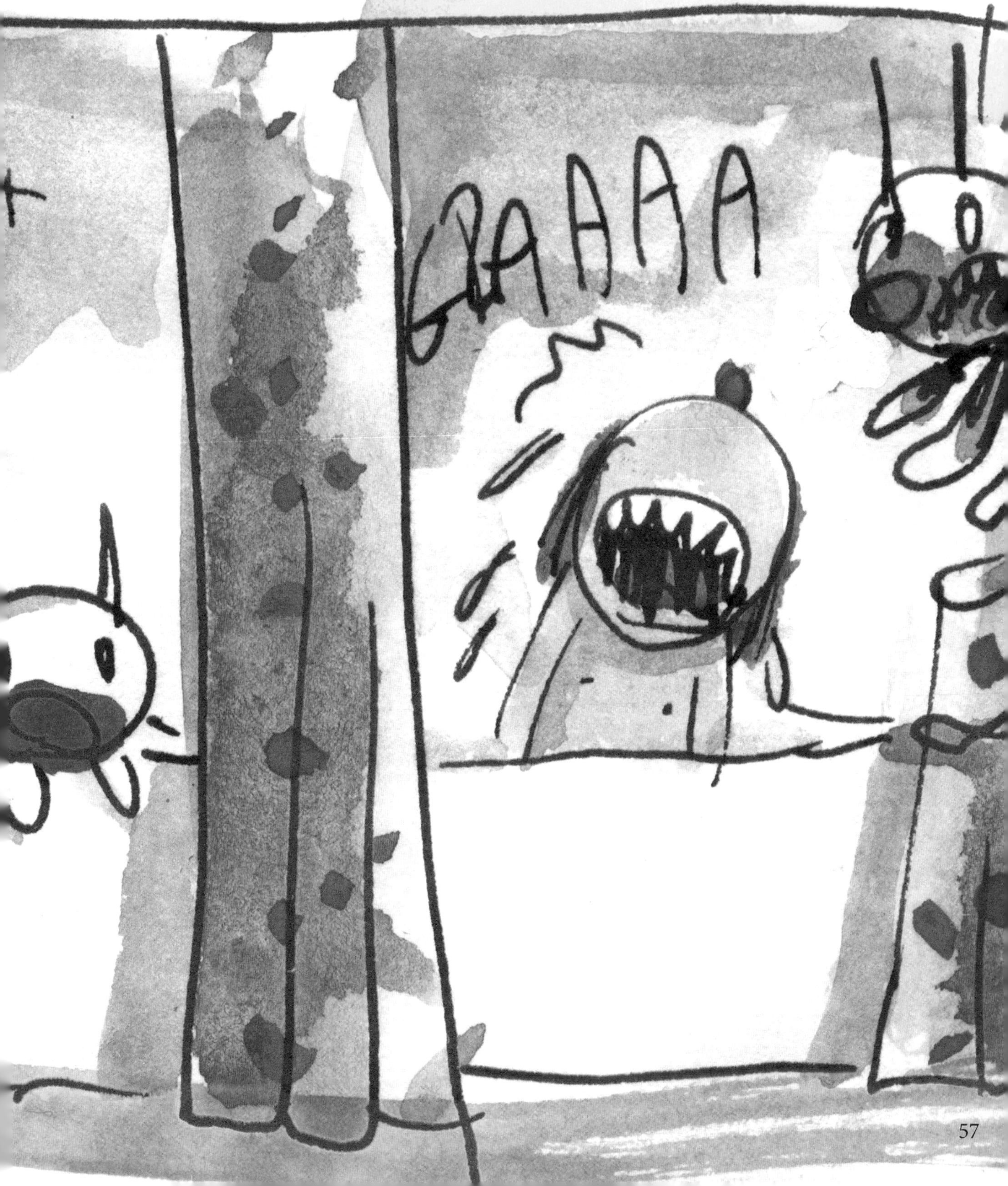
GRAAAA

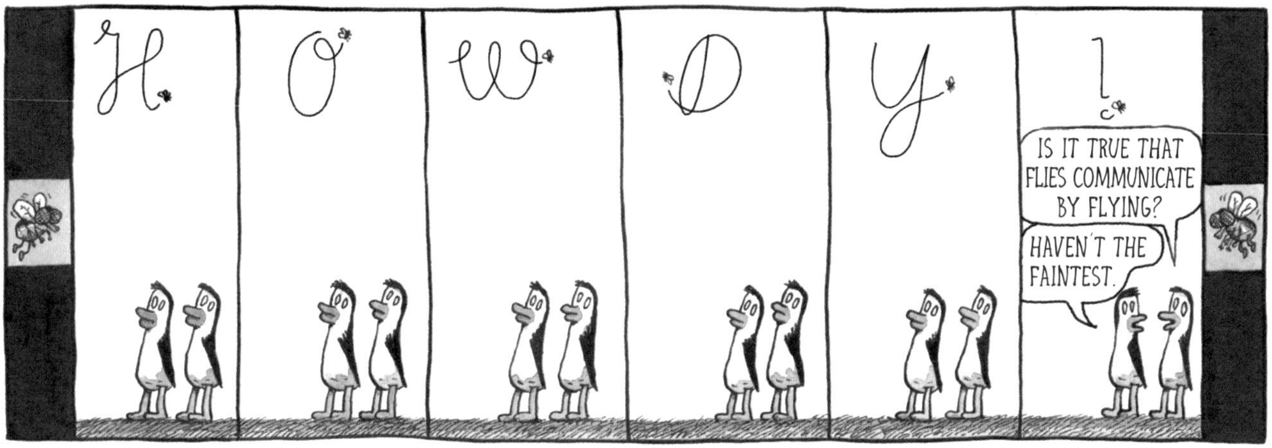
H O W D Y !
IS IT TRUE THAT FLIES COMMUNICATE BY FLYING?
HAVEN'T THE FAINTEST.

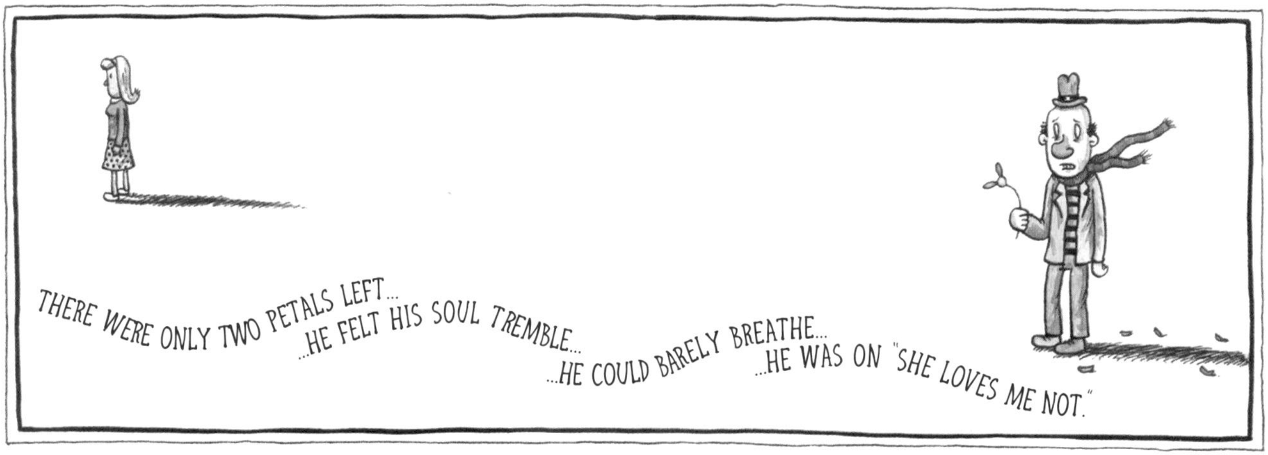
THERE WERE ONLY TWO PETALS LEFT... ...HE FELT HIS SOUL TREMBLE... ...HE COULD BARELY BREATHE... ...HE WAS ON "SHE LOVES ME NOT."

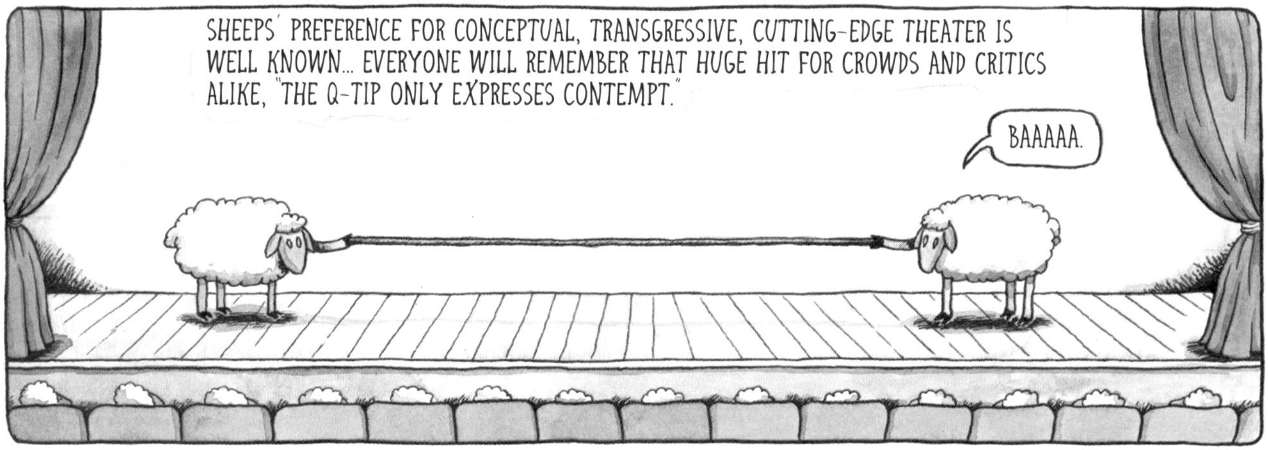
SHEEPS' PREFERENCE FOR CONCEPTUAL, TRANSGRESSIVE, CUTTING-EDGE THEATER IS WELL KNOWN... EVERYONE WILL REMEMBER THAT HUGE HIT FOR CROWDS AND CRITICS ALIKE, "THE Q-TIP ONLY EXPRESSES CONTEMPT."
BAAAAA.

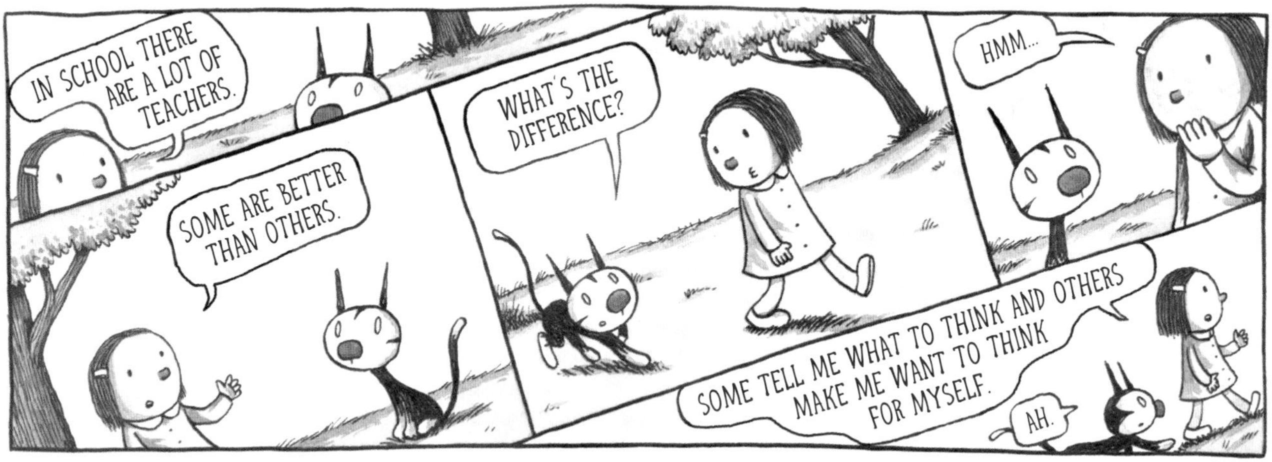
IN SCHOOL THERE ARE A LOT OF TEACHERS.
SOME ARE BETTER THAN OTHERS.
WHAT'S THE DIFFERENCE?
HMM...
SOME TELL ME WHAT TO THINK AND OTHERS MAKE ME WANT TO THINK FOR MYSELF.
AH.

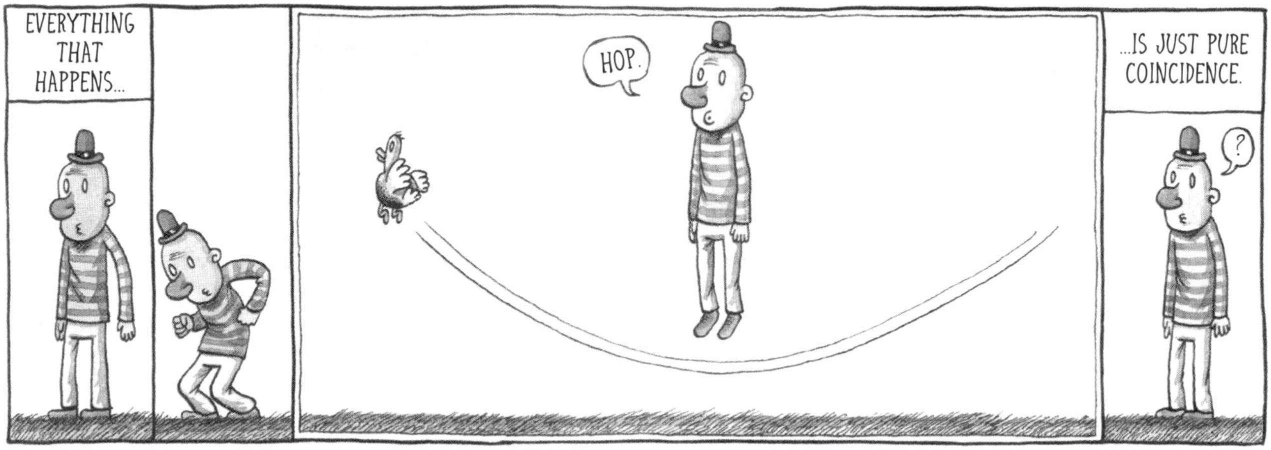
EVERYTHING THAT HAPPENS...
HOP.
...IS JUST PURE COINCIDENCE.
?

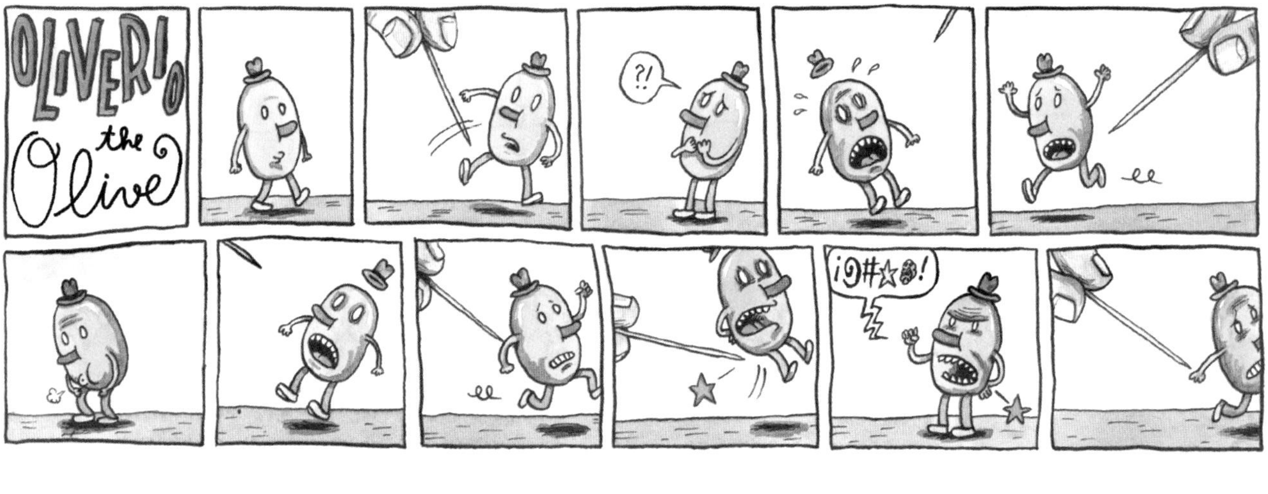
OLIVERIO the Olive
?!

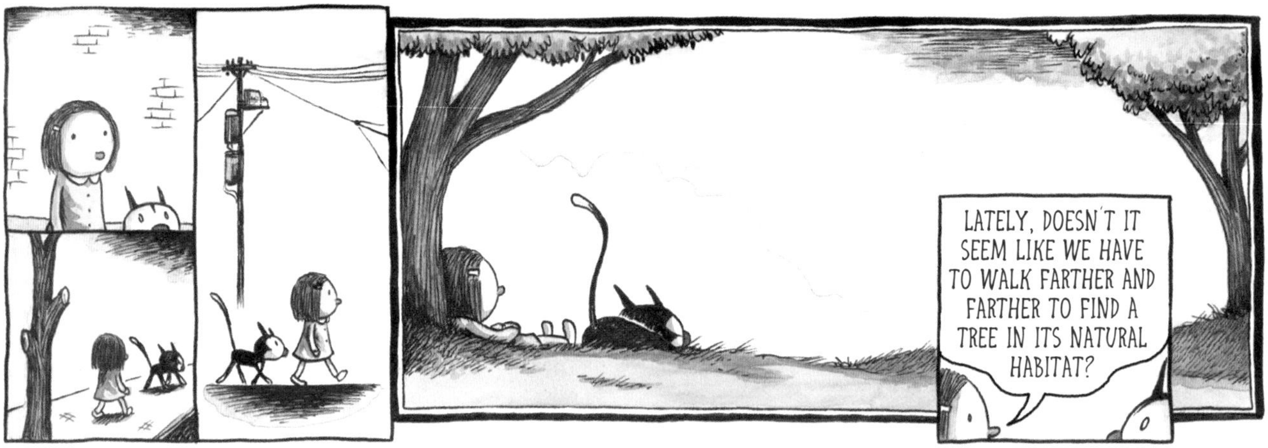
LATELY, DOESN'T IT SEEM LIKE WE HAVE TO WALK FARTHER AND FARTHER TO FIND A TREE IN ITS NATURAL HABITAT?

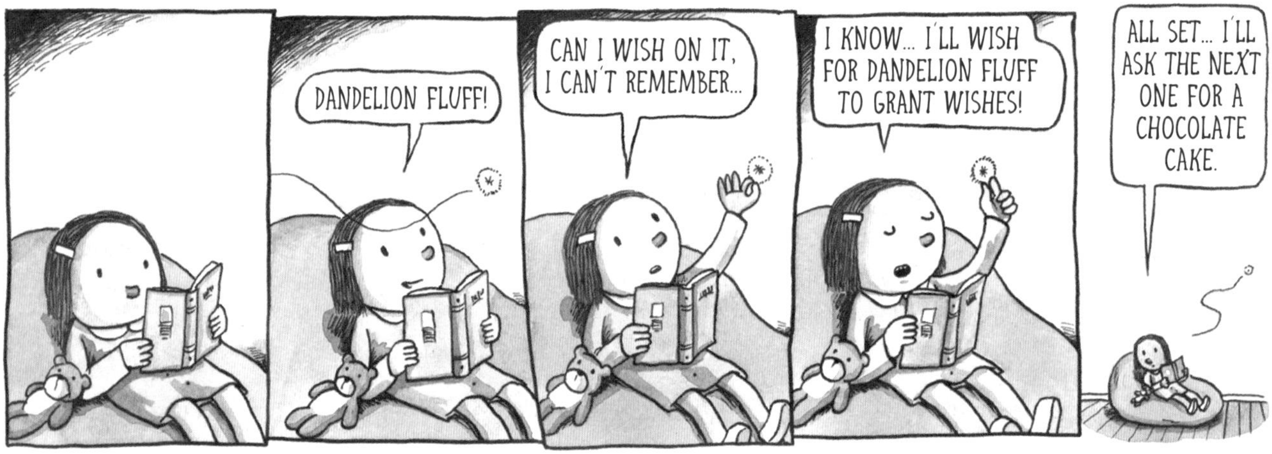
DANDELION FLUFF!
CAN I WISH ON IT, I CAN'T REMEMBER...
I KNOW... I'LL WISH FOR DANDELION FLUFF TO GRANT WISHES!
ALL SET... I'LL ASK THE NEXT ONE FOR A CHOCOLATE CAKE.

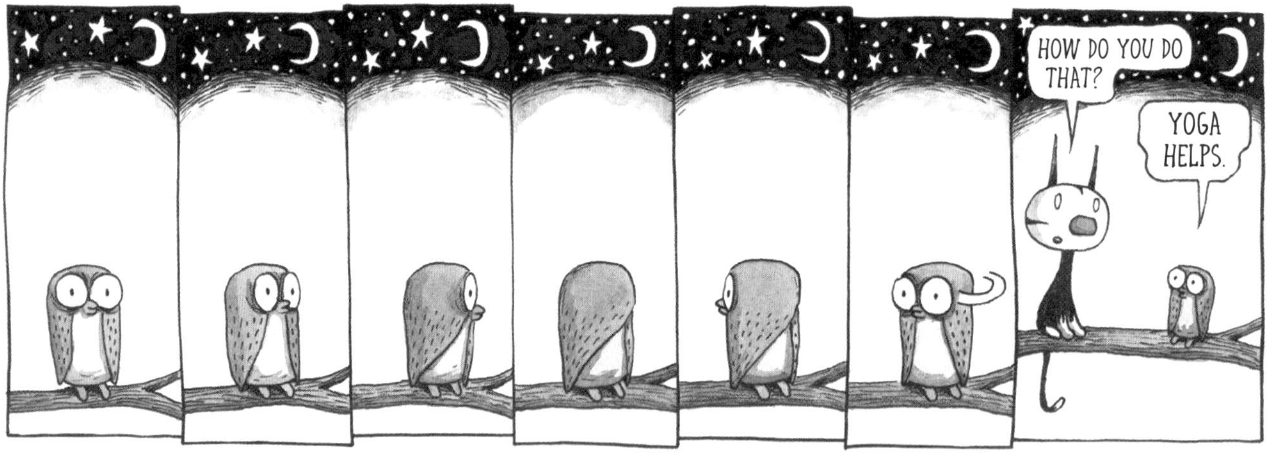
HOW DO YOU DO THAT?
YOGA HELPS.

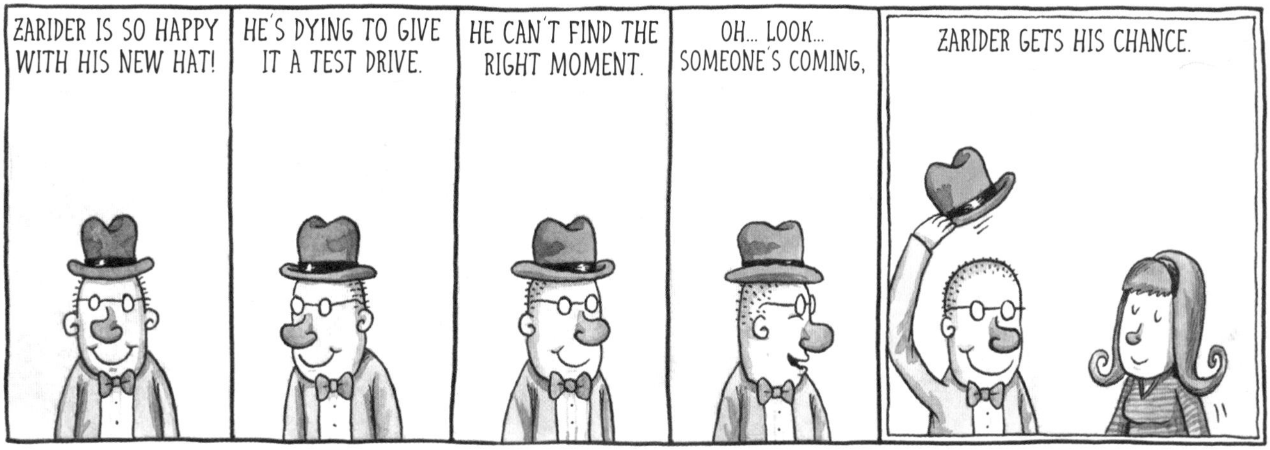
ZARIDER IS SO HAPPY WITH HIS NEW HAT!
HE'S DYING TO GIVE IT A TEST DRIVE.
HE CAN'T FIND THE RIGHT MOMENT.
OH... LOOK... SOMEONE'S COMING,
ZARIDER GETS HIS CHANCE.

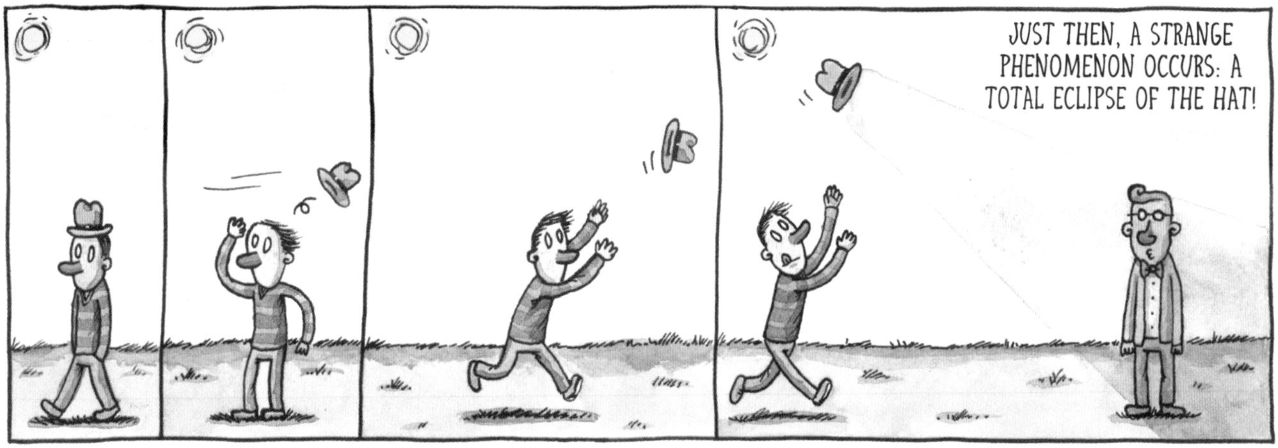
JUST THEN, A STRANGE PHENOMENON OCCURS: A TOTAL ECLIPSE OF THE HAT!

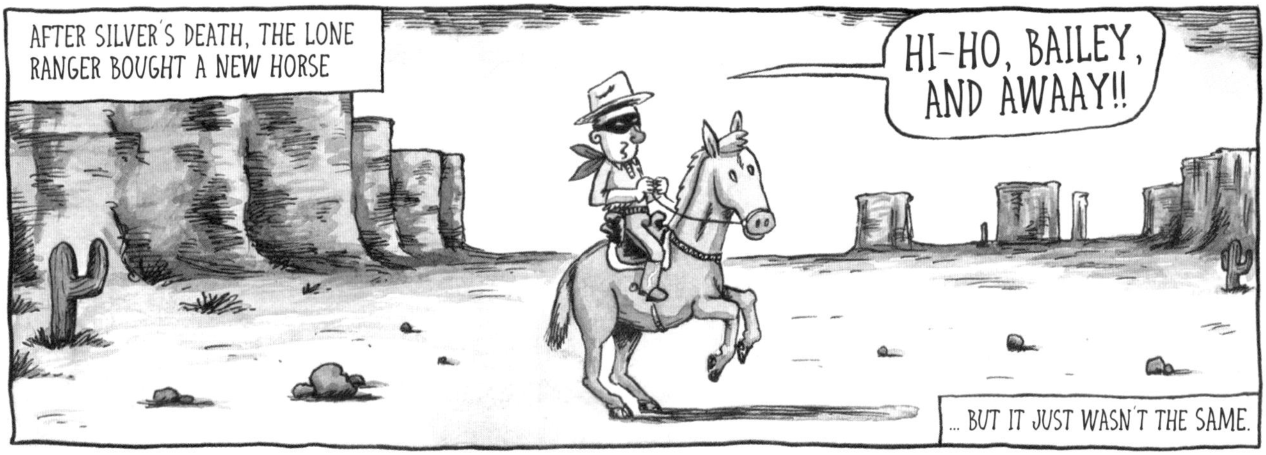
AFTER SILVER'S DEATH, THE LONE RANGER BOUGHT A NEW HORSE
HI-HO, BAILEY, AND AWAAY!!
... BUT IT JUST WASN'T THE SAME.

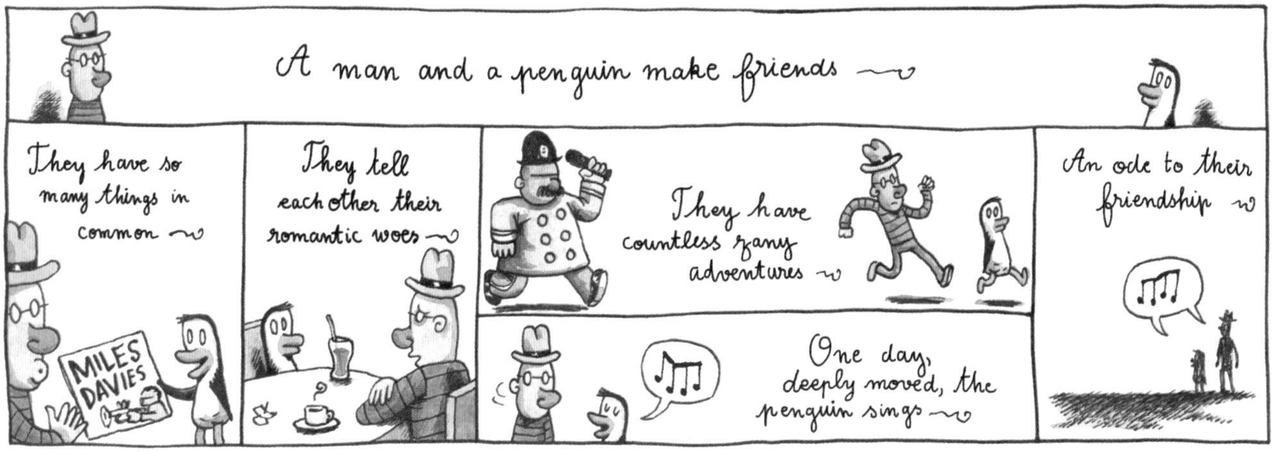
A man and a penguin make friends
They have so many things in common
MILES DAVIES
They tell each other their romantic woes
They have countless zany adventures
One day, deeply moved, the penguin sings
An ode to their friendship

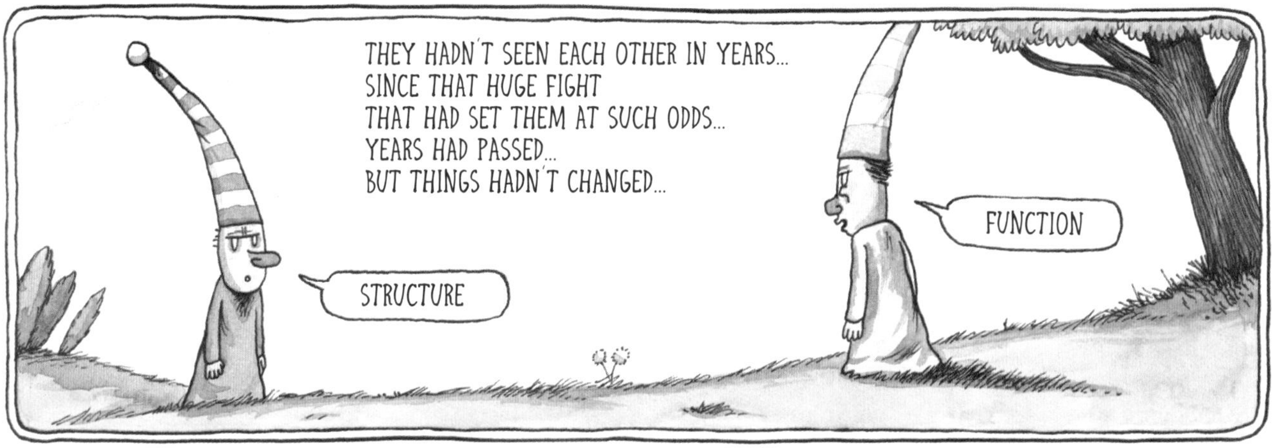
THEY HADN'T SEEN EACH OTHER IN YEARS...
SINCE THAT HUGE FIGHT
THAT HAD SET THEM AT SUCH ODDS...
YEARS HAD PASSED...
BUT THINGS HADN'T CHANGED...
STRUCTURE
FUNCTION

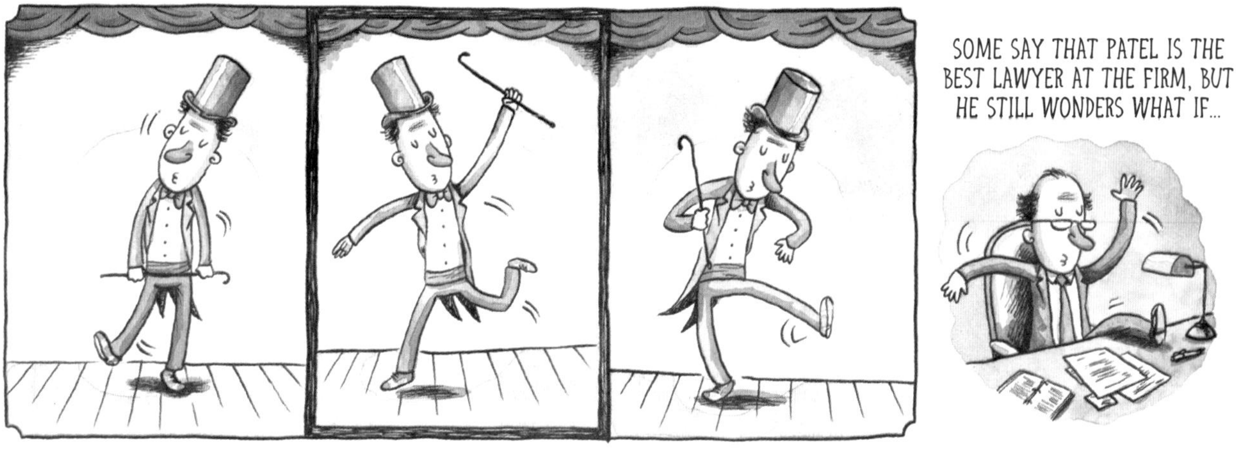
SOME SAY THAT PATEL IS THE BEST LAWYER AT THE FIRM, BUT HE STILL WONDERS WHAT IF...

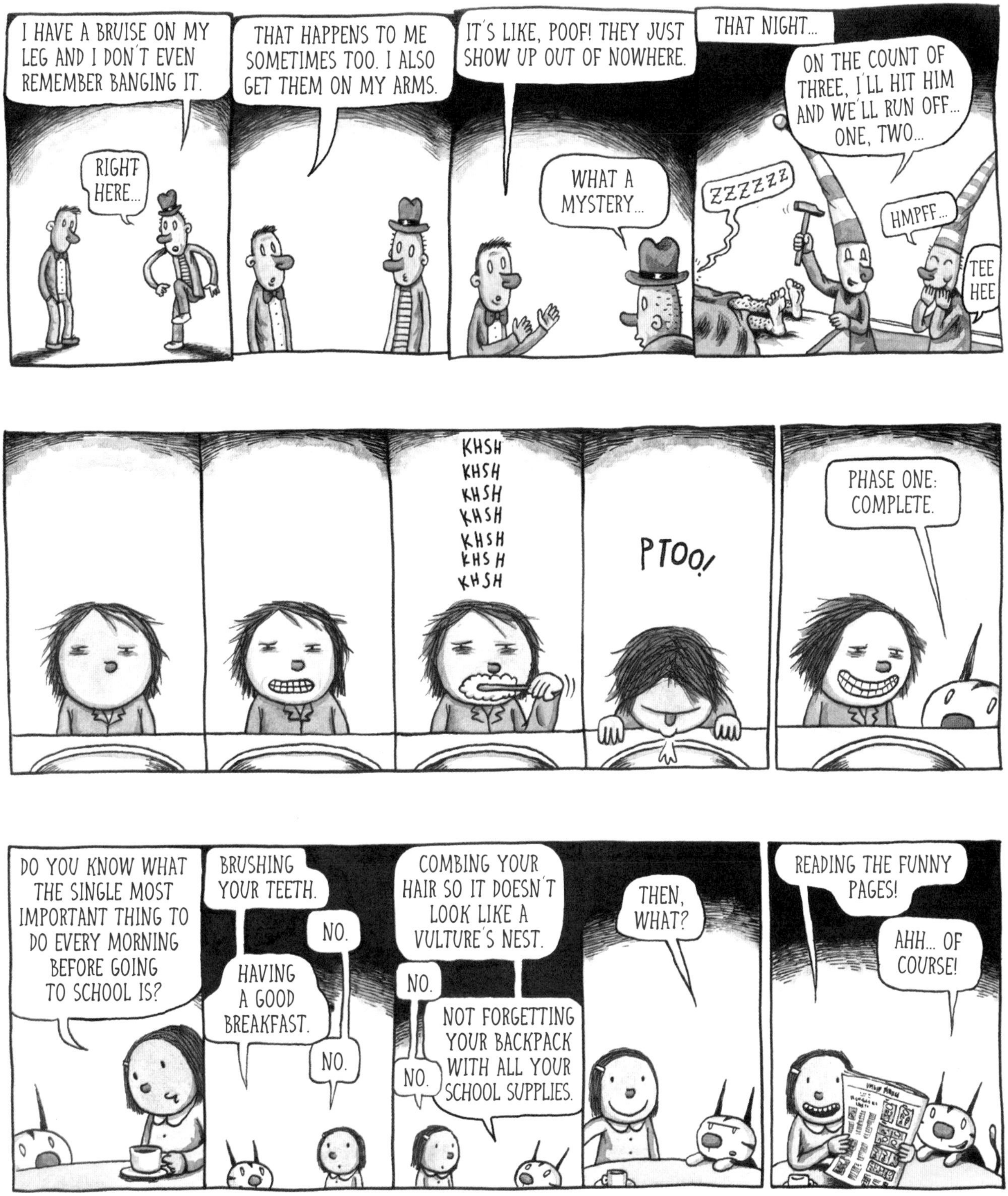
I HAVE A BRUISE ON MY LEG AND I DON'T EVEN REMEMBER BANGING IT.
RIGHT HERE...
THAT HAPPENS TO ME SOMETIMES TOO. I ALSO GET THEM ON MY ARMS.
IT'S LIKE, POOF! THEY JUST SHOW UP OUT OF NOWHERE.
WHAT A MYSTERY...
THAT NIGHT...
ON THE COUNT OF THREE, I'LL HIT HIM AND WE'LL RUN OFF... ONE, TWO...
ZZZZZZ
HMPFF...
TEE HEE
KHSH KHSH KHSH KHSH KHSH KHSH KHSH
PTOO!
PHASE ONE: COMPLETE.
DO YOU KNOW WHAT THE SINGLE MOST IMPORTANT THING TO DO EVERY MORNING BEFORE GOING TO SCHOOL IS?
BRUSHING YOUR TEETH.
NO.
HAVING A GOOD BREAKFAST.
NO.
COMBING YOUR HAIR SO IT DOESN'T LOOK LIKE A VULTURE'S NEST.
NO.
NOT FORGETTING YOUR BACKPACK WITH ALL YOUR SCHOOL SUPPLIES.
NO.
THEN, WHAT?
READING THE FUNNY PAGES!
AHH... OF COURSE!

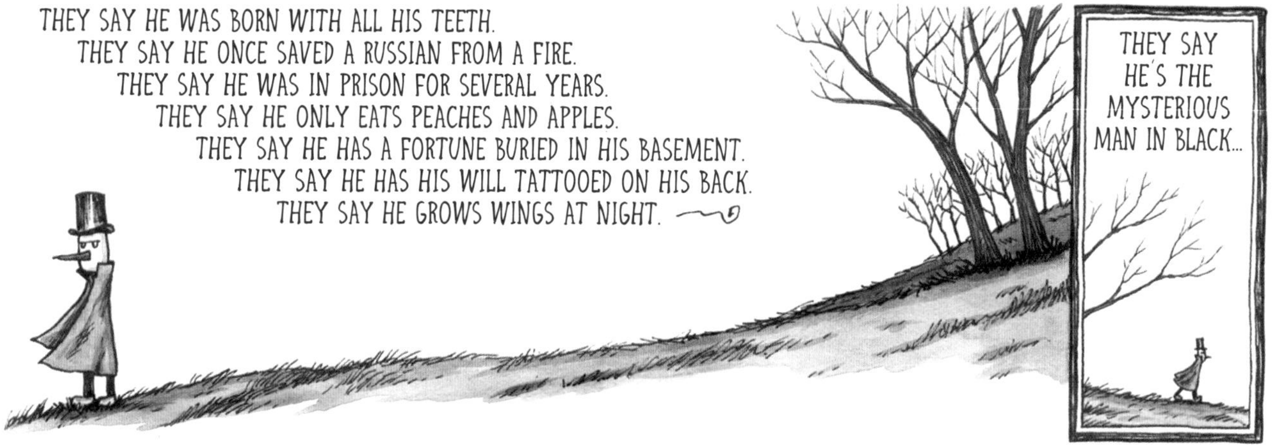
THEY SAY HE WAS BORN WITH ALL HIS TEETH.
THEY SAY HE ONCE SAVED A RUSSIAN FROM A FIRE.
THEY SAY HE WAS IN PRISON FOR SEVERAL YEARS.
THEY SAY HE ONLY EATS PEACHES AND APPLES.
THEY SAY HE HAS A FORTUNE BURIED IN HIS BASEMENT.
THEY SAY HE HAS HIS WILL TATTOOED ON HIS BACK.
THEY SAY HE GROWS WINGS AT NIGHT.
THEY SAY HE'S THE MYSTERIOUS MAN IN BLACK...

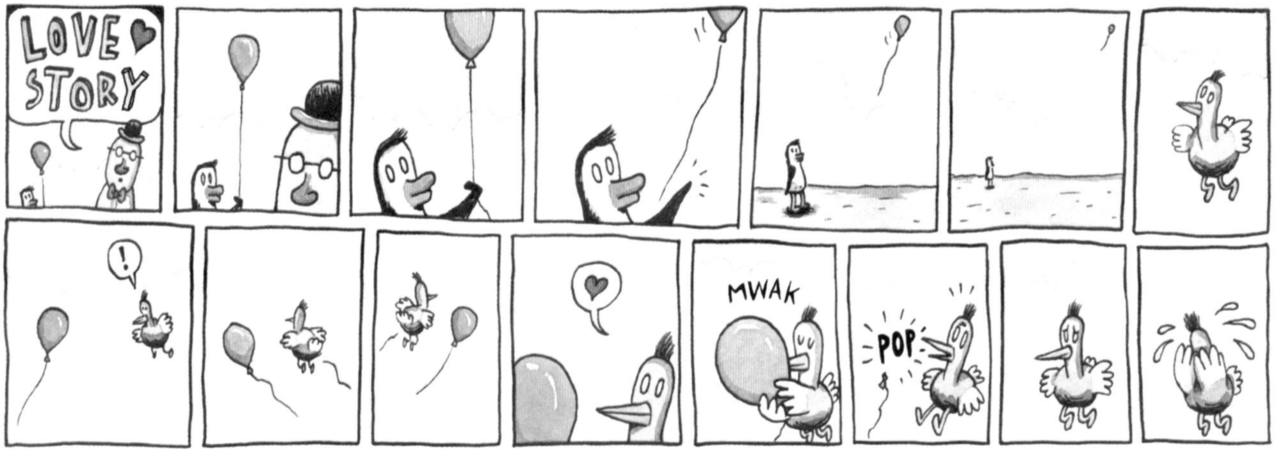
LOVE STORY
!
MWAK
POP

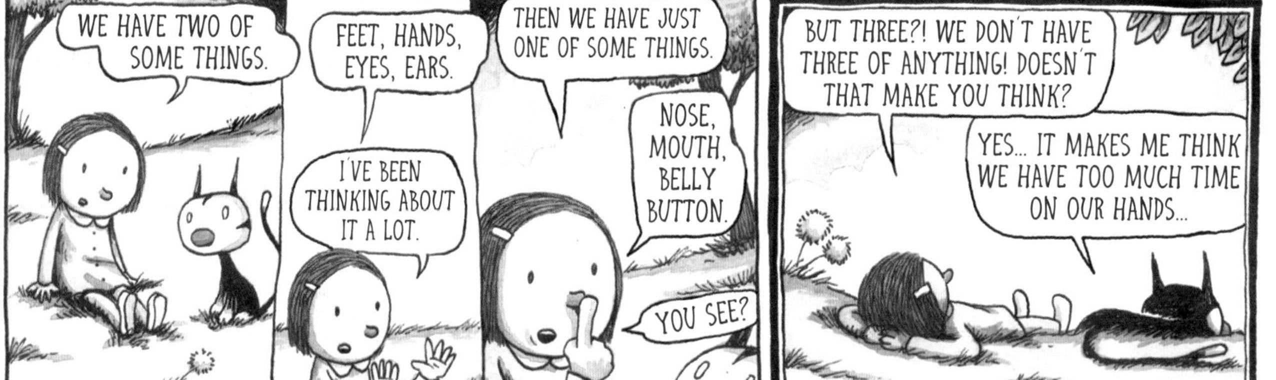
WE HAVE TWO OF SOME THINGS.
FEET, HANDS, EYES, EARS.
I'VE BEEN THINKING ABOUT IT A LOT.
THEN WE HAVE JUST ONE OF SOME THINGS.
NOSE, MOUTH, BELLY BUTTON.
YOU SEE?
BUT THREE?! WE DON'T HAVE THREE OF ANYTHING! DOESN'T THAT MAKE YOU THINK?
YES... IT MAKES ME THINK WE HAVE TOO MUCH TIME ON OUR HANDS...

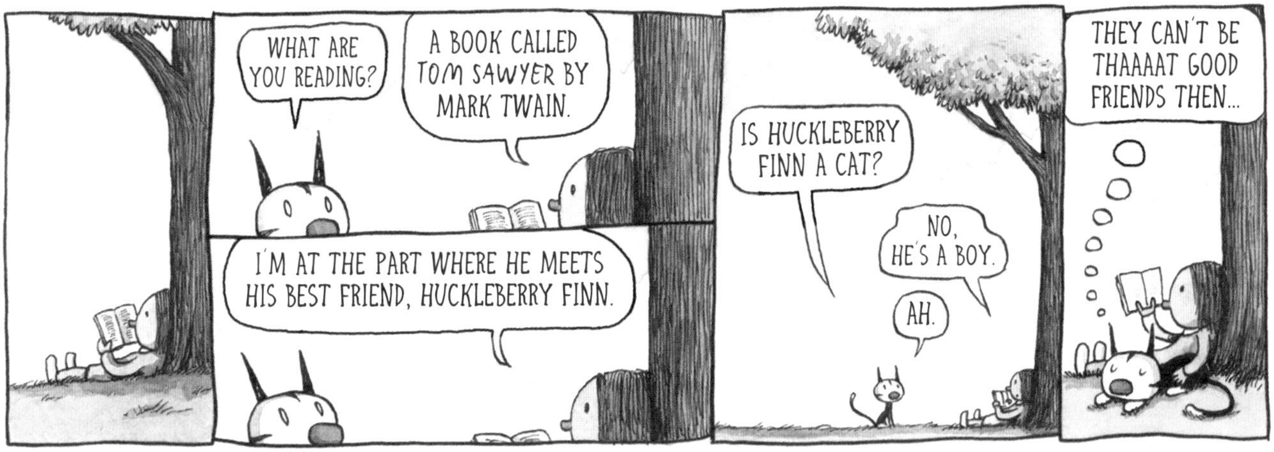
WHAT ARE YOU READING?
A BOOK CALLED TOM SAWYER BY MARK TWAIN.
I'M AT THE PART WHERE HE MEETS HIS BEST FRIEND, HUCKLEBERRY FINN.
IS HUCKLEBERRY FINN A CAT?
NO, HE'S A BOY.
AH.
THEY CAN'T BE THAAAAT GOOD FRIENDS THEN...

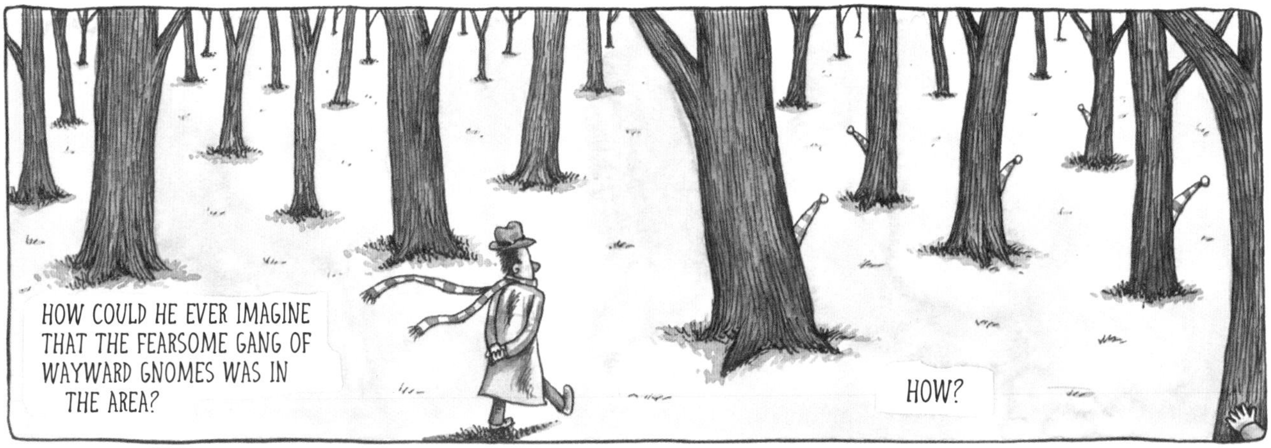
HOW COULD HE EVER IMAGINE THAT THE FEARSOME GANG OF WAYWARD GNOMES WAS IN THE AREA?
HOW?

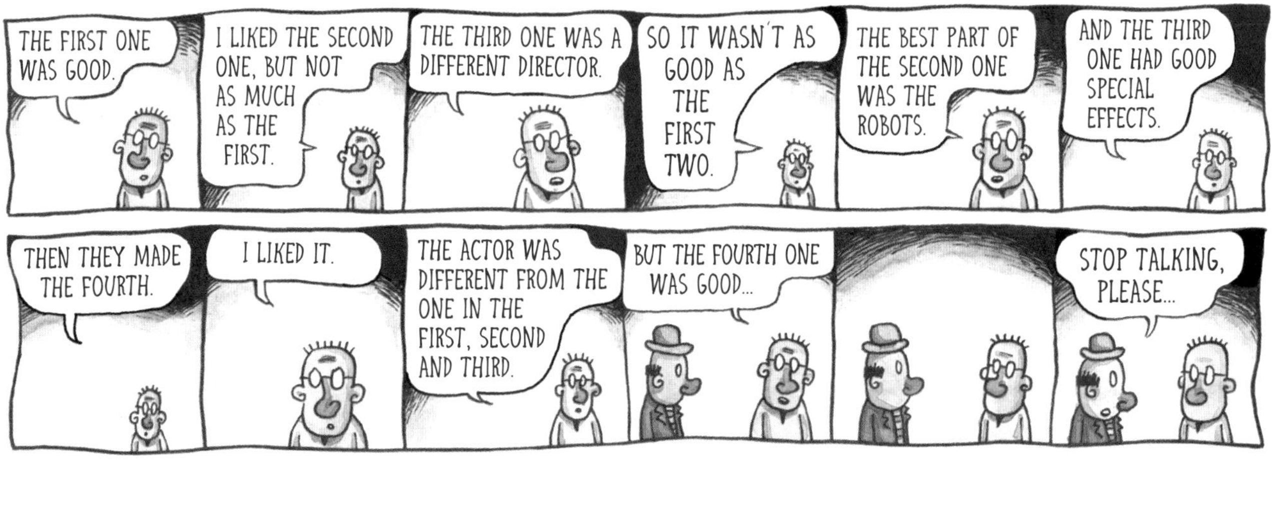
THE FIRST ONE WAS GOOD.
I LIKED THE SECOND ONE, BUT NOT AS MUCH AS THE FIRST.
THE THIRD ONE WAS A DIFFERENT DIRECTOR.
SO IT WASN'T AS GOOD AS THE FIRST TWO.
THE BEST PART OF THE SECOND ONE WAS THE ROBOTS.
AND THE THIRD ONE HAD GOOD SPECIAL EFFECTS.
THEN THEY MADE THE FOURTH.
I LIKED IT.
THE ACTOR WAS DIFFERENT FROM THE ONE IN THE FIRST, SECOND AND THIRD.
BUT THE FOURTH ONE WAS GOOD...
STOP TALKING, PLEASE...

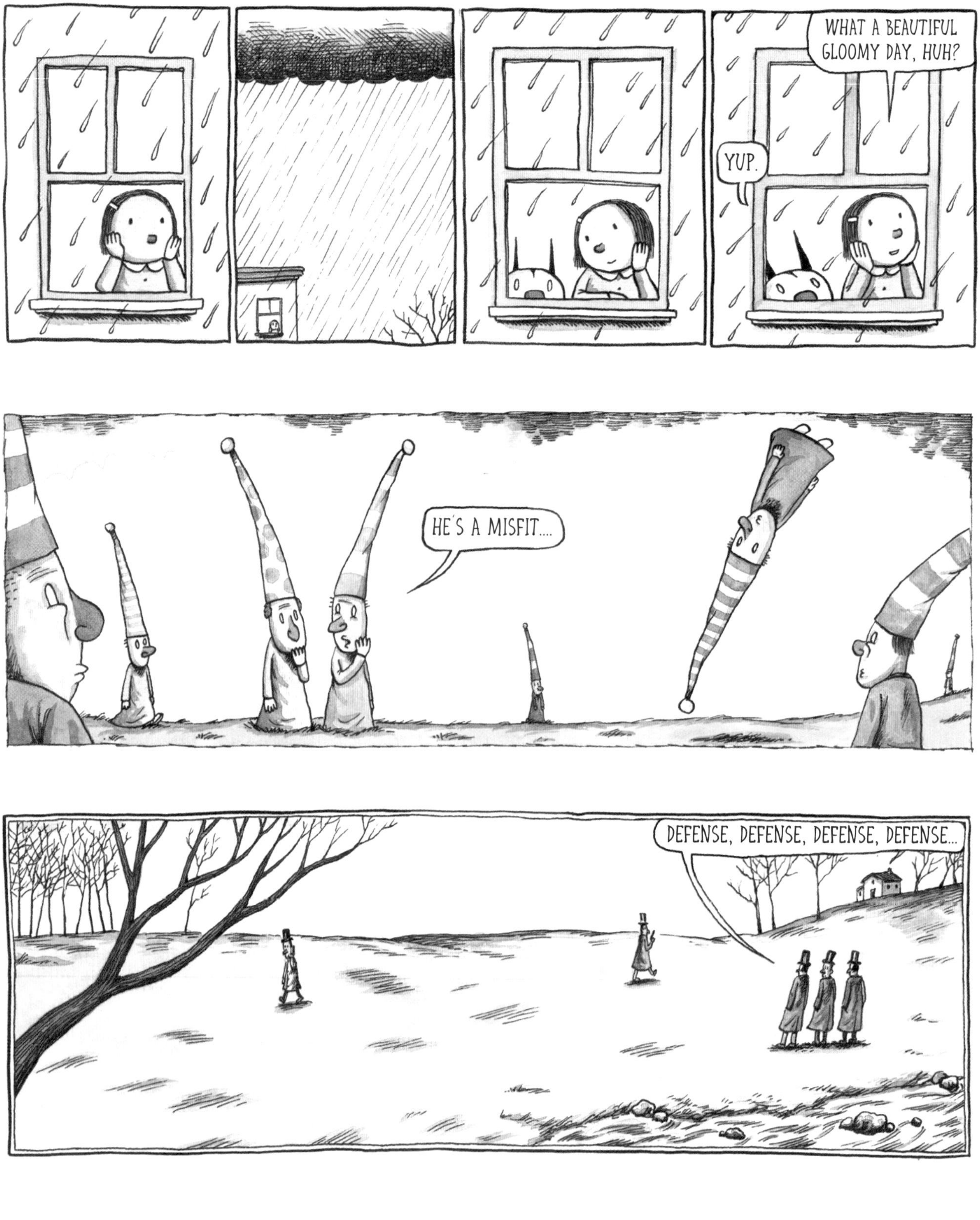
WHAT A BEAUTIFUL GLOOMY DAY, HUH?
YUP.
HE'S A MISFIT....
DEFENSE, DEFENSE, DEFENSE, DEFENSE...

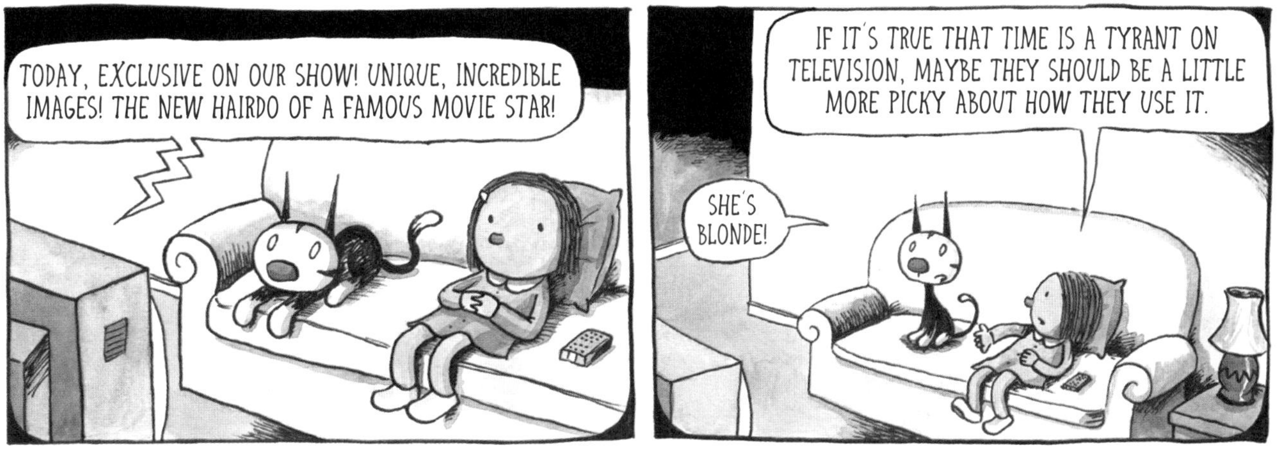
TODAY, EXCLUSIVE ON OUR SHOW! UNIQUE, INCREDIBLE IMAGES! THE NEW HAIRDO OF A FAMOUS MOVIE STAR!
SHE'S BLONDE!
IF IT'S TRUE THAT TIME IS A TYRANT ON TELEVISION, MAYBE THEY SHOULD BE A LITTLE MORE PICKY ABOUT HOW THEY USE IT.

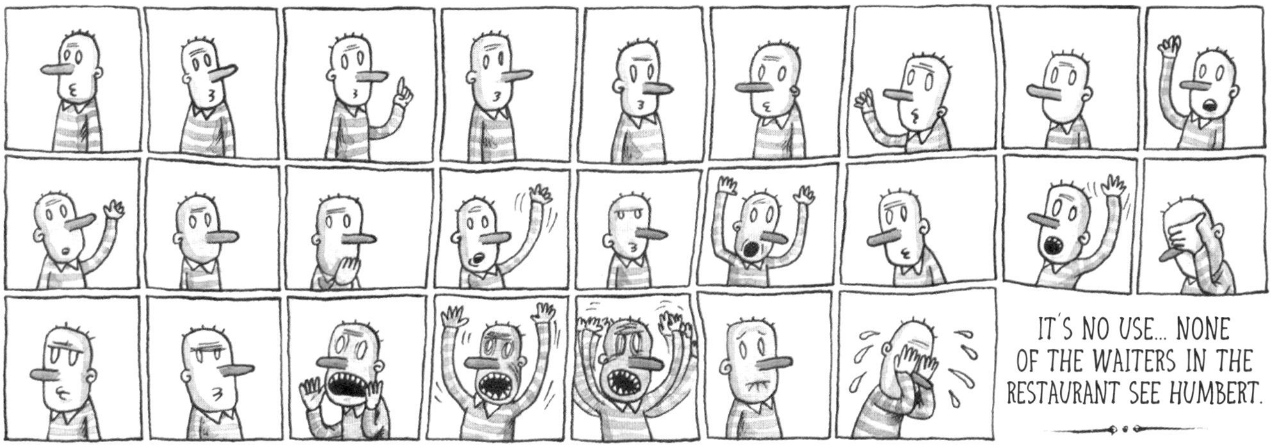
IT'S NO USE... NONE OF THE WAITERS IN THE RESTAURANT SEE HUMBERT.

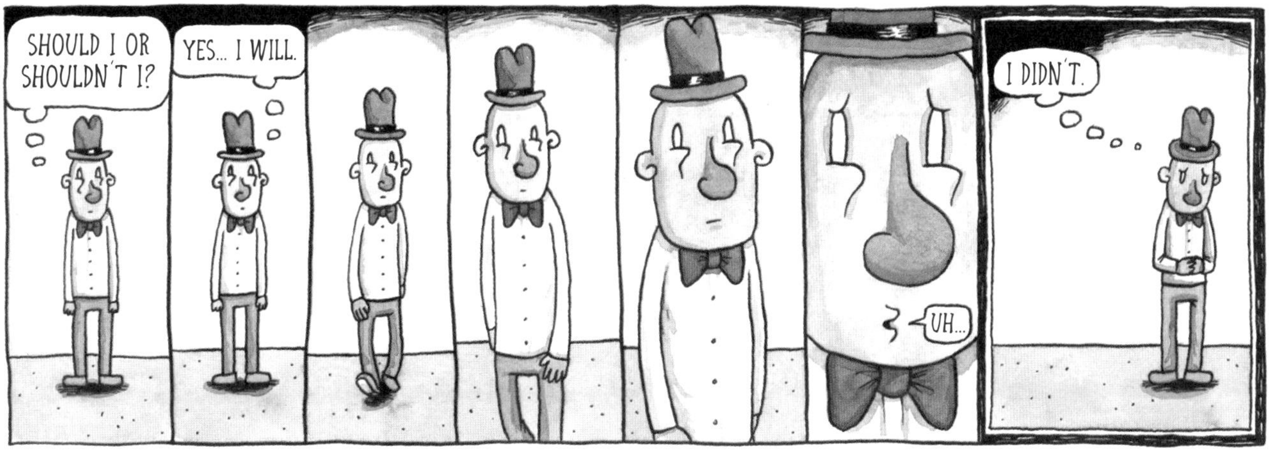
SHOULD I OR SHOULDN'T I?
YES... I WILL.
UH...
I DIDN'T.

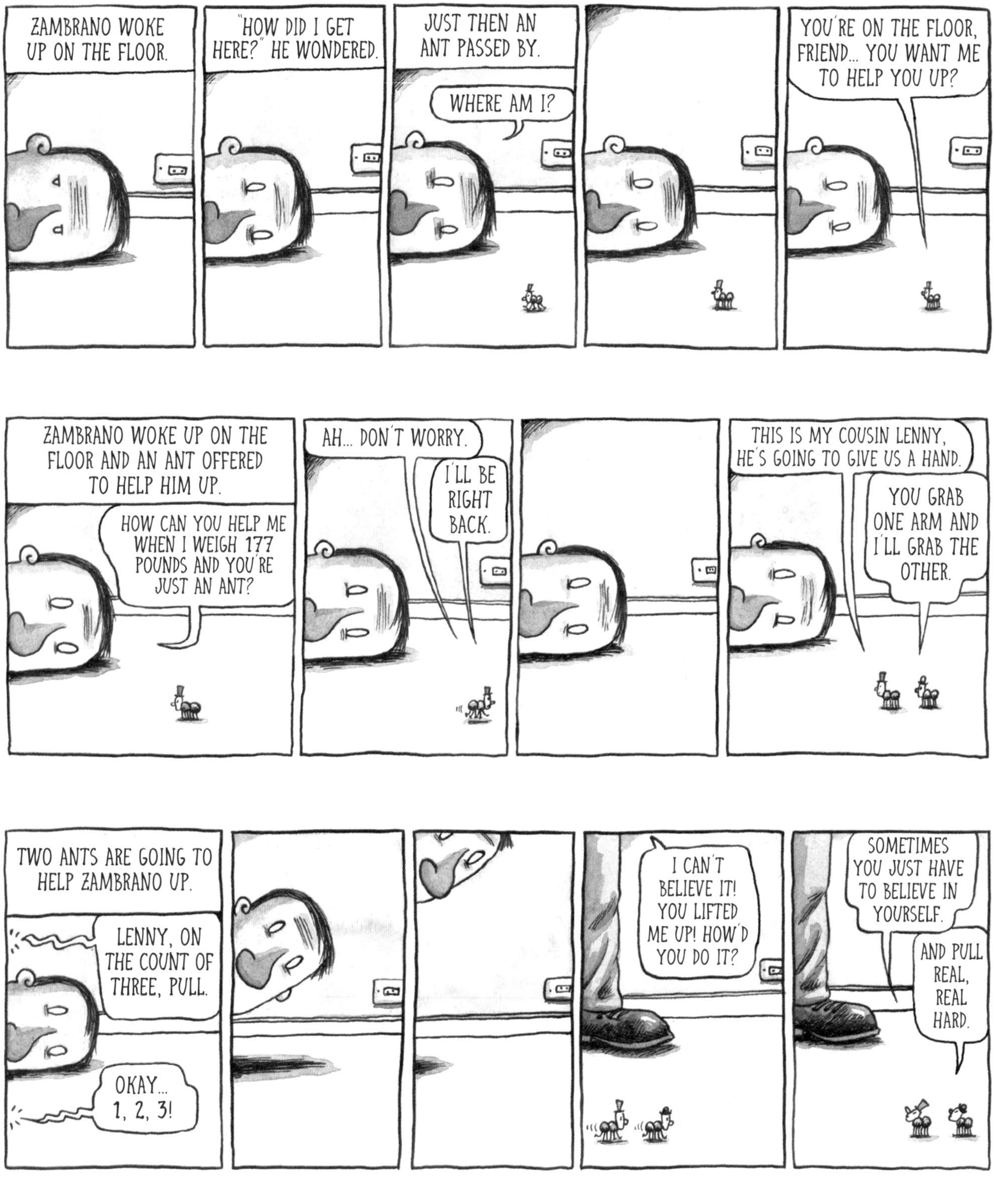
ZAMBRANO WOKE UP ON THE FLOOR.
"HOW DID I GET HERE?" HE WONDERED.
JUST THEN AN ANT PASSED BY.
WHERE AM I?
YOU'RE ON THE FLOOR, FRIEND... YOU WANT ME TO HELP YOU UP?
ZAMBRANO WOKE UP ON THE FLOOR AND AN ANT OFFERED TO HELP HIM UP.
HOW CAN YOU HELP ME WHEN I WEIGH 177 POUNDS AND YOU'RE JUST AN ANT?
AH... DON'T WORRY.
I'LL BE RIGHT BACK.
THIS IS MY COUSIN LENNY, HE'S GOING TO GIVE US A HAND.
YOU GRAB ONE ARM AND I'LL GRAB THE OTHER.
TWO ANTS ARE GOING TO HELP ZAMBRANO UP.
LENNY, ON THE COUNT OF THREE, PULL.
OKAY... 1, 2, 3!
I CAN'T BELIEVE IT! YOU LIFTED ME UP! HOW'D YOU DO IT?
SOMETIMES YOU JUST HAVE TO BELIEVE IN YOURSELF.
AND PULL REAL, REAL HARD.

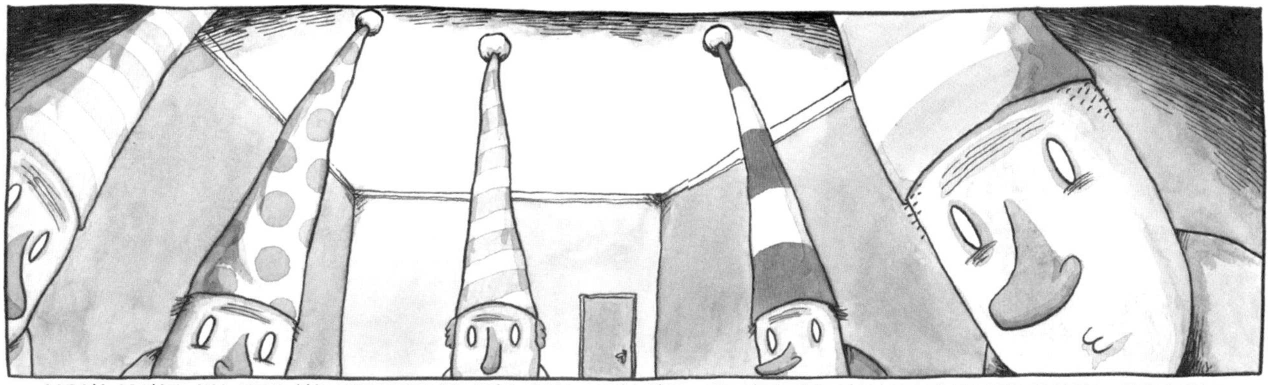

ORTON OPENED HIS EYES AND THOUGHT HE WAS STILL DREAMING... HE SAW THE GNOMES FROM HIS GARDEN... BUT WHAT WERE THEY DOING THERE, BESIDE HIS BED? AND WHY WERE THEY LOOKING AT HIM LIKE THAT? ...WHY?!

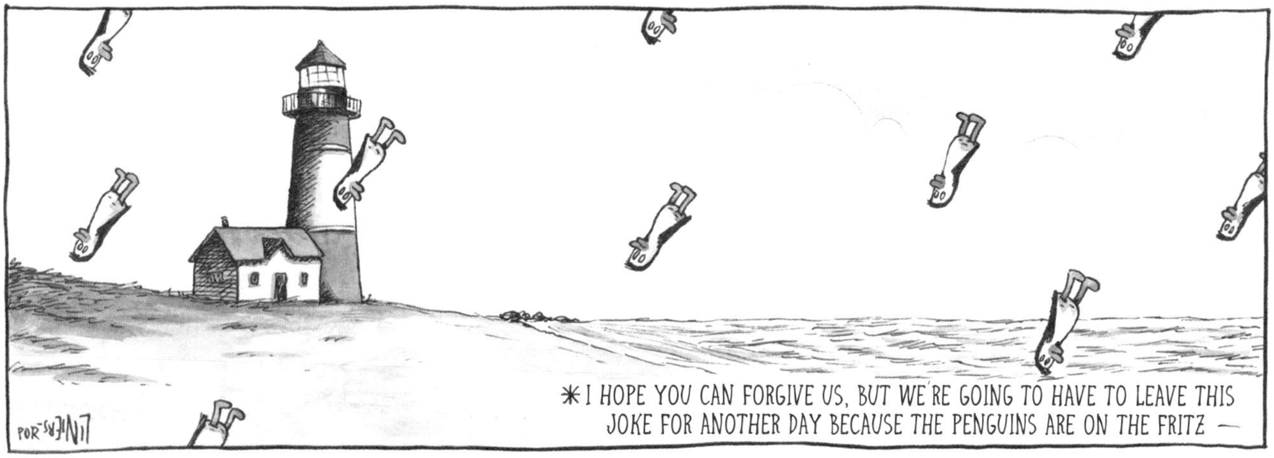

*I HOPE YOU CAN FORGIVE US, BUT WE'RE GOING TO HAVE TO LEAVE THIS JOKE FOR ANOTHER DAY BECAUSE THE PENGUINS ARE ON THE FRITZ —

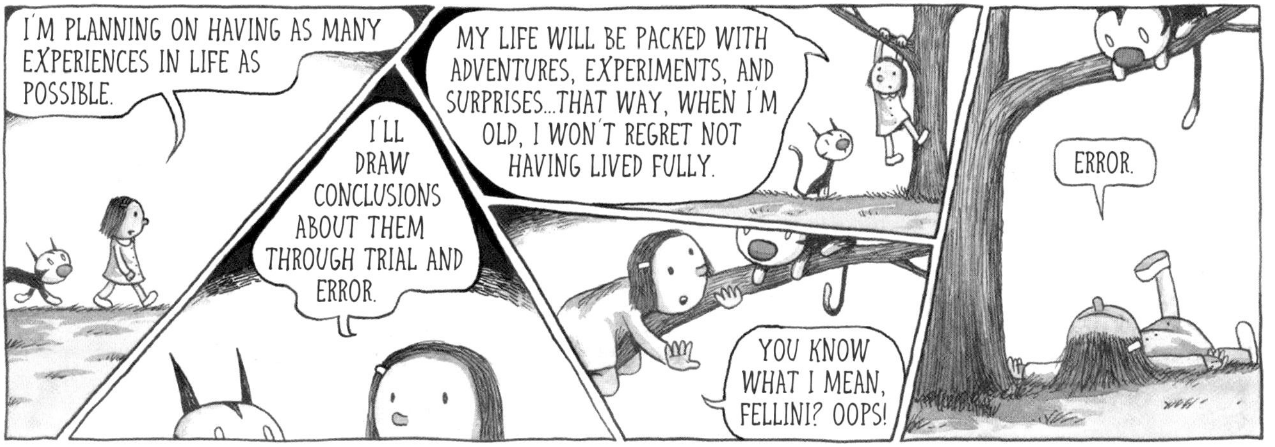

I'M PLANNING ON HAVING AS MANY EXPERIENCES IN LIFE AS POSSIBLE.
I'LL DRAW CONCLUSIONS ABOUT THEM THROUGH TRIAL AND ERROR.
MY LIFE WILL BE PACKED WITH ADVENTURES, EXPERIMENTS, AND SURPRISES...THAT WAY, WHEN I'M OLD, I WON'T REGRET NOT HAVING LIVED FULLY.
YOU KNOW WHAT I MEAN, FELLINI? OOPS!
ERROR.

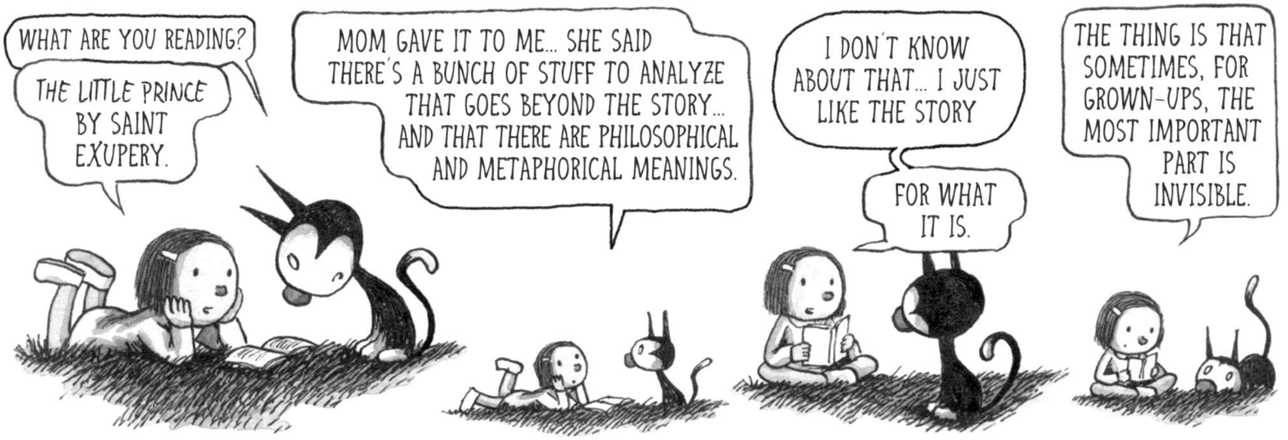
WHAT ARE YOU READING?
THE LITTLE PRINCE BY SAINT EXUPERY.
MOM GAVE IT TO ME... SHE SAID THERE'S A BUNCH OF STUFF TO ANALYZE THAT GOES BEYOND THE STORY... AND THAT THERE ARE PHILOSOPHICAL AND METAPHORICAL MEANINGS.
I DON'T KNOW ABOUT THAT... I JUST LIKE THE STORY
FOR WHAT IT IS.
THE THING IS THAT SOMETIMES, FOR GROWN-UPS, THE MOST IMPORTANT PART IS INVISIBLE.

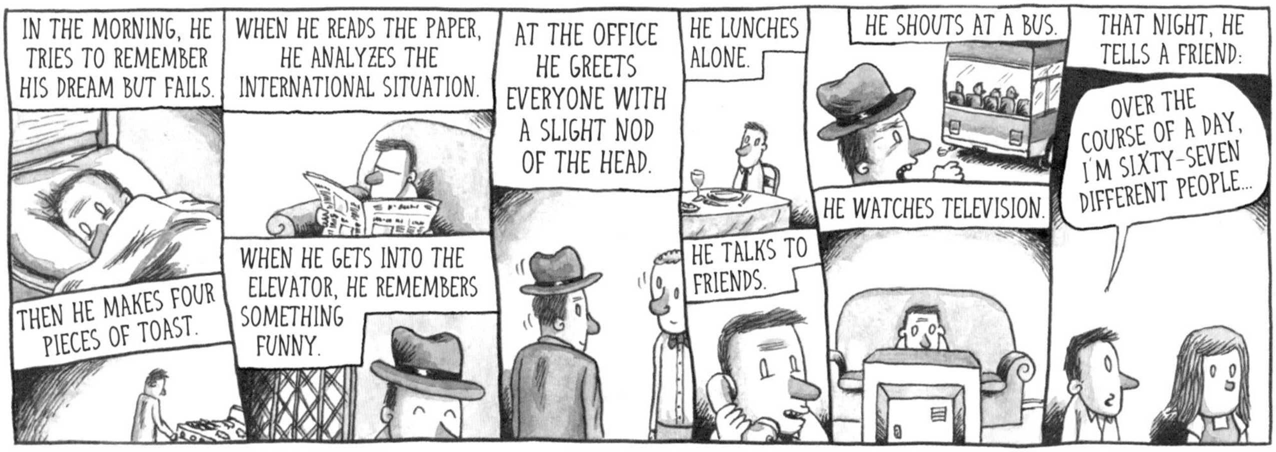
IN THE MORNING, HE TRIES TO REMEMBER HIS DREAM BUT FAILS.
THEN HE MAKES FOUR PIECES OF TOAST.
WHEN HE READS THE PAPER, HE ANALYZES THE INTERNATIONAL SITUATION.
WHEN HE GETS INTO THE ELEVATOR, HE REMEMBERS SOMETHING FUNNY.
AT THE OFFICE HE GREETS EVERYONE WITH A SLIGHT NOD OF THE HEAD.
HE LUNCHES ALONE.
HE TALKS TO FRIENDS.
HE SHOUTS AT A BUS.
HE WATCHES TELEVISION.
THAT NIGHT, HE TELLS A FRIEND:
OVER THE COURSE OF A DAY, I'M SIXTY-SEVEN DIFFERENT PEOPLE...

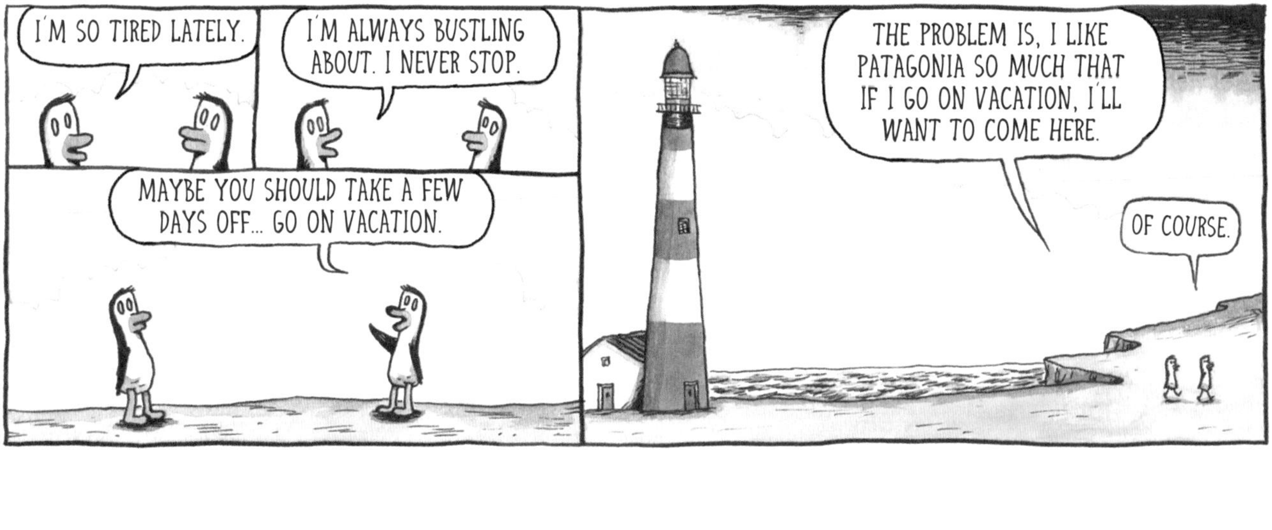
I'M SO TIRED LATELY.
I'M ALWAYS BUSTLING ABOUT. I NEVER STOP.
MAYBE YOU SHOULD TAKE A FEW DAYS OFF... GO ON VACATION.
THE PROBLEM IS, I LIKE PATAGONIA SO MUCH THAT IF I GO ON VACATION, I'LL WANT TO COME HERE.
OF COURSE.

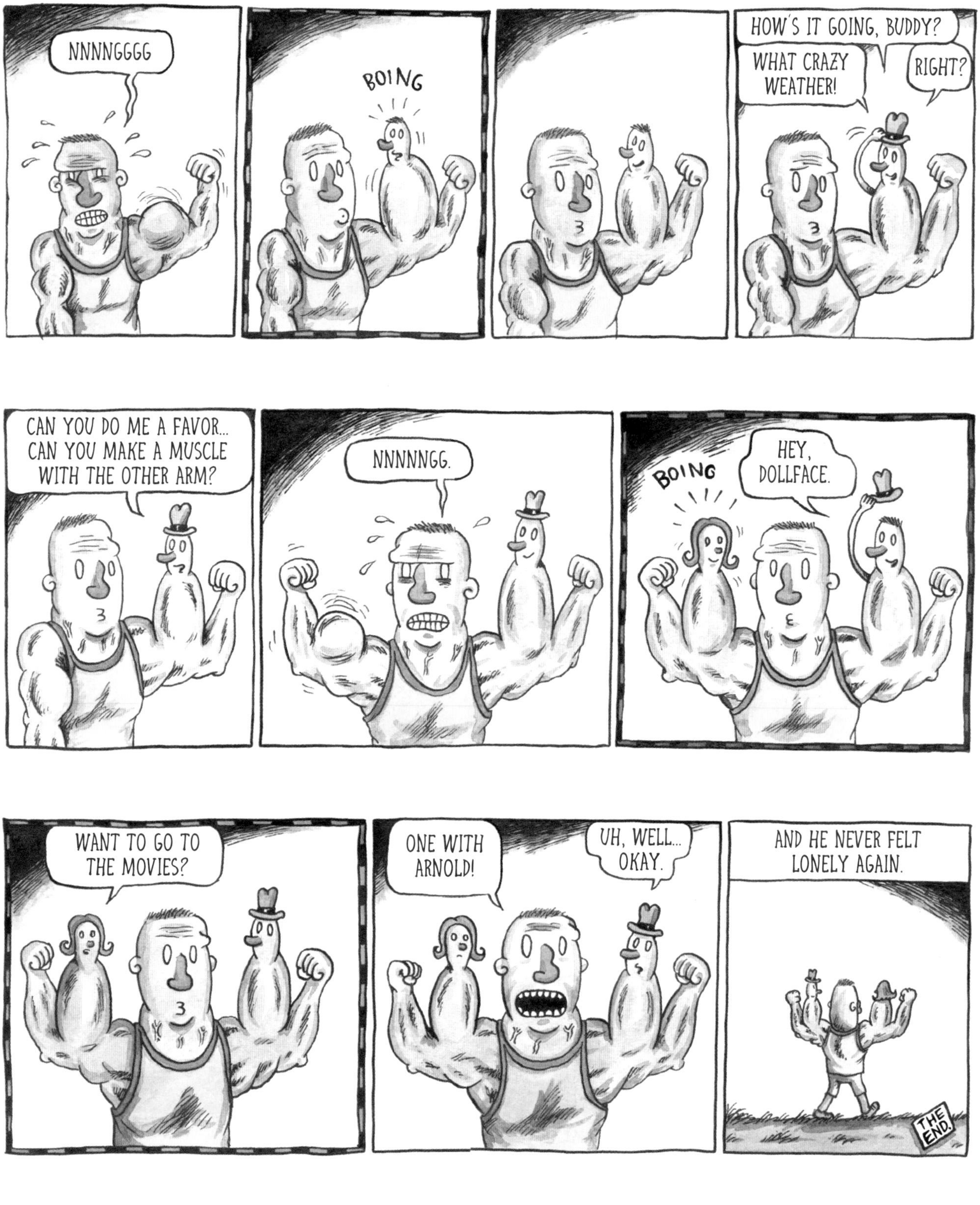
NNNNGGGG
BOING
HOW'S IT GOING, BUDDY?
WHAT CRAZY WEATHER!
RIGHT?
CAN YOU DO ME A FAVOR... CAN YOU MAKE A MUSCLE WITH THE OTHER ARM?
NNNNNGG.
BOING
HEY, DOLLFACE.
WANT TO GO TO THE MOVIES?
ONE WITH ARNOLD!
UH, WELL... OKAY.
AND HE NEVER FELT LONELY AGAIN.
THE END.

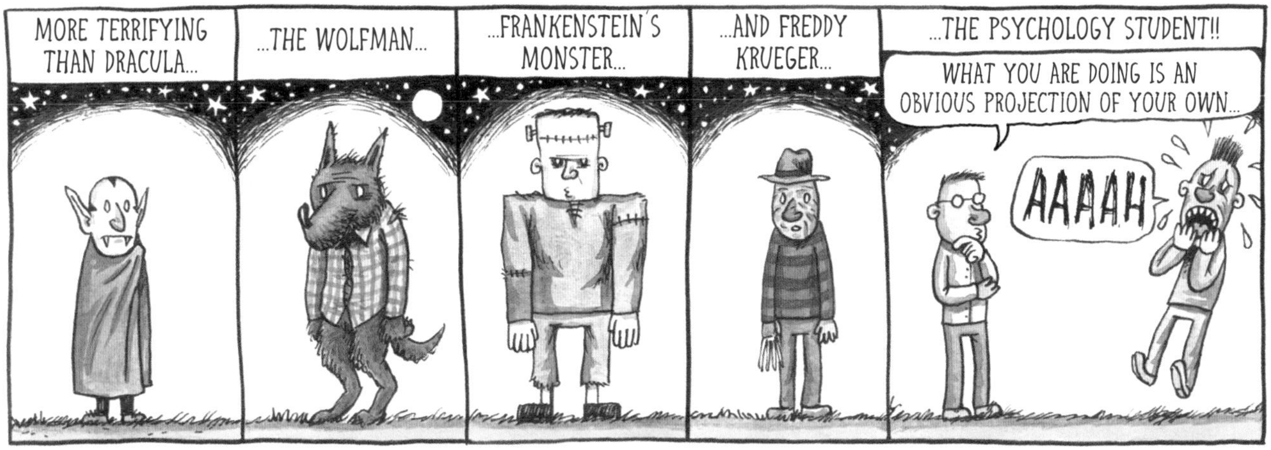
MORE TERRIFYING THAN DRACULA...
...THE WOLFMAN...
...FRANKENSTEIN'S MONSTER...
...AND FREDDY KRUEGER...
...THE PSYCHOLOGY STUDENT!!
WHAT YOU ARE DOING IS AN OBVIOUS PROJECTION OF YOUR OWN...
AAAAH

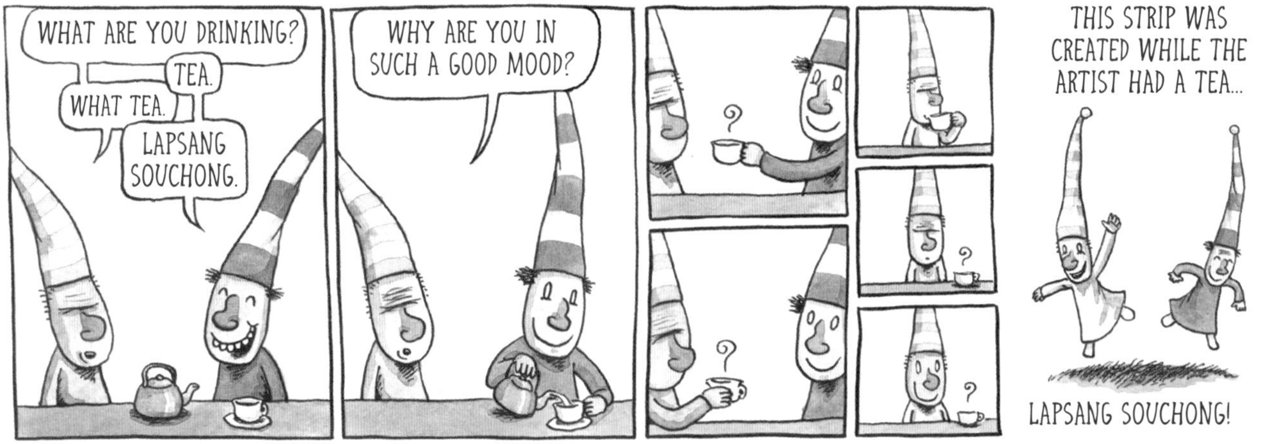
WHAT ARE YOU DRINKING?
TEA.
WHAT TEA.
LAPSANG SOUCHONG.
WHY ARE YOU IN SUCH A GOOD MOOD?
THIS STRIP WAS CREATED WHILE THE ARTIST HAD A TEA...
LAPSANG SOUCHONG!

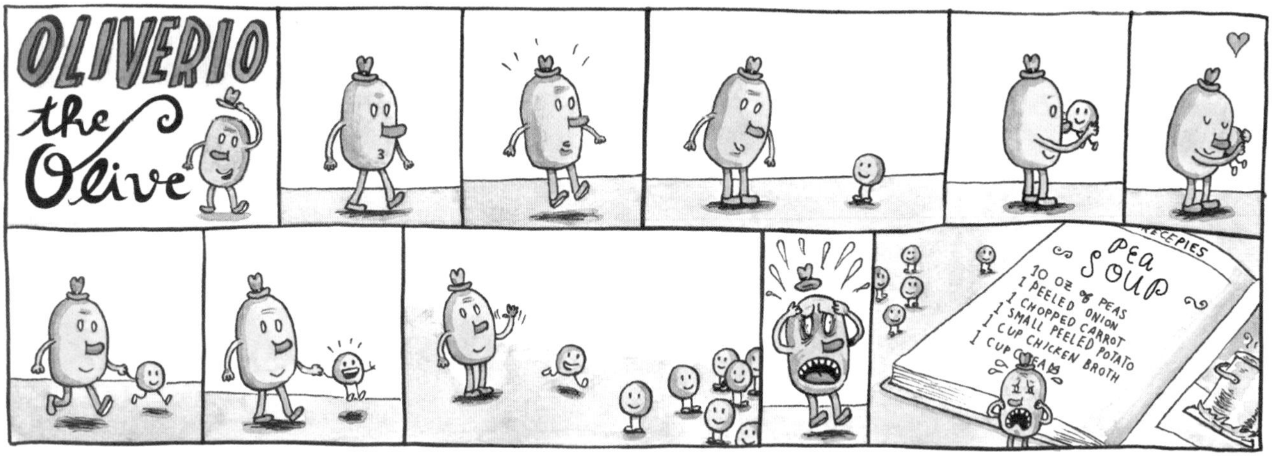
OLIVERIO the Olive
RECEPIES
PEA SOUP
10 OZ of PEAS
1 PEELED ONION
1 CHOPPED CARROT
1 SMALL PEELED POTATO
1 CUP CHICKEN BROTH

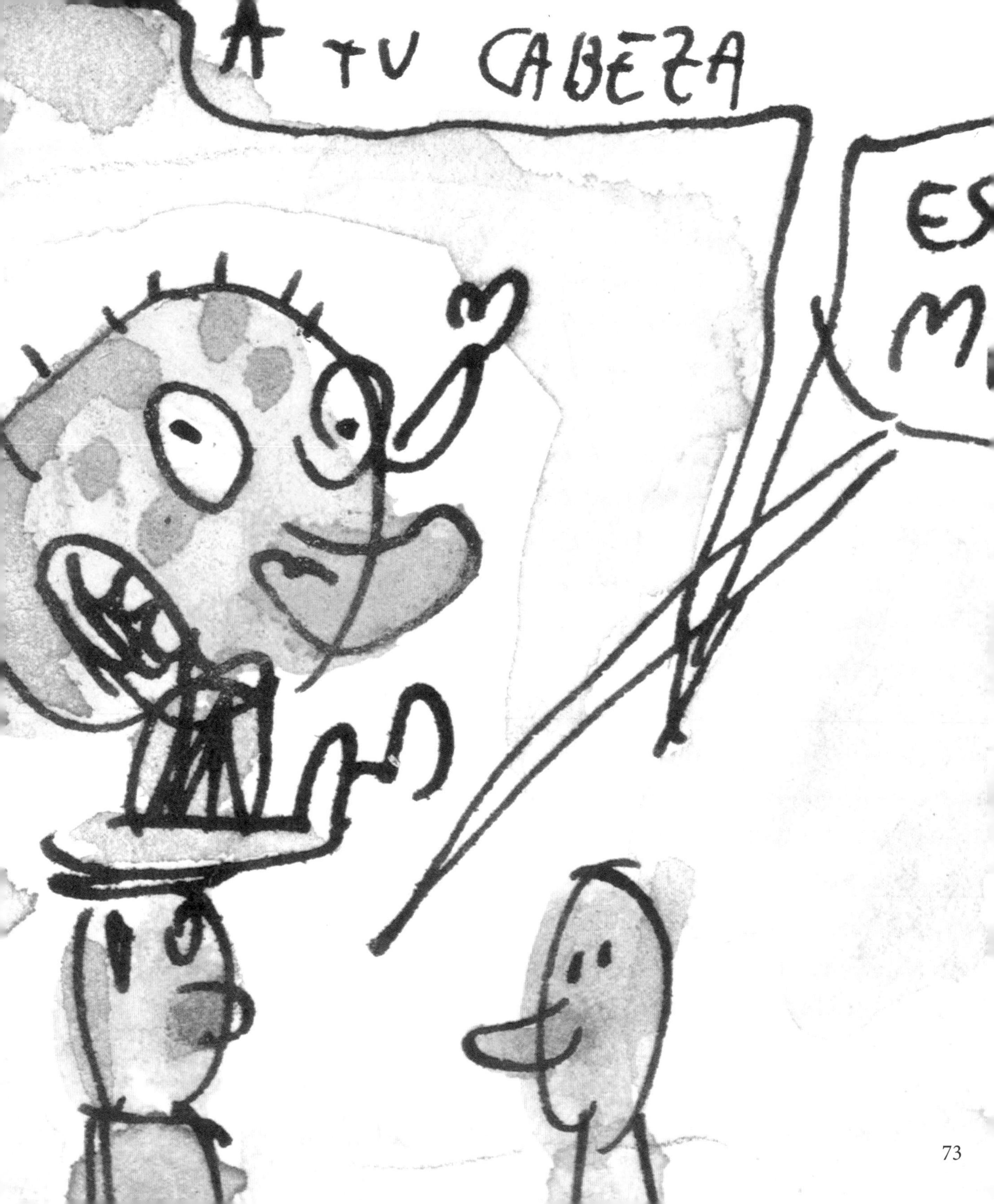
A TU CABEZA

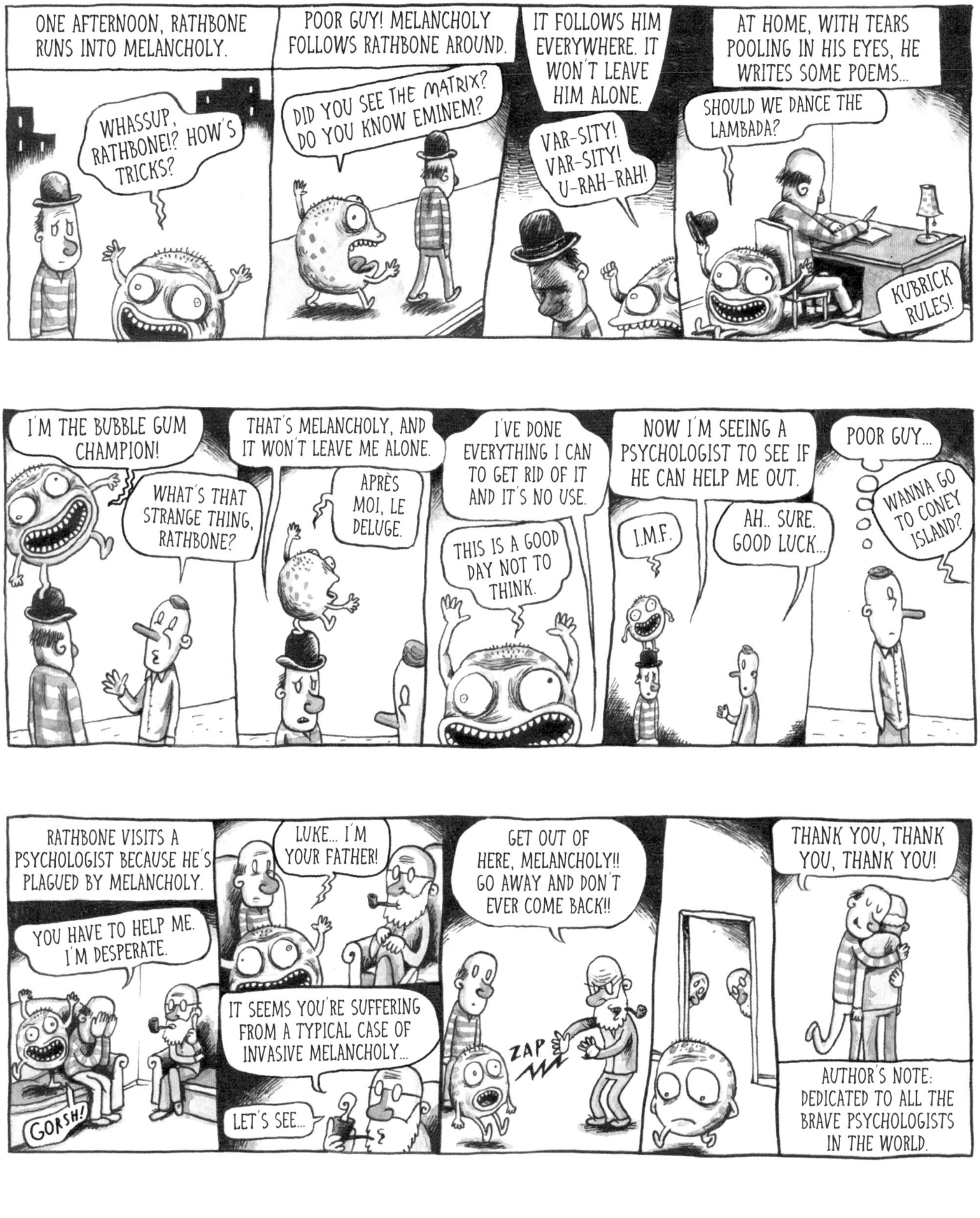
ONE AFTERNOON, RATHBONE RUNS INTO MELANCHOLY.
WHASSUP, RATHBONE!? HOW'S TRICKS?
POOR GUY! MELANCHOLY FOLLOWS RATHBONE AROUND.
DID YOU SEE THE MATRIX? DO YOU KNOW EMINEM?
IT FOLLOWS HIM EVERYWHERE. IT WON'T LEAVE HIM ALONE.
VAR-SITY! VAR-SITY! U-RAH-RAH!
AT HOME, WITH TEARS POOLING IN HIS EYES, HE WRITES SOME POEMS...
SHOULD WE DANCE THE LAMBADA?
KUBRICK RULES!
I'M THE BUBBLE GUM CHAMPION!
WHAT'S THAT STRANGE THING, RATHBONE?
THAT'S MELANCHOLY, AND IT WON'T LEAVE ME ALONE.
APRÈS MOI, LE DELUGE.
I'VE DONE EVERYTHING I CAN TO GET RID OF IT AND IT'S NO USE.
THIS IS A GOOD DAY NOT TO THINK.
NOW I'M SEEING A PSYCHOLOGIST TO SEE IF HE CAN HELP ME OUT.
I.M.F.
AH.. SURE. GOOD LUCK...
POOR GUY...
WANNA GO TO CONEY ISLAND?
RATHBONE VISITS A PSYCHOLOGIST BECAUSE HE'S PLAGUED BY MELANCHOLY.
YOU HAVE TO HELP ME. I'M DESPERATE.
GORSH!
LUKE... I'M YOUR FATHER!
IT SEEMS YOU'RE SUFFERING FROM A TYPICAL CASE OF INVASIVE MELANCHOLY...
LET'S SEE...
GET OUT OF HERE, MELANCHOLY!! GO AWAY AND DON'T EVER COME BACK!!
ZAP
THANK YOU, THANK YOU, THANK YOU!
AUTHOR'S NOTE: DEDICATED TO ALL THE BRAVE PSYCHOLOGISTS IN THE WORLD.

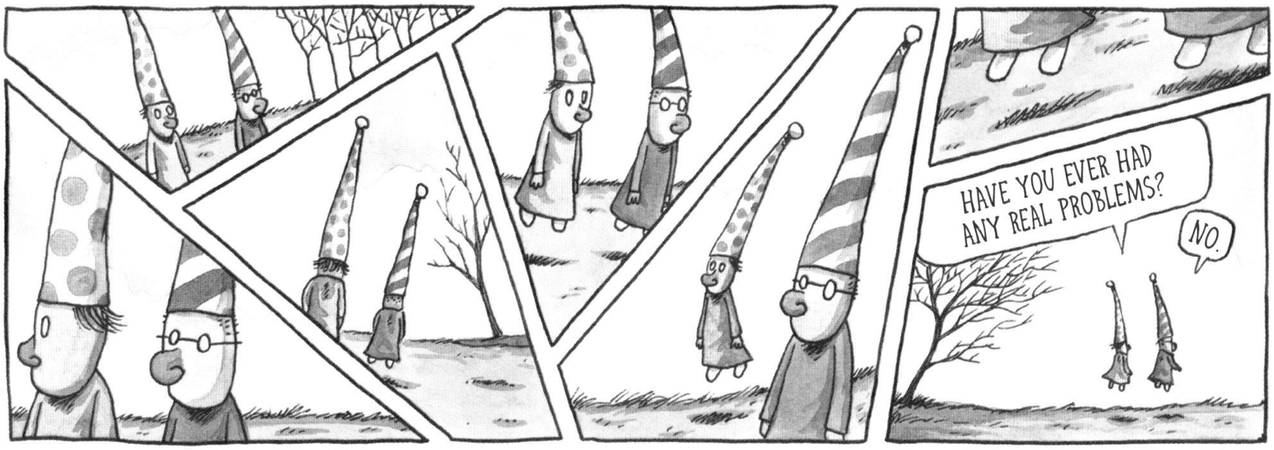
HAVE YOU EVER HAD ANY REAL PROBLEMS?
NO.

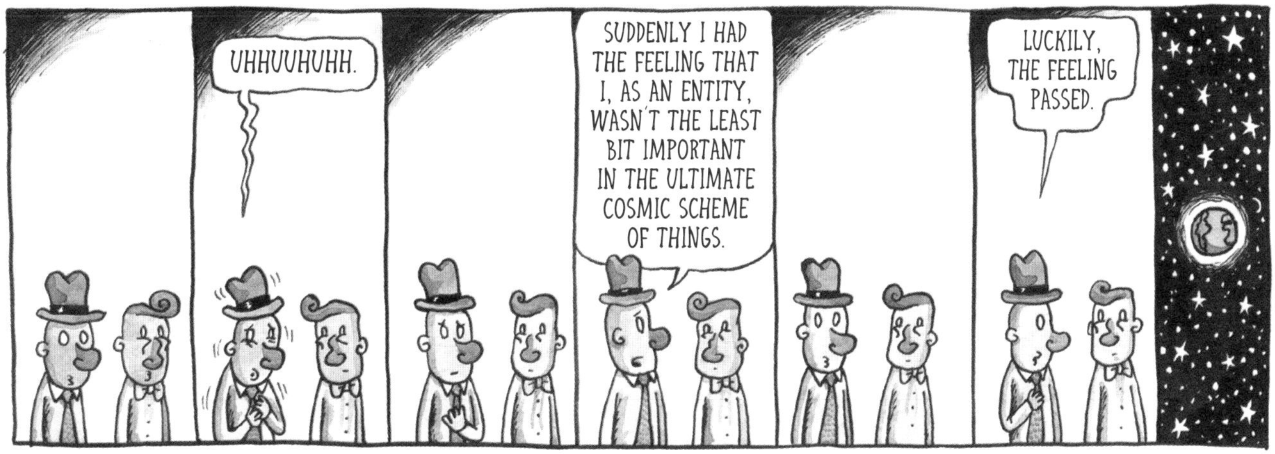
UHHUUHUHH.
SUDDENLY I HAD THE FEELING THAT I, AS AN ENTITY, WASN'T THE LEAST BIT IMPORTANT IN THE ULTIMATE COSMIC SCHEME OF THINGS.
LUCKILY, THE FEELING PASSED.

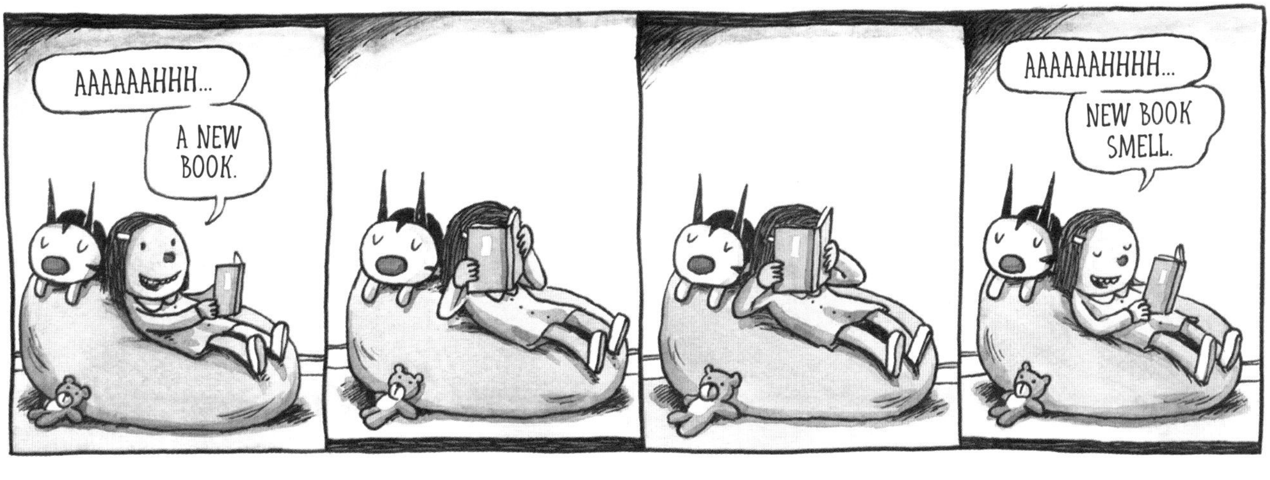
AAAAAAHHH...
A NEW BOOK.
AAAAAAHHHH...
NEW BOOK SMELL.

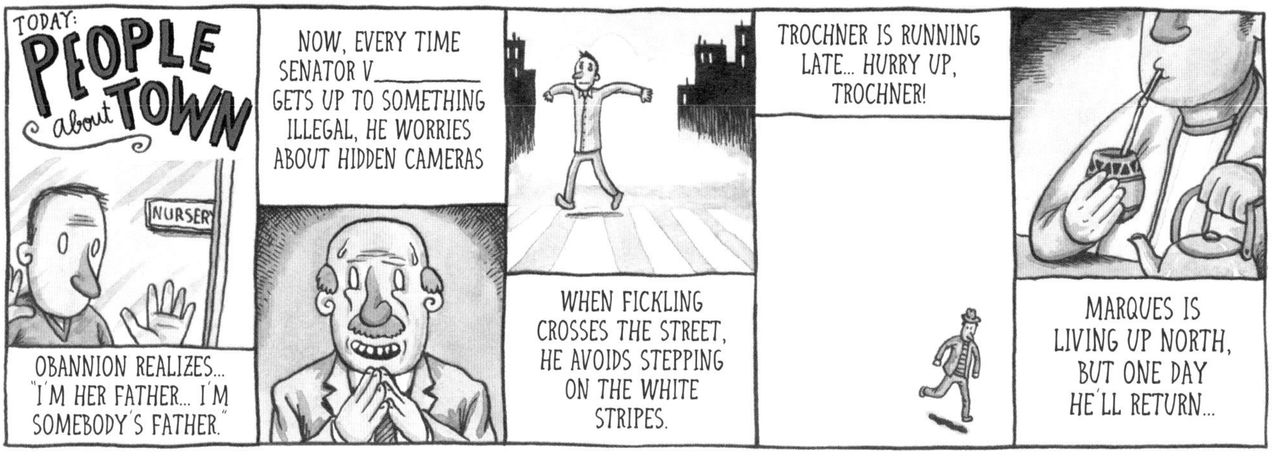
TODAY:
PEOPLE about TOWN
NURSERY
OBANNION REALIZES... "I'M HER FATHER... I'M SOMEBODY'S FATHER."
NOW, EVERY TIME SENATOR V__________ GETS UP TO SOMETHING ILLEGAL, HE WORRIES ABOUT HIDDEN CAMERAS
WHEN FICKLING CROSSES THE STREET, HE AVOIDS STEPPING ON THE WHITE STRIPES.
TROCHNER IS RUNNING LATE... HURRY UP, TROCHNER!
MARQUES IS LIVING UP NORTH, BUT ONE DAY HE'LL RETURN...

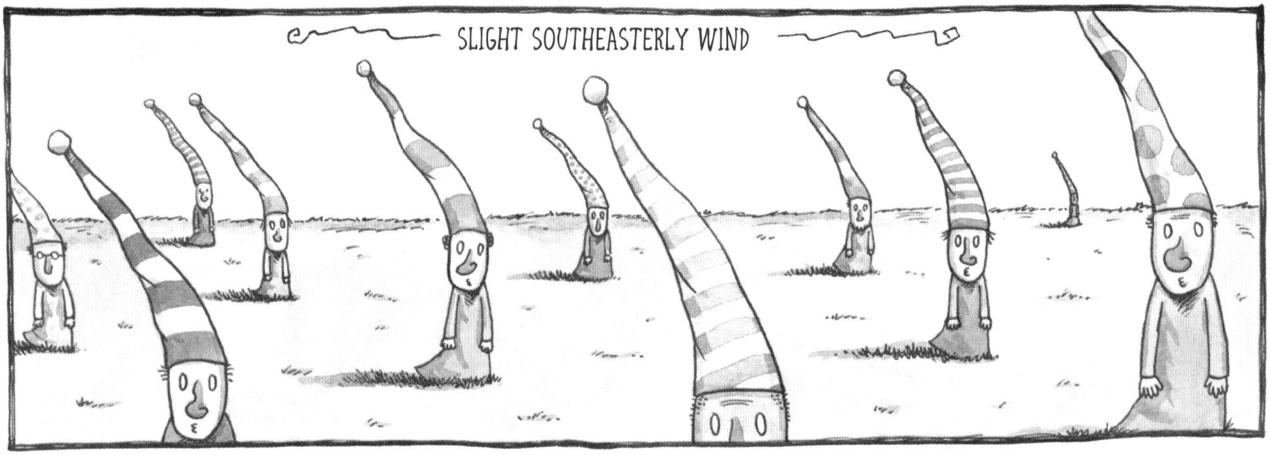
SLIGHT SOUTHEASTERLY WIND

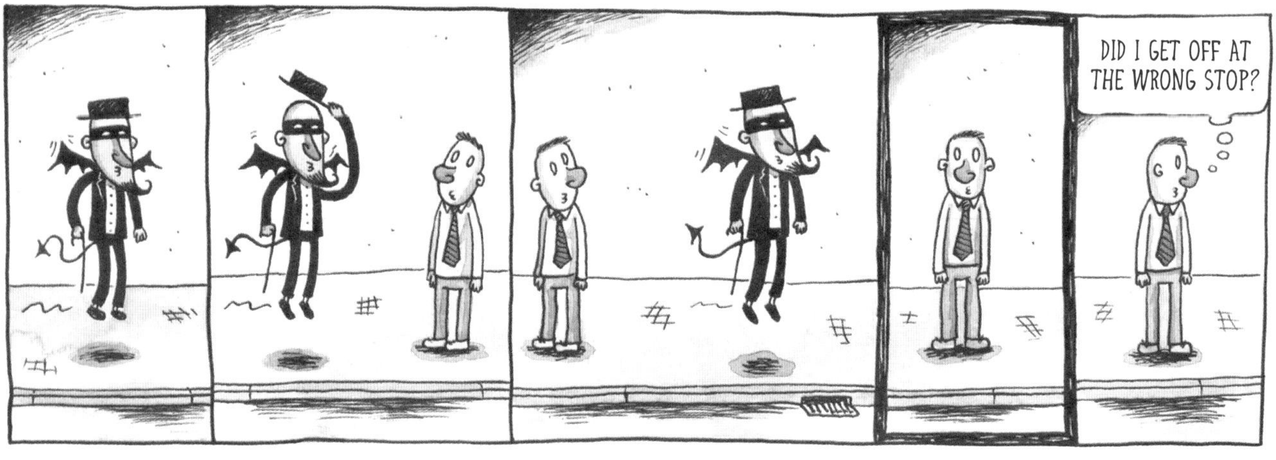
DID I GET OFF AT THE WRONG STOP?

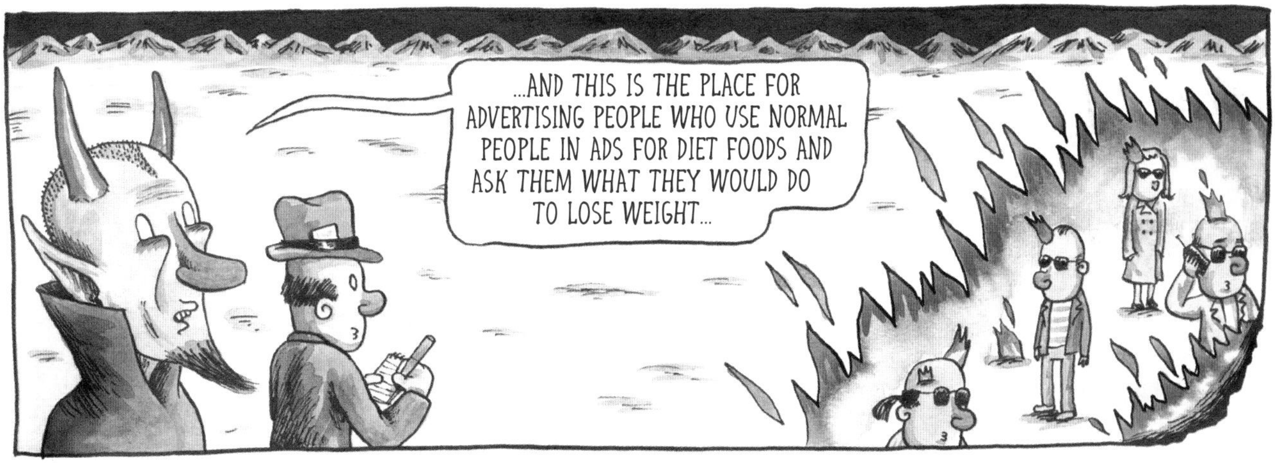
...AND THIS IS THE PLACE FOR ADVERTISING PEOPLE WHO USE NORMAL PEOPLE IN ADS FOR DIET FOODS AND ASK THEM WHAT THEY WOULD DO TO LOSE WEIGHT...

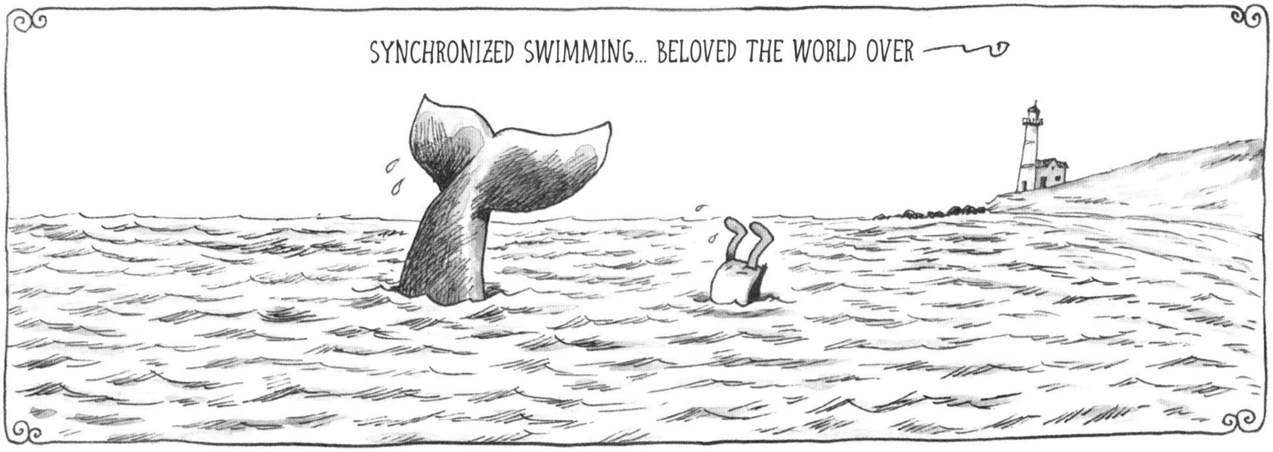
SYNCHRONIZED SWIMMING... BELOVED THE WORLD OVER

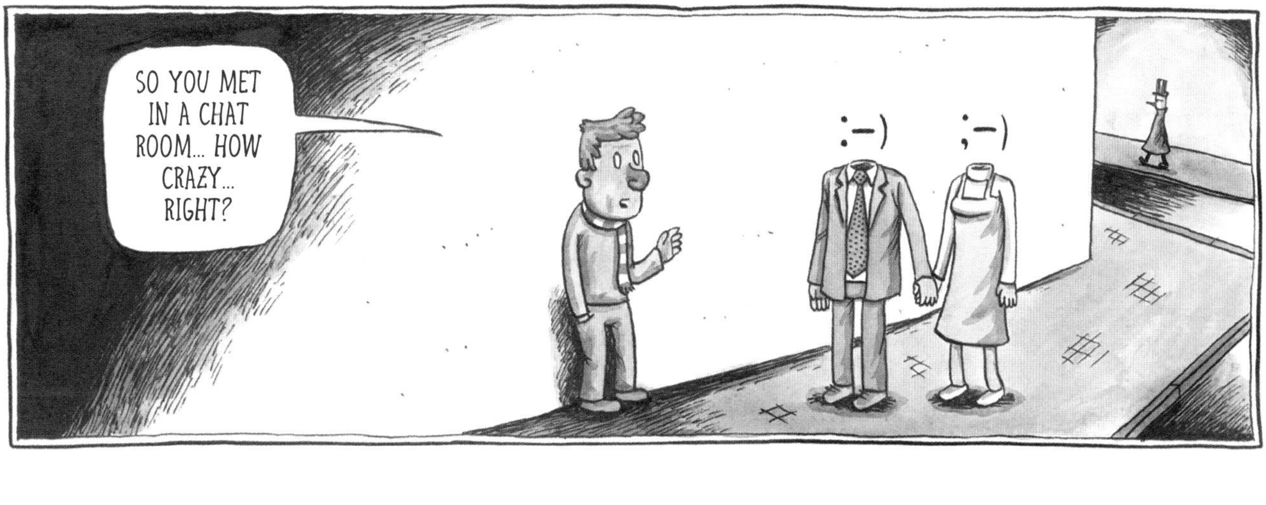
SO YOU MET IN A CHAT ROOM... HOW CRAZY... RIGHT?
;-)
;-)

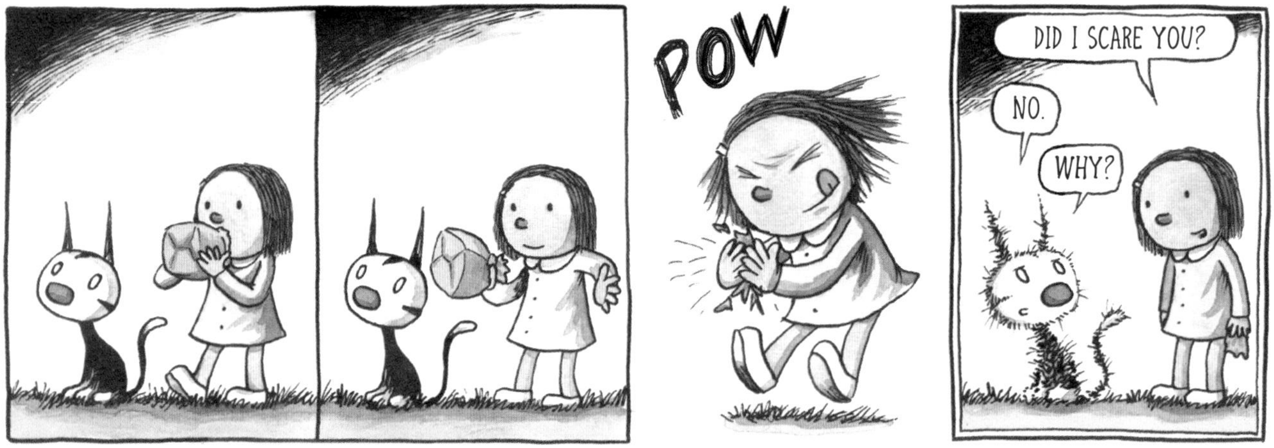
POW
DID I SCARE YOU?
NO.
WHY?

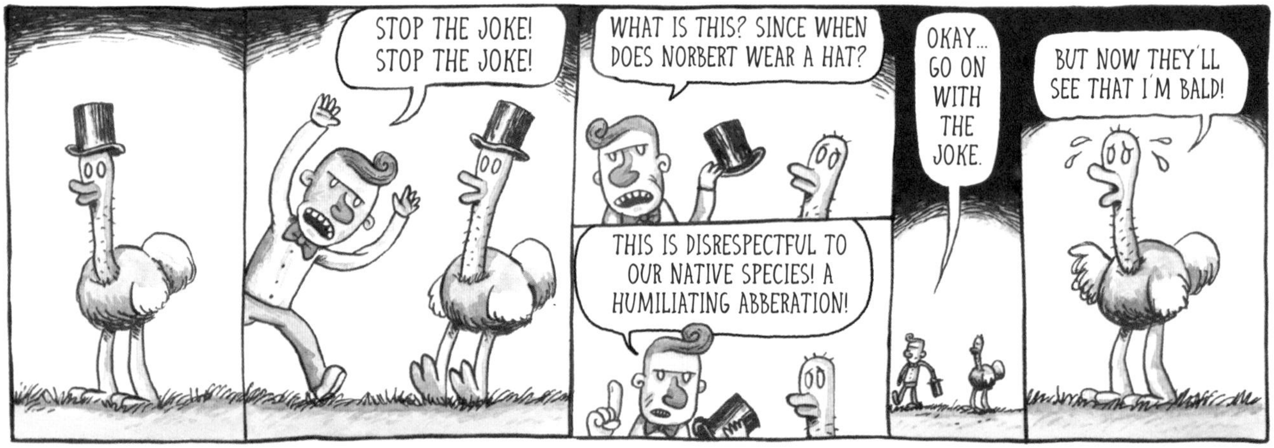
STOP THE JOKE! STOP THE JOKE!
WHAT IS THIS? SINCE WHEN DOES NORBERT WEAR A HAT?
THIS IS DISRESPECTFUL TO OUR NATIVE SPECIES! A HUMILIATING ABBERATION!
OKAY... GO ON WITH THE JOKE.
BUT NOW THEY'LL SEE THAT I'M BALD!

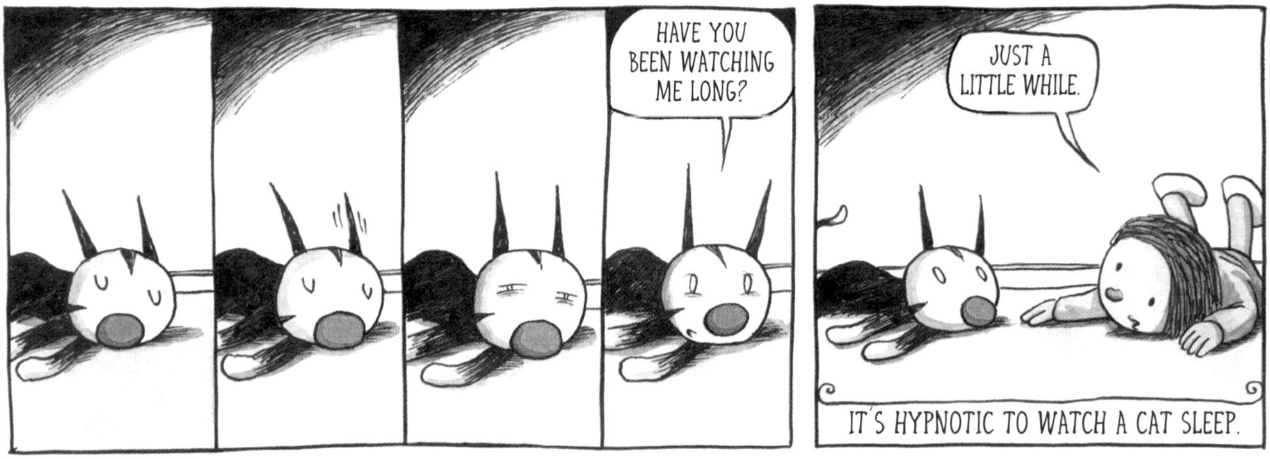
HAVE YOU BEEN WATCHING ME LONG?
JUST A LITTLE WHILE.
IT'S HYPNOTIC TO WATCH A CAT SLEEP.

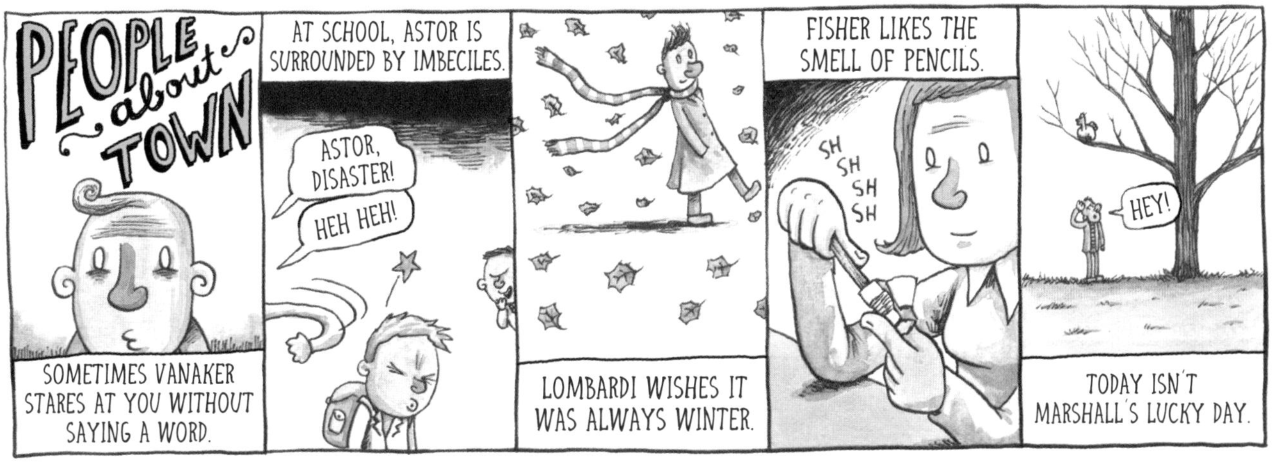
PEOPLE about TOWN
SOMETIMES VANAKER STARES AT YOU WITHOUT SAYING A WORD.
AT SCHOOL, ASTOR IS SURROUNDED BY IMBECILES.
ASTOR, DISASTER!
HEH HEH!
LOMBARDI WISHES IT WAS ALWAYS WINTER.
FISHER LIKES THE SMELL OF PENCILS.
SH SH SH SH
HEY!
TODAY ISN'T MARSHALL'S LUCKY DAY.

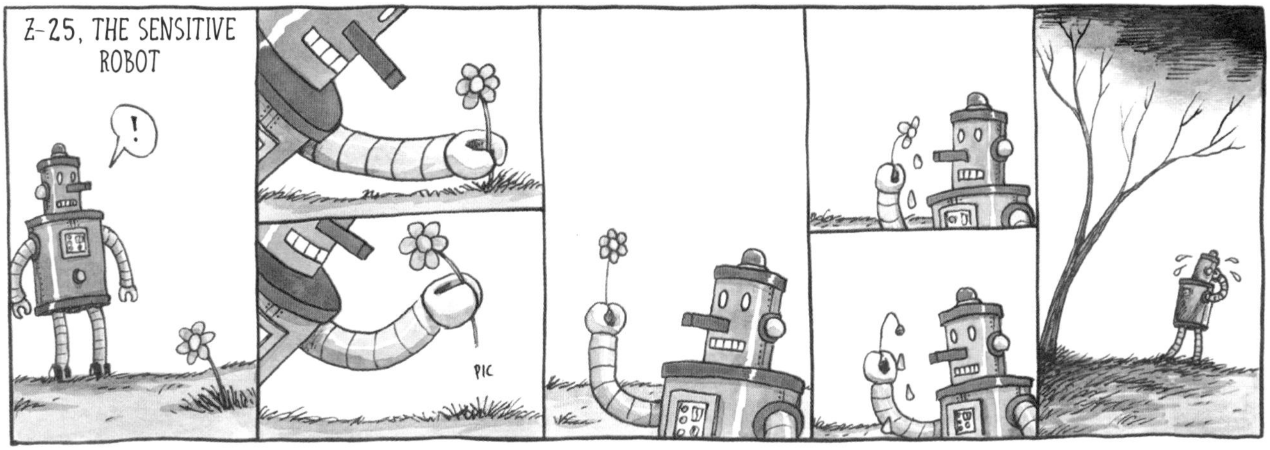
Z-25, THE SENSITIVE ROBOT
!
PIC

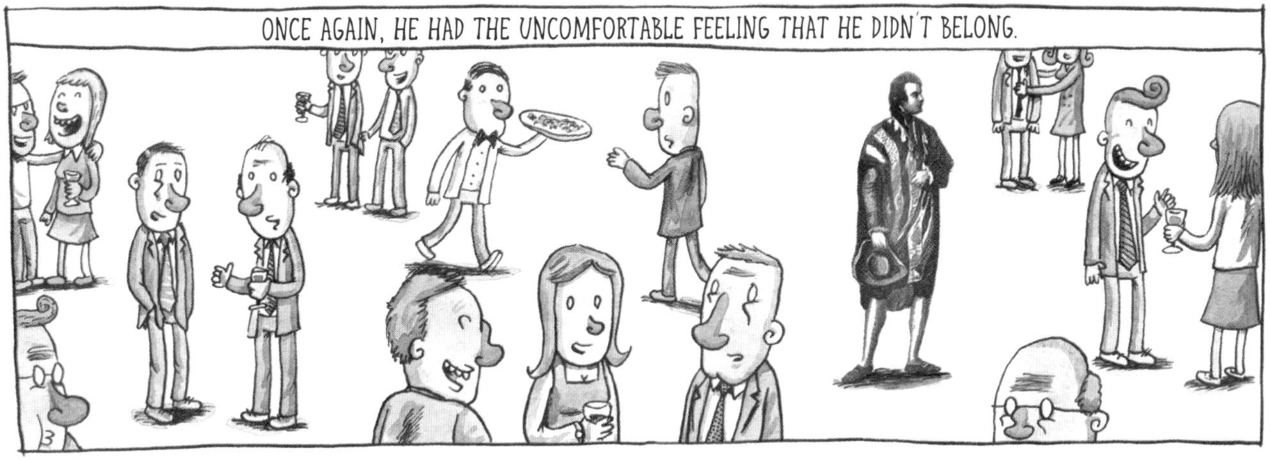
ONCE AGAIN, HE HAD THE UNCOMFORTABLE FEELING THAT HE DIDN'T BELONG.

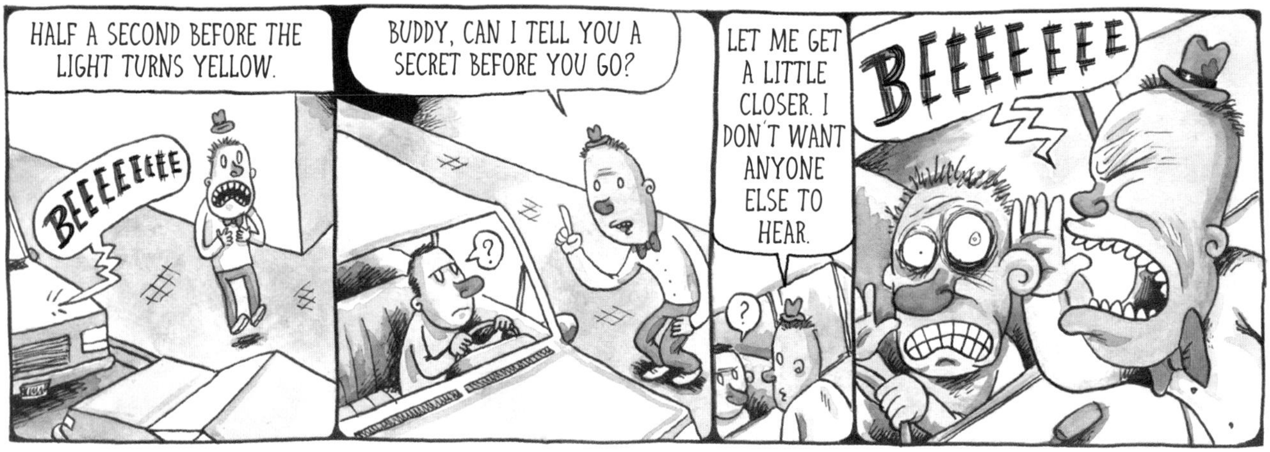
HALF A SECOND BEFORE THE LIGHT TURNS YELLOW.
BEEEEEEE
BUDDY, CAN I TELL YOU A SECRET BEFORE YOU GO?
?
LET ME GET A LITTLE CLOSER. I DON'T WANT ANYONE ELSE TO HEAR.
?
BEEEEEEE

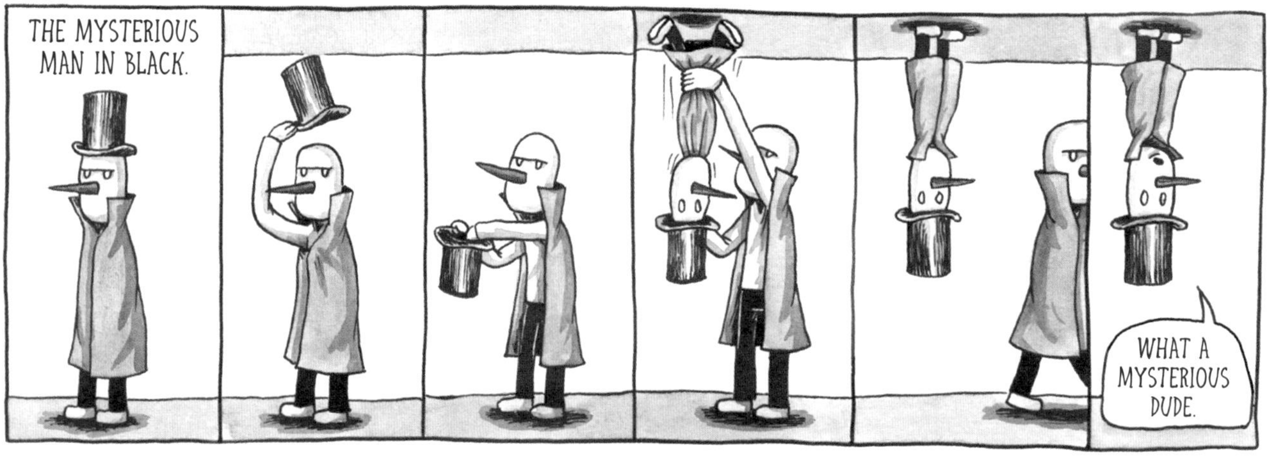
THE MYSTERIOUS MAN IN BLACK.
WHAT A MYSTERIOUS DUDE.

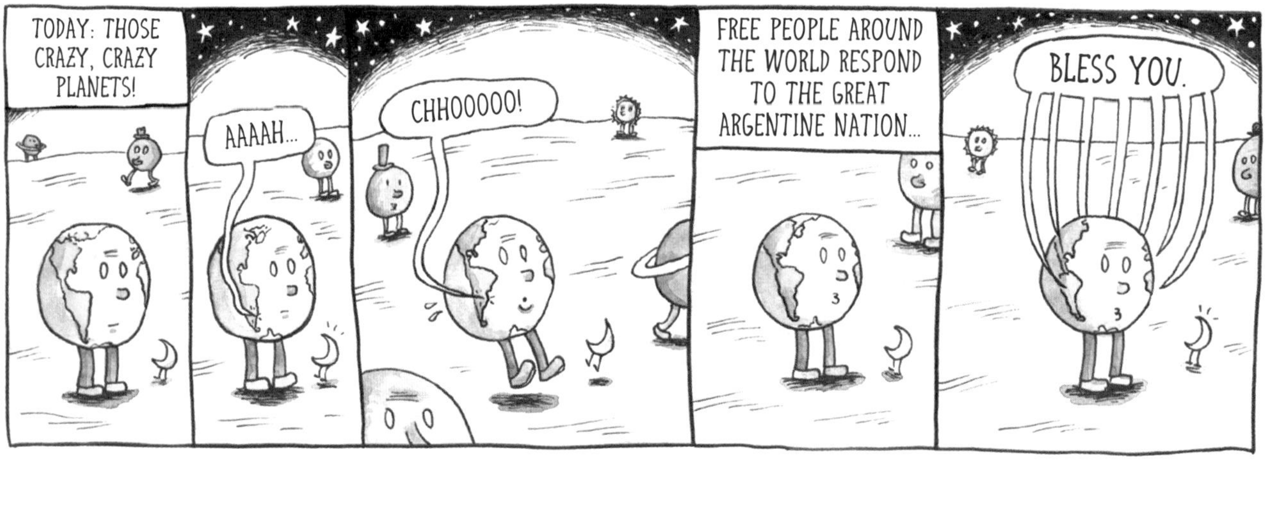
TODAY: THOSE CRAZY, CRAZY PLANETS!
AAAAH...
CHHOOOOO!
FREE PEOPLE AROUND THE WORLD RESPOND TO THE GREAT ARGENTINE NATION...
BLESS YOU.

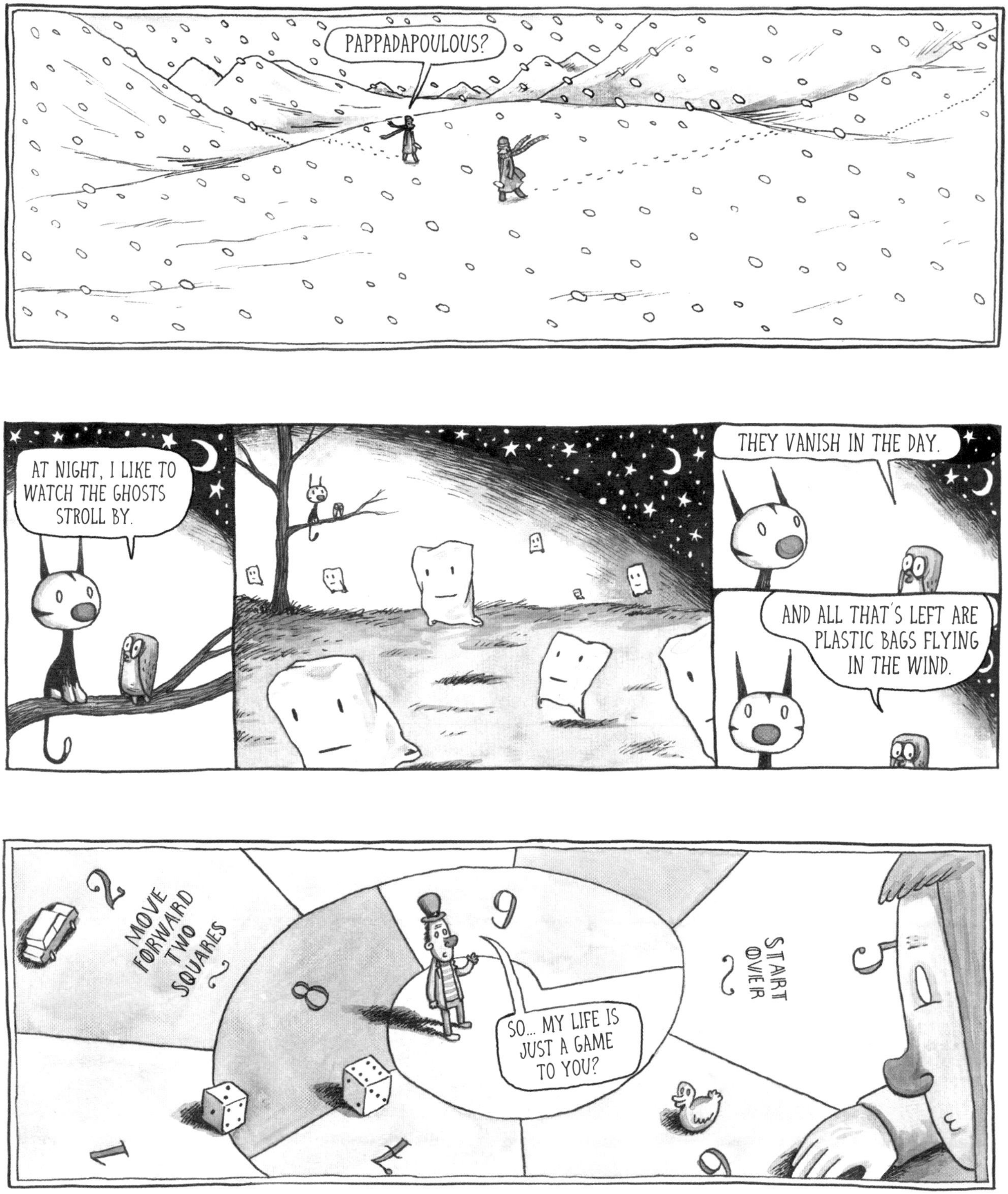
PAPPADAPOULOUS?
AT NIGHT, I LIKE TO WATCH THE GHOSTS STROLL BY.
THEY VANISH IN THE DAY.
AND ALL THAT'S LEFT ARE PLASTIC BAGS FLYING IN THE WIND.
MOVE FORWARD TWO SQUARES
START OVER
SO... MY LIFE IS JUST A GAME TO YOU?

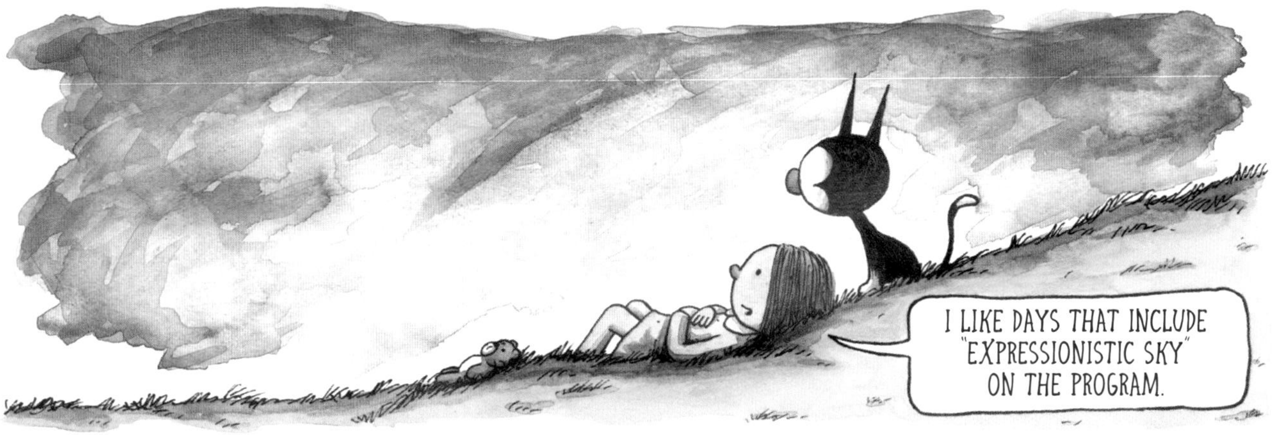
I LIKE DAYS THAT INCLUDE "EXPRESSIONISTIC SKY" ON THE PROGRAM.

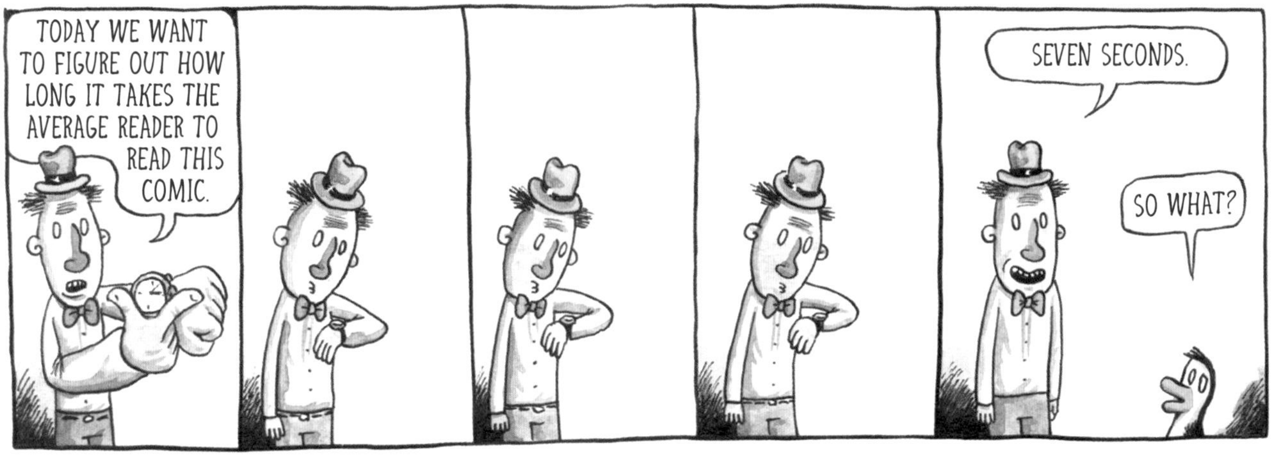
TODAY WE WANT TO FIGURE OUT HOW LONG IT TAKES THE AVERAGE READER TO READ THIS COMIC.
SEVEN SECONDS.
SO WHAT?

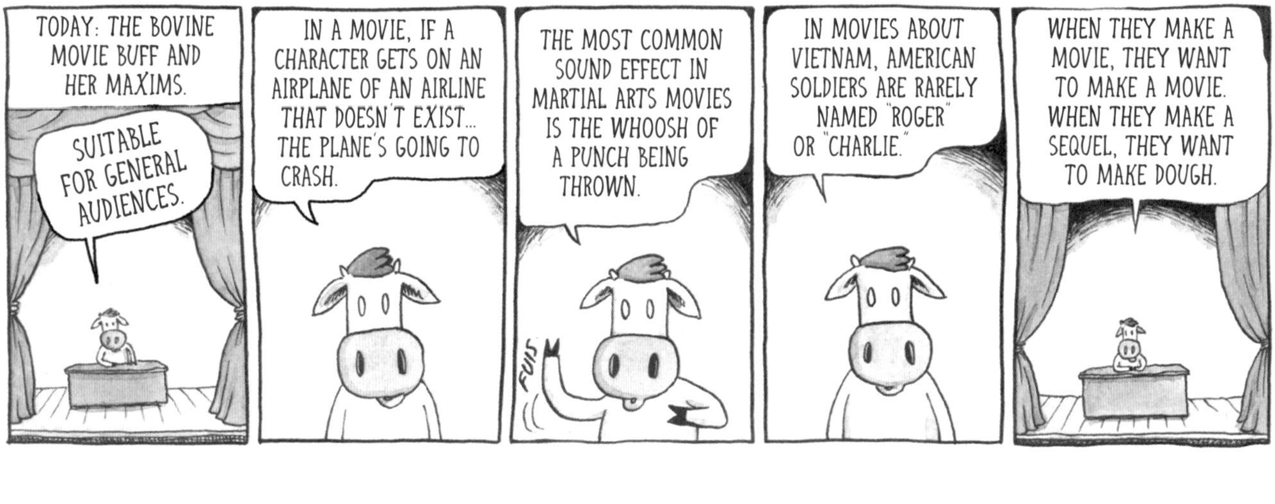
TODAY: THE BOVINE MOVIE BUFF AND HER MAXIMS.
SUITABLE FOR GENERAL AUDIENCES.
IN A MOVIE, IF A CHARACTER GETS ON AN AIRPLANE OF AN AIRLINE THAT DOESN'T EXIST... THE PLANE'S GOING TO CRASH.
THE MOST COMMON SOUND EFFECT IN MARTIAL ARTS MOVIES IS THE WHOOSH OF A PUNCH BEING THROWN.
FUIS
IN MOVIES ABOUT VIETNAM, AMERICAN SOLDIERS ARE RARELY NAMED "ROGER" OR "CHARLIE."
WHEN THEY MAKE A MOVIE, THEY WANT TO MAKE A MOVIE. WHEN THEY MAKE A SEQUEL, THEY WANT TO MAKE DOUGH.

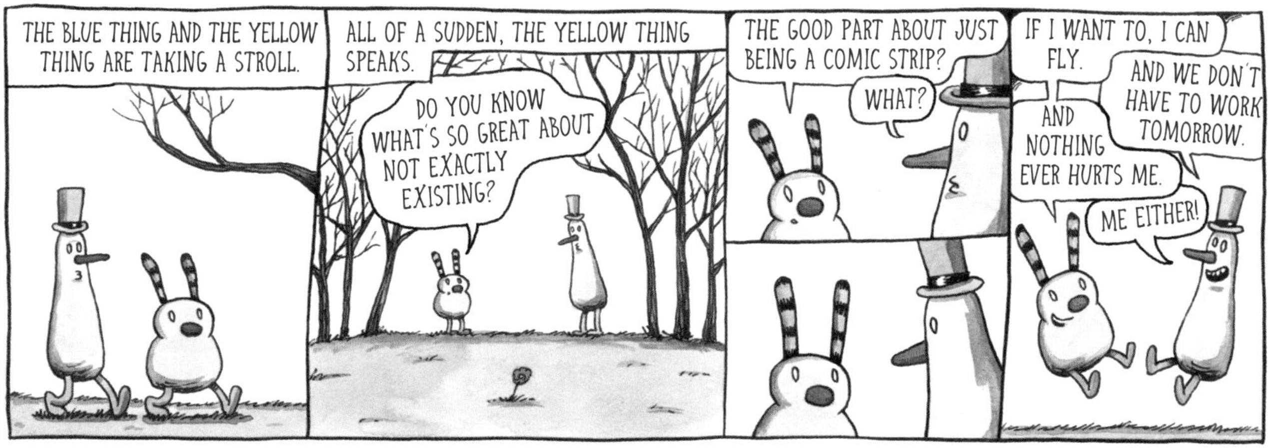
THE BLUE THING AND THE YELLOW THING ARE TAKING A STROLL.
ALL OF A SUDDEN, THE YELLOW THING SPEAKS.
DO YOU KNOW WHAT'S SO GREAT ABOUT NOT EXACTLY EXISTING?
THE GOOD PART ABOUT JUST BEING A COMIC STRIP?
WHAT?
IF I WANT TO, I CAN FLY.
AND WE DON'T HAVE TO WORK TOMORROW.
AND NOTHING EVER HURTS ME.
ME EITHER!

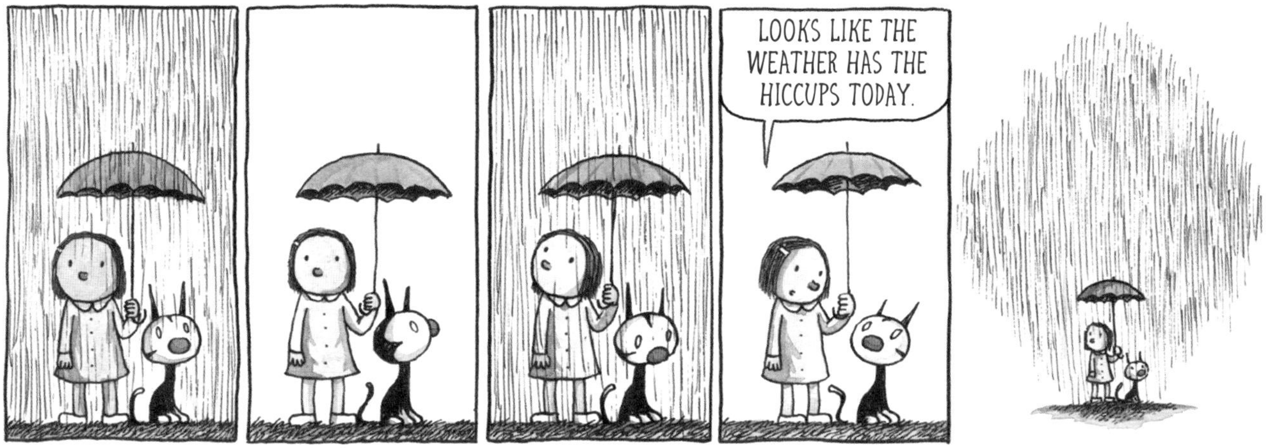
LOOKS LIKE THE WEATHER HAS THE HICCUPS TODAY.

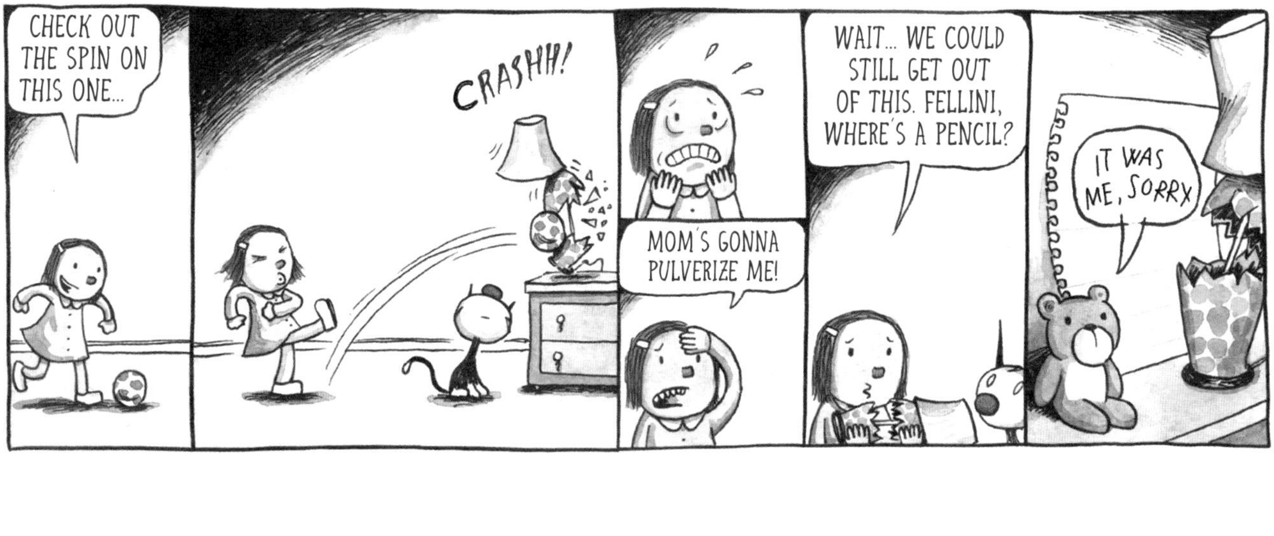
CHECK OUT THE SPIN ON THIS ONE...
CRASHH!
MOM'S GONNA PULVERIZE ME!
WAIT... WE COULD STILL GET OUT OF THIS. FELLINI, WHERE'S A PENCIL?
IT WAS ME, SORRY

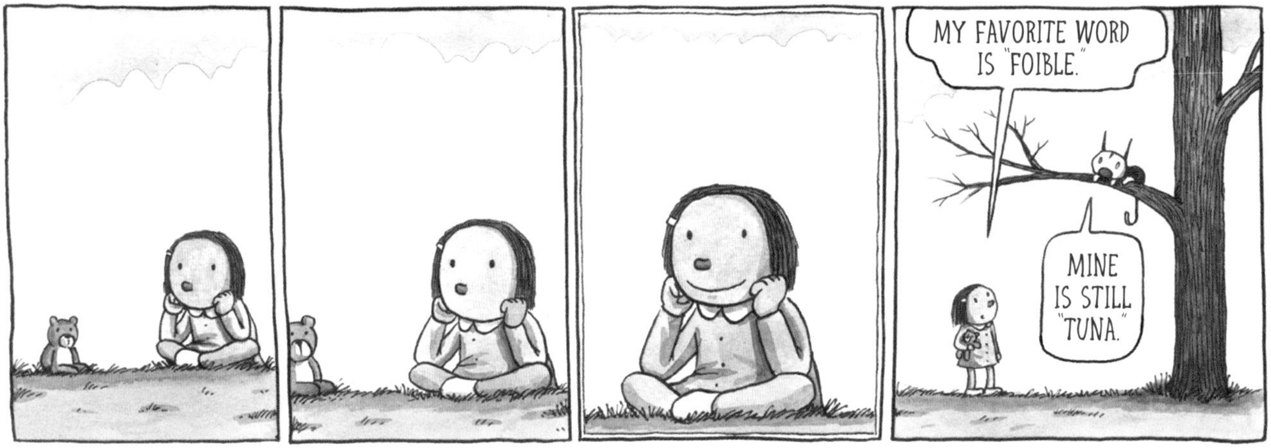
MY FAVORITE WORD IS "FOIBLE."
MINE IS STILL "TUNA."

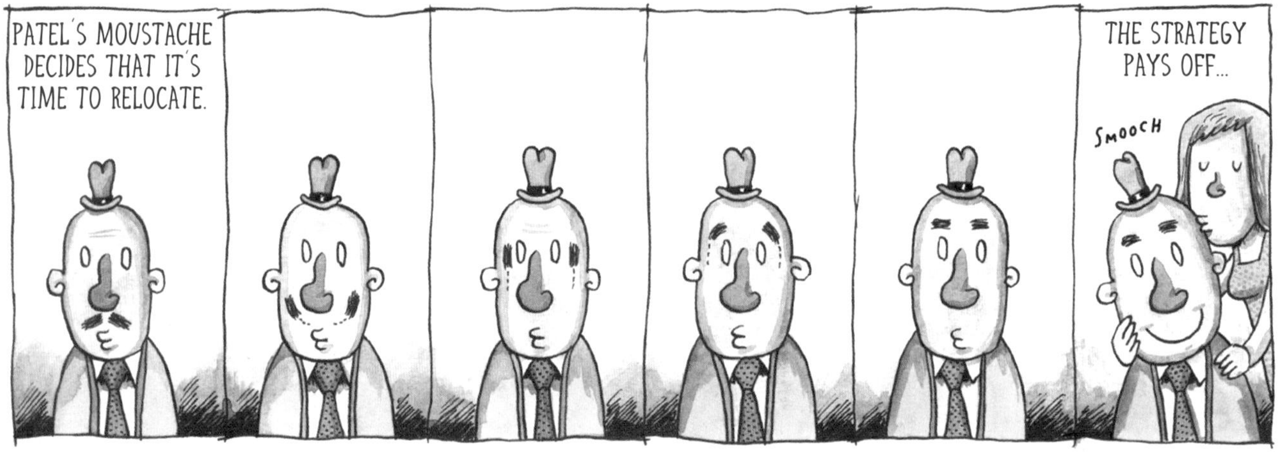
PATEL'S MOUSTACHE DECIDES THAT IT'S TIME TO RELOCATE.
THE STRATEGY PAYS OFF...
SMOOCH

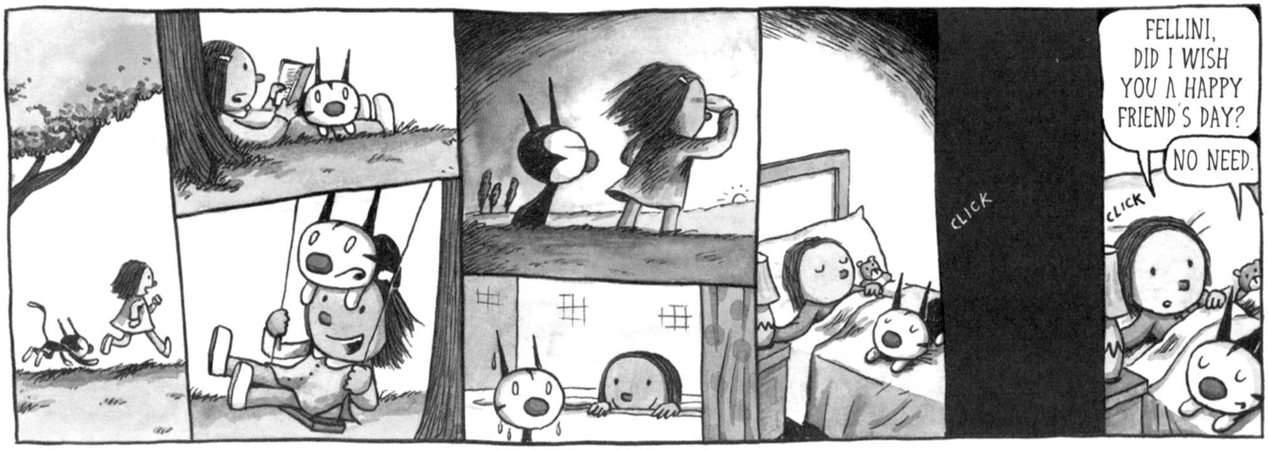
CLICK
CLICK
FELLINI, DID I WISH YOU A HAPPY FRIEND'S DAY?
NO NEED.

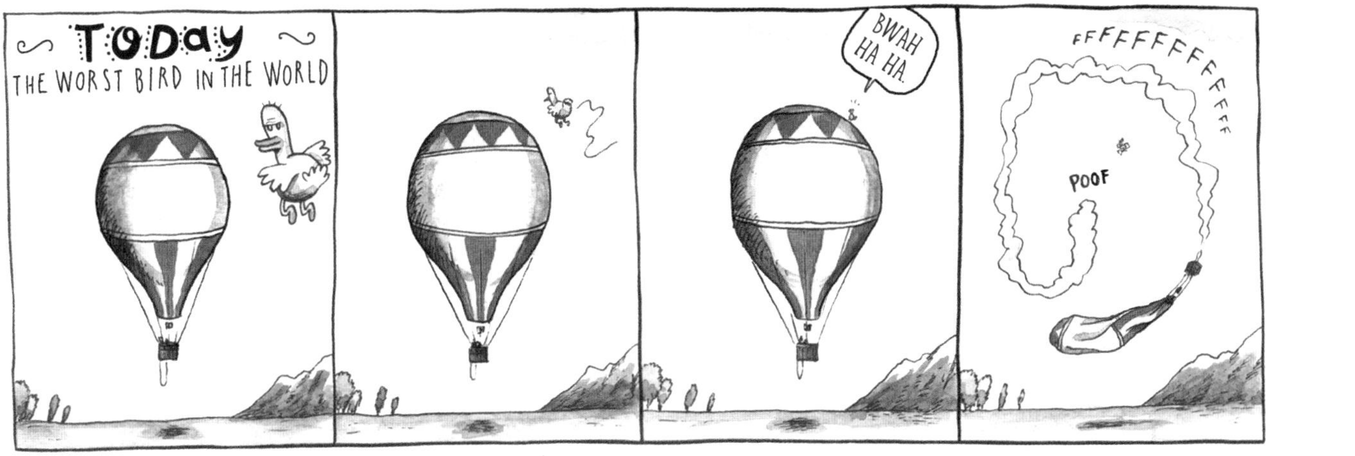
TODAY
THE WORST BIRD IN THE WORLD
BWAH HA HA.
FFFFFFFFFFFFFFFFF
POOF

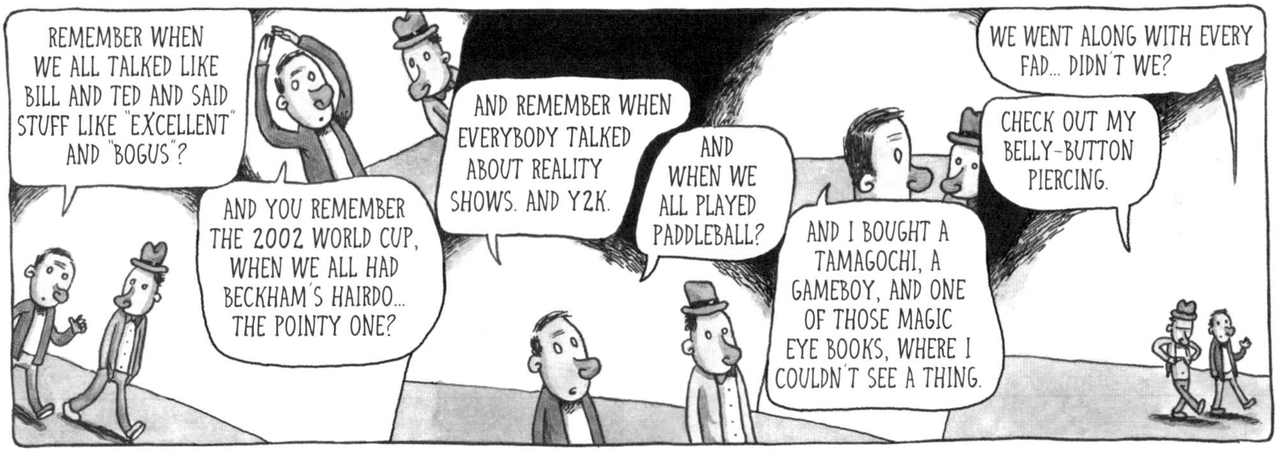
REMEMBER WHEN WE ALL TALKED LIKE BILL AND TED AND SAID STUFF LIKE "EXCELLENT" AND "BOGUS"?
AND YOU REMEMBER THE 2002 WORLD CUP, WHEN WE ALL HAD BECKHAM'S HAIRDO... THE POINTY ONE?
AND REMEMBER WHEN EVERYBODY TALKED ABOUT REALITY SHOWS. AND Y2K.
AND WHEN WE ALL PLAYED PADDLEBALL?
AND I BOUGHT A TAMAGOCHI, A GAMEBOY, AND ONE OF THOSE MAGIC EYE BOOKS, WHERE I COULDN'T SEE A THING.
CHECK OUT MY BELLY-BUTTON PIERCING.
WE WENT ALONG WITH EVERY FAD... DIDN'T WE?

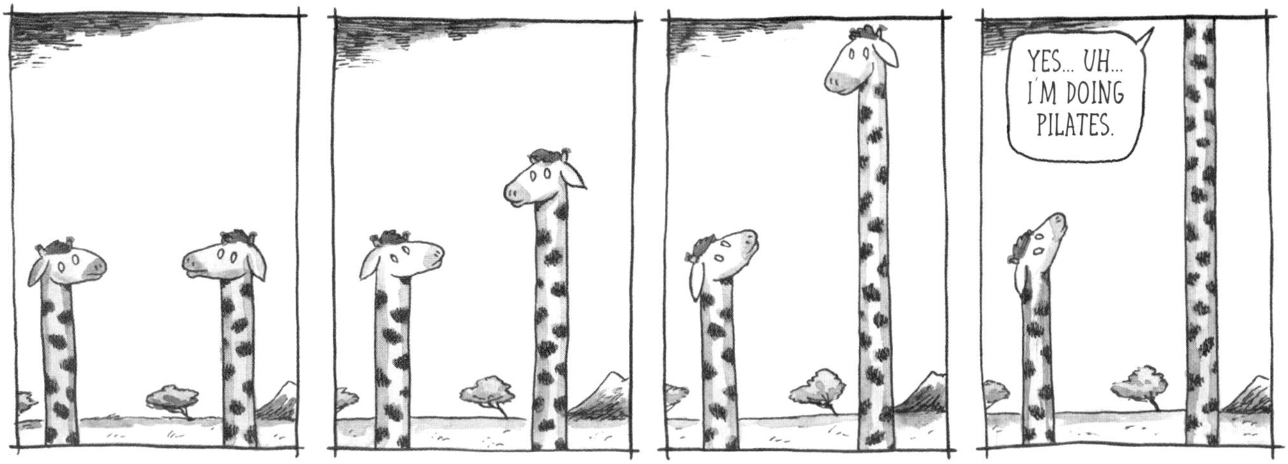
YES... UH... I'M DOING PILATES.

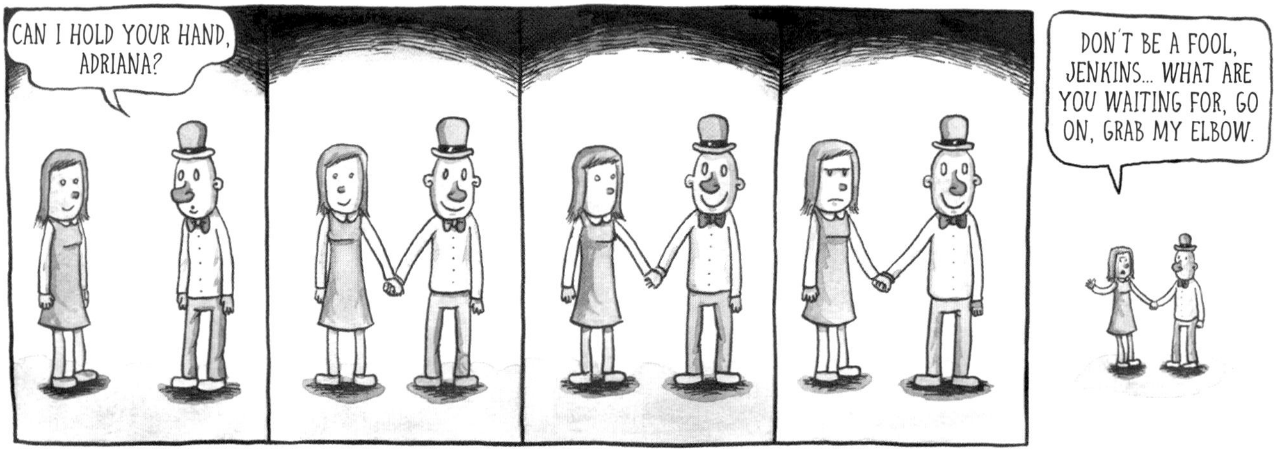
CAN I HOLD YOUR HAND, ADRIANA?
DON'T BE A FOOL, JENKINS... WHAT ARE YOU WAITING FOR, GO ON, GRAB MY ELBOW.

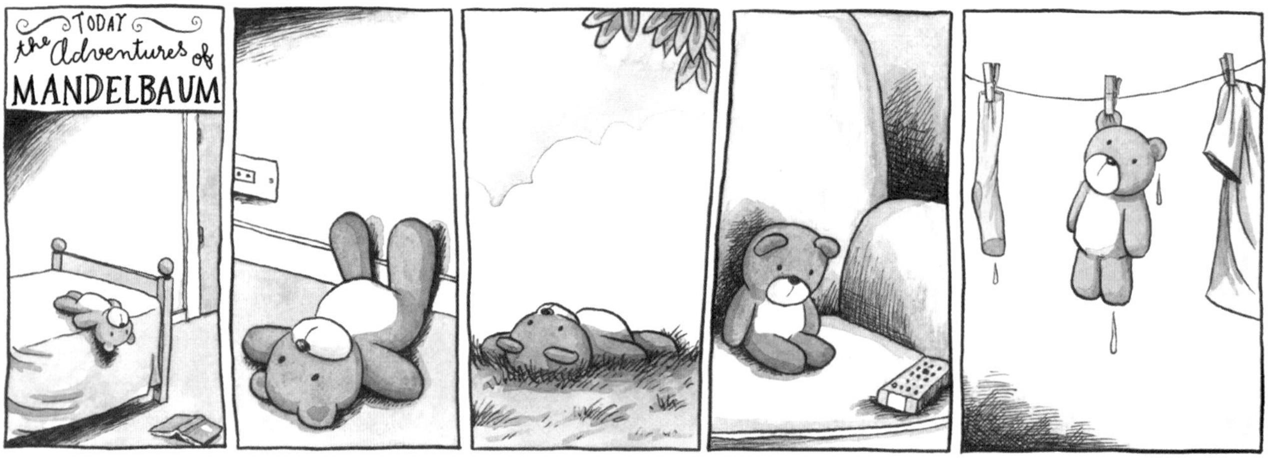
TODAY
the Adventures of
MANDELBAUM

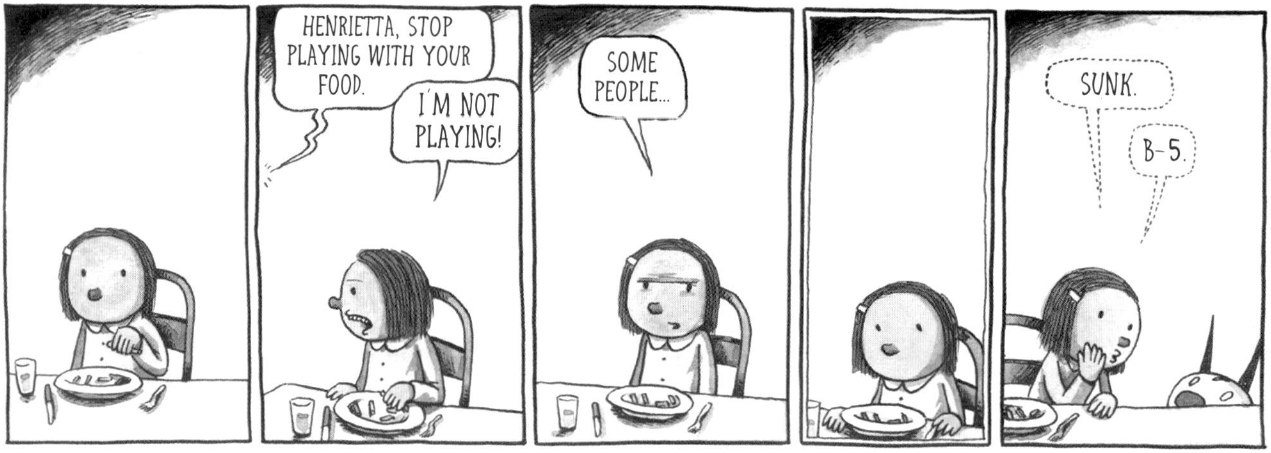
HENRIETTA, STOP PLAYING WITH YOUR FOOD.
I'M NOT PLAYING!
SOME PEOPLE...
SUNK.
B-5.

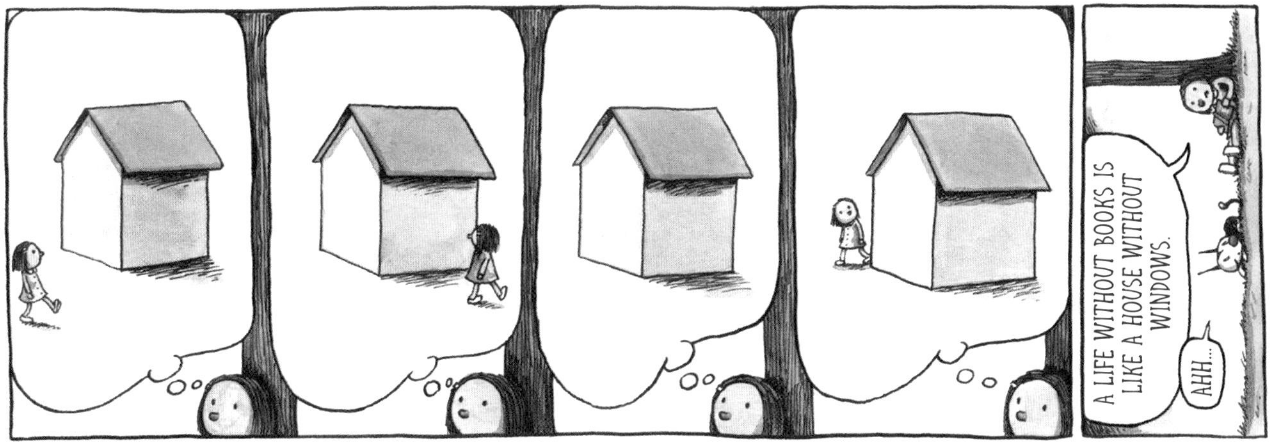
A LIFE WITHOUT BOOKS IS LIKE A HOUSE WITHOUT WINDOWS.
AHH...

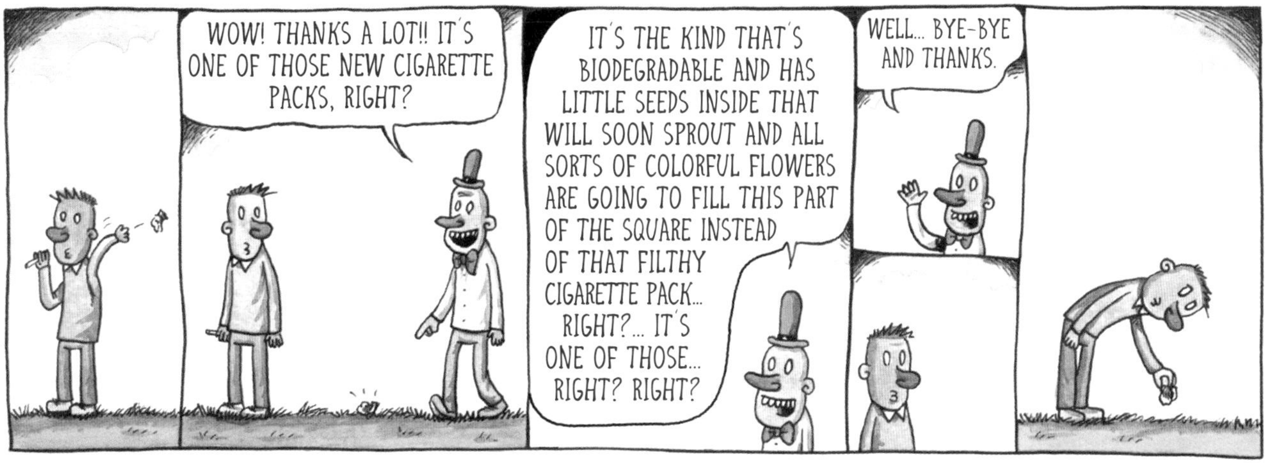
WOW! THANKS A LOT!! IT'S ONE OF THOSE NEW CIGARETTE PACKS, RIGHT?
IT'S THE KIND THAT'S BIODEGRADABLE AND HAS LITTLE SEEDS INSIDE THAT WILL SOON SPROUT AND ALL SORTS OF COLORFUL FLOWERS ARE GOING TO FILL THIS PART OF THE SQUARE INSTEAD OF THAT FILTHY CIGARETTE PACK... RIGHT?... IT'S ONE OF THOSE... RIGHT? RIGHT?
WELL... BYE-BYE AND THANKS.

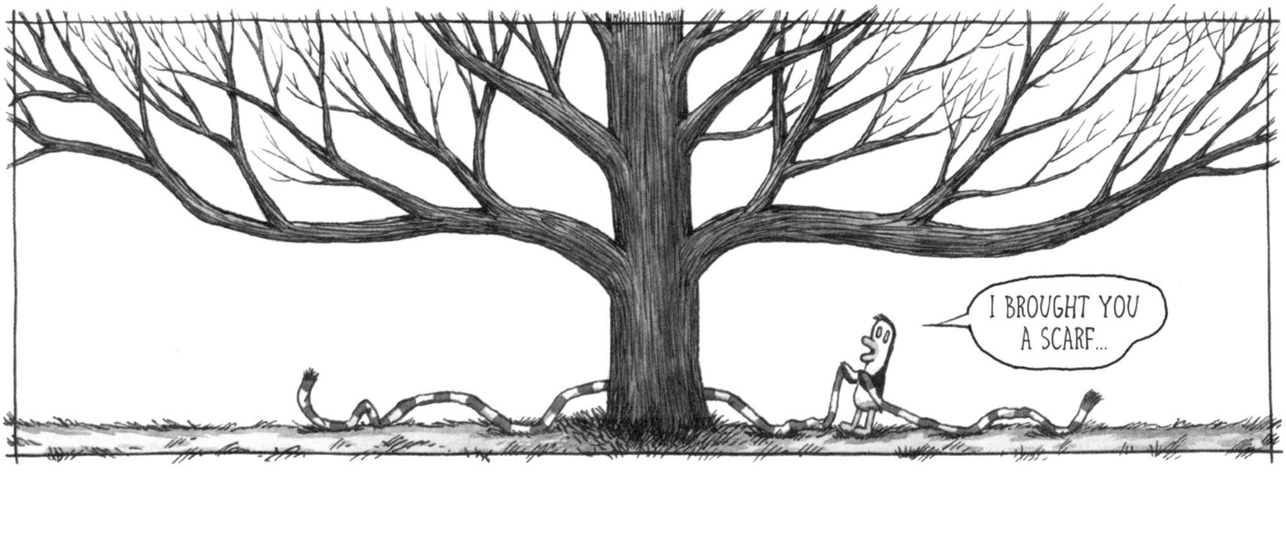
I BROUGHT YOU A SCARF...

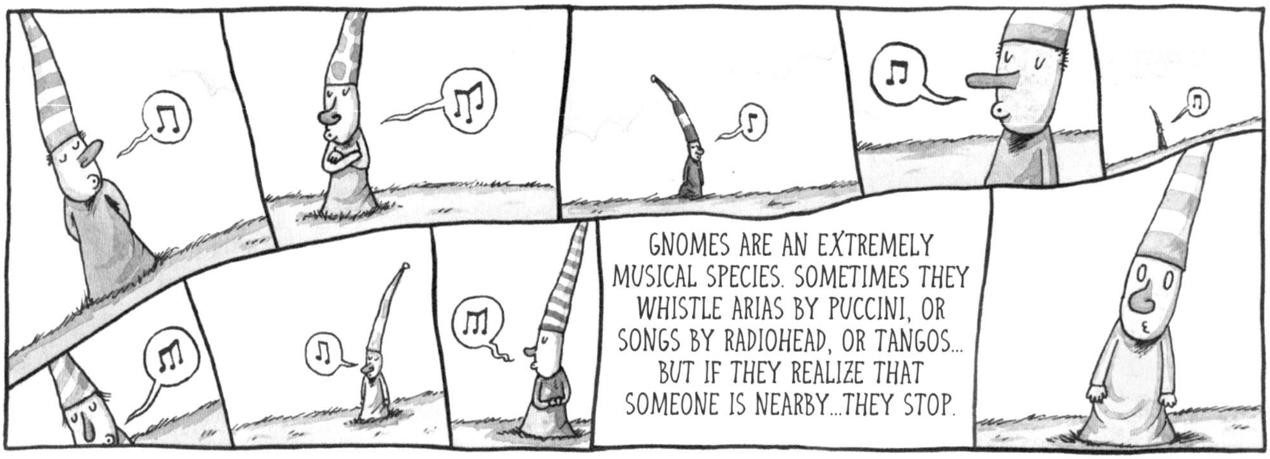
GNOMES ARE AN EXTREMELY MUSICAL SPECIES. SOMETIMES THEY WHISTLE ARIAS BY PUCCINI, OR SONGS BY RADIOHEAD, OR TANGOS... BUT IF THEY REALIZE THAT SOMEONE IS NEARBY...THEY STOP.

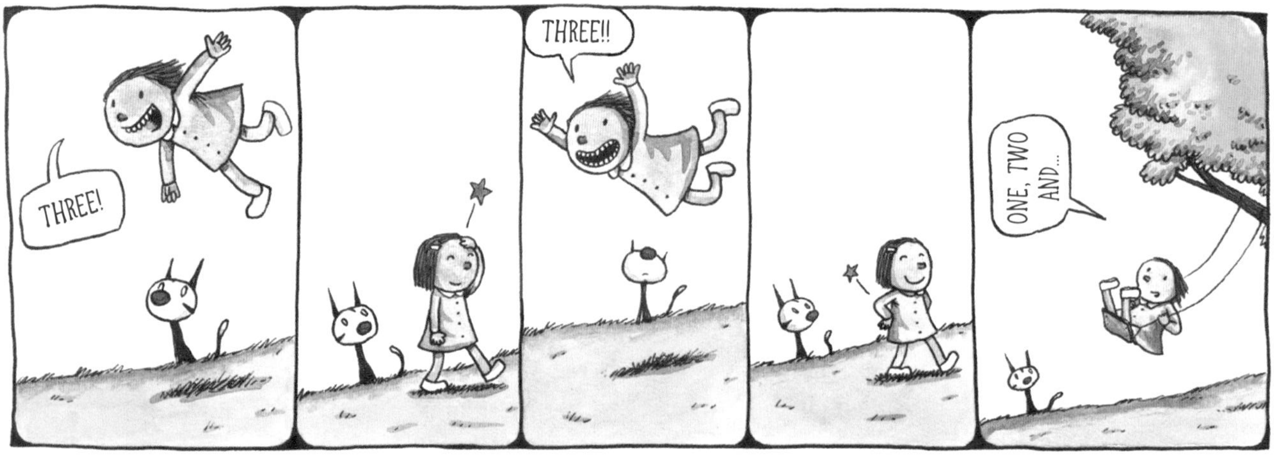
THREE!
THREE!!
ONE, TWO AND...

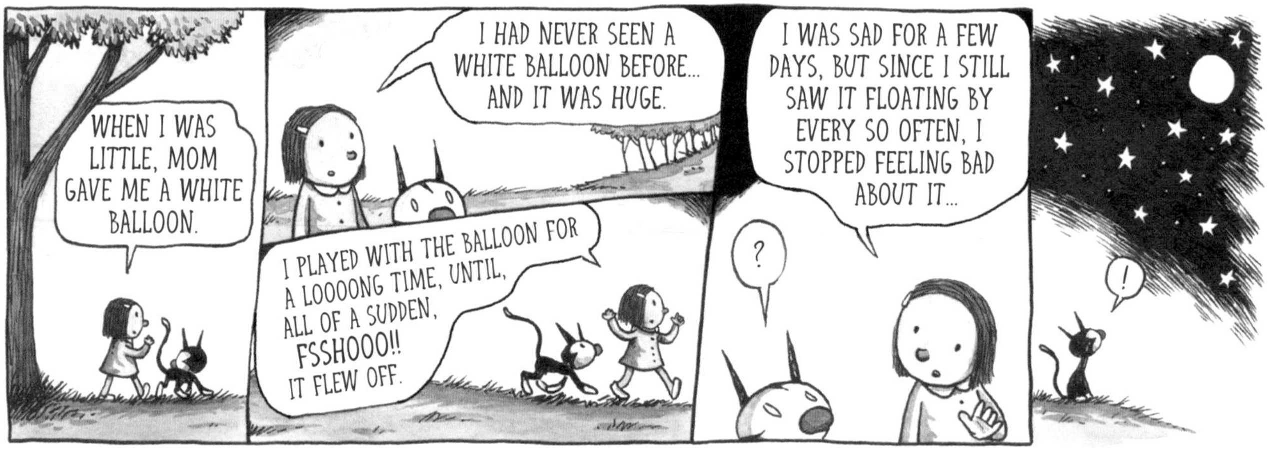
WHEN I WAS LITTLE, MOM GAVE ME A WHITE BALLOON.
I HAD NEVER SEEN A WHITE BALLOON BEFORE... AND IT WAS HUGE.
I PLAYED WITH THE BALLOON FOR A LOOOONG TIME, UNTIL, ALL OF A SUDDEN, FSSHOOO!! IT FLEW OFF.
I WAS SAD FOR A FEW DAYS, BUT SINCE I STILL SAW IT FLOATING BY EVERY SO OFTEN, I STOPPED FEELING BAD ABOUT IT...
?
!

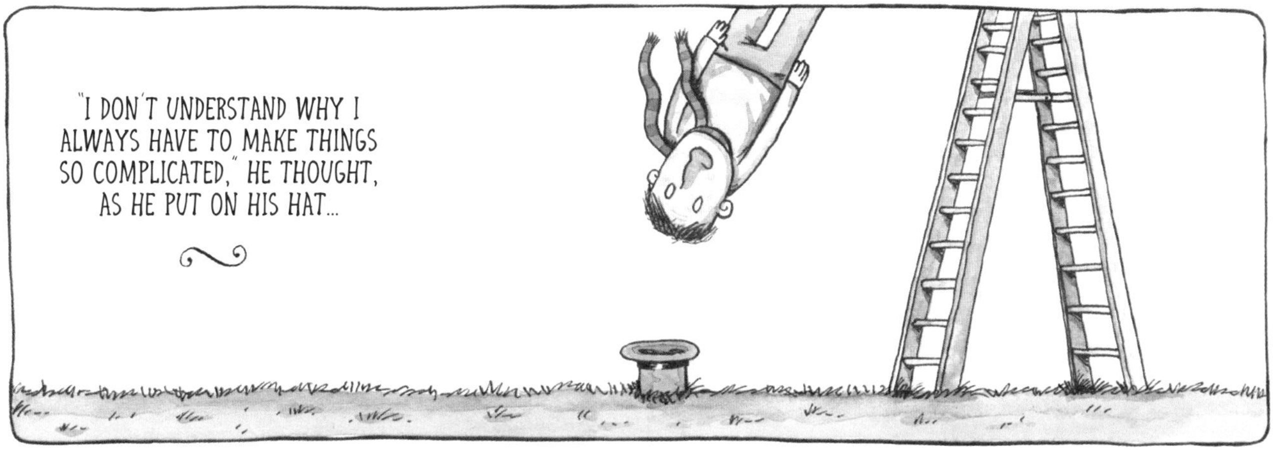
"I DON'T UNDERSTAND WHY I ALWAYS HAVE TO MAKE THINGS SO COMPLICATED," HE THOUGHT, AS HE PUT ON HIS HAT...

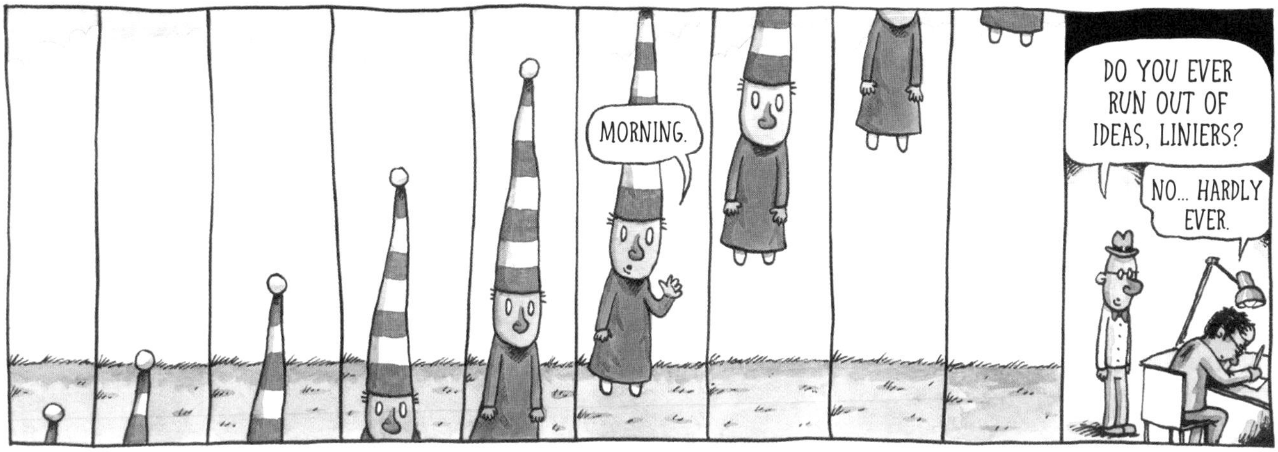
MORNING.
DO YOU EVER RUN OUT OF IDEAS, LINIERS?
NO... HARDLY EVER.

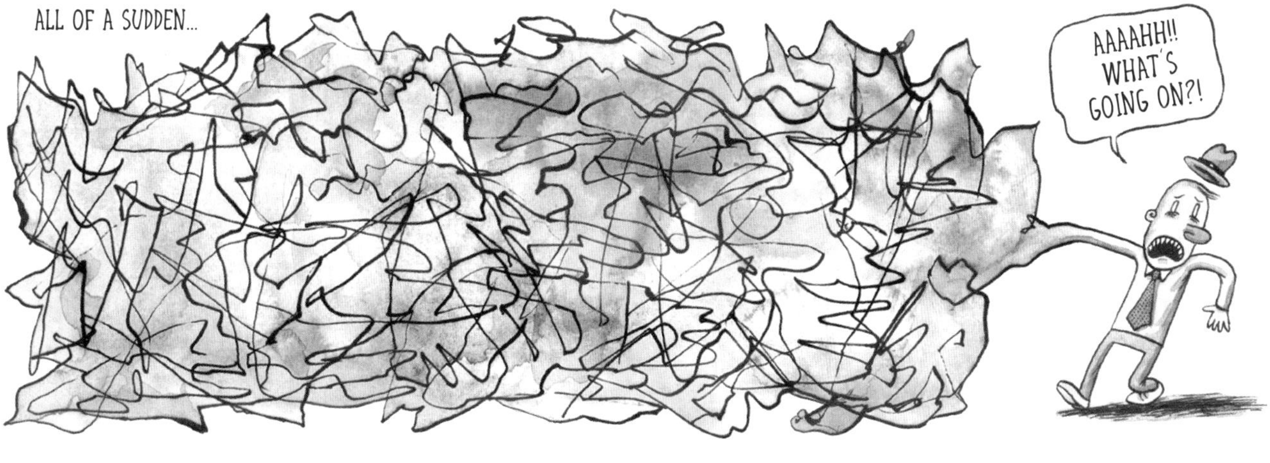
ALL OF A SUDDEN...
AAAAHH!! WHAT'S GOING ON?!

THE DANGERS OF FALLING UPWARDS

a short story

BY LINIERS—

THE DAY IS
SO NORMAL
THAT IT MUST
BE A THURSDAY

AND SANDERS IS
SUCH A NORMAL MAN
THAT HE MUST WORK IN
SOME SORT OF AN OFFICE

BUT SUDDENLY HE
FEELS LIKE HE'S
GOING TO FAINT

WHICH ISN'T AT ALL
NORMAL FOR SANDERS

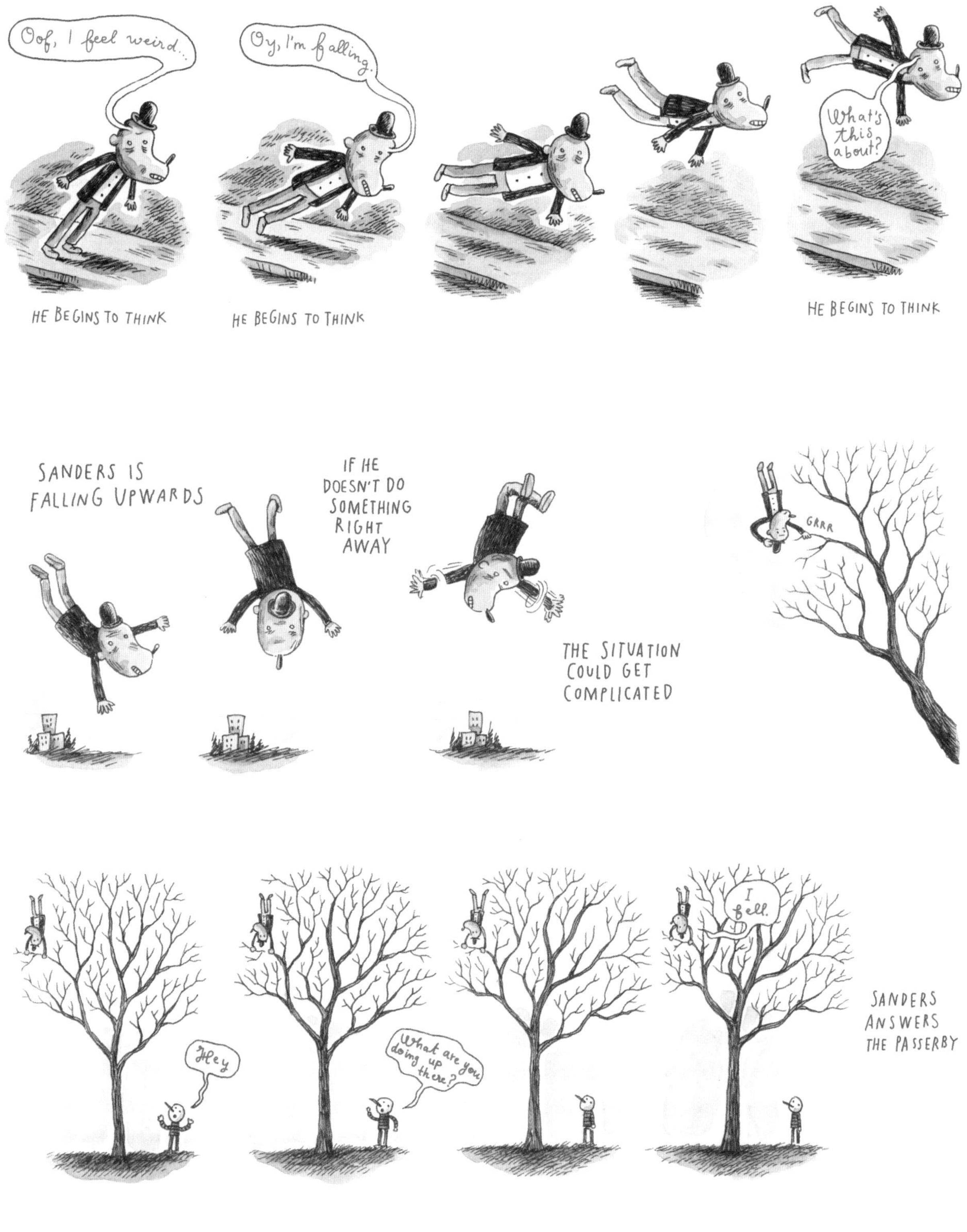
Oof, I feel weird...
HE BEGINS TO THINK
Oy, I'm falling.
HE BEGINS TO THINK
What's this about?
HE BEGINS TO THINK
SANDERS IS FALLING UPWARDS
IF HE DOESN'T DO SOMETHING RIGHT AWAY
THE SITUATION COULD GET COMPLICATED
GRRR
Hey
What are you doing up there?
I fell.
SANDERS ANSWERS THE PASSERBY

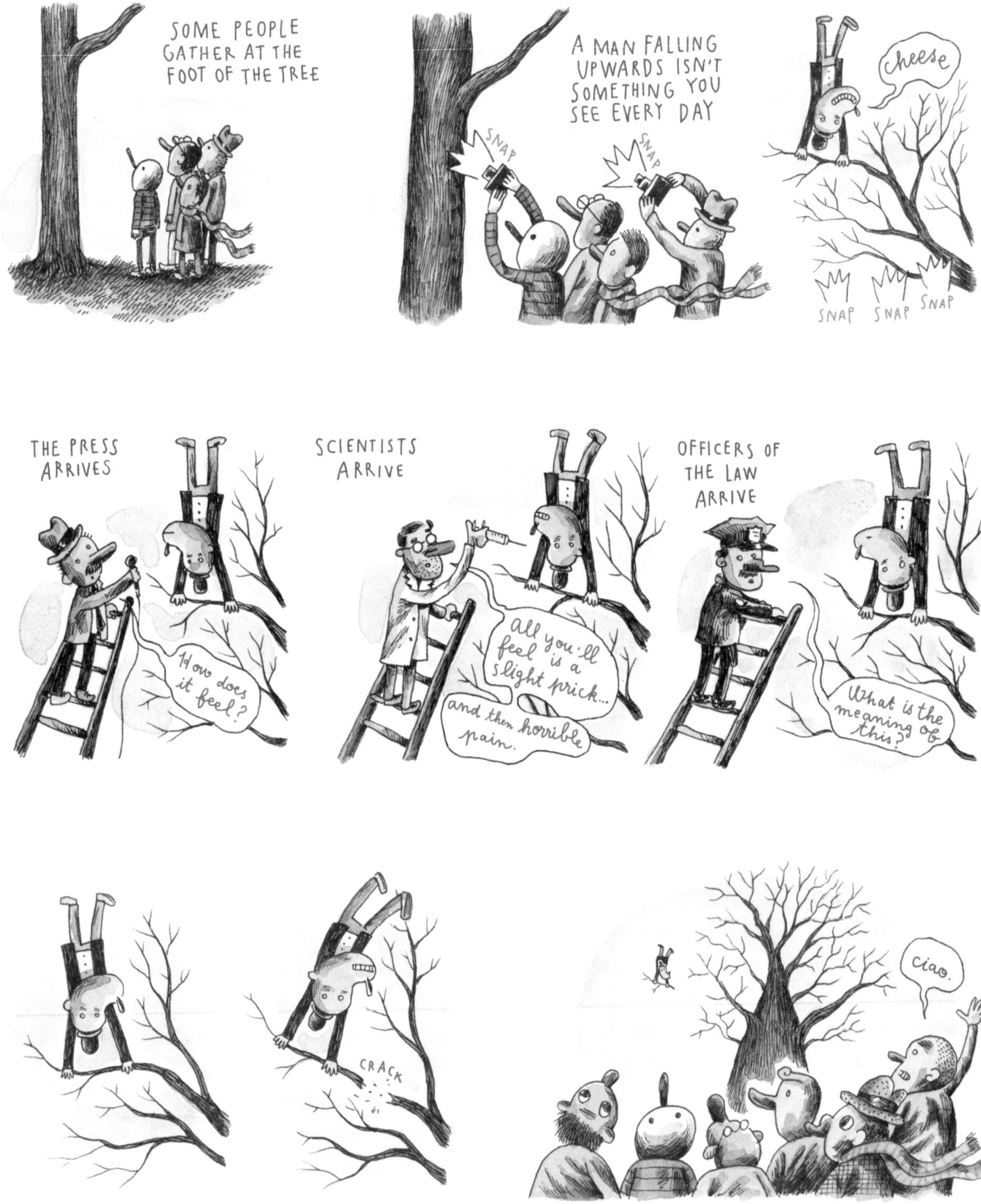
SOME PEOPLE GATHER AT THE FOOT OF THE TREE
A MAN FALLING UPWARDS ISN'T SOMETHING YOU SEE EVERY DAY
SNAP
SNAP
cheese
SNAP SNAP SNAP
THE PRESS ARRIVES
How does it feel?
SCIENTISTS ARRIVE
All you'll feel is a slight prick...
and then horrible pain.
OFFICERS OF THE LAW ARRIVE
What is the meaning of this?
CRACK
ciao.

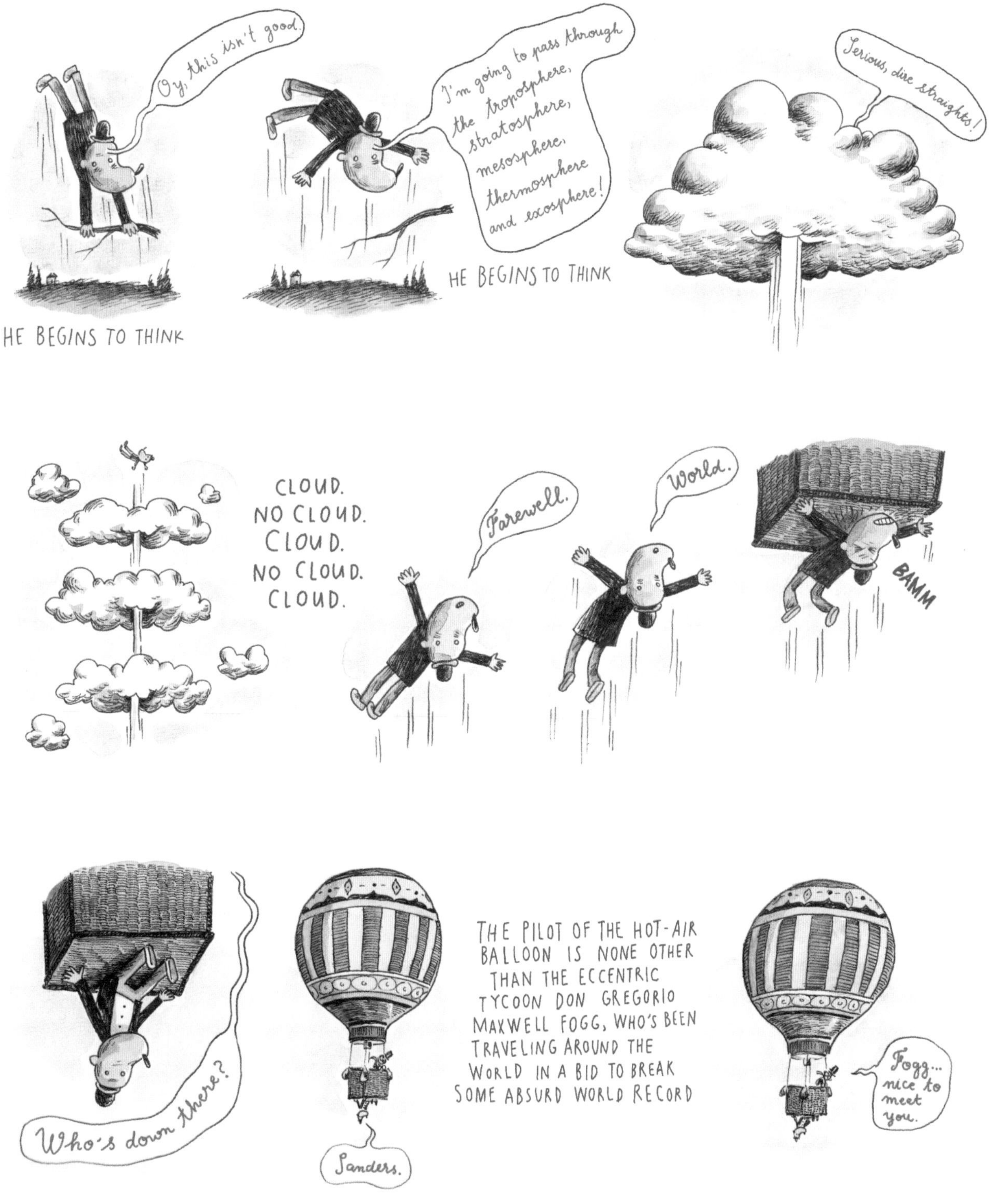
Oy, this isn't good.
HE BEGINS TO THINK
I'm going to pass through the troposphere, stratosphere, mesosphere, thermosphere and exosphere!
HE BEGINS TO THINK
Serious, dire straights!
CLOUD. NO CLOUD. CLOUD. NO CLOUD. CLOUD.
Farewell.
World.
BAMM
Who's down there?
Sanders.
THE PILOT OF THE HOT-AIR BALLOON IS NONE OTHER THAN THE ECCENTRIC TYCOON DON GREGORIO MAXWELL FOGG, WHO'S BEEN TRAVELING AROUND THE WORLD IN A BID TO BREAK SOME ABSURD WORLD RECORD
Fogg... nice to meet you.

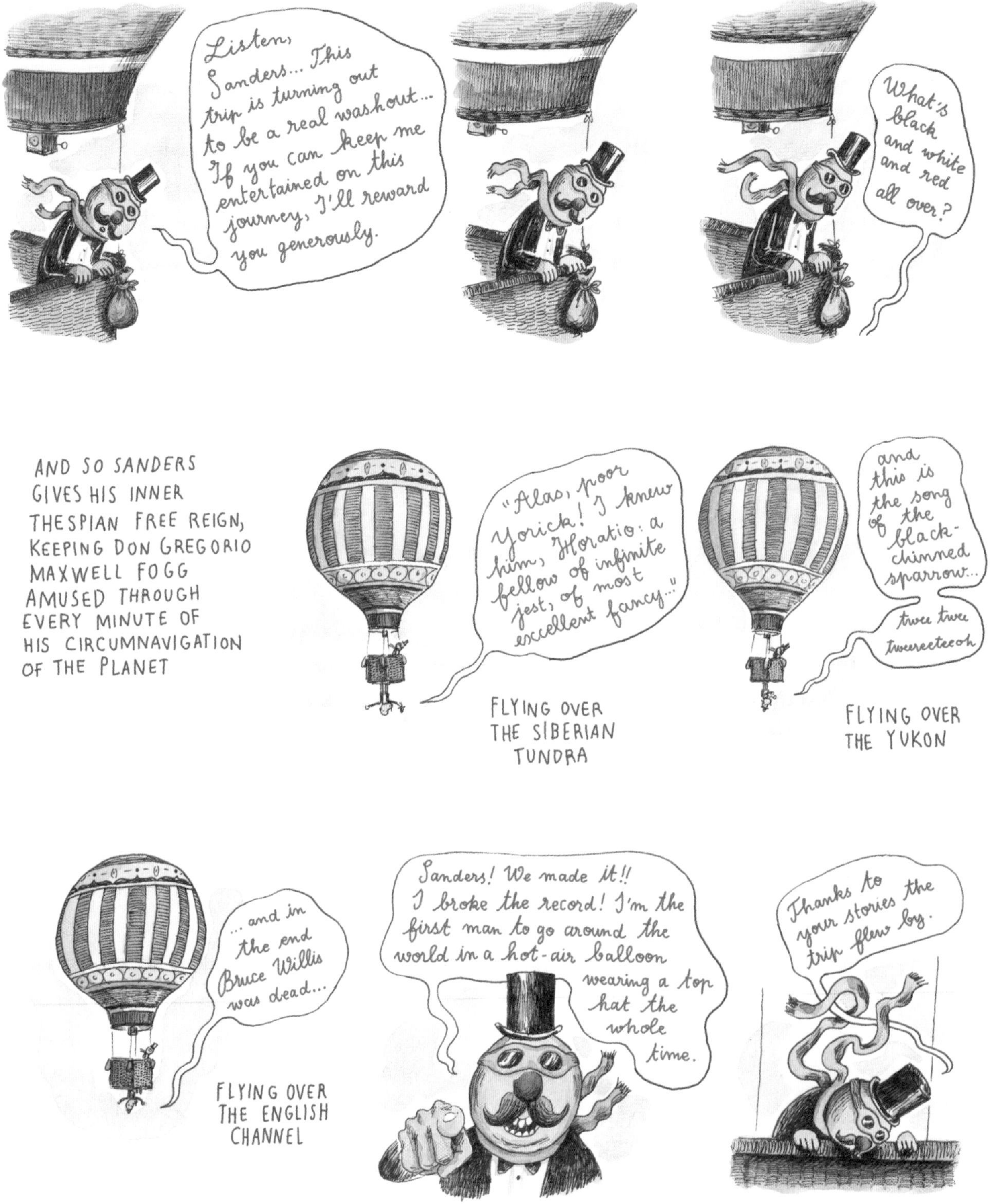
Listen, Sanders... This trip is turning out to be a real washout... If you can keep me entertained on this journey, I'll reward you generously.
What's black and white and red all over?
AND SO SANDERS GIVES HIS INNER THESPIAN FREE REIGN, KEEPING DON GREGORIO MAXWELL FOGG AMUSED THROUGH EVERY MINUTE OF HIS CIRCUMNAVIGATION OF THE PLANET
"Alas, poor Yorick! I knew him, Horatio: a fellow of infinite jest, of most excellent fancy..."
FLYING OVER THE SIBERIAN TUNDRA
and this is the song of the black-chinned sparrow...
twee twee tweeeeteeoh
FLYING OVER THE YUKON
... and in the end Bruce Willis was dead...
FLYING OVER THE ENGLISH CHANNEL
Sanders! We made it!! I broke the record! I'm the first man to go around the world in a hot-air balloon wearing a top hat the whole time.
Thanks to your stories the trip flew by.

THEY ARE RECEIVED WITH GREAT FANFARE. THEY'RE HEROES.
DON GREGORIO MAXWELL FOGG WON'T FORGET HIS PROMISE.
WEEKS LATER
This is your new house, Sanders.
As you can see, we've had it adapted to your particular situation.
You like it?
SANDERS IS OVERCOME WITH EMOTION
HIS TEARS FALL UPWARDS
?
PLOP
THE END

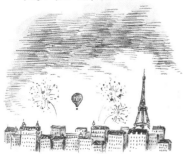

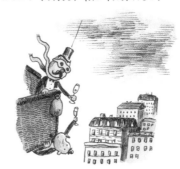

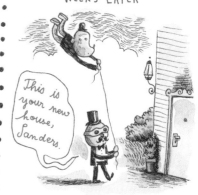

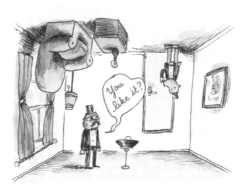

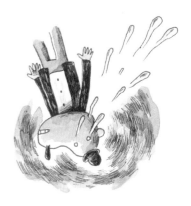

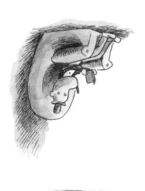

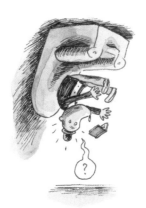

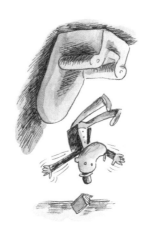

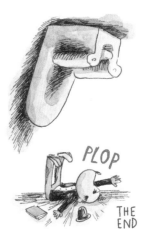

The Author (circa 1983)

Thankyouthankyouthankyou to:

Angie
Daniel, Kuki, Christian, and everyone at De la Flor
La Nación
Malba, Kevin Johansen + The Nada, Maitena
Juan Sasturain, Rubin, Ana Quiroga, Rodrigo Toso
No Tango
Hecho en Buenos Aires
Juanita, Santi, and friends both here and there...
Claudia Zoe Bedrick, for her wonderful guidance
Mara Faye Lethem, for finding the perfect words

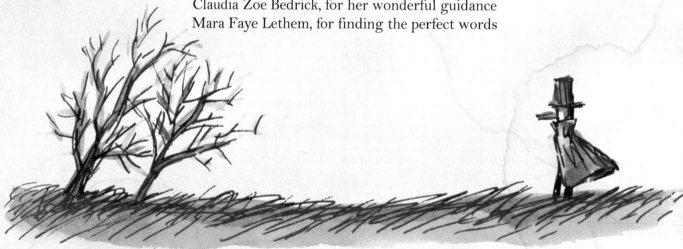

The comic strips in this book were published in the newspaper *La Nación* during 2003 and 2004.